THE LAST COWBOY

Daniel Uebbing

Robert D. Reed Publishers • Bandon, OR

Robert D. Reed Publishers
P.O. Box 1992
Bandon, OR 97411
Phone: 541-347-9882; Fax: -9883
E-mail: 4bobreed@msn.com
Website: www.rdrpublishers.com

Editor: Barbara Harrison
Cover Designer: Cleone Lyvonne
Cover Photo: "Cowboy" © Subjektiv from dreamstime.com
Interior Designer: Amy Cole

ISBN 13: 978-1-934759-13-4
ISBN 10: 1-934759-13-9

Library of Congress Number: 2008930750

Manufactured, Typeset, and Printed in the United States of America

The Cowboy's Lament

As I walked out in the streets of Laredo,
As I walked out in Laredo one day,
I spied a poor cowboy wrapped up in white linen,
Wrapped up in white linen as cold as the clay.

"Oh, beat the drum slowly and play the fife lowly,
Play the dead march as you carry me along;
Take me to the green valley, there lay the sod o'er me,
For I'm a young cowboy and I know I've done wrong.

"It was once in the saddle I used to go dashing,
It was once in the saddle I used to go gay;
First to the dram-house and then to card-house;
Got shot in the breast and I'm dying today.

"Get six jolly cowboys to carry my coffin;
Get six pretty maidens to bear up my pall.
Put bunches of roses all over my coffin,
Put roses to deaden the sods as they fall.

"Then swing your rope slowly and rattle your spurs lowly,
And give a wild whoop as you carry me along;
And in the grave throw me and roll the sod o'er me
For I'm a young cowboy and I know I've done wrong."

We beat the drum slowly and played the fife lowly,
And bitterly wept as we bore him along;
For we all loved our comrade, so brave, young, and handsome,
We all loved our comrade although he'd done wrong.

— Anonymous

· BOOK I ·

CHAPTER I

On the night of the murder, the moonlight spread a thin white glare over the rain-battered streets, and all was quiet. The cowboy strode into town at midnight. His face remained always shadowed under the brim of his hat. He clunked his old horse to a bar down the Main Street of Stricland, Oregon, a lonesome, law-abiding town, furrowed in the mountains. Dismounted, he stood outside the bar in the rain. The fluorescent glow of the beer advertisement in the window did not reach him but fell to the sidewalk where he could see a homeless man sleeping in the commercial red. Standing there over the broken man, the cowboy cast that mysterious silhouette of his in the window; his steady shadow carved against the light. He tied his horse loosely to the rail among the line of beaten up trucks and cars out front, and he kicked through old-fashioned "for show" swinging doors. He'd had a bad day.

In the bar, only the lawmen were up drinking. Well, most were already passed out on the tables or in the booths. They were all tired of dealing with domestic disturbances and kids with drugs and petty small-town stuff. Their uniforms were all loose and dirty. The cowboy saw a limp hand holding an empty bottle. He saw the pointy boots kicked up on the bar. The sheriff in the corner crossed his legs, eyeballing the cowboy sharply from under his hat.

His spurs clinking in the thudded aftermath of each step, the cowboy went to the bar. The marshals started to wake and look him over. A fat woman, the sheriff's wife, opened her eyes in bed upstairs, went to the top of the stairwell, pressed her cheeks against the wall and listened.

"Whiskey," ordered the cowboy.

He had to shove aside two drunks to make way to sit. The bartender nodded and poured the stranger his whiskey. The cowboy shot it down and ordered another. He wanted badly to get drunk, go to sleep and disremember his entire past life of quick fixes and reckless wanderings. And if he still remembered them the next morning, he would simply deny himself, settle down with a pretty girl and build his home in America.

The only thing worth anything to him was something of a faded memory: a rickety swing set, endless blue sky, fields of wheat and rye, and muscular horses and ponies to ride; lassoing calves and broncs, his Pappy's old gun lying in the grass, and a beautiful girl from his boyhood, chasing her in the tall grass and the sunflowers — all out there in old Kansas. The girl was the main thing. She was like a song stuck in his head that kept playing louder with all the anger of all the years and distance growing between them; and yet he could not remember the rhythm or sing along. So he drank his third shot of whiskey, hung his head over the bar and felt the cool, dry relief hit.

The bartender squeaked the glasses clean with his shirttail down at the other end, eying the cowboy also, wondering where he'd seen him before. The cowboy saw him and gestured him to get over there and get him another drink.

"Keep 'em comin," he said.

"Last one, cowboy, we close up pretty soon," the bartender replied.

The cowboy looked around at the drunken lawmen. The bar was all black oak, dense with rain. On the wall over the shelves of liquor behind the bar, the antlers of a great elk protruded. A rank yet crisp smell distilled the air. A dim showcase light lit up the liquor shelf. The whole place was dimly lit.

The cowboy looked at the bartender.

The bartender looked away toward the sheriff. "Say, haven't I seen you around?" he asked the cowboy, glancing at him.

"No, I reckon not. I'm a stranger to this town," he said as he lit a cigarette.

"I coulda sworn..."

The cowboy said nothing.

The bartender introduced himself.

"Well," the cowboy said, nudging his empty glass to the edge of the bar, "let me tell you something, Jimbo, while you're fetching me another drink. I also need a bed and a whore, a good clean whore. Hell, where are all the women in this town anyway?"

"Come again?" the bartender said. He was a frail, bald man in suspenders.

"Man, that's all I need right now, just one last thrill, a bed, and a good woman. Probably have to settle for a whore at this stage, but that don't matter. Just get me a clean one, the cleanest you can find, and I'll take that bottle of whiskey, too," the cowboy said. He leaned back, tipped his hat down over his eyes and rested his hands behind his head.

The bartender started to chuckle. "There are no more rooms here."

"Make room."

"All right. And how were you planning to pay for this?"

The cowboy touched his gun.

The table creaked as the big, drunken sheriff managed to get out of the booth and make his way to the bar.

"Sheriff's coming," warned the bartender. "You better pay up and leave, cowboy."

The sheriff stood next to the cowboy at the bar. He imposed his big, taut face and his beady eyes down on him. The cowboy leaned back, kicking his fancy boots up on the bar. The sheriff knew his kind right off: a bad seed, wouldn't pay for anything, thought the law didn't apply to him and wouldn't go out without a fight. The cowboy slumped down in the chair with a good five shots in him. He looked up at the sheriff, snarled his dry lips, dragged long on his cigarette, cocked his head back and exhaled, shooting smoke straight up.

"How's it going?" the sheriff asked the bartender, coughing slightly from the smoke.

The bartender gestured his eyes toward the cowboy and leaned into the bar, nervously. "All fine and dandy, sheriff," he said with a cough.

The sheriff looked at the cowboy. "Well, what do we have here? A cowboy, eh?"

The cowboy sighed.

"Tell me, are you the real article, or are you a fake? Are you a romantic bastard cowboy? Are you a rootin' tootin' gun-slinging, son-of-a-bitch cowboy? Are you a bank robbin', rag-assed renegade cowboy? Ha haa! Or are you one of those performing arts, pussy cowboys?"

The cowboy did not want any trouble. "Sheriff, you are drunk and talking out your ass," he said.

The sheriff scratched his whiskered chin. "Yeah, you are one of those acting cowboys, aren't ya? This is all an act, ain't it? 'Cause no one talks to Jack Miller like that, son! 'Talking out my ass.' Do some rope tricks for me and the boys! Go on, get your little rope from your little horsy out there, ha, ha!"

By this time, the sheriff's men were all up and crowding around the cowboy. The cowboy kept smoking his cigarette coolly and sipping whiskey. He took a glance over their puny, drunken faces and wanted to kill them all. "I ain't about to kill no drunken sheriff," he said.

"No, you wouldn't kill anyone, would ya? Wouldn't harm a fly. Say, what are those pistols for, cowboy?" said the sheriff.

Two silver pistols gleamed in his holsters. The cowboy had the full attire: heavy leather pistol strap dampened with rain and ware, buckled cockeyed to the left as his dominant left hand would rest on the butt of his pistol in a cocky, defiant threat; damp, trodden Stetson covering his eyes; long trench jacket with the collar up; scraggly bandanna around his neck; rugged, hard, unshaven face; big Adam's apple; whiskey-gulping cowboy.

"Them pistols ain't loaded," he said with a smile.

"I didn't ask if they was loaded," the sheriff said. He was what the mothers of the town called a "bear of a man" whose shoulders shook when he laughed and jiggled his belly. He wore a red and black flannel (tucked in tight over his beer belly) and a thick belt with golden steer horns on the attachment emblem. Proudly pinned over his heart, his tin star badge cast a little white light dancing on the ceiling.

"What are those guns for, I said? And what is a cowboy stranger like your kind doing in my town with those guns? Son, you better start talking. And where'd you get that pretty little hat and those pretty little boots? Ha haa! It's a cowboy, boys! A regular Roy Rogers! Boys! Get over here. Get a load of this guy, he's a cowboy!" He turned back to the cowboy. "Come on now, son, answer my question. What are those pistols for?" he said.

The cowboy looked up at him real slow. "There for killin' law," he said, "big, fat, yella law."

"Killin' law, huh?" The sheriff looked around the bar to see if any civilians were hanging around, saw he was clear, and furrowed his brow, his raging eyes down on the defiant cowboy before him. "Just what I thought. Well, let me tell you something about killing law!" And he backhanded the cowboy hard, knocking him to the floor.

The cowboy reached for the whiskey bottle on the bar as he got back up, but one of the sheriff's men bashed a beer bottle over his head. This gave the sheriff ample time to rip a barstool from its floor hinges and raise it over his head, so high he nearly fell back over. A pair of his less drunken men had to catch him and push him forward. His men loved it. They kicked the cowboy down on the ground, hard in the gut, in the face, and they spat and urinated on him.

"Better to get pissed off than pissed on, eh, cowboy," the sheriff said, and he came down with the barstool on him. The metal leg hit his blocking arm. He grabbed his throbbing arm and looked over in delirium and saw the fat figure of the sheriff's wife sitting halfway down the stairs, watching through the rails.

The sheriff hovered over the cowboy. "I thought I killed off the rest of you cowboys a long time ago, 'spose I missed one." He grabbed the cowboy by the collar, pulled him up and punched him down. The cowboy hit the floor hard. The glasses in the cabinet rattled.

The bartender watched through his fingers, ducked down behind the bar. "Sheriff, should I call the police or someone?"

"We are the damn police!"

"I know, I know. I mean, shouldn't you arrest him or do you want to take his name?"

The cowboy crawled on his elbows to the floor. The sheriff met him there with his boot and kicked him all the way up and back down on his back.

"No need," said the sheriff. "No, I'll tell you what we're going to do. Stand him up. Stand him up straight."

Two men picked the cowboy up by the arms and held him before their sheriff: his head hung, his left eye swollen, his mouth bloodied.

"Now that's more like it," said the sheriff, "the cowboy in the raw. Let's have it, cowboy. Right here. Right now. Law against outlaw. Showdown. Just like in the Old West. The way they used to settle things. Now tell me, how many drinks have you had?"

The cowboy was unresponsive.

"How many!" the sheriff demanded, and he slugged him in the gut.

The bartender couldn't take it anymore. "Five, he's had five!"

"Five, huh? Well, looks like you got some catching up to do. I've had, I'd say ten worth, but every man here knows I'm a fair man so I'll drink one with ya and we'll call even."

The men roared with senseless laughter, rocking back in the booths and pounding the tables with their fists and circling the cowboy singing, "You've done it now, cowboy; you're gonna get yaself kilt now!"

The sheriff and the cowboy stood man to man. The bartender brought them their drinks.

"Thanks, Jim," said the sheriff, still looking at the cowboy as he took his whiskey.

"Anything for my sheriff," replied the bartender, and he gave the cowboy a smirk as he went back behind the bar for cover. The cowboy spat out shards of glass and teeth and smiled in his bloody contempt.

The sheriff even scowled in disgust at the cowboy spitting, and he ordered a man to bring the tobacco basin. As he finished spitting, he said to him, "You walked into the wrong damn tavern, cowboy, acting like some vermin rebel. Your kind don't last, not in the town of Stricland anyway, that's for sure. Ain't that right, Jim?"

"Yes, sir," said the bartender, poking his head out.

The cowboy shook off the men holding him up. He took his drink from the sheriff and drank it. "Let's get this over with," he said.

The sheriff drank his whiskey and smiled at the cowboy before him. He knew that either way, he'd never see a real live one again. And he admired him a bit — reminded him of his boyhood playing cowboys and Indians in Wyoming. But he knew that he must die. No man comes into his town and orders whiskey and women and does not pay. Every man pays his price in this town.

"WHHHooooowweeeeeee! We gonna have ourselves a showdown, boys!" cried one of the men. And they all crowded out and lined the streets.

The cowboy stepped outside and went over to his horse to load his guns. Some of the men were taunting and bickering at the big horse. He brushed them back and took the bullets out of his strap and shoved them into his revolvers, growing angrier with each one. He couldn't believe he had to do this. All he wanted was to get drunk and laid, and lie in bed smoking a good cigar late into the day and figure out his new life, his journey back home.

The sheriff's wife saw the cowboy loading his guns from inside. She went to the fireplace, stood on her toes and reached above it for an old family rifle on display under the elk head. She ran upstairs with the gun, crying hysterically for her son to get up. To her right in the dark corridor beamed a night light where the children slept. She realized this and hushed her manner but still moved frantically to the door at the end of the hall where she stood, knocking and whispering as loud as she could: "Open this door!" She could hear her son inside, messing around with some girl. "Who's that?" she heard the girl say between moaning and the mattress springs squeaking. "Nobody," her son told the girl, and the moaning went on. The boy's mother barged in.

"Ma, what the hell?"

"Shut up, boy! You, missy — out! Here's your gun, son. Your daddy's gotten himself into some trouble."

"Goddamn it! Again?" He pushed the girl up off him, escorted her by the arm out into the hallway and went to the bedside drawer, where he retrieved some ammunition.

"Should I just wait here?" asked the naked girl, covering her breasts with her arms and peeking in the room.

"Yeah. Turn off the light, will ya, and close the door," said the sheriff's son. And she did.

From the bedroom window the sheriff's son, called "Bucktooth," had a good view of the scene below. As his mother told him the situation, he took aim at the cowboy.

Below, the men had lined the streets, sitting on the cars and staying drunk on account of the bartender out distributing a round of beers. The bartender made sure every man had a bottle and ran back inside for cover.

One of the men saw the homeless man by the door, kicked him awake and told him to get lost. The homeless man squelched off, cursing under his breath and spitting down the alleyway. Shrouded in his rags, he sat against the wall with just enough view to see the action.

The cowboy and sheriff stood in the middle of the street, face to face. The small old buildings lining the wide flat street looked like black blotches, crammed together with an uneven roofline against the mountainous night sky. The pale streetlights and the moonlight on the pavement reflected off the car windshields parked on the sides. The yellow streetlight on the cowboy's end flickered on and off. Otherwise, all else was black and vacant. The cowboy's effacing road, if he got out of this scrape alive, led back up into the mountains. The sheriff's path faced the distant ocean. The rank smell of the bar tinged with a brackish offshore mountainous air and faded into the cool night.

"All right, gentlemen, you know the rules," said a deputy to the cowboy and the sheriff. "Fifteen steps and fire at will." And the deputy stood on the roof of a car and fired a crisp echoing shot into the dark sky. Both men turned out from each other, and they waited. The gunman on the car looked at both men, smiled, slugged back his beer and fired the initiation shot. And the duelers began to walk.

At step five, the sheriff stopped. His jaw hung and his eyes bulged like a kid about to get caught in a prank. He silently drew his gun, turned and pointed it at the cowboy's back. He smiled hugely, licking his lips. "Just like the movies, cowboy," he snickered, "just like in the movies." All the men stood and watched, hushed. The homeless man came to the curb and leaned against the streetlamp. He wanted to yell out to the cowboy and almost did, but he knew that they would have killed him.

The cowboy kept walking. Step eight. Step nine. Step ten. He did not notice the sheriff's steps had stopped for he was not listening and figured it really did not matter if he lived or died. Yet as he walked, a chilly wind swooped down from the mountains and caught his chin and he thought of Kansas, and the wide open fields of his boyhood there, and that pretty girl who lived miles down the road and yet still the girl next door; and on the pure whim that comes so naturally to him, he decided once and for all that he would go back there and live truly, with her. He opened his eyes and caught a white sparkling reflection off the car window. He drew his guns, turned and bent his knees and fired five shots all in one motion. He hit the sheriff in the wrist, (knocking his gun back firing) thrice across the gut and once in the neck. The sheriff's badge fell and clinked loudly in the broken silence of the night, dancing its white sparkling law everywhere and dying gradually, dwindling off to nothing, as he grabbed his throat and choked down to his knees — his eyes bulging — and then all the way down, the tin star rattling, still.

The men watched blankly, dropping their bottles shattering on the street. They had whiskey and beer in them for courage, but they had no will of their own. They had lived corruptly under the protection of the sheriff, and they could not conjure up what to do now that some cowboy had ridden in and shot him to death right before their eyes — gunned down for the dirty mongrel that he really was.

The cowboy gripped his guns and seethed in the last of his cigarette. "Take a shot," he said, "anybody." He looked around in disgust. "Yella! All of ya! You're all yella! Come on, ya yella bastards! Take a goddamned shot!"

"Kill 'em all, cowboy!" came a ravaged voice.

The cowboy slung his guns to the street corner. He saw the homeless man standing under the streetlight, giddy in his toothless joy.

"Kill all these bastards!"

The cowboy gave him a smile and twirl-holstered his guns.

The homeless man saw him walking away and kept shouting at him. "You go all the way, man, you kill 'em all! You've got to free us good men. You hear what I'm saying? You've got to free us. You're gonna be the one. You. You are the only one who can. Ha ha! Kill 'em all, cowboy!" And he ran away down the alley, laughing.

From the window above the bar, the sheriff's son steadied his aim. He saw below, the cowboy getting away and the stunned cowardice of the men letting him. His arms quaked. His hands trembled. He aimed for the heart, right through the back, but his anger got the best of his concentration and the gun jerked up as he squeezed the trigger a split second too soon between breaths. The cowboy heard a noise from the window and looked up, and for an imminent moment the two locked eyes, the cowboy looking up and the son of law raging down unto him.

The sound of the shot split the night. And all the lawmen and the bereaved son saw the cowboy go down. The men started to cheer and run to finish off the fallen cowboy. But he got up. Yes, he sprang up cussing, and hobbled over and slammed against the side of a car, one hand holding in his guts. He pointed his left pistol and fired up at the window. The sheriff's son ducked under the ledge under the raining glass. He popped up and let off another shot, clearing out the remaining shards of the window with the barrel. The cowboy dodged, letting his legs collapse out from under him. His back hit the side of the car and his bum on the street. The shot hit the car window above him. He got up again, shaking the glass from his face. "Pig-f—- whores!" he shouted. The sheriff's men crouched back behind the cars. The cowboy ran, humped down, his right hand compressing his wound, his left waving his gun at the window, "Don't you shoot me, you bastard," he said. And he ran to his horse holding his bloodied gut and looking up at the window.

13

Under the short arcade where the cowboy had his horse, the sheriff's son had no shot.

Some townspeople and extra men now had come to help and look on, standing armed yet unaware in the street. The cowboy rode off through the crowd as fast as he could, the horse raising its legs over the men, trampling, pushing forward and neighing wildly. His good old horse ran right to the edge of town as fast as she could, as the cowboy bellowed off his last rounds into the night.

He pulled up at the edge of town before the dark path up the mountains and looked back. He clamped his wound with as much strength as he could muster, yet still blood leaked over his thick hand. Thankfully, for as far as he could see back to the town, the lights were starting to turn on in the homes one by one, but no one was actually coming after him, yet.

He lifted his head to the dark mountains before him, kicked up his horse and began to ride. The horse broke into gentle stride, as if she felt her rider's wound. The cowboy flipped up the collar on his jacket, pulled his hat down and leaned in, hunched over on the horse.

He looked back at a wooden sign as he passed it in the rain at the edge of town. "WELCOME TO STRICLAND," it read. He checked his wound and gasped, looking over his shoulder and back at the sign. "Goddamn Stricland," he said. And he tossed his cigarette, spat blood to the sign and moved out.

As he left, the lights of the town turned on, one by one. The good men grew anxious for answers and held close their loved ones. All the good townspeople felt the break in the law and they feared it. The danger had begun and they would fear it until it was killed, until they knew it was killed, saw it die, this cowboy stranger, who sat now humped over, grabbing his gut with one hand, and the other limply holding the bridle. He lost consciousness for a moment and fell bleeding into his horse, his hand slipping down around her neck. The horse whinnied him awake.

"All right, girl," he said, "you're all I got. Take me home, girl, take me home." And he touched her mane and her broad neck and kicked her up, riding back up and into the mountains.

◆ ◆ ◆ ◆

CHAPTER II

M eanwhile, back in Kansas, on the eastern outskirts of a small town called Fort Plain, in an old, blue-faded house with white shutters barely hanging on, with an old church across the street, and a big red barn out back with the paint all twisting and curling off into itself, emitting black slits where the wind sifts through it and all the hollow wooden structures of the town, the abandoned silos, the old store fronts on Main Street, all surrounded in waves of endless wheat fields and prairie, a young lady crept downstairs barefoot and in her nightgown. It was nearly dawn. She went to the kitchen where she made herself some tea, and she washed her face with cold water from the sink. There were many dirty dishes on the counter. She frowned over the mess and told herself she would take care of it after she snuck outside and did her secret thing she did always in the morning.

But she had to be careful not to wake her mother. She moved to the door, stopped at the creak in the floor, waited to hear if she'd woken her, and moved forward again. And then for a second there, she lost herself with a gust of wind through the screen door, and she was a child again and could not wait. She pushed out the screen door and jumped off the front porch to the day. The screen door slammed behind her. She knew she had done it. She sat given up on the front porch and pulled a cigarette from her bosom. Smoking, she heard her mother stilt the whole house upright with her feet on the cold floor as she ached up from bed and then release and creak about upstairs.

"Angie! Angie! You haven't been smoking them cigarettes, have ya?"

"No mama!" Angie called. And she snubbed out her cigarette in the flowerpot.

"Angie, I want you to water them flowers!" crabbed her mother from upstairs.

The house stood frail and thin as a skeleton in the wind and voices carried far and easy as did sight. Miles down from her spot sitting on the porch, Angie could see the town stirring about in the dusty Main Street in the early morning. The townspeople were happy and earning their money. All the employed and school kids were up and getting ready for the day. The factory started up with its cloud making. The flat white factory building was the closest to the house, and the wind always swept the smog eastward over it, and the chemicals glowed all pink and yellow in the clouds. Mixed with occasional tornado wind and current polluted wind, the dilapidated house stood through many-a-mighty trials, but still stood, only slanted a noticeable fraction to the east. It was still a pretty old house — just bent — like a flower in the wind. Out passing the factory northward, Angie could hear already the construction workers drilling, up extra early to work on the new Commercial Avenue — a four-lane highway taking the want-to-be-urban country teenagers to the city and the mall, lined with billboards and restaurants and minimalls and commercials of all kinds, cutting through the plains.

A hollow metal bonging sound tolled out, lonesome in the wind, against the flagless flag pole out front of the old blue house by the road, looking over all of Kansas, all the sunflower country and beyond. Angie heard it and ran up and around the house impetuously. She always felt as if she had to outrun something, and then be alone and safe from it, having survived with some secret love in her. She sat now on an old rickety swing set with weeds and dandelions and tall patches of grass sprouting up from the crimson rusty poles in the earth. A cold, smoothed-out oval of wear dipped down on the bare, trodden-down footpath beneath the swing. She swung sadly and dangled her feet in the dustless dirt. She could see the barn and the sun breaking the sky behind it, a sudden long yellow crevice spreading instantly over the gray land. She looked down and watched the empty swing beside her sway in the wind.

"Angie!" her mother called. She was downstairs now. "I want ya to do the dishes and raise that flag before ya head out to work, dear. We gotta be strong now. Gotta show our patriotism now."

"Yes, Ma," Angie groaned. She held on tight to the rusty red chain of the swing and let her head hang back, and she squinted through the white daylight to look at the clouds.

"Hey, I don't wanna hear no groanin' and complainin'!" Angie's Ma said. She was outside now, looking for her daughter. "Where are ya? Always flouting about, getting me all grumpy, grouchy, grinchy — moanin' and groanin' in the mornin'!"

Angie's Ma went around the other side of the house slapping her thigh — a little thing she did with her anger.

Angie looked down at her legs dangling. They'd grown too long to glide without holding them up, and they dangled in the bare earth. She looked beside at the empty swing again, swinging in the wind as though some friend had just jumped off it and run inside. She kicked back against the earth and swung back and flew forward off the swing to the grass with a sudden rush of wind, as she had done so many times long ago, her Ma calling her in for dinner when Pa was still there.

She skipped around the house singing, "Heart and soul...la, la, la... heart and soul..." — the old song she used to play on the piano. And she saw her mother, the big, flushed, pale-skinned, white-haired, hardly probable Englishwoman, bent over a weed- infested garden in the front yard, a stiff brocade sticking up the back of her dress, and her underskirt clearly wedged up her butt. She was a very uptight, high-strung lady, especially since her husband had left her five years ago, left her with half his pension money (some 20,000), left her to take care of Angie — the twenty-three-year-old, uneducated, dreamy girl, with a mere $8.50 per hour wage coming in from working in the factory. Too old to yank her bent self up, the mother of the household, Madame Sherman, as the good old folk in the town still respected and often times, she thought, tormented her with in remembrance of when she had money and a complete family with her husband the most skilled and envied farmer in all of Kansas, let her daughter sneak by and into the house once again.

"Mornin', Ma," Angie peeped as she went. "Goin' to fetch the flag like you said."

"Aaagh, morning, honey," Madame Sherman croaked, her glassy

blue eyes breaking a bit and crying as she looked at her hand holding a chunk of earth with the gangly weed roots sprawling out with the worms, slithering and falling. She looked a long time at that earth.

Angie came quickly out with the American flag all folded up in a triangle. She swept it out like a blanket and let it fly in the wind, and she danced around with it in the front yard.

"Stay away from the road," her mama warned. She straightened her back painfully and sat up on the top porch step where the flowerpot sat smoking a thin tendril. She picked out the butt and flung it away. She could see the tip of the flower, a speck of life in the soil, struggling to grow, charred black over the green. She spat on her fingers and cleansed as best she could. And she sat and watched her daughter.

Angie draped the flag over her and held it around her chest as she pulled down the hoist and hooked up the flag. She let it loose and hoisted it up in all its grandeur and glory and sorrow rippling.

"Now that's a good girl. See, what good you've done? That's some good color there, some good color, that flag. Now come on in, darling, I'll make you some breakfast before ya head out. Come on now, child."

"I'm a gettin', Mama, I'm a gettin'," Angie said. She heard the screen door close and felt Ma watching from behind the screen. And together they awed for a moment at how big the flag was. A bronze eagle spread its wings in flight, ornamenting the tip of the pole like a vigilant guard over the homeland, its eyes stone and open. Angie seared her big blue, wistful eyes to the flag — as though it were her only child to survive — her light brown hair coming loose from under her nightgown and catching the westward wind. The star-spangled iridescence and the long broad red and white stripes ran a wave through and through with a following one; for a moment in between, Old Glory stood firm and rich, against the wind.

"He will come," Angie whispered. "He will come."

◆ ◆ ◆ ◆

CHAPTER III

"Murder! Murder! Murder!" a woman screamed. The sheriff's wife ran out to the streets and managed to pick up her husband's big dead head and embrace him. She wept into him long and hard. The men stood around again, not knowing what to do, touching her on the shoulder and saying useless normal things like, "It's gonna be okay."

"You better hang him! You kill him right!" she snapped.

The men, however, held scattered intention for actually going after the cowboy. In their minds the sheriff had lost, and the cowboy had won, and that was that. And so they felt fine letting the dueling cowboy get away, leave room for the sobering tragedy to sink in, they figured, and wait for new leadership to arrive. But no one could stop Bruce "Bucktooth" Miller, the stolid son of the dead sheriff, from taking his chase at revenge. He sat in the semi-dark basement of the bar, secluded off to corner, holding his rifle across his lap, figuring, his face blank and slack-jawed, showing his long yellow front buck tooth jutting out like a thorn.

Old Bucktooth had lived a sheltered twenty some years, hunting, fishing, drinking, "sowing some wild oats," as his mother called it, with the ladies lately and knowing that he had a job as a lawman always waiting for him, without schooling or nothing, on account of his father. And now all that was gone. So he sat and took in the noise of the room: the policemen interviewing, nodding their heads, talking to the men scattered about, some having to sit down to tell their accounts.

Outside, sirens roared. The rest of the legitimate police force and ambulance and skim press of the small town arrived. Quickly, an orange plastic cautionary line formed the perimeter around the site, tied from tree to tree along the sidewalk. Flares burned on the street, where a line of officers stood holding back the crowd. The good working fathers went out and looked on and talked. Some children ran out of a home to the street. A policeman caught them. But one child got by and stood for a moment with his hands on the cautionary line. He could see through the legs of the medics the moonlit gloss on the hump of the sheriff's belly lying in a puddle as they lifted the body onto a gurney and into the ambulance. Nobody noticed the boy.

Chett Bradshaw, the thin, big-headed, smart-mouthed top deputy on the force, stood just beyond the flares, wrapping up his interview.

"Mr. Bradshaw, do you have any idea who did this? Some sort of cowboy we're hearing?" asked the reporter.

"Yeah, that's what we've been hearing so far. Strange. But a ... we'll get him. Thank you," he said, and he jogged into the bar like an athlete.

On his way in, he passed a woman holding a crying baby in the flashing siren light.

"It'll be all right," Chett said to her.

"Just what this country needs," said the woman, sardonically, "another murder."

Chett smiled a wry line, which vanished as quickly as it came, and he went down the stair shaft to the basement of the bar. It was all hollow and dark down there. Some policemen still lingered, interviewing shadows of men in the back room. In the forefront, under the pale light of a single bulb on the ceiling, five men sat around a table, twirling their guns, talking low and slow, loading up. Chett entered and all heads looked to him and waited. Bucktooth sat silently, smoking a cigarette in the corner, petting his rifle.

"All right men, so this is the crew. Come on, boys, don't look so blue! We've got justice on our side. Justice. And we will bring justice to this *cowboy*."

"Revenge!" cried one of the men. "I say we head out and blast the bastard right now!"

"Hang the son of a bitch!" said another.

"Now let's not get carried away here, men," Chett said, wriggling his big head. It was amazing that he could stand up straight with that head. He walked around the table and took a look at Bucktooth. The stocky young man sat vacantly, in a spell, petting his rifle. His sweaty yellow hair stuck to his head under his hat as sweat beaded and streamed down his neck and his chest. His eyes pierced the air. He cocked his head to one side. A pale streetlight showed through the little window above him, a thin trapezoid-shaped ray down over him, cutting his red face in half, and blinking in and out of the darkness, as feet walked back and forth outside.

"This cowboy is going down, but we've got to keep our heads," Chett said, receiving a silent wave of aggression from the men in the shadows.

"This duel or whatever it was is over," Chett continued. "Now we've got to hunt down this varmint, using proper police procedures, all right? Indifference can be worse than hate," Chett said, looking right at Bucktooth. "I understand your thirst for revenge. And I tell you, rest assured, we will take this cowboy down. The rest of the force, along with a few U.S. marshals who are already interested in this guy, will be heading south — they think he's heading for Mexico. Well let me tell you, he won't taste one margarita. We've got stencils being made, posted up all over the place; this guy is wanted on national TV — all over America! Hell, we've got cars, this guy's on a goddamned horse!"

The men chuckled. Bucktooth remained silent.

Chett looked at the guns on the table. He was not one for guns and killing, but he was smart enough to act it before the men — those durable men of beards and beer bellies and farts and tobacco and rigid obedience and brevity.

Bucktooth sat still in the corner. He looked up, tipping his hat back and up against the wall, revealing his scruffy head of dirty yellow, sweaty hair. He could see out the small basement window above him the legs standing around and walking. He could hear the policemen interviewing the folks outside. A clock ticked somewhere in the dark on the wall, yet it felt right behind him always, ticking away each instant he strived for, losing it again and again, and swallowing and sucking in his intemperance, biting his quivering lip firm, lifting up his stubborn chin to the men. At minutes end, he pounded his fist into the wall beside him. The ticking continued. He heard it all like white noise; saw it all in glimpses under his hat, the policemen nodding and taking notes. It all meant nothing, helped none. His father was dead.

"Did you see his face?" Bucktooth heard one man say.

"Naw, man, but this guy was a killer right out of a movie, let me tell you," said another.

"He's on a horse. About 15 hands high; I'd say 1,200 pounds, a big strong horse."

"What kind of horse?" asked the officer.

"I don't know. It might've been a dunn or a quarter horse or what-ever cowboys ride, shit!" exclaimed another.

Through all this, Chett saw Bucktooth sitting irascibly in the corner. "All right, that's enough, that's enough!" he announced to the legitimate policemen. "He's dead. That's the story. Our good sheriff is dead. The cowboy killed him. Now we know what has to be done. Let us do it."

The policemen understood and left the men.

Chett's continued trying to conciliate the men. He was a temperate man of the "legit" half of the force, not referred to as "lawmen" under the sheriff in the old-fashioned town, but of the ones who did the actual mundane work of the job without all the booze. He'd grown accustomed to appeasing the slightest demand of others. He had a bad marriage, bad kids, etc. He used to always keep his head down and never had a convic-tion about anything in his life. And he always stood by the law. And since that night, he'd had one hell of an overdrawn inferiority complex under Sheriff Jack Miller and was actually secretly happy that he was dead. His work was his life now. His one goal was to prove himself by scooping up this leaderless band of lawmen and bringing them back into the legiti-mate fold of reality — yet at the same time, prove to these rough men that he could handle things, prove it to his wife, society in general. Get promoted. Get even. Get respect with a round of beers. Kill the cowboy.

He went over to Bucktooth and put a hand on his shoulder. "Son, I'm gonna get you your revenge. I will," he said.

Bucktooth looked up real slow, his face hard, eyes fierce and cut-ting. He sat slumped over as if he'd been wounded, thinking of his father when he was young, petting his rifle. "I reckon I can kill 'em my damn self," he said.

"That you will, son," Chett said. He turned back to the men. "Now, gather around here, boys."

The men obeyed.

"We were made for this. We have justice on our side, and justice is always justifiable, like I always say. We'll kill this cowboy legally, boys."

The men snickered. Most didn't know what he was talking about but understood that they were to kill the cowboy and that Chett was trying to be funny about it, and so they shrugged their big shoulders in laughter.

"We'll kill him just like the old days. Us seven — hell, the Magnificent Seven! The posse of discipline, law, system, we'll kill this cowboy before summer breaks. What is it, April 8? He'll be dead by June at the latest! Perfect for television! Now what do we got? Come on, what do we got?" he asked his men and presumed his position at the head of the table.

Some men sat or stood off to the side, moving in under the light and huddling in the posse. All men accepted Chett as their new sheriff without a grunt of argument and slammed their guns to the table.

Spivey, a thin marksman with a mustache, reported as the guns hit the table. "Bo's got a .38; Mitch's got a .22; Freddy's got the big .45; I got my .44 magnums, a bunch of carbines, sawed-off shotgun, believe it or not, buckshot 12 gauge, double-barrel Spencer rifle, and a pair of Smith and Wesson six-shooters…. aah, and some dynamite, and that's about it."

"Ammo?"

"Boxes of it," said a man, and pointed to the back end of the basement.

"Good. Target? Who is this cowboy?"

"Nobody got his name."

"The bartender did. Where is he? Get him down here."

A man went to get him and came back five minutes later. "He won't come," he said.

"What?"

"He won't come. He's too scared."

"Scared? Get him down here! Spivey go with him," Chett ordered.

Minutes later the bartender appeared, trembling down the stairs. The men had to hold his arms so he would not faint.

"Have a seat, Jim," Chett said to the bartender. "Butch, get him a drink, will ya?"

"Yes, sir."

A dry whiskey materialized before the bartender's eyes before he sat down. He picked it up and looked at the amber-bronze liquid.

"It's whiskey, Jim, drink it," Chett said.

As soon as he finished it, another took its place.

"What is this cowboy's name?" Chett asked, leaning in to him over the table.

The bartender sweated profusely. "H-He,"

"Drink your drink, Jim. Good. Now, he only told you his name. What is it? Just tell us. We're gonna kill him. Just tell us."

"H-he,"

"Henry?"

"Sounds like a fake."

"No," said Bucktooth from the corner. "This asshole's straight up, he ain't no fake." And all heads turned to Bucktooth, then back to the bartender who had gathered his nerves.

"He didn't say his name," said the bartender.

"He didn't say," Chett said, leaning back and thinking, fingering the whiskers on his chin. "So, no name — just some nameless cowboy... stops in and kills our sheriff."

"Where do you think he's heading?" asked a man.

"East," said Bucktooth.

"Yes, east," Chett agreed.

"East?" Spivey objected. "Why the hell would he go east? What the hell is east? Boston, New Jersey? No way, this cowboy's going south! He's gonna make a run for the border. Let's get goin'. What are we waiting for? I say, he ain't gonna taste one margarita before I. .... "

"Spivey!" Chett shouted. "Sit down. The kid here knows this cowboy; he's looked into his goat eyes. And I am in command. You shut up and tag along."

Spivey slowly sat down.

Chett turned to Bucktooth and looked off a bit. "Yeah, that's right, kid. East. All that land. Naw, he won't hide, will he, kid? He'll go east without a care, and we'll meet him there."

◆ ◆ ◆ ◆

CHAPTER IV

In Kingston, Nevada, Sasha the whore ducked out of the rain into a bar on the corner of the casino-lit strip. Her dyed blonde hair streamed wetly down her cheeks. She wore a mini-skirt with black panties and a tight, red blouse with her tan bosom all snug and busting out. Her soft-skinned, dainty arm held a black leather satchel. Her lips glossed pink, and her eyes painted black and blue with mascara, she clacked her high heels across the floor and leaned in over the bar so her legs and bottom bounced up playfully. She swung like this, chewing her gum, waiting for the bartender who was talking to some guys down at the other end. He saw her and smiled. The short, stumpy, white-haired man always looked to her like some old familiar uncle. The men smiled as well, and one gave a wave. Sasha blew one last big bubble, then took her gum out, stuck it under the bar and lit herself a cigarette. She sucked in on the cigarette quick and hard and let the smoke come out her nostrils and the corners of her mouth. She could not stop moving, fidgeting, tapping her fingernails on the bar, swaying her body over it and her dainty ass up in the air, her head down to the cherry wood and her finger gesturing for the bartender and the men.

Finally, the bartender came over and poured her a brandy. "How are ya, Sasha?" he asked without looking at her. He was a portly man with two chins and three strands of hair waxed over his bald head. His voice wheezed and his chubby hands grabbed quick, as if he'd tended for many years to deep pockets.

Sasha held her round glass in her palm and swirled the brandy. "What do ya got for me, Sam," she said in her Southern twang. "It's raining fucking cock 'n' balls out there."

"I hear that," said the bartender. He wanted to tell her a little rain was good for the land, but he held his breath.

"Speaking of which," he said, tipping his head to the two men down the bar.

"No, Sam, don't say those two. Not them. They're rich psychopaths, just looking for a trashy piece like me they can rip up and eat."

"Sasha, they're legitimate businessmen. They just closed a big deal, and they're looking for some celebration. These guys make the world go round, baby. Cut 'em some slack, huh? Look at them. They look like nice guys."

"Yeah, easy for you to say, you don't have to fuck them," she said, and she looked over at them. Both men sat at the short end of the bar by the wall. The dim lights over the bar shined down over the two men. She could see one's smug smile, and the other's wry, lustful eyes, their loosened neckties and white collars.

"Goddamn it, Sam, he saw me."

"Good. Let him. He wants you."

"Can't you get some regular scrungy guys? I mean what are these kinda guys doing in this part of town anyway?"

"There looking for a special girl like you."

"Probably got wives."

"That's never stopped you."

She adjusted her boobs and looked over at the men again, then back at Sam.

"Oh, I don't feel up to it, Sam. Not tonight. I don't look ... rich enough for these guys. Why didn't you tell me it was gonna be like the president and vice president?"

"Hey, that's bull right there," Sam said. With one chubby hand, he lifted her chin. "You look great. Look at you, regular high-class Southern girl — just like that one movie — what was it?"

"Oh, why is everything a movie?"

"Forget it. You are *you*. Here, look at yourself in the mirror." Sam moved out of the way and directed her attention to a small circular mirror on the wall. Sasha caught herself in it. "See, look at that. Look at those eyes, always moving. Finally you stop and find yourself, and just how beautiful you are. Blonde, luscious, white, rosy cheeks, Sasha you are my number one girl."

A smile slowly took her. And soon she was having drinks with the men and laughing hysterically, sitting between them, letting them touch her on the neck and legs. She even let them slip down one of the strings of her halter top. But at that point, Sasha fixed herself and stood up. The men looked at her, bemusedly for a moment, on the verge of laughing in her face. Sasha suggested that they get a room.

On their way out, a young boy ran into Sasha's lap as she walked through the dark parking lot with the men. The boy hit both men in their stomachs. They backed off, holding their stomachs in mock pain, dying of laughter.

The boy looked up at his mother and burrowed his head into her lap. Sasha ran a hand through his hair until she got to his ears and pinched them outward, the soft white lobes. The boy cried. He cupped his ears, stepped back and cringed, facing his mother.

"Aah, man, she's got a kid! A kid!"

"Let's get out of here," said the men.

"What?" Sasha said. "This is not my kid! I have no idea who this kid is, just some street dirtball begging for money — wait!" she called after the men.

The men gloated with laughter.

Sasha saw that they liked it and continued. "I have no idea who this kid is, really! Some nerve he's got, hey he thinks he can afford a girl like me!"

In the roar of the men's laughter, Sasha whispered fervently down to her son, "You want money, boy? You want toys, huh? You want food?"

The boy nodded sadly.

"Then run away, boy, run away. Momma's gonna be okay. Get! Get on now. Back to the car, wait for me there. Get!" she shrieked. And the boy ran off between the cars and down an alley between two empty warehouses.

The men then took Sasha to a tall hotel down the street. Their room was on the third floor. The boy followed his mother from within the shadows. He knew her by her walk and the sight of her legs flickering through the strangers'. He kept a good ten paces away. He followed them into the swanky hotel and through the lobby. He saw his mother's legs in the small crowd of drunken, rich people and uniformed ushers. He followed her into a crowded elevator where he stood in the middle of everybody, gazing up at the golden ceiling, smiling at glimpses of himself and his mother in the gold. He was a skinny boy, with a mop head of blonde hair over his eyes.

He kept his distance, still a good ten steps from his mother as the men took her out of the elevator and began walking down the long narrow hallway of yellow walls and red tapestry decorated carpet. He heard the men stop his mother at the room three doors away from the open window at the end of the hall.

"This is it," said one of the men. He unlocked the door with a strip of plastic and the other pushed the boy's mother into the room. She went with a feeble yelp of resistance, and she thought she saw her son's head peeping from behind a ledge down the hall as the door slammed.

The boy had heard the slam but didn't know where it came from. He ran to the end of the hall. The wind blew the long silk, white window curtains into his face like a dreamy mist as he passed through them to the veranda overlooking the city. In the middle of the veranda sat a rich white-clothed table and the leftover mess of an extravagant multi-course dinner for two, and a black telephone. The boy's eyes widened. "Boy, oh boy!" he exclaimed, "boy, oh boy. oh boy!" And he dug in on the leftover food.

An hour later, his mother still hadn't come out. He put his head down on the white table and waited, looking at the phone. Dappled with sleep, he collapsed his face in his arms, knocking over the phone with his hand. The receiver lay on the table, quiet as he fell into sleep. After a few seconds, the phone started with the phone-of-the-hook warning sound.

"Hello, sir, is everything all right?" came a man's voice from the phone.

The boy nearly thought it was his old man as he woke from dreaming. "Hello," he said sleepily into the receiver.

"Who is this?" said the voice.

"This is no one," said the boy, and he hung up and went to the ledge of the veranda where he rested his arms. The rain had stopped and the desert night air settled in aridly.

Down in the square of desert between him and the next hotel, he saw a bison grazing like a statue in the dark. To his left, he viewed the wide-open desert and distant purple mountain ranges. The bison must have wandered on over, separated from the herd, or likely the last living one, run away from a circus somewhere, he thought. He could see its thick, curled-up horns and its bulk of mane and muscle agleam slightly as it wandered closer to the street and the light of the hotel.

The first floor down, a buffet of food lined the outer ledge of the hotel where the boy could see a sliver of rich folk partying. Soon he heard them laughing and making jokes. One said, "Now, just don't make it mad whatever you do!" And that was exactly what the boy decided to do. He drew his slingshot. He knew his time was short before they found him. He'd only have a couple of shots to piss off the bison. A given-up sadness clouded him and any chance he thought he had of saving his mother. But he fought it, slinging and reloading, stretching back and aiming as best as he could, nailing the brute right between the eyes, trying to get it angry as hell, so it would charge for the hotel, knocking it over and killing all except his mother, whom he would ride through the cinders and save. But the big dumb animal wouldn't move and very quickly he ran out of stones. He threw the phone, a few dishes, a chair and was trying for the table when they grabbed him and took him away, detained in the lost child area behind the desk, where he sat in a room alone, waiting for his mother.

◆ ◆ ◆ ◆

CHAPTER V

The cowboy escaped that murderous night to his grandmother's house atop White Willow Mountain just across the border into Idaho. His horse knew the path well. Every now and again, he would wake at the strong gallop and look up at the tall, silent, black trees shifting massively in the wind and harrowing down on him. And then he'd fall back down onto the horse, letting her take him up the mountain, all dark and green in the night.

He reached the summit by dawn. His grandmother's cabin sat secluded in the pine trees overlooking a snow-capped peak, a good stretch of rugged land as the fog clears in the morning, and several towns nestled against the foot of the mountain. All the people of Stricland on the western foot had once dreamed of venturing up the mountain at one time or another and making their homes there, but none had actually done it for one reason or another, but primarily on account of the mysterious old witch who lived up there in a cabin. Now that mysterious old witch, who was really a very nice old lady, stared out her kitchen window behind the sink, running lukewarm water over her paper-skinned hands. She saw her grandson come out of the trees and into the pale light, dying on his horse. She smiled knowingly.

The cowboy made it to the door and fell off the horse. His grandmother opened the door and met him on her doorstep with her little smile.

"There's my handsome grandson," she said.

The cowboy squinted up at her. She stood over him with the sun around her like a halo. The sight of her in the doorway and the old wooden smell coming out from the cabin was a composite of everything he remembered as home. Even though he grew up in Texas, she was family and the only one left who gave a damn.

"You've done it again, I see," she said.

The cowboy swallowed in pain, nodded his head slowly up to her as she scolded him. "Granny, I'm dyin'. Granny, this time, I'm really dyin', I am…" he gasped.

"They didn't piss on ya, did they?"

"Granny, I'm dying here!"

She bent down and sniffed him. "Oh, heavens! They did pee on ya!"

"Granny!"

"Oh, yes, I know you are. I know. We's all dying a little bit these days. Come on in, everything is ready for you."

◆ ◆ ◆ ◆

He awoke in water. His grandmother heard him gasp.

"Water too hot?" she called from the kitchen.

He looked around dumbfounded. He sat in an old-fashioned bathtub with his legs dangling over the end. He was not in a bathroom, just against a log wall parallel to the window across the small cabin. The window took up nearly the whole wall with a terrific mountainous view. The smell of old mothballs saturated the air. He took in the modest cabin interior, remembering the place all at once: the miniature furniture, the split-logged wooden staircase that angled nearly straight up like a ladder to the cots on the small platform above. He remembered details that led to little stories, like how he'd get up at the break of dawn and throw on his trousers, boots, and shirt, and head downstairs — but every morning his grandmother would beat him to the day, already down in the kitchen rattling pots and pans, fixing breakfast.

He looked over across the sleepy cabin floor to his old hat on the mantel in the dulled silver mountain light. The hat looked so far away as he gazed at it lazily, remembering his whole life as a kid and thinking a bit about his situation on the run from the law again, now that he'd killed that fat sheriff over in — whatever that town was — goddamned shithole, he thought. He reached for his hat. It sat just out of reach, but he squeaked around to the end of the tub like a kid, splashing and dripping water all over the dusty floor. He grabbed his hat and shoved it down over his eyes and sank down into the water, blowing bubbles.

As he came to the surface the second time, a more recent memory hit him: the hollering, throwing back whiskey, feeling the whiskey burn on his wound as his grandmother would lash it on, lying on the dinner table saying, "Granny, 'taint no need bothering, I'm gonna die from this, I'm dying fast..." as his grandmother skillfully carved out the bullet in his side and patched him up.

He sat now in that tub a few days later, yet he could still see a blur of metal scattered out on the table and he could smell the iodine twinge through the thick mothball air. He saw his grandmother bustling back and forth from the kitchen to the dinning room. The cabin sat neat and empty with small clutters of books and things here and there. His grandmother replaced the metal scalpel and bin with a yellow flower in a vase on the dinning room table and bustled away humming. Old pictures of very old relatives and such cascaded down short walls around the table. A fire crackled under the kettle. A fringe of some faded flowery decoration lined the ceiling like an attempt at wallpaper. The cowboy rested his head against the curved white edge of the tub and followed the flowers down the ceiling with his eyes.

"Granny?" he called eventually from the tub. His harsh, savage voice had now completely transformed into something so boyish and innocuous, ringing throughout his grandmother's cabin. He tried to stand up but the stitches in his side wouldn't allow it. They felt like they'd rip open as he seethed through his teeth, easing back into the hot water. He saw his grandmother then bustling about outside, tending to her magnificent flower garden of every color — an extraordinary feat of growing them at that altitude. Now, they had spread themselves and grew wild down the mountainside. He watched her water them and walk over, disappear behind the wall, and he heard her come in, walk across the hollow wooden floor to look at her grandson, as he'd hoped she would, but no, rather she walked right by the tub and into the sowing room, giving him only a glance.

The cowboy tried to turn around and talk to her, but his wound wouldn't allow it. The healing incision bled a bit in the tub, the drops puffing outward in the water, the stitches getting all soft and loose.

"Granny, is this gonna leave a scar?" he called tilting his head back in the sunlight.

"Yes," she replied. "Everything *you* do scars you, boy, you ought've learnt yer lesson by now. Soon you'll be no skin, all scars. The scarred cowboy."

"Hey, I ain't scared of nothin'!" the cowboy said in his big dumb Texas grandson tone.

"Scarred, I says!"

"Oh."

"No, Henry. If there is one thing you ain't, and I mean truly ain't, is a coward. No Dunn ever was. Even when all the cowards came a'sweeping through America, no Dunn ne'er changed. Some men I know are so afraid of being a coward that their cowardice is that they are afraid of being one." She smirked and tooted a high-pitched, satirical laugh. "That explains why no Dunn ne'er been able to hold a job and do well any-more. Generations back, your great-granddaddies marked the history books with their good doings, working the land and the ranches and such, driving cattle all across the desert. Stopping in the little cracker-box towns, finding love..." she trailed off nostalgically, ceasing with her sowing and looking up into a time capsule in a ray of sunlight through the window.

Silence settled in the cabin. Henry and his Granny thought about their lives in separate rooms. Dust floated around Henry's head. He blinked. He had blue eyes. "Say, is Pa still in Texas?" he asked. The ces-sation of his voice cut the stale air.

"No, he and Grandpa moved back to Kansas."

"Well, I'll be goddamned!"

"Yup."

Granny sat in her rocking chair, quilting and looking out the win-dow. A gray luminescent knowledge lay on her from the mountains and the clouds. The west slope of the mountain was rocky and gray and white, with trees spurting in between the boulders. The tip of a tall pine withered upward to a bent point. Its lower boughs tapped, hypnotic and tranquil, against the window.

"You now, Granny, I think I might go back there to old Kansas."

"And why in the hell would you want to do that? Damned place."

"Watch your cussin', Granny."

"Oh, mind yourself, boy."

"I aim to go back and marry that girl next door, what was her name?"

"Oh, it's been too long. I don't recollect anybody out there, dear."

The cowboy grew silent, fingering his chin and trying to think of that girl's name. He'd mutter every now and again, "some sort of song, some sort of little name..."

"What are you muttering about?" Granny stopped her rocking, waddled over and looked in the next room at her grandson as he leaned his head against the soapy tub.

The cowboy kept figuring. "Aah, nothing Granny," he said. "Nah, I reckon she's been married off by now." But he reckoned harder.

As he thought, his grandmother lectured. She screeched a chair from the dining room and sat down beside the bathtub with a sterile air about her as she washed her grandson with a soapy sponge over his broad back and shoulders.

"You know, cowboy Henry," she began, squeezing the sponge over his arched back, "you can't just go around gunning down everybody that gets in your way. You've got to respect folks. Respect the law. You keep killing people like this, in this drunken rage against society or rebellion or whatever you might call it, hell you might end up killing somebody you love. Ever think about that?"

The cowboy shoved her away playfully, and she gave up trying to clean him and went back behind the wall into the sowing room. She sat rocking swiftly in the old chair by the window, looking out over America.

"Nobody ever taught it to you so I guess I ought to at least try," she began again, tersely. "The world will kill you. Especially this world and this government we got set up here. It'll kill you if you keep on like this. All this courage, bravery, independence, whatever you call freedom, the world will kill. And don't go thinking you'll get a gun-blazing bloody legend death either. They'll arrest you and put you on the magazines and TV, and you'd be just another American scandal, just like that one actor who went crazy, whatever his name was...

"And then they'd send you to jail and raise a big controversy on whether to kill you or not, but the truth is, and you'll know it right well, they already have. Yes'm, it all depends on which state they nab you in. These United States ain't united in law, you know. You can kill in one and get killed in another. I tell you this America, they're all aiming to kill each other and they're all bound to do it at the same time. And you, you think you're something special, cutting through society and all with this cowboy get-up. Well, let me tell you right now: sooner or later you'll be a part of this rat race, too. Sooner or later they'll break you, they will."

"Naaaah! Get outta here!" the cowboy said hoarsely, and he flapped his hand at her through the wall from the tub.

"Don't think I don't see what you're up to," his grandmother continued. "Think you got this great childhood love waiting for ya back in Kansas. Has it ever occurred to you that maybe some of the men you kill might have a damned childhood? I mean, we're all in this together, Henry. You're just making it worse. Think you're making some big change. Think you're some big pioneer American legend, big cowboy stud, but you's just like everybody else. Same arrow in your heart."

The cowboy broke from his trance of thought. He had decided what to do.

"Granny, get me a towel, will ya?"

Granny came in.

"Durn it, Granny, why don't you have a washroom with walls around it like normal folks do?"

"I like to look out the window when I bathe. No need for walls."

"Well it is one pretty view," said the cowboy.

Granny came in with a towel and told him to stand up. The cowboy moaned, half-embarrassed, like a kid. "Come on now, cowboy Henry," she chided. "No need for embarrassment with me! I've seen this naked hinny plenty a times!"

Henry stood up slowly, smiling a half-smile, covered with bubbles and only his hat on his head.

"Granny, don't call me Henry," he told her with his eyes closed as she dried his face with the towel.

"What? Why? It's your name. You don't like your name?"

"Nah, just, I don't know … it ain't really a cowboy name. Don't seem fit to me. Don't seem tough."

"It's a king's name. It's tough. Henry. What's wrong with Henry?"

"Aah, nothing I guess. Just don't tell anybody my name, I mean if they come up here asking, don't tell them my name, all right? Tell them my name is … Custer."

"Well, all right. I don't know what your father would say about this cowboy nonsense or Ulysses, for heavens sake!"

"Say, where is old Grandpa Ulysses?"

"He's with your Pop in Kansas."

"Well, what the hell's he doin' there?"

"Henry, I don't know. What the hell is anyone doin' anywhere? What are you doin'? That's what I want to know. Where are you thinking about heading anyway, straight for Kansas?"

"No, I figure I'll go south for one last thrill."

"Oh, God."

"Then north to find work. Keep the law off my back for a while, while I earn up some money. I'm not going back to Kansas empty-handed, Granny. I'm not going back without some money. I'll tell you that right now."

"Well, arms up, cowboy," she said. And she continued to dry off her grandson, scrubbing his torso good and clean with the towel. Henry stood and let her with his arms in the air. Granny soon got down to the stitches on his lower left side. She carefully rubbed them off with the moist towel. A fresh, red scar about three inches long blazed.

"A little scar. Not bad," Granny said. She wrinkled her soft blue eyes and admired her grandson before her. She felt somehow that she would never see him again. As he got dressed, ate a square meal and loaded up his horse, she continued giving him supplies of water, food, and advice. She was a very knowledgeable woman: 80 years of hearing and seeing in the world to a stubborn, old-fashioned mind, uncorrupted by the hypocrisies of our time. Yet now she had been broken. Years back, her husband was arrested for fraud and tax evasion. She'd told him money wasn't worth it, but he said she didn't understand and he went to jail — a smart man. When he got out, they separated between mountains and a desert and plains of land. Now, she mutters around alone, getting talked about when she'd go into town, and some youth would sneak up on her house on Halloween and the whole recluse bit, mopping around, thinking of old times, looking out the window saying, "even the old get divorced nowadays, even the old."

The one thing that kept Henry with his grandmother a good half-hour more was a shave. He hadn't had one in a month. He stood by the window shaving, glancing at a handheld mirror, the water basin and the lather balanced finely on the tall mantel. The placid iron-silver light of the mountains hit him through the solaced setting sun and the thin window.

After his shave, he had his last hot meal, sitting across the table from his grandmother. He'd look up and his granny would be grinning at him like she was hurt inside and he'd say, "What's the matter, Granny?" And she'd say, "Nothing." Now the cowboy had heard a bit here and there about what his grandmother had told him about the world killing a fellow and such. He could sense her concern, and he knew that this very well could have been the last time he saw the old lady. He knew it could very well have been his last home-cooked meal. She had prepared the hot broth and steak and potatoes and milk and watched him from sitting on the bench across the table with her hands folded, and her eyes glowing, and the whole rest of her body stiff and surrendering, as she watched her grandson chow down her carefully prepared meal.

Afterward, the cowboy went out and tied the tin basin to the surcingle on his horse, clanging with the other little pots and spoons and forks like bells in the wind. Granny made her way down the doorsteps and draped a thick red patch quilt over the saddle. She told him that the centerpiece in the quilt came from his great grandfather's Confederate uniform from the Civil War. Henry thanked her for all, kissed her on the cheek, straddled up, and smiled goodbye.

And so he began his journey. The cowboy's old granny waited out in the cold that evening, watching her grandson ride off east down the other side of the mountain, with the Home of the Brave awaiting him all in the distance and its huge slabs of gray rock, jagged at the edges in the forefront, his horse going over them, in between them and sloping down the iron rock, with him and the horse the color of bronze and gold blur, and then only brown, the horse swaying in steady rhythm already, taking him back home. He had made his farewell, and he did not look back. But at the edge of the crest, he arched his shoulder around and lifted his hat. He pulled back the reins on his wild-tempered horse and she rose into the air kicking her front hooves and neighing as the cowboy held on and waved his hat. His granny waved back and smiled a broad happy line in her wrinkles. And she let her hand surrender him with her blessing, descending to her side.

"That's boy's gonna cause one hell of a ruckus," she said softly after him, "hmm, hhmm, one hell of a ruckus."

◆ ◆ ◆ ◆

• BOOK II •

CHAPTER VI

Back in Kansas, Angie went to work. Inside her cubby box, she found a pink slip. Due to the recession, the factory had downsized, laying off 100 employees that day. The young brunette came home crying. The next day her mother went just a few miles down the street with her daughter still whimpering at her side, to the old gas station located on the road into town. There old lady Sherman knew the owner; hence, her daughter Angie got another job.

While working one hot day behind the register, a sickly, pale-skinned, bulky young man named Ken entered the store. He wore a small thick golden hoop earring, loose jeans and no shirt. His body was flabby and big. His hairy potbelly hung out in his boxer shorts, which stuck out of his jeans. He drooped his belly down and sucked in, trying to flex his flab but only belching loudly in the effort, as he strutted around grabbing a candy bar and a bag of chips from the shelves and shoving them into his pockets. He made his way to the refrigerator in the back and grabbed a case of beer.

As he went to the register, he straightened his back and said to himself, "Damn!" as he saw Angie sitting behind the counter, reading a book and twirling her hair.

"Hey there, pretty lady," he said. And he slammed a case of beer on the counter, planted his hands on the table and leaned in as though he were at a bar.

Angie looked up. "Oh, I didn't even notice you!" She stood up, flustered in innocence and embarrassment. Her hair curled in brown rivulets — and if you noticed, closely and calmly, when the sun hits them in the center, a certain sparkling crimson shine swayed in the curls.

"Didn't notice me!" Ken blurted.

"No, I'm sorry," she pushed a button on the register. "Damn thing. Shoot. Where's Bonnie?" She looked back at the little office for her manager, Bonnie. She was alone. She hit the right button and the register drawer popped out and frightened her. "Whoa, there she goes!" she said. "Sorry about that." She had this constant sorry syndrome — a habit of apologizing for everything ever since she was a child. "Okay, so a case of beer .... okay ...will that be all?" she asked, glancing back at Ken.

Ken ripped open the cardboard case, took out a beer and popped it fizzing open, spilling onto the counter. He gave her a crazed grin with his lazy turtle face, arched his head back and guzzled the beer. Angie stood awkwardly, again looking to the back room for help. After slurping down the last of the beer, Ken crunched the can in his hands and tossed it toward the trash. He tucked his chin into his chest, showing his rolls of fat, and belched a long, groaning, smelly one.

"Pard' me," he said.

"That's 26 dollars and 59 cents," Angie said. She lifted her chin up and to the side sternly and looked at him in her uptight, professional manner the manager and also her mother had her practice for these types of situations, with particularly this type of customer. She could hear herself in her mind telling her mother all about how she handled it after work.

"Twenty-six dollars for a case of beer!" Ken exclaimed.

"And on account of one *Whack Attack* magazine, one bag of chips and a candy bar," she said, the corners of her lips pursing and dimpling her cheeks, her hips tilted to one side, and herself all cool and relaxed. She pointed to the top wall where a security camera rotated in an electronic buzz.

"Well, I'll be damned," Ken said, "times are a-changin'."

Angie smiled a bit and took a step back from the counter.

"You've been watching me this whole time? Huh, what's a pretty little thing like yourself working in a dump like this anyway?"

Angie didn't answer. Sweat beaded on the back of her neck under her hair. Glancing over the empty aisles, her eyes found the Coca-Cola clock. Bonnie wasn't going to be back for another hour. An hour: such a long time in a young life, she thought.

"Say, I tell you what, I'm gonna be fair to you," Ken announced. "This ain't right. We don't even know each other's names and we're already fighting over beer. Here: I'm Ken." He extended his hand.

Angie blushed and took his hand. "Angie," she said. "And one more thing, you're not supposed to enter the store without a shirt on. Sign says." And she pointed to the sign in the window.

"Don't miss a thing, do ya?"

She shook her head, wrinkling her eyes and smiling.

"Say, I'm having a little get-together later on, what do you say you come on over, drink some of this here brew with us?"

Angie smiled brightly now. Her cheeks blushed. She had not been asked out in the longest time. "Okay," she said sweetly, catching his beady eyes.

And Ken gave her the address and time and went out. As soon as he stepped out and the door closed behind him, she heard his yell muffled through the plexiglass door, with his arms outspread to the sky, "gawd, I love that girl!"

After work that day, Angie skipped home singing. She found her mother watching TV. The TV set was an old-fashioned one perched on an old wooden mantel low to the floor. The walls in this TV room were a light pink. The carpeted floor dipped down into a smooth brown tiled kitchen floor and in between the rooms was the front door, blue like the rest of the outside of the house with a white-square-checked, half-circle little window frame at the top of the door.

Angie hopped under the cherry tree out front and up to the old wooden porch, where she could see a litter of cigarette butts smothered against the top step and some even in the flower pot where the poor rose struggled to grow. She peered in through the door window and watched her mother falling asleep in front of the TV, the remote control about to fall from her limp hand on the sofa arm.

"Hello Mama!" Angie said, coming in lively.

"Angie, Angie, where are you?" her mother said, waking up. She rubbed her eyes.

"I'm here, Mama!" Angie said. And she went over to the sofa, wrapped her arms around her mother and sat down beside her. "Whatchya watching?"

"Nothing, nothing ... some bombing on the news, the Middle East, you know they're ripping it up where it all started. ...Oh, I'm so happy you're home!"

"Oh, me too, Mama!"

"I woke up and for a moment there I'd thought I'd lost you."

"Mama!"

"Yes, dear. You've been gone for such a long time, it seems, and I woke up with the sleep in my eyes like I couldn't see and I couldn't remember who I was even, and I remembered, and thought maybe you'd found a better fix than coming home to this old shack, living with me. Thought you'd run off on me."

"Oh mama, never!"

"You know that feeling when you wake up after a deep slumbering and you don't remember where you are, or who you are even?"

"Well, I don't know Mama, but I'm here now, you have me now."

"I know, I know."

The mother and daughter cuddled on the sofa under a blanket.

"Mama," Angie said, "I have been invited to a party."

Her mother's face stiffened in frown.

"This nice boy named Ken —"

"Ken Strover?"

"Yes, that's the one."

"Works down at Ken's Body Shop fixing up cars and such?"

"That's him."

"Oh, you stay away from that boy, darling, he's a troublemaker."

But Angie pleaded with her mother all through dinner. And eventually she said, "All right, get outta here!" And the daughter hugged her mother and ran upstairs to get dressed and put her makeup on to go out.

The party was held right in the middle of a field. There was no bonfire. Angie just drove out to the vast empty country in her Poppa's old pickup and turned right — barely missing it — down Ken's long stone driveway at around midnight to the lights of cars parked out on the plain. Ken's old man gave Angie a smile as he directed her to keep going down the driveway and into the little valley.

The cars formed a circle of headlights shed on a patch of grass blown down sideways in the wind. Ken and his friends and their girlfriends guzzled out of a keg from the trunk of one of the cars. All the cars were decked out with fluorescent lights glowing underneath them on the grass, tinted windows, and of course the old boom-boom stereo system bumping and vibrating from music through the cars.

"Here's my ho!" Ken cried, as he saw the pickup truck approaching. He chastened himself as she arrived within hearing distance. "Here she is," he said, "my girl! I knew you'd come!" He rushed over to her door and tried to help her down out of the truck, but Angie didn't see him there and jumped down by herself.

"Oh, sorry," she said.

"Don't worry about it," Ken said. His face looked all shadowed under the eyes and pale in the car light. He escorted Angie into the circle. Her Poppa's pickup truck she had parked just outside the circle of cars. Throughout the night, she glanced over at it sitting in the dark and she thought of leaving as Ken boasted to his friends. Ken stood on a car and flexed his muscles. Spat. Guzzled beer. And he grabbed her and, dancing with her drunkenly, spun her round and round — the car headlights whirling. He bragged mostly about his money and how his dad's auto shop was raking it in and ripping people off. He kept calling Angie his girl. She drank two quick yet tall beers, then sat drinking the third one slowly. Sometimes one of the couples started necking and falling all over her and she'd have to slide off the hood of the car and out of the way. Some went off to have sex in the little dip of a grassy valley. One of the girls asked her if she wanted another beer. "Got one," Angie said, lifting up the tall can. "What's that beer doing not empty?" said a boy a few minutes later. "Drink, drink." And he tipped up the bottom. "There you go," he said, and he went off laughing with a groupie. Angie wiped some beer foam from her mouth with the back of her hand and her sleeve.

"Hey that's my car, goddamn it!" Ken shouted at a couple getting naked in his car. He opened the door and kicked them out.

One girl walked off drunk, looking into space. She wandered aimlessly across the valley and through a cornfield, feeling tips of the stalks like she'd never felt anything before on her fingertips, gazing over the hedges, tickling herself, shivering and walking out into the heart of nowhere (which ain't too hard to find in Kansas).

And then Ken and Angie were alone. Angie moved to the hood of one of the cars, sipping her beer. Ken went and knelt before her. He gawked up at her, his jaw hung and curved in like a spout, drooling.

"Ain't you having fun?" he asked.

"Yeah," Angie said, and she bobbed her head slowly and looked off to the stars. The wind took up her hair then. Ken's bald head remained an immobile white marble in the dark before her.

"Hold still," he said, "I want to give you a kiss."

"W—."

Ken, owing allegiance to the class that the kids from the city would call "white-trash" as they drove through the trailer park areas of Fort Plain; Ken, the bulky, white, homegrown son of a mechanic, known to the town's parents and the local police as a troublemaker, responsible for all the parties and complaints from parents of young girls, thinking that he had her with his rehearsed "hold still" line, darted in, grabbing her head, pulling her hair in the back, pressing himself into her on the hood of the car, and thrusting his squirming tongue in her mouth. Angie shrieked. Her slender arms crossed her heart. Her face shivered up and back in utter, helpless resistance.

Ken withdrew. "I ain't humping you, I'm just kissin', honey," he said with his fetid beer breath.

"Taint no respectful kiss! 'Taint no right kiss. You got to respect me! I'm a lady. I'm a. ..." Angie's protest trailed off into tears.

Ken stood up over Angie who lay on the car hood, her arms crossed at her heart, her hands stiffened outward in defense. "I'll respect you when you suck my cock," he said. And he muttered off.

"Put a few more beers in her, Ken," suggested someone sitting against a car in the dark.

"Yeah, that's what I'll do, sho, that's exactly what I'll do!"

"What the fuck's a bitch for?" laughed the kid in the dark.

Angie slipped down off the hood of the car feeling the cold metal slide on her skin through her white dress, which stretched out thin. She walked across the car-lit space to the figures in the dark standing behind the cars. The car light illuminated her white dress ethereally. "I'm going home now," she said like a goddess. She could picture herself walking right through that crowd and getting in the truck and driving straight home to Mama. And she almost believed it. Then someone threw a bottle at her. Another grabbed her by the hair and slammed her face into the hood of a car. Then they held her down by the neck from behind. They held her head still and her moth open under the keg nozzle. She was indeed a slender soul.

Angie awoke lying in wet grass. She couldn't move. She heard the boys talking, but she couldn't move her head to see them. Ken stood over her in his dark jeans and shirtless. His head tilted down to her. At his side he held a beer bottle by its neck. A chill shimmered through her. Her arms broke out in goose bumps. She tried to sit up, but it was no good. A sharp pain clenched in her, disallowing movement passed a certain point. Her mouth hung open sticky with something.

Ken waited, looking down on her, slowly grinning. "Stupid bitch," he said. "You don't even know."

"No ... I am innocent," Angie said. "I'm a virgin, a virgin till I marry. That's the way of the Lord. I am a virgin. I am innocent." And with this she tried to get up and ached back down to the wet earth. Her dress stuck to the back in the dew. Ken and his boys, and even some girls, laughed. Shortly, Angie heard them leave, their cars booming away with their stereos. She heard clearly the voice of an African-American artist shouting, "I keep my bitches drugged up on that ecstasy!"

Angie let her arms fall over her head and watched the stars hopelessly for a long time. She looked over and saw the fringe of flowers beside her house and a bit of a blue color of home in the dark and she cried. She did not want her mother to know. They just dumped me here, blaring that nigger music, surely mama heard, she thought.

And so she lay like this. Eventually a star shot off free through the stagnant night web. She witnessed it lying there, and with but a tingle, felt something stir in her. And in the strong resolve of her heart, she found the courage to stand up. With her inner thighs bruised, she hobbled, careful not to close her legs over the spot as pain shot through her at the slightest bump in her path, closing her legs a fraction together.

She made it to the swing and sat down, rested her head against the chain and lifted her feet up enough to drift. The swing creaked shrilly into the cold night. Her own home looked for a moment unfamiliar and frightening to her, standing like a big dark cut-out gap in the night. The sky grayed over the land and then reddened in the distance into the dawn as she fell asleep, one milky white undamaged arm raised up on the chain and her poor sleepy child's head rested on it, leaning against the rusty chain and swinging gently, letting her feet dangle to the ground.

Overhead and way up, a big old airplane streaked across the sky as a dirty breeze roused her to the day. The tiny sediments in the air tickled her face. She blinked her eyes in the wind. And suddenly she remembered a secret promise — something no one else could remember save one. And she let a slight smile take her back, drifting in the wind. And she waited.

CHAPTER VII

The cowboy rode southward around Hell's Canyon, Snake River, and the Seven Devils Mountains, through the long green and yellow potato plains of Idaho, the farms, and the cracker-box towns, with his Granny's blue mountain fading distant on the range. He rode through meadows and woods and he avoided the roads, only crossing them and riding along them every now and again.

He figured now that somebody was definitely after him. He could smell his trace in the air. But for the most part, he really didn't care. Not caring had always worked out for him in the past — always got him into trouble but always out, somehow. And things would turn out the way he liked. He'd shrug it off with a smile, some beer, and a good laugh, and call it a good old time; brag about it to anyone who asks, "Say, ain't you that cowboy?"

He rode along the highway in the sun at midday. He could hear the ceaseless, hollow rushing sound of cars. He kicked up his horse and galloped up the embankment and for a while rode along the road. Then the land dipped down to a gutter. The horse jumped clean over the polluted creek and rode up again to the shoulder with the cowboy flailing wildly. But only his hat could be seen over the guardrail from the highway, bobbing up and down. Kids in the backseats of minivans and cars and all different shaped SUVs stared out their child-lock safe windows and caught glimpses of the cowboy as they zoomed by. They'd twist around in their seat belts to get a better look. "A cowboy!" they yelled. "A real cowboy!" And their parents would smile and nod and say, "Yup, this is the cowboy land," until they had enough and they'd quiet. But the kids knew what they saw. They'd sit in the backseat whispering to each other and dreaming about one day getting a leather Indiana Jones jacket and a gun and being a cowboy when they grew up.

A quiet kid in a car seat saw the cowboy clearly from the far opposite lane. He saw him through the cars and the sticks of guardrail flying by. "Cowboy," he said, and he pointed and smiled out the window. The kid's father turned back to him and played with him, talking in his baby-talk voice, "Yes, cowboy! That's right, you cute little bump!" The mother smiled and looked at her child in the rearview mirror, her eyes sparkling happy.

And then the broad raspy voice of the radioman cut out the music:

"We interrupt this program for an urgent message: the unidentified killer/cowboy is at large and loose somewhere in the Northwest. Police say he is riding saddleback on a large bronze horse with a golden mane. He is dressed like a cowboy. He is wanted for the murder of Sheriff Jack Miller of Stricland, Oregon. If you have any information, call your local police, or call the FBI hotline toll free at 1-800---- And beware, he is to be considered armed and extremely dangerous."

The cowboy was sighted again in Las Vegas. As he rode in that night, tourists took pictures of him. He cursed and shooed them away, and he actually fired his guns in the air, but they just kept coming, snapping pictures with their little Japanese digital cameras, saying, "Oooh, aaah, what a spectacle!"

The cowboy glared at them and then got into some heavy cussing. Most of the prudent tourists had young ears to protect and promptly left the cowboy be, discarding him as an R-rated attraction.

The cowboy saw the cons flashing in fluorescent lights for changes and games and money. He pulled a fistful of dollars from his inner vest pocket and went to gamble. He got lucky on blackjack and doubled his money, then won the first three hands at the poker table and lost it all.

"Horse shit!" he said to the dealer, and he punched him, slammed his head into the table and lifted the whole table up and over, the chips and cards and that big green table burying the dealer. A couple of monkeys in suits threw him out. When it came to gambling, he just did not know when to quit or hold back.

◆ ◆ ◆ ◆

Down on his luck and money, he walked the streets of Vegas looking for a woman. The lush pink lights of the Hotel de Sensual at the end of the block blanketed a growing crowd. The crowd heaped out from the lobby into the street, where the traffic had stalled to a patrolled one lane of sports cars and limousines.

The cowboy had strung up his horse in an alley beside the hotel. He shoved his way through the crowd, but the crowd was stronger. It carried him zigzagging, floating around the blur of pimply faces and capped heads. The cowboy saw some cute girls smiling at him in the pink light. He noticed that it was a fairly young crowd. He tipped his hat to the girls like a gentleman and brushed by them, grabbing their behinds and saying, "Pard'm, doll," and, "Watch out now, darling." All the girls were scantily clad, exposing tan, sweaty, tempting flashes of skin — thigh and bellies and breasts — to the cowboy's eyes. And they all wore tight colorful clothes that he loved. He loved the groups of these girls, swimming through them, touching them. And then there were the lone ones, the really awesome ones and the hottest, in the cowboy's opinion. Only trouble was, they usually had some boyfriend nearby. The cowboy rubbed himself up against a sweet girl with a cheery smile as he squeezed by. He tipped his hat to her and looked her over good from head to toe. The girl blushed and let him look. Her sexy gloss of sweat filmed over her perfect young face and bosom. Her jeans were tight and stems nice, too. But what really got him was the butt. Butts were in, it seemed. Everything else was great but butt, oh man, the tight pants and the perfect bubbly butts! And then that cherry red tight shirt stretched out over her breasts. He was sprung, and he couldn't help but to gawk down at her breasts, snug and tan and sweaty, with a pink light of the Hotel de Sensual shinning lightly over the soft beautiful bundles of pure American flesh.

"Hey dolls, what are these girls here to see," he asked the girl's breasts.

"Oh, um, Courtney Roundapple," replied the girl, sweet as pie.

"Courtney's round apples?" asked the cowboy.

"No, Courtney Roundapple, the singer."

"Right. Thanks, sugar," he said.

The girl's boyfriend overheard this conversation, the cowboy calling his girlfriend doll and what not. He took one last zoomed-in picture of the gigantic holograph of Courtney Roundapple's round apples that alone took up three stories of the hotel, and he stepped forward from the dark spot into the pink light.

The cowboy tipped his hat in farewell to the girl and got another smile out of her cherry lips. He grimaced at the boyfriend and took one step out of the girl's space, and the crowd swallowed him up again. He looked back and saw the girl hit her boyfriend and fold her arms as he went back to ignoring her, gawking straight up at the holograph of the sexy pop star on the hotel.

The crowd spit him out, and the cowboy shook his limbs free and straightened his hat. He walked down the middle of the empty road from the pink light that dissolved into the dark where there was a tall thin building lit from the base like a golden shaft erected in the night. At the foot of the building, a water fountain spurted and sprinkled in a certain cool, corporate sapience like the statue of a boy pissing on the crowd from inside a futuristic time capsule.

There was a small confetti-strewn stage with a podium (like a politician had just been through on the campaign trail), a giant TV in the background set up against the building, and a tall pole in the center holding a windless American flag. Bouquets of flowers and letters and such laced the perimeter of the stage. The cowboy took one big step up onto the stage. A dry wind stirred the graffiti across, clearing a path as he went over to the flag. He looked at the flag, then climbed its stone base and looked out to the lights of Vegas. The vigil was empty save for the cowboy looking out to the crowd under the flag.

Behind him the fancy fountain spurted from the statue of a daydreaming boy, urinating upward, the water shimmering an azure blue pool. The cowboy lifted his head a fraction and gave a look at the lush light of Courtney Roundapple impaled against the building. The young Hollywood skin glowed, hazing her image over the idolizing crowd.

"Hot damn!" said the cowboy, "Now that's what I call a woman!"

Just then fireworks shot up and the giant television filled with color and digital life. An image of the American flag materialized on the screen, the red, white and blue rippling hugely over the electronic dots — all those ones and zeros — and the cowboy's silhouette cast its lean shadow, sticking up right in the heart of the flag, his boldly chiseled form: the ready hand at gun-side, the shadowed face, the rigid Stetson outline cut out in the flag.

The American TV light beamed out, slicing around the cowboy. He turned his head to the fireworks, a flashing light sparkle at the edge of his sharp shaven face.

A fat, short tourist with a large family and a camera around his neck witnessed the sight.

"Dad, get a picture of the cowboy!" screamed the kid.

"Wow, gang! The last cowboy, right here in Vegas!" said the dad, flashing his camera. The cowboy grunted. The American family went back into the night, heading toward the crowd.

As the cowboy stepped down from the stage, the TV changed to a music video of Courtney Roundapple. He heard loud screams and an arch pathway forged out into the crowd. The screaming fans backed up in somewhat nervous humility as a black limousine pulled up to the hotel. The driver got out, ran around and opened the back door of the limo and out stepped Courtney Roundapple in the flesh. The press lined the sides of the stairway, snapping pictures of the celebrity, taking note of her pink and purple extravagant Buchetta dress, exposing her signature round, bursting soft, silicone-ample breasts. The cowboy could not contain himself. He plowed through the crowd to the front line and whistled at the sexy pop star/singer/actress (actor to be politically correct)/artist formally known as Bitch. Courtney Roundapple turned around, her sparkling hair swirling over her shoulders glamorously in the myriad flashing camera lights; her dress splitting a bit at the seams, revealing in the hot celebrity light a tan, juicy thigh. Her eyes danced quickly from head to head — wondering if anybody had seen — her eyes landed on the only cowboy head in the crowd, and she smiled tritely at him.

"I'm all yours darlin'!" called the cowboy from the crowd. He raised his arms high up over all, hailing her and fingering her come to him, smiling broadly.

Courtney whispered something to one of her tuxedoed servants while smiling at the cowboy. The servant saw the one she wanted and nodded. Courtney turned again, her hair swishing around, sweeping a gasp of humility through the crowd as she continued her strut up the red-carpeted stairs to the hotel.

The cowboy, disenchanted as soon as the celebrity girl left, wandered through the crowd, skimming his hand along the police barricade that separated the crowd from the star. He always kept his head down under his hat as the policemen passed like statues. He made it around to the side of the hotel and went down the alley, where he found his horse. In the puddles down the alley, the horse looked oddly smaller than it was. When he was halfway to his horse, a side door clanged open before him. A short, fat Italian man with a little ponytail and a nametag emerged. The man's name was Vincenzo.

"Hey, you're with the crew, right?" Vincenzo asked.

"What?" the cowboy winced.

"The crew. You're that cowboy guy, for Courtney right?"

"A-yeah."

"Nice outfit. Come with me, man, you're late."

"What the hell," thought the cowboy. And he followed the little fast-talking man through the noisy kitchen of pots and pans and fizzing and cursing, up the silent elevator, and down a swanky red-carpeted hallway. Vincenzo knocked on Miss Roundapple's door several times. "Women, can't live with 'em, can't shoot 'em," he smirked back to the cowboy.

The cowboy gave a good laugh at this. And when the door creaked open, he was still laughing. An advisor talked through the crack and the golden chain lock to Vincenzo's big greasy face: "Miss Roundapple is not to be disturbed," she said.

"Who is it, Jane?" came a sultry voice from inside.

"Yo, it's Vinny," Vincenzo called through the door. "I brought you a present."

"Oh, is that my cowboy?"

"Yes, honey, it's your cowboy, come to sweep you off your feet," Vincenzo exclaimed in hope of a raise.

"Oh, my cowboy!"

And so the cowboy was let in.

"Let us be alone," Courtney said from bed.

Vincenzo walked away down the hall muttering. The cowboy looked after him in confusion before he entered the room.

"You're the massage therapist, right?" Miss Roundapple asked. She was sitting up in bed watching TV with her back against a pillow propped up on the headboard. She had hardly glanced at the cowboy.

"Yeah," he said in a daze, looking around at the hotel room. He'd never seen such a ritzy hotel room. And he never saw that guy Vincenzo who plucked him out of the streets and into it again.

After having sex with Courtney Roundapple, the cowboy lay next to the young star in bed. Courtney sat up and turned on the TV. There was some urgent news on. She flipped to the music video channel to catch herself on TV. The makeup artist came in and did Courney's face just as the cowboy roused up in her for another go. "Keep your head still," ordered the makeup artist. "Close your mouth!"

And so the cowboy humped Courtney Roundapple while her makeup artist painted her young face. He humped her so hard that her round apples juggled up and down like Jell-o, so far that Courtney could kiss and suck her own nipples.

After the second time, the young star praised the cowboy's large cock, yet was not allowed to suck it on account of the makeup artist not wanting her perfectly clayed face to ruin. So the cowboy and the star sat in bed and talked. People bustled about the hotel room, in and out, carrying racks of outfits, posters, fruit baskets and suitcases. And every now and again the makeup artist would come in and perfect Courtney's full red American-girl cheeks, and someone else would adjust her boobs.

"So what would you like to know about me?" Courtney asked in her cute, artificial, high-pitched voice.

The cowboy was dead tired from sex and loving it, his hat down over his eyes, snoozing alongside Courtney in bed, leaning against the headboard.

"I don't wanna know anything you haven't already told me, doll," he told her from under his hat. His clothes and his boots lay on the floor. The thin white bed sheet blanketed his legs and his big toe stuck out at the end of the bed.

"Yes, they're fake," Courtney blushed.

"What?"

"My boobs, they're fake. Everybody wants to know. I'm not ashamed of it either. They look good, don't you think? I mean, everybody in America has a right to beauty, am I right?"

"Well, darling, those are some fine boobies," said the cowboy boyishly, and he grabbed her boobs.

Courney went on to tell her life story. The cowboy kept caressing her boobs. In the part of her story when she was just about to thrust into stardom, Courney turned her little head and yelled, "Jane, where the hell is Ramad? I need a fucking massage!"

She then explained in one breath to the cowboy that she had Vincenzo get him just because she had never slept with a cowboy before and she told him that he was the massage therapist, part of the crew, so it wouldn't leak out — a little fun she has with random people she wants from time to time but not too often — too risky, could ruin her career, plus she's supposed to be promoting chastity on the side.

She jerked back to the conversation. "So anyway, what's it like to be a cowboy? Rob banks? Sweep women off their feet? Stuff like that?"

"Well I ah. ..."

Courtney's publicist entered the room. "He'll be here. Chill. Here have a Pepsi," she said and handed her a soda.

"I fucking hate Pepsi! Get me a fucking Coke!" Courtney demanded. "You want anything?"

"I'm good," said the cowboy.

"Sure?"

"Ahh, got any whiskey?"

"Yuck, whiskey!"

She was starting to get on his nerves, although he did enjoy humping her.

Before the cowboy could sip the first sip of whiskey that he loved there was a knock on the door. Ramad came in, dressed in lion cloth African clothes. He was a big black man with shiny black freckles and a big loveable brown face. He wore one of those crazy African leopard-skin caps.

"Ramad, my dear! How wonderful to see you!" Courtney cried in her sexy fake Southern twang.

"Yes, yes," boomed Ramad. "It is good to be seen, especially by the likes of your sweet kind, my dear." And he stepped toward her. "Would you like to do it on the bed," he said in his deep, suave as hell voice, "or on the floor this time?"

Courtney chose the bed. Ramad grabbed her by the ankles and laid her belly down, giggling.

"Hold it," said the cowboy. He was a racist. "What the hell's going on here?" He stood beside the bed. "So this is it, you're gonna throw me out just like that for this big gumbo nigger — hell no, you tell this Negro to leave."

"Ramad, you don't mind, do you? Couple of minutes," she said to him with a little wink and a mocking desperate face.

Ramad gave the cowboy a look and left to wait out in the hall. All the servants had cleared out for Miss Roundapple's massage. There was no one in the room except Courtney and the cowboy.

"I love ... humping you," he began and knelt beside the bed. Ramad heard this and laughed from outside in the hall. Courtney blushed. The cowboy kept on, his face broken, his speech stumbling and desperate. But he did not take his hat off for her. To her, he looked like an action figure, a toy, something right out of one of her commercials or music videos.

A V-shaped shadow slanted starkly, covering his face, leaving a halo of yellow hotel room light around his rigid frame.

"Will you, Courtney Roundapple, marry me?" he proposed.

She blushed and turned away. "Aww, you don't even know me."

"I know, baby, I know. But I could get to know you; I could get to know you real fast! See, I know this is all very sporadic of me, but I'm just downright tired of chasing women. It's high time I settle down, raise eight or nine children, you know, have a family. And I figure since you're so damn pretty and hot in the sack and all, I might as well ask 'cause I know I won't see ya again if I go, and you know me: I always bet my money on the long shot..."

He was losing her. "Yeah...." Courtney said.

"There's this 24-hour drive-in wedding chapel I spied on my way into town. Again, I know this sounds crazy, but fuck it, let's be crazy, darling. Huh? What do ya say? I'm just too damn tired of running around. I'm getting too old for this shit. I want to settle down and have a family. A son, daughter. Whole bunch of youngins. Raise 'em right. Little cowboy and cowgirl all running around on a little country ranch somewhere. You know, the American dream. My granny don't think it exists anymore on account of all the bullshit, but I still believe it does."

"Oh how sweet," Courtney remarked cordially.

And just then her ADHD kicked in. She lost interest in pretending to listen to the cowboy as her Pepsi commercial came on TV. "Ahhhh! That's me!" She swirled her luscious head back to the cowboy. "Of course, I'll marry you! You are, like, my man," she giggled. "Here," she said and reached over to the bedside table, pulling out a rolled-up poster from a box. Courtney unrolled it carefully on the bed. It was a poster of her in a sparkling gold and white dress. The dress slit down around her breasts and up at the edges, revealing those American thighs, and it cut off torturously at the edge of exposing what the cowboy now had witnessed to be a red slit of definitely deflowered vulva. *Courtney Roundapple Live in Las Vegas* read the red cursive caption on the black backdrop. Courtney signed it across her breasts with a black marker, folded it in half and handed it to the cowboy with a trite smile.

"Here you go, cowboy," she recited.

He took the hint and the poster. The last he saw of Courtney Roundapple in the flesh was her sitting on the bed leaning against the headboard (that had rattled against the wall) her leg posed stylishly, carelessly bent, her wretched Southern voice yelling something to her advisors and servants, watching TV, her night-slip stuck with sex sweat to her healthy thighs and buttocks. And Ramad walked in, and the pop star smiled benignly at her next visitor. The big black man boomed in the room, blocking the cowboy's last glimpse of the superstar and closing the door.

◆ ◆ ◆ ◆

Disgruntled, the cowboy went looking for a whore. He went to the red-light district where the girls danced in shop displays and in the streets in the red light. A whore stopped him with her leg as she leaned against the entrance to a cheap motel.

"Hey cowboy, looking for some late-night pussy?" coaxed the girl. And he was hooked.

Five minutes later, the cowboy stormed out of the motel, disgusted with himself. His whore staggered behind him through the parking lot, dropping her purse and having to bend down in her tight skirt to pick it up and scrape up all the change she could off the street with her long fingernails. She stood and fixed her hacked-up skirt. The cowboy had not yet paid her. She was itching to work up the nerve to ask him as she staggered behind, tripping over her high heels, her hair and self all tossed in the desperate dishevelment of the business of sex and money.

At the first whimper of money, the cowboy grabbed a fistful of the whore's hair and slammed her face into the pavement. He left her face down in the parking lot, bleeding from the head. And he went to find a better whore.

◆ ◆ ◆ ◆

He got drunk with a bum named Milton. He was all lips and gums and one hell of a chomping "grill" for teeth. Milton told him his life story and had the scars to prove it. The cowboy nodded and drank along. He'd heard it all before.

"Take a drink, kid," he'd say, as Milton told of his family dying in a car wreck. Now, this old bum was a black dude, but the cowboy didn't care about that racist thing anymore. He suddenly, in his drunken depravity, shed his strict racist disposition to bum a few drinks from a bum.

Milton told the cowboy he would make a good priest. "No, no, no … hell no," said the cowboy, taking a swig and shaking his head. "Hell, partner, I was just about to ask you where I could find a good virgin whore! Haahha! And you think I should be a priest! A damn priest! I'd be banging nuns three at a time! I'd be humping the altar and gad knows what other sacrilege! Jerking off in the confession box to some slut's confessions. No way man, I could never contain. Man what a sad sight that'd be: the poor priest whacking off!"

"You're drunk, cowboy," said Milton. "What's this virgin whore yous talking about?"

"Oh, the virgin whore! That's what I'm after in this town! Yeah, man, I keep getting these dirty cunts, pussy looks like it's been blown open with a 12-gauge — always gotta ask 'em if they got AIDS before we do it, right? And they get all sore at me. Not like I got a medical record on 'em, but their word helps, I guess. It just ain't no fun doing whores like that knowing that it might be your last. You know what I'm saying? I don't want to cash in over some goddamned whore!"

"So you want a good, clean virgin whore?"

"Yeah, I don't want no virgin neither. I don't want no prude girl who pops her cherry in three minutes — although those are mighty sweet little things. I need a stasis, stranger. You know what I'm saying? I need a balance betwixt the whore and the virgin. A good, clean virgin whore!"

"Yeah," Milton said in awe.

And with this, the poor Milton and the cowboy laughed up a good knee-slapping hoot on the corner of those dry Vegas streets under the arcade of myriad bright commercialization that kept pulsating deals and bargains and discounts and lies, and the huge red sign right above them in the center flashing SEX SEX SEX in the night.

The movie got out and the perverts flooded out of the theater behind them. Milton went into the rushing crowd to beg for money. The cowboy would not do this. No matter how much liquor he tanked in his belly, or how much despair he packed in his heart, he would beg from no man, especially no damn pervert.

Instead, he wandered away from the crowd, down the empty street of empty shop displays. Sparse folks were left squandering the streets that night, sparse good folks anyway. The cowboy walked through the prostitutes with their jeers and legs curving out into the streets, the hipsters, solicitors, gangsters, bums, punks, and all kinds of bastardized societies all clashed together and destitute in the bowels of America. He saw one kid with a green Mohawk. "Goddamn Injun," he said to him. And they got into a scuffle. The cowboy knocked him into a spell. His Mohawk came in handy for grabbing a good grip on as he banged his head against a thick-glassed, square, white-lit showcase window in an ivory marble building. An extravagant diamond engagement ring filled the punk's final conscious sight as what was left of his blood-drooling face slid down against the showcase glass. The cowboy took a closer look at the ring through the smear of blood sludge. He tried to remember that girl's name from back home.

He then dragged the heckler/punk by the Mohawk into an alley, beat him to a pulp (the way the cowboy's old pappy had done to him when he was a kid), spat on him, cursed him and cut off his hair with a flint knife.

◆ ◆ ◆ ◆

He stopped at a bus stop — a glass chamber on the side of the street — and looked up to the orange highlighted times for when the next bus would come. A black car with tinted windows roared by, bumping its stereo system. The cowboy looked down at the noise, then abruptly over his shoulder on sheer instinct. He caught a boy trying to pick his pocket. The boy ran away. But he'd gotten a glance at his face and saw that he was young, so he didn't think much of it. He walked down slowly in the direction the boy had fled. He saw a prostitute grab the boy as he tried to cross the street. The prostitute bent over, leaned her sharp, quick, little face into the boy and scolded him in a fierce enough whisper so the cowboy 20 feet away could hear. "Never cross the street without holding my hand, boy."

"Yeah, let's both get hit by a damn car! Let me go!"

"Don't give me that smart mouth, boy!"

And the prostitute ran after the boy across the street — both nearly getting hit by a car, the horn wailing.

The cowboy smirked at this and went over and leaned against the smooth wall of a clothing store. Although he felt fatigue setting in, his mind all waned down and his pockets empty, he did not allow himself to slide down against the building. A poor man sat leaning against it a ways down. "Buildings are getting smoother. Used to be all rough brick. Says something about our great economy, now don't it? Ga-head, man, give up. Slide down. Feel this smooth cold concrete on your aching back and the wet cold of the street on your bum.

The cowboy lit a cigarette. He walked off toward the main square of Vegas by the big fountain that spurted its grand midnight finale. There, it was all sports cars and limousines again and beautiful people under the glamorous white, red and blue lights.

The poor man who had attempted to tempt the cowboy into giving in chuckled a high satirical chuckle and continued scratching his gutted-depravity against the incorporated concrete building side with his fingernails. He plopped his hand down in a puddle and scratched through the rubbish at the bottom of it and found a penny. He cleaned it off and examined it, even straining his eyes enough to see the old Lincoln Statue in there. The wretched man decided that with this single insignificant penny, with the trust of God, the e *pluribus unum*, he'd get up and make it in America. Then he gave up while trying to get up, as a limo splashed a puddle on him as it drove by. But he saw the cowboy figure walking steadily away around the corner and decided to try again sometime.

On his way, the cowboy passed another gray, dimly lit shop display — glowing like a neutral gap in time, an oblivious vacuum attracting the hopeless like flies in the void of night. Behind the thin glass set perfectly square in the center of a colorless table was a modern black TV set with a sales tag on it. The thick black wire snaked around the side and back, arched perfectly, plugged into the wall. The cowboy drew near to the glass, the gray static glow on his face. His hat tipped back against the glass. Behind the glass, and behind the screen, Courtney Round-apple danced, looking right at him through the screen and the glass, and drawing him forward with her fingers. She was doing a live, lip-synced concert, with fired special effects, a live snake around her neck, and red lights galore, giving the stage a certain hellish look.

"Hey, you're the guy looking for a virgin whore, right?" came a gruff voice.

The cowboy startled backward, almost tripping over his own feet. He could not believe he let his guard down for a girl on TV; let a low-life pimp creep this close to him downwind — well, there was no damn wind in that cool Vegas night — that must've been it, he thought, as he left his fingerprints and frosty breath evaporating on the glass.

"Yeah," said the cowboy, grabbing his belt, gathering himself.

"What do ya got?"

The fat pimp told the cowboy he had a "good, clean, young virgin whore fresh out of high school and ready to get fucked."

"Good," he told him.

And he followed the fat pimp down the side streets and alleyways. Turned out, the virgin whore was not in. They waited, looking up for her shadow in the red-lit window of her apartment, but it never came.

"Where the hell is she?" said the pimp. He held a stack of money in his fat, greasy hands. He realized this in his heroin haze and put it away before the weary cowboy could see it. He turned to the cowboy, looked at him without looking at him and said, "All right, tell ya what,: you gotta place to stay? Here, I'll tell ya what — you can crash out at the company shack at the edge of town, and when you wake, the young virgin whore will be tendering ya — satisfaction guaranteed."

"All right," the cowboy said. "Tell me where this place is. I have to get my horse."

◆ ◆ ◆ ◆

The shack sat in the dusty decadence of the northwestern outskirts of Las Vegas, across the street from a large, flat flea market. The roof over the shack sagged over the brown wooden walls. Inside the bedroom, with its dusty wooden floorboards, sat an old-fashioned bed with a stiff, yellow cover. The other room was the TV room, and that was it. There were no pictures on the walls, nothing else in the small whore shack. It was the perfect place for the cowboy to lie low for a while.

He awoke the next day on the stiff bed, sat up and stared at the blackness of the TV screen on the dresser against the wall. He rolled over and fell off the bed onto the floor. A cloud of dust puffed up from under him. Dust particles floating in a yellow sunray washed the stale room through the curtain lace. He watched the air. He rubbed the sleep out of his eyes and stared down the ceiling. A board in the floor under him stuck up into his back, telling him to get up, but he didn't listen. The gradual pain persuaded him to jerk up. He cursed and rose to the day and hammered down the loose floorboard with his foot.

He turned on the TV. The news was on about the Texas Seven — seven killers and bank robbers had been arrested and sentenced to the death penalty. They were all seven the cowboy's old partners he used to ride with.

He changed the channel. He was on the next one. They showed a black cowboy head outline in the corner of the frame as the newswoman spoke of his mysteriousness, the last sighting of him in Vegas, the murder, the reward, and his effect on the American people. Then there was a commercial. The TV filled with lush mountain landscape of a perfect world with only one person in it: the driver of the new $46,000 Cadillac SVG or whatever the hell they called it. A broad, average voice exclaimed, "Keep America Roll—"

The cowboy turned off the TV.

Soon the virgin whore arrived. The cowboy heard her talking softly to someone in the next room. He stood up from the bed, leaving his dent in the made old-fashioned bed. His dent dipped — an imprint of the cowboy in the cloth — and then rode up with a little *wush* sound, filling whole and solid again, as he went to the door, opened it, and cast his shadow over the mother and the kid.

"Who the hell are you," the cowboy croaked, his first words of the day.

"I'm—"

"You ain't no virgin whore. How can you be a goddamned virgin whore if you got a goddamned kid?"

"He ain't mine!" pleaded the mother, denying her son again.

"Sure he ain't."

"Do you wanna fuck or not?"

The virgin whore pushed her son to the TV and turned it on. She wore those high soft heels, soundless on the floor, and pink toenail polish. Her legs were white and smooth and freshly shaved without the pantyhose. And the rest of her is history. The cowboy took one good look and convinced himself without argument that she was undeniably — denying only the kid and some jackass father somewhere — indeed the one and only virgin whore.

The cowboy laid her down, closed the door, and plucked her tight-strewn, shaved cherry. Slept. Revived amorous again. And rode the virgin whore like a bucking bronco. At noon he bent her over the dresser. The virgin whore looked at her face in the mirror as the cowboy thrust violently into her from behind, slapping her ass, calling her a bitch, sending flesh rippling, vibrating throughout her body, banging his pelvis against her cushioned butt, which let out some curt farts with the thrust. At the climax, the cowboy grabbed her hips and slammed them back — the hole bleeding a stream down her leg. His hairy chest was

61

illuminated yellowish in the sunlight through the curtains. He thought of all the careless human carnage that elated the cells of all the natural sinners scrounging and scorning the earth dry — scorned already into the earth as he climaxed and shook his dick around in her ass, squirting cum on her cheeks and sloped slender back until she was good and lathered.

The virgin whore looked into the rattling mirror banging against the wall. Her reflection wavered dizzily up and down, back and forth, WHACK-WHACK-WHACKing against the wall. She felt lost in a carnival funny mirror that makes you look fat and skinny and short and everything you are not. A tear rolled down her cheek. The cowboy grabbed her head back by the hair and whipped a splatter of thick cum up on her lips and face as he pulled out and her tear drowned out in the thick milky-white spludge.

She grabbed some cocaine from her purse and snorted up as the cowboy inserted again into her butt. He continued his slow, rising undulations into her again. He got her going again until her body was rocking and the mirror was rattling against the wall. Her hands trembled, clasped under the cowboy's heavy hands, pressed into the dull edge of the dresser wood. The cowboy was quite amorous. She offered him some coke and he did a few lines on her butt and the small of her back, and for another good twenty minutes the mirror on the dresser rattled against the wall. The boy watching TV in the next room heard the terrible shaking and rattling, and his mother screaming and moaning and yelping. The cowboy swirled his hat over his head and yelled, "Yeeeeehhaaaaa! Ridin' cowboy!" Then he ordered the virgin whore to say the same.

"Yeeha. Riding cowboy," she said with only a hint of false conviction. "How fucking corny is that?" she thought.

"Come on, girl, say it like you mean it!"

"YEEhahhaa! Riding fucking cowboy!"

"That's it!"

And slowly he calmed to a stop, leaned over the naked girl bent under him, and caressed her smooth stomach with a shiver from the girl; and then he grabbed two handfuls of soft breast. As he poked her lightly in the tranquil aftermath, her breasts flopped back and forth in his hands.

"My name is Sasha Hill," said the virgin whore.

The cowboy rested his chin on her shoulder and said nothing. His jaw bent, his voice box croaked the cool sigh of finishing.

"But that's not my real name," continued the whore, with a harsh snort of coke.

The cowboy pulled out with a long, death-like sigh and fell backward onto the bed.

Sasha stared at the mirror. Blood trickled from her nose. She let her head fall to the dresser table and snorted vehemently the last line. The cocaine sprinkled in her blood, which was now all over her lips and chin and mixed in with the drying cum. Her dirty-blonde, slick, streaky hair — she had washed out the bleached blonde when the pimp said he needed a virgin whore — fell to the sides of her lowered bubblehead. She perked up and stared into the mirror. Her eye veins bulged a fiery red. She jolted around to the cowboy who lay in the bed.

"Do you love me?" she said. "Do you love me?" She crawled up to the cowboy's sleeping face. "Tell me you love me, tell me you—"

He slapped her. She fell off the bed and crawled to the corner. She sat weeping, her knees huddled, her arms cringing around them.

"My real name is Sasha Rhodes — I changed it to Hill 'cause it sounds more professional, don't it? I'm from Shitville, Arkansas. I changed my name 'cause I wanted to be an actress."

"Well, you're doing plenty of acting now, that's for damn sure," grunted the cowboy, and he turned away from her to try and get some sleep.

"I wanted to go to acting school in California," Sasha continued. "No one would take me. I don't got the money! I don't got no fucking money!"

"Hey slut, do me a favor and shut the fuck up! Will ya? I'm try'n' to sleep."

But the whore went on complaining, crying, flopping her hands in her lap and her head in her hands. The cowboy warned her twice more to shut up, but she was so wound-up on account of the powder and had completely cracked her superficial shell right before the cowboy, she was now hemorrhaging all her true repressed self onto him, free of the constricting bureaucratic bullshit thath had hindered and confined her life. For some reason, she saw something in the cowboy she could not describe but felt, knew in her heart that he was different somehow from the others. The cowboy wanted nothing to do with her.

Sasha gathered her strung-out courage, looking into the crevices and tiny prints in her hands that some kindergarten teacher long ago in her childhood had told her made her special and different 'cause no one else had her print mark in the world; and she stood up. She went to the next room to check on her son. She could've left — she no longer cared about the money — but she wanted to talk to somebody, see if he could heal her heart.

"Hey, get back here and kill each other," said a cartoon character with a giant, multicolored head on the TV. The boy's eyes impaled dark and blank against the screen. The images reflected, moving fluidly, colors of tiny dots in the thousands configured, programmed, moving constantly, set to cut to commercial.

"What are you watching?" said the boy's mother, and she reached over him and changed the channel. "There's the ball game. You like the ball game," she said. But the kid did not like the ball game. The pitcher kept on wiping his brow and throwing over to first, as the crowd waited in commercialized anticipation for the slugger to launch his 100th steroid-induced home run.

He'd heard his mother do it again. She left him again with a kiss on the head and slammed the door. And he had heard her fighting with the cowboy, who told her to shut up and hit her down to the floor.

Sasha re-entered the bedroom — quaking inside, shivering on the surface. Her skin felt like sullied leather, stretched thin and stained. Trying not to cry and failing miserably, she made it to the corner again, pressing herself into the walls as far away from the cowboy as possible. The cowboy got up, turned on the TV and sat up in bed watching the news, right in time to see the picture taking up the full screen of his shadowed silhouette and some off sketch of his face. It shrank to the corner of the screen and the anchor came on with his broad voice. "If you see this man, identified only as 'the cowboy,' you are instructed by the FBI not to assist him or shelter him in any way, despite any alleged benevolent gestures or his supposed iconic disposition as a cowboy, his contumacious behavior will not be tolerated."

"Whatever Americans think they see in this so-called 'cowboy,'" said FBI director Frank Fondman, "make no mistake, he is a killer; he is public enemy number one to the American people."

The cowboy clicked off the TV. "Bureaucratic bastards," he muttered. Sasha crawled up on to the bed to his face under his hat. The cowboy opened his eyes and met her crazy, cocaine-inflamed pair.

"I don't see it in you," Sasha said. "You could never kill. You're not a killer. You're not the guy on TV. You ain't the guy they're looking for. Everybody thinks that you're this ruthless killer, all mysterious under that hat of yours, but if only they could see what I see. You're really just a little kid under there." She tipped up his hat. "If only they could see what I can see. ..." She kissed him, all slow, soft and romantic-like. And then she withdrew and searched his eyes for a change. The cowboy smiled and brought her to his chest. He looked at her little hand clasped in his. He watched her tiny head rise and dip with his hearty breath. Sasha could hear his big heart beating steadily. The cowboy stared at the hat on the bedpost. His guns were in their holsters slung over the opposite bed post above him, secured between the wall and the headboard. He calculated simply in his head the exact action he'd have to make to get to his guns. He'd have to reach across the pillow and grab the Colt that jutted out the closest by the butt. All this he thought while staring all lonesome like at his old hat on the post in the shadow-washed room.

"Get my hat, will ya, doll?" he said at last.

She reached back, grabbed it and put it on her. The hat fell over her eyes, and they laughed. The cowboy stopped laughing first and looked at her, and she put on his hat good and loose over his head, brim over his eyes.

"What is your name?" she asked him.

The cowboy was silent.

Sasha slung herself back to him and laid her head upon his chest. She hugged his neck under the sheets with her frail hands.

"I want you to tell me. I want you to tell me everything, and I want you to take me away. I want you to quit killin' and whorin'. I want you to father my kid."

The cowboy opened his eyes.

"Father him right," Sasha said, arching her back up and looking into his eyes.

"Get off me. I'm sleepy," he said. And he shoved her off and down to the floor. The sun had heightened and changed its angle through the window over the bed, throwing a hotel-stale, pale luminescent ray to the corner where Sasha sat in the heat. And she started her complaining again, the kind the cowboy could not stand. At one point, the whore-turned-good said in her whining Southern voice, "Why, why, why does my heart yearn for you — some cowboy stranger — wanted for murder? Why this love for you? Speak, cowboy! Tell me why? I am good — a good girl. Why must my heart suffer for you, you rude, bad man!"

"Because you're a damn slut in your heart," the cowboy consoled. "Now shut up!"

And the whore began weeping again. The cowboy couldn't stand it, so he reached across the dusty pillow and shut her up. Nobody heard the shot. Except the boy.

"Shit," said the cowboy, and he went back to sleep as the bloody mess of the virgin whore dried in the sun, attracting flies.

About an hour later, the cowboy awoke. It was 3 o'clock in the afternoon. He gathered his stuff, washed up and opened the door to leave. Before him in the doorway stood the boy. The cowboy cast his dark shadow over him.

"Your mother was a whore, kid," he told him, and he shoved the boy aside and went out into the dry, dusty day.

The boy did not look in the room. He kept looking at the cowboy's hand swaying at his side. He sprang after him and grabbed the stranger's hand as he crossed the street.

"What the hell?" the cowboy said. "Git off me, kid!"

A car hit the kid's jeans flapping in the wind as it whizzed by. The kid grabbed hold of the cowboy's hand a second time. The cowboy shook him off again, flailing his arm up in the air like swatting off a fly. The boy held on tighter but had to let go. It was actually the cops that did it. The cowboy saw them in a swath of desert haze forming a blockade down the road, stopping all vehicles, holding wanted ads asking good Americans, "Have you seen this man?" and "Do you hold contempt for the United States government?"

It was then the kid grabbed the cowboy's hand a third time and grasped it tight.

"All right, kid," he said, "I'll let you tag along, but you better not cause me no trouble, and I'll tell you right now, you ride with me, there's bound to be one hell of a fight."

With this, the cowboy looked down at the kid's hand in his. He lifted it up closer and saw the little pink fingers, and he grimaced and shook his head. And so, without any other choice but the destined money-scraping current borne ceaseless against the wind, the cowboy and the kid crossed the road, saddled up and rode out to the desert and the red-scarred mountains, off on their journey, cutting, zigzagging and hopefully straightening out home across America.

◆ ◆ ◆ ◆

CHAPTER VIII

O n their way out of Sin City, the cowboy had a little scrape with a burly, bearded Angel who said he came from hell and rode a motorcycle. He had stopped at a gun shop, kicked the door in, smashed the display window, and stole a shotgun. He then went to the back workshop, where he found a vice and a metal-cutting saw. He sawed off the long barrel, leaving about a five-inch snout.

The pungent Angel in black leather and chains and silver spikes around his bulky neck heard the noise while sleeping outside by his motorcycle on the side of the store and trudged in, grunting.

"What the hell's going on back here?" he growled.

The metallic clang of the sawed-off hollow barrel hitting the concrete floor in the workshop rang out, shuddering to a stop as the cowboy completed his work. He loosened the vice and grabbed the freshly sawed-off shotgun. He could smell the distinct scent of burnt, cut metal in the air. He rested the gun on his shoulder and walked toward the closed door where he'd thought he heard something through the saw cutting. The door opened and he met the Angel's fist.

He staggered to his feet and the Angel punched him again, knocking him back into the dull vice head. The cowboy grabbed his back in pain. The Angel hit him a third time, and he slammed into the wall and crouched down. The Angel was much bigger than the cowboy. But the cowboy saw the boy watching the fight through the dusty window, and so swiftly he revived. He was sick and tired of getting beaten and thrown around by these big, ugly law-abiders.

"You're that cowboy," said the Angel. "Well, I'm gonna pound your face in, partner! I come from hell, cowboy!" And the Angel grabbed him and threw him into the boiler room to fight.

The cowboy hit the Angel with a hard left hook. Knocked him again with his right, straightened his back and arched a fully extended upper cut. The Angel broke through the metal doors, slamming back into the shop. The cowboy picked up the shotgun while the Angel plugged him in the head as he tried to get up and shoot. The gun went scratching across the shop floor all the way to the door. The kid looked down at the gun behind the dusty glass door. He looked at the cowboy reaching out to him as the Angel applied a chokehold. He knew what to do.

The Angel let the cowboy go and stood him up leaning against the counter for a good wailing. And he wailed him a good one. And just then, the kid stepped in and picked up the gun.

"Don't move, fat man!" he said. "Get you hands up before I blow a hole out the back of yer head!"

The cowboy figured he'd keep the kid around for a while after all.

Without reproach the kid aimed the gun right at the Angel's chest. The big Angel tried to coerce, then sweet talk the kid, but the kid warned him not to take another step.

Meanwhile, the cowboy came to and found some shotgun shells that had fallen out from the smashed display window that the Angel had hurled him into. He grabbed handfuls of shells and stuffed them in his pockets.

The Angel drew near the kid. The kid kept his eyes open and squeezed the trigger. The empty click of the unloaded gun echoed. The Angel made a sinister slow smile. He was nearly upon the kid. The cowboy stood up and exploded out with his Colts. Blood spattered out from the Angel's mid-section. He backed away and hit the wall, leveling shelves of merchandise. And he crashed into the dusty floor.

While the Angel was down, the cowboy slung on back-up ammunition over his shoulder. His arms were bare and red and muscular from the fight. He wore only his hat, jeans, boots, and holsters full of his trusty .45 Colts.

He went over to the kid. He wanted to say something to him but didn't know what. He took the gun from him and loaded it.

The Angel croaked and sat up. The cowboy looked at the kid.

"We might as well test it," he said. And he went over, kicked the Angel back down and dragged him out to the desert.

Outside, the cowboy could hear sirens in the distance. He looked at his horse grazing, then at the Angel's chopper. He didn't have time to mull things over. He had ridden that horse since he left home ten years ago. But he reckoned it'd be a dead give-away to the cops. So he reluctantly unloaded the stuff he needed, discarding his granny's patch quilt, and he threw the Angel's stuff out to roll with the tumbleweeds. Then he packed his stuff in the black case at the rear of the motorcycle.

Now the Angel came running at the cowboy, seeing him mount his motorcycle. The cowboy shot him in the knee. The Angel stumbled forth, tripped over his broken leg and fell to the desert floor like a slain bull, sliding over the rough desert under the mounted cowboy.

The cowboy rolled the Angel over with his foot.

"Come on, kid," he called.

The kid climbed on back.

The cowboy looked down at the fallen Angel. The Angel breathed heavily, pig-eyed and afraid. He looked everywhere in the haze except to the shadowed figure above him. Then he saw. It spoke.

"How do I get this thing to go?" it asked.

The Angel said nothing. He gazed at the cut-out cowboy figure and the slouched kid and snarled his upper lip. The cowboy shot the Angel in his other knee and asked his question again.

"Kick it up," gasped the Angel.

And the cowboy did. "Kick it up — I like that," he said. The chopper purred between his legs. The cowboy angled the black shining gun down at the Angel. The gun seemed to slope and bend in the Angel's bloody hot gaze. "Don't think I'm gonna forget you, pretty Angel," said the cowboy.

"The handle, turn the handle," the Angel gasped.

The cowboy did, reviving his memory on the damn things, and the bike jolted forward, then stopped.

"Some fine last words," said the cowboy. And he slanted the sawed-off shotgun back to the Angel's chest and put him out of his misery, the pellets plastering him to the cracked, dry, desert plate.

CHAPTER IX

The cowboy and the kid rode that chopper, cutting through the desert, splitting a V-shaped line of dust in the rising swath, plowing their path onward. The cowboy's old horse, sadly, kept following them, stretching her body long, muscles gleaming in the sun alongside them, carrying the heavy empty saddle. The cowboy stopped and hauled off the saddle to wear out in the desert and one day in a museum (he figured), and he slapped the horse and shouted, "Get on now! You're free! Get on!" But the horse wouldn't go. She whinnied and shook her huge snout at the machine horse. She could see her reflection in the shiny, silvery, long metal tubes that held the front wheel and also multiplied a thousand times in the spindles.

The big nameless brute sweated under the blistering sun. The cowboy fed the old beast grain and oats from his palm. He loved that horse. He petted her mane and looked fondly at her big eyes. And he whispered into her ear, her secret name and spirit. That didn't work either. So he pulled out his pistol and fired once near her rear end. And the horse ran off free and angry, not ever going to be caught, least not without a fight, a few good kicks in the jaw to whoever tried to saddle-win her. The cowboy watched her riding away with the wind, out to the sun atop a distant plateau. She raised her body up with her front legs twirling and neighed goodbye to her old master. Her outline cast out against the sun.

And so the cowboy and the kid went on, riding fast and right down the middle of the desert granite road. They cut onto a smooth black-top section of freshly paved gravel. The bike flew along, its front wheel chopping out to the flying road, and the engine shot sound yards ahead and always growing and passing in a huge and present rush and then growing distant again, as it seemed to all the sparse desert critters along the road.

The kid hadn't said a word. The desert wind bit into his gaunt face as they flew out of Vegas.

"Yeeehhaaa! Whhoooweee! Hot damn! What a horse! Come on, kid, you gotta be loving this!" cried the cowboy in the wind.

The kid said nothing.

The cowboy tightened the drawstring on his hat, the little wooden holder pulled up to his whiskery chin. His mullet flew free behind him. His straight hair was smoothed back over his ears with a little spit and ear wax. His hat's brim flapped down and in on the sides in the quick, stale, speed-made wind. The kid's loose, worn blue jeans flapped in the wind by the engine. He had worn the same clothes for weeks.

They rode that chopper through the Southwest, arriving at the Grand Canyon by approximately May 1. The cowboy kept stealing gas, food, and money and getting shot at occasionally by the drunk, red-neck lawmen in the cracker-box towns. It was in standing over the deep red-scarred Grand Canyon when the raw and humanly divine American dream sprang from the wide chasm and the thinning, dried, distant river below.

"I am free!" he shouted to the canyon walls. "I am sober! I am wide awake! I am an American! I am a cowboy! And my granny was born on the fourth of July! I gotta drunk pappy and a dying grandpappy and my girl Angie back home in Kansas! I love Angie! Yeah, that's her name. Angie! Angie! Oh hell yeah! I love America! I love home! And I'm going back there, whooo! I am going home! I love beer and whiskey! I love — kid, get over here and yell out something to the great gods of America!"

The kid walked to the cliff and looked down. He could see some brown dead weeds sagging over the edge, gas-stained against the rock, as if a car had run over them on its suicide path. Some green trees further down, closer to a little waterfall spouting from the canyon wall reflected a shimmering green off the red rock and the river.

The cowboy looked down at the silent kid. He crouched next to him. He wouldn't have been surprised if the kid attempted to murder his ass right then and there, kick him over to fall into a rocky cowboy heaven.

"Look, kid," he began. He quickly bowed his head in shame and cursed the earth. "Goddamnit! I sorry I shot your mama, okay?"

The kid said nothing but looked out over the gorge.

"Beautiful, ain't it?" said the cowboy. He knew to shut up and enjoy the view.

Then he said, "I'll tell you what kid. ..."

The kid turned with a spark of eagerness in his eyes.

"Yeah, yeah," said the cowboy, nodding, "I see it in you already. Kid, I'm going to make you a cowboy. The best damn cowboy in America. I'll need a backup, see, supposing I get killed, which is liable to happen before the end of this chase, and I'll need you to carry on the cowboy way, keep its spirit alive. Now, I'm sorry I killed your whore mother, but hell if I didn't, some asshole would've sooner or later. The world is full of assholes. Hell, there's two assholes setting on this very cliff, but imagine all the assholes all over America and all the bullshit, that's what you shoot through, got me?"

The cowboy set his hat on the kid. It fell over his eyes. The cowboy lifted the brim for him with a rare, gentle hand.

"You hear what I'm saying, boy? I'm going to find you a mother. I'm going to make a cowboy out of you. And you and your mother and I are going to be the great, complete American family, settled in Kansas. Boy, I'll tell ya, wait till you meet Angie! Wait till you meet her! She's my wife back home — well, we ain't really married yet, but I just know she's back there waiting for me and it's high time I oblige her, head back home to settle down. Boy, I remember lying in the grass with her when I was a kid! 'Round your age, too. Angie, Angie, boy she could play the piano. ... I remember...

"She's gonna raise you right, kid, tender you sweet, too! And I'll teach you everything you need to know about being a cowboy. You already got that stoic thing down: 'Talk low, talk slow, and don't say much.' Works quite fancy for you. Hell, look at that poker face! Look like you already done kilt all the fake assholes in America!"

The cowboy was ecstatic. He stood up and walked the edge of the canyon. He calmed and crouched down again. A strong gust of wind blew the gasless motorcycle over, crashing to the ground. The cowboy scowled at the useless machine horse.

"All right, come here, kid," the cowboy swallowed his intemperance. "Kid, do you want to be with Angie? Do you want to go to Angie, kid?" With this the kid turned his head slowly to the cowboy and walked the edge in the setting sunlight. He crouched beside him, imitating the cowboy's limp hand over his squatted thigh and every tough grimace and snort and grunt of his stiff, ossified face.

"The first rule about being a cowboy is: don't let anybody tell you what to do. Don't trust nobody. Don't listen to nobody. Don't ever let nobody push you around or shit like that. No official man in a suit, no men in uniforms and badges, no men with papers that say they can tell you what to do, or assholes who sit behind benches and podiums and tell you to go to jail and die. I mean, unless you got it coming. But no fake shit. Or dipshits on TV. Don't trust 'em; don't listen to 'em. No law. All right? Don't let law and money hold you down. We ain't bound by shit. Law and money don't mean nothing. And all the assholes that cultivate law and money follow suit. And don't trust girls, neither. Do not, do not, go chasing your heart on some skirt. Do not. Now, I know that's kind of like more than one rule, but the main thing is? What?"

"Don't let anybody tell you what to do," the kid recited.

"Beautiful," remarked the cowboy. "Now, go get my gun."

The kid went to the fallen chopper and fetched the cowboy's gun.

"Now, here's whatchya wanna do when some two-bit dandy starts up crampin' yer style. See that cactus yonder?"

Before the kid could turn to look, the cowboy shot the head of the cactus clean off. The shot echoed throughout the canyon.

"Damn," said the kid.

"Hoo-boy! Did I just hear a cuss come out of that little mouth of yours? Hoo-baby-doll!" The cowboy almost choked with laughter. Then he handed the kid the gun. "Here, now you try. Come on now. No more sling shots." He saw the boy's sling and tossed it over the canyon. Quickly he grabbed back the gun from the kid and fired three shots at the slingshot as it fell in midair. The last shot took off the slingshot's arm; the other bullets he sent sparking against the distant wall somewhere, shriveling into the red earth.

"Gimme that gun," the kid demanded, and he took the gun back. He pointed at the cactus's arm. The lone, prickled shrubbery stretched its ancient arms out to the sides like an old man reaching. The cowboy sat back on his elbows among the pebbles at the edge of the cliff with a smile in his eyes.

The kid missed. The gun jerked back and hit him in the teeth, bloodying his lip.

"Naw," the cowboy chuckled, "let me help you here, kid."

He sat up and aimed the gun over the kid's shoulder. "Hold on tight, this is a mighty big gun for a youngster. Yank ya right out of your pants if you ain't steady. All right, hold it steady, two hands, now you have it. Now squeeze the trigger. No need to pull it, just squeeze it nice and gentle, like squeezing a broad's titties — just let the gun do the work."

The cowboy squatted beside the kid. All at once, they both felt it when the kid had it and he squeezed his little finger around the trigger. The bullet zipped out and cut off the cactus's arm concisely, only a recoiled inch above where he'd aimed.

"Nice shot, kid!" said the cowboy.

The shot rang out throughout America, breaking invisible dimensions in the big blue sky.

"All right, kid, what do ya say we go test out rule number one? Get some eats, little bit of money, women. Don't listen to nobody who thinks they can deny us! What do ya say?"

"All right," said the kid.

And the cowboy chugged a beer with the kid and threw the bottle into the canyon, drew his gun, shot and smashed the bottle right in its belly, exploding copper glass in midair and then shedding down and away with the slight wind. They picked up the chopper and rode it as fast as they could on fumes. They rode through the desert on the canyon's edge, the cowboy still slugging back beers, tossing the empties to smash on the road, passing beers back to the kid and reloading his gun.

◆ ◆ ◆ ◆

They didn't get far. Just a ways down the road, the chopper sputtered clean out of gas. The cowboy kicked the bike down in the dust. He wanted to throw that mechanical horse out over the ledge of the canyon. He could understand running out of horse and mortal dying and he could forgive it — hell, he'd sent plenty to die — but he could never understand or mouth any forgiveness for the death of the machine. He wished he had not let his horse go.

Anyway, the cowboy and the kid walked along the Grand Canyon in the sweltering rising heat after the sun had nearly set and had baked the earth all day. Each lookout point they passed with the good Americans paying their quarters to look out the binoculars and opening up their picnics out the back of their SUVs, the outlaw cowboy resisted the urge to rob and slay them (if he had to) on account of a little pact he'd made in his head: no more killing in front of children. And all the good American families had a litter of children. Instead, the cowboy waved and one family even gave him and the kid some water. "Look, kids, a cowboy!" said the dad. After some show and tell for the kids, the good American man shook the cowboy's hand and said, "This was just great, thanks a lot." And the good American man let go of his hand and sent him on his way. And without the words, the cowboy enlightened himself simply in that beneath all the commercial bullshit people are good enough to help each other from time to time. And he and the kid did enjoy that "Purity Guaranteed" bottled drinking water.

They saw a rest stop on the side of the road yonder. The cowboy smiled. He figured they'd head over, camp out and wait till the store opened the next morn. He knew the kid had something in him on account of witnessing that stunt he pulled with that Angel guy back in Vegas. Tomorrow, he'd find out what it was exactly.

"Come on, kid," he said. "I wanna try something."

And they strutted to the heat-sweltered brown box of a building off the exit in the distance, the cowboy and the kid.

◆ ◆ ◆ ◆

They entered the little tourist shop at high noon. The heat beat down, crackled the desert plate and rose up in thick, wavering gusts. The souvenir shop was empty of customers. It was a small pueblo-style building with fake windows on the two floors above the customer floor. A heavy-set, bearded hunter worked the shift. His legs were kicked up on the counter. He flipped through a dirty magazine, folding out the foldouts and all.

The cowboy walked in first, nodded at the clerk and walked around hatless, checking out the bread and snack aisle. The kid walked in second, bandanna over his face, the cowboy's Stetson setting on his head, gun out and pointed at the huntsman.

"Gimme the money," said the kid.

The clerk looked up slowly from his magazine.

The kid looked at the cowboy in the aisle. The cowboy mouthed silently what to say.

"This is a holdup," said the kid.

"No shit," said the clerk. "Damn kids," he muttered to himself, raising his hands mockingly, just to be safe. "Kid, what the hell are you doing with that gun?"

"Shut up! Git your hands in the air! Reach for the sky!" ordered the kid, aiming the barrel at the hunter.

The cowboy loved it. He walked out with his hands up in mock fear and said, "You better listen to him. He ain't the type that jokes around when it comes to money."

There was a pause. The kid looked at the cowboy. The cowboy looked at the kid. The clerk looked back and forth at them. The kid snapped his mean face back to the clerk. That straightened him back up right with his hands up.

"Line," said the kid, still looking at the clerk.

The cowboy's mind had wandered a bit.

"Line," said the kid louder, his eyes piercing at the clerk over the muzzle.

"Oh, yeah, yeah, aaah..." And the cowboy whispered the kid's line.

"Gimme the money!" said the kid.

"That a-boy!" said the cowboy.

"Reach for the sky, fat man!"

"All right, all right! Let me just put my hands down to get the money," said the clerk.

"Slowly," warned the kid.

And so the kid and the cowboy robbed their first store together. Not only did they get some 350 dollars in cash, but also a pack of cigarettes, a case of beer, and various snacks. The security camera caught the whole thing — the cowboy and the kid stealing bounty from the commercially charged, commerce-clenched, beautifully true and inconsequential American dream.

◆ ◆ ◆ ◆

Now they needed a couple of horses. The cowboy was still bummed that he'd let his old steed go. That horse could run for miles on end.

They hitchhiked their way back toward L.A., the cowboy taking advantage of the kid's cute little face, telling him to lay off the mean one. "Time to lie a bit and get ahead, kid — goddamn cops are on our ass!"

"Yeah, well why the hell we goin' back to the city?" asked the kid.

"Yeah, kid, you gotta know when to hold up, know when to fold up, know when to walk away, and know when to gamble."

He put the gun to the driver's head and told him to take them to Vegas. Driver ended up jumping out of the moving car out of fear. The cowboy moved over to the driver's seat in time to veer out of the oncoming traffic, which hit the poor bastard who had picked them up. They muscled their way back to America's playground in a '67 Mustang.

Once in Vegas, the cowboy got on a roll and won three grand, then blew his money on whores and drunken gambling all over again. He lay in a motel of drug dealers and prostitutes, watching his hat sadly setting on the TV. The old, rugged hat held all his thoughts of women, money, beer, whiskey, and Angie from the weathering times. Angie. She was the one constant, heavy stone in his heart that cleansed all sin with just the thought and kept him going, breaking through and quitting the games he couldn't win. The cowboy stood up sober enough from the bed, donned his hat, put his boots on and decided to change his life once and for all.

He passed through the beaded curtain lace and found the kid in the next room with the whores. He sat watching the TV screen. The teen-aged whore kept hitting the buttons furiously, playing some video game in which the main character was a sexy lady spy with enormous graphic jugs, traveling the world killing the bad guys to attain some secret disc. All the special effects were computer-enhanced and top-notch. "And if you press up, over, up, up, down, a, b, c, right, left, she'll sit down on the bed, take her shirt off and moan — oh my god, that is why so many guys love this game, that just like totally occurred to me just now!" the whore explained to the cowboy in one teenage breath.

The teenaged whore saw the cowboy standing in the doorway, looking around. "Wanna fuck?" she asked him, glancing at his eyes and then back to the game.

"No," he said. "Come on, kid, we're leaving."

Two mother-whores were painting makeup on the kid's face. They sat on either side of him on the bed. They had covered his face with their hands when the cowboy came in the room. "Tadaa!" they said and unveiled the prostitute-painted kid.

"Awww, gawd!" said the cowboy, biting his fist. And he took the kid out of there. The whores laughed them out. "He looks so cute!" they jeered. "Isn't he a little hottie?"

Outside in the streets under a huge cowboy fluorescent figure smoking a cigarette 200 feet tall in old downtown Vegas, the cowboy spat on his fingers and tried to wipe the makeup off the kid, but it was really thick and he only made it look worse.

That early morning, they walked around and looked for a place to sleep. The cowboy was mad. That's just great, he thought. And then he said aloud, "My kid's just another freak in L.A. Man, that fucking pisses me the fuck off!" And he spat again on his hand to wash the kid.

"We're in Las Vegas," said the kid, cringing his eyes shut at the cowboy's forcible, spit-cleaning hand.

"Yeah, yeah, it's all the same to me, kid."

◆ ◆ ◆ ◆

Penniless, the cowboy and the kid slept in the gutter. At least the cowboy did. The kid was still all perky and to look at him jumping around in the trash with all that goddamned makeup on his face didn't help the cowboy get much sleep, rolling around in the newspapers. He'd thought about just robbing some helpful dude's trailer or something and crash there, but he was too tired to pull any of that. And then out of the blue, came the luckiest break. The morning came and the day grew slowly late and hot as they wandered hungry and bored around the downtown shopping malls.

They went into a department store, up the elevator and took a long nap on one of the beds in a furniture store until security kicked them out. They then wandered around for a long time and eventually found themselves in some grocery store or flea market, drifting down the aisles and gawking at the food. The kid swiped some ice from the fish cooler and walked around sucking on it; reaching and grabbing stuff off the aisle, saying, "I want that, I want that... I'm hungry!" And then the cowboy would have to explain to him all over again about what he'd spent their money on. This gave him a headache. He was tired and hungry and guilty — he was guilty.

He tried to explain to the kid the difference between sex and love and that all people need sex. Most times you respect your sex partner, but sometimes it's kinky not to, or sometimes your sex partner could just be a downright annoying bitch like your mamma, he thought. The son of a woman like that don't need no explaining, he figured. But he told him anyway: you respect your sex partner in the sense that you give her what she wants and she gives you what you want, a business relationship is all. After telling him all this he thought he might have to tell him about the birds and the bees, but he didn't ask. "I guess people just fit together then," was all he said.

"Yeah, kid," the cowboy said, relieved.

He didn't think the kid even heard his mutterings in the first place. The kid kept on grabbing stuff from the shelves, and it was starting to attract attention and piss him off; so he turned to the kid and just sort of nicked his nose a bit with his fingertips.

"You hit me!" cried the kid.

"I didn't hit you," the cowboy said.

"Yes, you did!"

"Kid, I did not hit you," he said again.

"Yes you did! You hit me! You hit me on the face!" the kid said very loudly

. Everybody in the store was giving the cowboy the old child-abuser scorn. And the kid was crying. It was terrible.

Then some grandmother came up to the kid and gave him a hug. She just thought he was the cutest kid. She didn't seem to notice the cowboy who walked behind them. He got a little jealous — thought that maybe the kid liked the old hag. Then the kid arched his head back to him for an instant and gave him this look like someone just farted a silent but deadly one as he stuck out his tongue. Right then, the cowboy could tell that he really wanted to get out of there, and he almost burst out laughing because it was the cutest desperation look. But the grandma kept patting the kid's head, pinching his cheeks and patting his hinny sometimes. He just looked as if he were screaming inside: "Get me outta here!"

The cowboy mouthed to ask the lady if she'd buy them some food. The kid asked if they could have a ride instead. Must've gotten the wrong message. But that was fine and dandy by the cowboy. He didn't feel like shopping with the grandma from the beginning. He knew grandmas: always take forever shopping, especially for a kid.

Anyway, she said yes immediately and soon they found themselves riding in a leather-seated Cadillac and driving out of Las Vegas back into the desert. The kid sat in the front, of course, and the cowboy in the back like he wasn't even there. He had his hat over his face and pretended to take a nap, which didn't seem like a bad idea with all that spacious leather backseat and the sun shining mildly through the thick car glass. But he stayed awake and mouthed tips to the kid for talking to Grandma Hot Tub — that's what she said her name was on account of the hot tub at her house that her grandchildren loved and hence all called her Grandma Hot Tub. She looked like a Grandma Hot Tub anyway.

Eventually the kid asked her, in a very cute way, if she had any money she might like to donate to their cause.

"And what cause is that, dear?" asked Grandma Hot Tub.

"To get us to Kansas so I can find me a new mother," said the kid.

"Oh, yes, dear. Of course, dear! Thank you for reminding me! I almost forgot!" And then she reached into her purse, maneuvering the wheel with one hand and driving a little bit off the road and sometimes into the next lane, which was pretty scary on account of her going so slow. And the other cars would zoom by them, as she pulled out from her purse a fresh one hundred dollar bill.

"That should buy you some candy, dear," she said, stuffing the bill into the kid's belly.

Now the cowboy wasn't sure if she knew exactly what bill it was, but she had six of them and she handed over all six. After every half hour, he'd get the kid to ask again and every time it was a one hundred dollar bill. It was amazing. She was like a living money machine at their disposal, printing at the touch of a button. Only trouble was that every time Grandma Hot Tub went to get another bill, she'd swerve all over the road, and as slow as they were going they were like sitting ducks out there on Route 15. There were some pretty close calls. But Grandma was oblivious. "Oops," she'd peep, as she swerved back into the lane among the passing, horn-wailing cars. So the cowboy mouthed to the kid to get the hell out, and he just said, "This is our stop right here, ma'am." They were right in the middle of the desert, but Grandma stopped. She said goodbye to the kid, wished them good luck with their search and then let them go. They watched her car for a long time while they walked until it disappeared in the distant heat-waving air.

◆ ◆ ◆ ◆

After a while they came upon a little corral in the middle of nowhere. All it was really was this old wooden fence around a couple of horses, and the owner or nobody else for that matter was around. And it was real hot, so the cowboy just had the idea that they would borrow one of the horses and ride along on it for a while — just like a *real* cowboy again. So he snuck up on one and tried to jump on it, but it moved. He got up and dusted himself off and tried again, but it moved again. Damn thing just kept on moving and eating hay and smelling like manure. Then he finally raised the kid up to straddle the horse, and it didn't move at all except for a slight twitch of the tail. He too claimed a good sturdy horse and climbed on.

Then trying to get the damn horse to move gave him a hell of a time. He thought about shooting a round off by its rump after petting and horse whispering didn't do no good. Finally he kicked it in the belly in his frustration, and the damn thing took off. They ran in circles for a while around the fenced-in ranch. The horses were pretty wild. It was pretty exciting for the kid, watching the cowboy ride like on a bucking bronco, but they weren't getting anywhere. Although he loved fast action, and killing law, and whoring, and gambling and scraping, that damn pale horse nearly put the fear of death in him. He saw the kid and felt a mite concerned his horse might follow suit. But the kid somehow leaned in real close to his raging horse, clamped his arms and his body against its neck and whispered into its ear, calming it completely, talking it into jumping over the fence. It did just that, and the cowboy's horse followed, and they were on their way.

Now it was a very hot day, so hot the air shimmered as though the earth's crust burned over a charcoal grill; it must've been a mirage or something because one moment they were riding along an empty highway and the next the road was packed with cars — one big line of traffic that never ended — and all the cars were traveling west, and the cowboy and the kid were heading east. The kids in the back seats of the minivans and cars watched them as they galloped along, and they were so real — the kids — they would press their hands against the windows and watch the cowboy and the kid for as long as they could — riding in the opposite direction, sweeping by and away impetuously, the horses kicking up a haze of dust along the road.

◆ ◆ ◆ ◆

After riding late into the day, they came to a house where a man sold them his pickup truck for the horses and some cash. The kid watched his horse clunk away by itself along the road. He wondered where it would wander. The man just wanted to get rid of his rusty old truck, which he had setting out front of his little shack in the tall grass with a for-sale sign on the dash. The kid knew the man wouldn't look after the horses. Half partial to his horse, the kid finally ceased looking after it from out the back truck window. He shrugged and figured the best thing for his horse, which he'd named already, would be to let it go free. The sad thing was what it did with its freedom, just clunking along, kicking up dust and looking at them with his big sad eyes as they drove away.

"Plenty of horses in Kansas, kid," the cowboy said, "prettiest horses ya ever did see. Let's just get there."

Their truck was good, but once again even the cowboy missed riding. He tried not to remember it because it made him regret the deal for the truck. He loved riding under the sun with the people looking at him from their cars, and the kids wishing they could ride with him instead of sitting in the back of the cars. Everybody seemed to really wish they could just ride with the cowboy and the kid.

Anyway, this rust-bucket truck actually had a decent engine and a fairly sturdy frame. It shot out, churning the highway back. The kid sat in back holding onto the side of the bed. He stuck his head out and let the dirty breeze blow through his hair. The cowboy caught a glimpse of him through the mirror. A little blond streak in his dirty blond hair cut back over his scalp in a blade's shape. The cowboy admired this unique trait and thought just how crazy the whole thing was and how much progress they were making already on his new life and journey back home — just him and the kid, heading east, searching for Her as best they could with 300 dollars in their wheels and another 50 in his pocket.

The cowboy clicked on the radio. The old, classic song from his boyhood rang out: Harry McClintock's *The Big Rock Candy Mountains*. It satisfied something deep in him as it croaked from the old radio box, but it wasn't the song that he couldn't remember from the beginning — that piano song that he couldn't remember — no, that song remained unsung, piercing like a gallstone in his brain.

But for those three minutes or so, they sang along, the cowboy looking back at the kid always and then glancing back at the road just in time to see the original Big Rock Candy Mountains open up to the right, snow-capped and distant as the road sank into the evergreen valley. Green fields furrowed down in rippling shadows of hills everywhere. After a few miles the color changed in the fields from green to a more pale green spaced out only in patches between brown and tan desert, and the wind howled out coldly dying to the distant mountains and through the sparse grass. The kid climbed in through the rear window and sat next to the cowboy. The cowboy still pondered simple things, trying to recall memories and such.

They bumped along the road now that turned from a smooth black top abruptly to dirt. The cowboy broke out of his trance and realized that they were literally under the snow-capped mountains. All around was mountainous. A metal cage kept the bulging belly of the mountain on the side of the road from sagging amid the bent "falling rock" warning sign.

The rugged mountains brazed an iron metallic color. Bubbly graffiti messages marked the rocks in some spots. One said: Crucify your mind! And another: Yossarian lives! And there were pictures of dragons and butterflies and naked women.

Deep in the mountains every now and again, there'd be a cave. The kid asked about the caves. The cowboy told him that the Bat Cave was back there. But the kid didn't seem to know what he was talking about. He decided he ought to take him to the movies one day. It was a sin that this American kid didn't know who Batman was. He began to express this opinion, but he had to keep his eyes on the road, see. The road would curve around narrow corners of cliffs leading to a rocky death, and they'd fly up and around them at 80 mph because they would just come up on them out of nowhere in the midst of conversation when the cowboy's foot was heavy with excitement. So he told the kid to shut up while he drove. And just as he did, the road smoothed out into just smaller, spread-out curves and was soon totally straight. He regretted shutting up the kid. But he didn't want to reverse any command over him, he thought. Or maybe it was just too awkward to submit him to any further dominance - nah! It never gets awkward between me and the kid, he thought.

Besides, the cowboy loved it when the kid got all scared and awkward feeling. It reminded him of when he was a kid, and he knew that those were the times when he could get him over it, make him a man like throwing him in the pool to learn to swim. And then the awkwardness of being young would be only a memory in him, and he'd push other kids over the edge with a certain mean, bad-ass disposition. That's why the cowboy loved the shyness in the kid and the way he would quiet himself and tense up inside, shoving his hands in his pockets. Then the kid would do that long blank stare out the window as the world whizzed by.

"Hey, why don't you open your window," he said to him at last, rolling down his. "We're in the desert now."

The kid ignored him. He could tell he was just fishing for a good coax to cheer him up. He didn't really know where the hell they were, only that it was hotter and the land looked barren and dry, rooted by cactuses and indigenous sage, all dry and stiff — roamed by tumbleweeds. The cowboy used to dream of venturing across the fabled West as a kid. Now he was in it but this kid partner of his was still all awkward and quiet. All the same, that's what made the space in the cab of the truck so cool. The cowboy loved to watch the kid squirm in his seat, dying for something to say, dying to grow up in an instant and break out into the world.

The cowboy laughed and said, "Kid, you need a woman."

Then it started getting a little cold. The cowboy put up his window and tried to think. At least he thought they were in the desert. He remembered they had come to this intersection, but he just kept going straight through it, which was north and not the desired east toward home. So he reckoned that explained the snow on the mountains and the green valley up north in the Sierras.

He pulled out his old compass. The unbalanced needle swerved round and round.

"Damn thing." He threw it out the window and looked at the sun. "Hey, do you know where we are kid?"

The kid shrugged, still sore about things.

"We're right in the middle of America."

"Yeah?" peeped the kid, twirling back his hair with his finger.

"Yeah, kid. The old Wild West. The American dream in action. The wide-open desert. This is the fun part, kid."

"Yeah?" said the kid, sitting up a little.

"Hell yeah, kid," he said. "Hey go ahead now, roll down that winda, the desert is hot, man, and this road, trust me, this road is long."

He could see he bought the excitement of it all and had cheered up. He rolled down his dusty window and leaned his head out and let the wind enthrall him. He pulled back in and looked at the cowboy in a half-smile for approval.

"What the hell was that?" he said. "Go ahead and stick your head right out there and catch a good breeze, man; stick your whole head out there, just like when you were riding in the back, remember? You climbed through the damn window when I was steering around that curve — I've seen ya! Ya little rascal."

The kid couldn't believe he wasn't mad at him for that. The cowboy admitted that he had been getting madder and madder since those whores, but now with just himself and the kid and with the whole world wide open and free to them and just cutting right through everything as fast as their old truck could sputter, he didn't think he could've been more content progress-wise.

Even so, it was getting colder. The sky reddened toward night, and he knew they wouldn't last too long with their heads out the windows.

◆ ◆ ◆ ◆

A great headache came over the cowboy then. He reckoned it was one of the pangs of sobering up finally or just the pure boredom of driving through the desert. It's only cool until you realize that it's a desert, he thought, as he drove. Yet something gave him solace the way the orange horizon spread and shed light up into the darkening blue sky. This was home, huge, full, and beautiful.

They drove onward with the kid still sticking his head out the window and everything seemed fine. But the cowboy just couldn't think for some reason. He thought nothing for gaps of time. And then came the faint high-pitched memory of voices: "*You get a job on your own then, ya hear? Don't come back till you do... Oh, Henry, come back, please, come back. ... You're gonna be the best-looking cowboy in Kansas, the best one.*" This was the first time he started noticing that something was wrong with his noggin — might be related to the time when he got hit in the head with a shovel in a scrape back home, he reckoned, as they passed an old, rough-weathered man standing on the side of the road looking west, his white beard stiff in the western wind, his clothes, apparently lost in Gallop.

With a gasp of cold air thrust into the cab, the kid came back in from the big wide world and looked at the cowboy and smiled. His face was all red.

"Had enough?" the cowboy asked him.

"Yeah," he said. And he rolled up his window.

It took forever for those western skies to set and die. Now it was a dark red crevice and the deep starry blanket of night weighed it down further into a sliver. But it only expanded in width. That sun just spread out like a warm blanket, dissolving up into the blue levels of stratosphere all the way across as though you could ride out there to the Sunny Land any time you liked.

"Where does the sun go down?" the kid asked.

The cowboy told him what he knew about the moon and the stars and such, but the kid didn't understand.

"Well, it looks like it sets itself right over there behind those trees."

"You wanna go looking for it?"

"Yeah!"

"Hell yeah, once and for all we're gonna go catch that sun."

And off they went chasing the sun. The cowboy drove right off the road, flew over the little embankment and landed in the desert, bumping over the tumbleweeds.

◆ ◆ ◆ ◆

CHAPTER X

Well, you wouldn't believe it, but for a while there it actually did seem like they were going to find the sun, and that the kid was really right about things all along. There was this huge burning light they saw in the distant dark. That's all they could see: just this big orangish-reddish fire in the night, and it wasn't no campfire. Too big to be a campfire. It looked as though the sun had fallen onto the earth.

As they got closer, it got bigger and the kid imagined it was a crashed alien ship, or a plane or car crash, or even a house on fire. The cowboy drove faster. The desert had smoothed out and the truck seemed to glide over it, streaking a curtain of dust into the night. It's funny how a fire can attract people, like when he was a kid struck by the fire burning in the fireplace, watching it, the fire dancing in his eyes and the heat on his face. The cowboy wasn't sure if he wanted to watch it or help pull people out. He just wanted to find out what the hell it was and then he'd decide.

Well, too bad for the kid. It turned out not to be the damn sun, but rather this huge bohemian bonfire in the middle of the desert. So there they were, all the bohemians, sitting around the bonfire, each with their own blaze reflected in their eyes; and their brains working fluidly behind the eyes; dressed in their crazy outfits, many involving very few actual garments; under their various hats, including a few cowboy hats.

The cowboy stopped the truck. The kid and he got out and walked toward the Bohemian's Cove. There was a big hand-shaped rock behind the fire. A slope littered with bohemians ran through the fingers of the red, hand-shaped little mountain of a rock, which seemed to reach up from the earth.

Between the hand and the fire, the bohemians sat in groups around smaller fires in the flat, soft sand. There were the hippies writing po- etry and passing around the crazy Indian pipes of opium and weed; the occultists and the religious bohemians; the English; the Scandina- vian gypsies; the crazy Brazilians and their sex and Lance Perfume; the old society-beaten beatneaks with their nonconformance; and the few modern, anti-establishment, natural-born killers, popping pills, defy- ing the metaphysical world; and there were the college dropouts; the government AWOLs; a few real Indian bohemians with all their cry- ing, incomprehensible, alcoholic satire — all sitting around their preju- diced flames. And in the far corner sat the savage intellectuals, talking in turn, ripping each other apart, writing books about how the devoid American culture empties by separating and pitting against itself and the terrible fire that erupts when the fires collide, and then solving their own elaborate problem by using the verb "aestheticize" metaphorically; all perfectly sane in the grove of insanity, giving birth to the end of the world and the salvation of mankind with words, feelings, dreams, drugs, and everything that is true, beautiful, and free in this bohemian rhap- sody, basking in the eternal ephemeral.

"Hello," the cowboy called out to them. All ceased movement and noise and turned their heads to the cowboy and the kid. They were awed by them with such enchantment as though they were gods, Amer- ican gods.

He saw one of them stand up, a black outline in the middle of the big fire. The mysterious way he turned around like that, all centered in the fire and looking as though he were emerging from the hellish pit, intrigued the cowboy to move forward against his better judgment. He knew from somewhere that you can't trust a crazy bohemian for more than his crazy ideas can merit trust. However, they did need a place to spend the night, and the desert was cold and desolate.

"Hey, man," the cowboy said to the one standing up, whom he assumed was the leader of this revel. "Mind if me and my boy here sleep by your fire for the night?"

"No, not at all."

"Much obliged. We won't be a bother to ya."

"Who's we?" asked the shadowed bohemian.

As the cowboy moved forward, he felt the eyes on him. He got a good look at the one standing up. He was wearing a cowboy hat, and for a crazy moment he thought he'd run into himself. The firelight made the cowboy bohemian's face look red, and he was a lot younger than he sounded.

"Aw, it's just me and my partner here. We ain't disclosin' no names. You understand."

"What shall we call you then?" the apparent leader intoned clearly.

"Call me Clyde," he said dryly, reaching into his arsenal, "and the kid, call him…" He looked down at the kid at his side. The kid stood like an heir to the American throne, a future boy king standing 5 foot 3 over his humble serfs.

"Call me kid," said the kid.

At these words, a gasp of awe shot through the crowd. And then, for a few moments things got real quiet as the bohemians looked them over in the firelight. There were so many of them. They all huddled in for a closer look at the strangers. They crept toward them around silent boulders in the dark like prowling animals fixed on their prey. The kid looked away and nestled his face into the cowboy's side. He was tuckered out already from all that slow action, looking around and such.

The cowboy made his way through the groping bohemians and went to the other side of the fire, where there weren't too many laying around.

"Where ya from, Clyde?" asked the leader bohemian.

"L.A.," the cowboy said.

"Aah, the westernmost city of civilization, no wonder such a generic concoction would stray this way," said the leader. He wore a green bandana around his head.

"Huh?" the cowboy grunted.

"I'm just fucking with you. So Clyde, tell us about this boy of yours," said the leader, sitting down on the other side of the fire.

So the cowboy told them about the boy. They all laughed. He never did know what was so damn funny. They were all stoned though, he knew that much. Then the conversation swerved all over the place, and they were all arguing and talking very loudly. It was hard to sleep. The kid was bundled up in the quilt behind the circle of bohemians and on the border of the dancing firelight. The cowboy got set up by the fire in a broken lawn chair that let him lay almost all the way back and stare at the stars. Man, what a beautiful night it was, a romantic night. You would think bohemians would have the mind to shut up and enjoy it. That's all they ever write about: the stars and the moon. And the moon always is the angry, white-knuckled mother of humanity or God or something, thought the cowboy. To him the moon was her, especially the crescent one of the present night. And you know, like a wise man once told him, if you reach for the stars as best you can, you might not get one star but you might get the moon. He would've shared this sentiment with the bohemians but figured they wouldn't listen to no lost, beaten-up cowboy telling them about the stars and the moon.

He watched them talk from under his hat and pretended to be asleep. Now they were talking about feminism and masculinity in America. One guy said the women were screwing up the old traditional system and ultimately stiffing the American man by being sluts instead of nurses and secretaries. Sometimes the professions go hand in hand, the cowboy thought. But man, he loathed the word "slut" — sounded so completely degrading to his sacred image of Angie running innocently through the grassy plains of his boyhood. If anyone called her that, man that son-of-a-bitch wouldn't have any face left when he'd done with him. Anyway, this led into women being the sin of the human race and how Eve first took a bite out of the apple in Paradise. One man said something about how sin perpetuates from baby to baby because we're all born through bloody cunts — the deserved pain of original sin. Another ignoramus backed this up saying that in a perfect world, men would have the babies.

There were many more men in the discussion than women. The few women were extreme, hard-faced feminists and not very pretty. They really overreacted to the men and totally blew their dignity by talking like whores. It was as if the men had lured them into a trap.

Finally, a strong feminine voice from the dark spoke out. "You men are just jealous," she said, "you know you couldn't *breathe* without us."

"Goddamned right!" the cowboy said suddenly, sitting up.

The woman turned her eyes toward the cowboy in the darkness. Two white beams in her dark eyes caught him as she stepped into the

firelight. She had a dark beauty about her, along with a dense air of es-
trogen, like the smell of birth. Wearing this long, dark silk dress, her tan
body moved swiftly through the clear night air.

"Are you in need of a woman?" she asked the cowboy.

"Yes," he said.

"May I ask why?" She swayed her hips, put her hands on them and
struck a poised pose, waiting to attack his answer.

"To love," he said.

"Ah, to love, to have and to hold — is that it?"

"Well, to make a family I guess."

"To make a family...."

"Yeah, it's just me and the kid right now, need a woman to complete my family," he said.

"Oh, to complete your family, ha!" she mocked, walking around the
fire to him. "To watch over your little boy there."

The bohemians stirred in the semi-darkness.

"Yes," he said, looking at the fire. He didn't know what was
so complicated.

The lady continued to walk around the fire, looking at the cowboy
the way that she did and questioning him like a lawyer. She couldn't find
one sexist chink in his armor. A bit macho in manner perhaps, but that
was a rarity to her: a man's man who is cavalier and simple and not a pig.
She wanted to know everything about the cowboy and his kid.

The court was adjourned and she sat next to him, whispering back
and forth. When this happened, the rest of the bohemians went back to
their discussions. Some of the quiet ones took their chance at offering
their world-saving ideas.

Meanwhile, the lady and the cowboy slowly recessed deeper into
the shadows, away from the fire, cuddling up together under this thick,
wool, plaid blanket under the cliff of the rock — the edge of the palm
on the hand. The whole camp nestled against the crazy hand-shaped
mountain that the bohemians may have summoned themselves. The
little rock mountain jutted up silently, hidden in the night yet ever present, and cold, and stiff in the air like a god you could turn and smack
your face into. They leaned against it now, a good few yards away from
the others. The stone was smooth against their backs. Her skin was
like the silk he uncovered. He told her this, and she rubbed her cheeks
against his. They could see now that the guys were passing around this
foot-long, feathered Indian pipe. She wanted to go smoke it and said it

was hers, but the cowboy refused. He wanted to stay in the dark with her and cuddle and fall asleep in the silk.

"You crazy, helpless child," she said, and she slid a flower into his mouth. The cowboy chewed and swallowed, and then she fed him some mushrooms. She watched his eyes widen. He put his head back against the cool smooth stone and then flopped over to go to sleep. She picked him up. She was a pretty strong woman, not big strong, more like veiny, skinny, tall, stubborn-opinionated strong. She was a Navajo Indian, straight from the reservation, known in some parts for her painting of a Navajo child in one of those sacks the mothers carry on their backs.

She took the cowboy's hand and led him up a trail to the summit of the mountain. He started dancing along the way. The rest of the bohemians were dancing around the big fire now, and the cowboy tried to run into it all and jump over the bonfire, but the lady reached her arm across his body and pulled him back against the side of the mountain. She looked him square in the eye and held a moment long enough to express, "Cowboy, I need to talk to you, okay?"

"Okay, doll," he said, "whatever you say, just let me grab us a couple of beers."

"All right. I will be waiting for you."

The squaw lady went up to the small summit. The cowboy ran down among the guys not dancing, jumped over a small fire and asked, "Any of you fellas got some beer?" Nobody answered. Finally one guy in the back searched a watery cooler. "Yeah, I got some," he said and he tossed two cans over the fire.

"Thanks, man," the cowboy said.

"No problem, man. Hey, be careful with that one."

The cowboy looked over his shoulder. He saw the squaw sitting modestly atop the mini-summit. She sat wrapped in a blanket, her body shaped like a soft, round upside-down plum against the rough-grained rock — swaying in the red sky.

The cowboy looked back at the holy man with the beer.

"That woman's an elitist feminist liberalist," emphasized the man.

"My kind of woman," said the cowboy.

He turned with a big smile, and with mad, rushing, feverish fervors of distant and near sweeping airs of fear of the world and feminists in him, and hallucinating herds of slaughtered cattle, marched like he would in a funeral procession up the winding path, lethargically stepping over passed-out bodies and sleeping ones, too. His brain seemed to disconnect from his spine or the other way around. He remembered there was this one passed-out guy he could see when close to the summit, strung out, buck naked, belly down on top of this huge, egg-shaped boulder. Foam from his mouth slowly wet the dry face of the boulder. If he woke up and rolled over or moved in the slightest direction either way, he was bound to fall a good ten feet to a pit between that rock and the little mountain. Man, the place really was the bohemians' playground.

When he reached the summit, the moon rose on cue over the open desert.

"Cowboy?" she said. She turned to him and reached back to let her hair down. "Like Tom Mix or John Wayne, huh?"

"Aye, something like that," he said, stepping toward her. She was at the edge of the summit. All that rose above them now was one peaking slab of rock that had been around since the dinosaurs (jutting up as likely, the middle finger) pointing up toward the stars.

Designed on the side of its slab in sharp, glittering white chalk was a picture of a massive Roman orgy.

"Aye? Are you a pirate now?" she said with a false English accent.

"Aye, a pirate of the land, a pirate of love," he said. And he grabbed her waist inside her dress and kissed her. "It's funny how you can go from happy to sad," he said, corny as hell, "it's all in the drugs, I tell you, the drugs and the women, they'll drive a man mad." He was no good at acting like a bohemian.

"You a poet and you didn't know it," she said.

He pushed her up against the orgy stonewall and kissed her with tongue and felt her breasts and legs, and the next moment they were dancing on the small platform of the summit, leaning against each other like beaten boxers late in a match. And then some guy and his girl came up to take the view. They kicked them out. Well, she did. And then they went over to the edge and took the view.

They sat with their feet dangling over and dwindling away into the blackness, crossing together like two kids in love. He held her hand in a rather awkward bending position behind his back, but it didn't hurt. He figured the bohemian in her would appreciate the unorthodox.

His mouth dropped open and fell to her shoulder. He just wanted to go to sleep and be carried off into that good night, sleeping on her and not knowing her name or anything — just staying totally neutral and innocent of the whole thing, pretending he was in love.

But she would have none of it. She shoved her shoulder and bounced his head back up until he felt her denying him. He opened his eyes.

Boy, she sure had a lot on her mind. She must've been just dying for a gullible guy to come along so she could bring him up there and pour her sad life story all over him, as well as her unpublished, crazy theories.

He knew he wouldn't be able to remember all the details, but he knew she was an Indian. And she thought the backbone of America, or the childhood of America, as she put it, was a tragic one right from the beginning because really the land didn't belong to the whites in the first place. And she told stories about her family on the reservation, and how they don't believe in money or having a Social Security number. He told her he didn't know if he had one, and therefore didn't, as far as he was concerned.

"See, I knew you were different," she said. "Right from the very moment I saw you, I knew. You're free, aren't you?"

"How can you tell a thing like that?" he teased.

"'Cause you're a cowboy. All cowboys are free. You've got a real cowboy hat even." She took it off him, put it on and looked at him without embarrassment. It actually fit her pretty good. Her straight black hair jetted down at the sides. If only she'd have smiled under the moonlight in that hat. He leaned back to look at her better. And he smiled softly to try to get her to smile like it was contagious, but she looked away.

She gave his hat back and told the long, sad story of her husband, John, who had left her after only one year of marriage. She really stressed this only one year. And she stressed how it never did feel like they loved each other or that he was ever there. The cowboy said that's not too bad 'cause she hasn't really lost anything. But she had heard it all before and said she hurt more by never having anything.

"I just gave in," she said. "I gave in to the tradition, the institution of marriage. You know? Yet at the same time, I betrayed the tradition of my people; I married a white man and had a kid…."

And it went on and on and was really boring. The cowboy fell asleep a few times. When he awoke for the last time, she'd finally stopped talking. She sat at the far side of the ledge, holding her knees up to her chest, still awake, eyes bloodshot, staring into the early, red-creviced dawn.

The cowboy figured he'd leave her be and go find some exotic drugs for breakfast. As he walked down the twisting dirt path back to the camp, he passed a low-ridged shadowy cave. He looked over just in time to catch a flash of bare white flesh —the thigh of a young girl walking in the dark. She caught his eye and gave him a cute little smile and a wave. "Morning, miss," he said. Then he saw a pale white glob asleep all over each other, exhausted. They must've really had themselves one big Roman orgy in the secret cave. And oh man, what a luscious blonde that one girl was! The cowboy wanted to jump right in the sea of them and swim around fucking at will. But then he probably would've gotten the virus. Why is there always some sort of human ailment limiting our fun? After a night with the bohemians, this was how he was starting to think. Always asking why and trying to answer his damn self, and thinking about the problems of the whole world and all of humankind. He'd heard them tell a thousand stories about childhood and romance, and those were nice. But what interested him were the God-rebelling, uncompromising nonconformists — man-against-the-world bohemians. It's like they just can't sit still without finding some unconventional, inventive itch to scratch in the back of their heads and bitch about. He loved it.

When he got down there, this one guy wearing Joseph's technicolored dreamcoat was dancing around the fire, which blazed in red embers, crackling against the enclosing dense morning. The dreamcoat bohemian, swirling his cape around and getting in everyone's face, told of his great vision that came during the night. He had long, rock 'n' roll, blond hair and a short, skinny build.

"Imagine," he began, "an innocent world where all living things grow freely and all people love each other and help each other compassionately. A world without gas prices or cars sales or alarm clocks or traffic lights — see, we'd take 'em all down, you know why? 'Cause we won't need 'em."

The leader bohemian sat leaning against a hippy-decorated Volkswagen van out away from everybody. He rolled his eyes and sighed under his hat and went back to sleep.

The idealist went on with his vision: "In this world you won't have to go to work, you won't have to go to school — why? Somebody tell me why you have to go to school? I'll tell you why. Because society man—"

"Don't give us this bullshit again!" someone said.

The dreamcoat bohemian went on. "They say you have to go to school, graduate from high school, and then get held down for four years of your life for a B.S. degree, and then you can get a job and start making enough to buy a car and a place to live and have cable TV to keep feeding you, training you in how to get bald sitting around getting fat, hoping for games that you can't change, and you have a family and then sell your kids into society again and again. You see, this is what the world will do to you. It's a whole bunch of "isms" — traditionalism, machoism, slutism — and they'll hold you down, have you sprawling like a worm on a spinning platter, and they'll hold up a huge mirror so you can see yourself in this state, they'll, they'll, man they rule you with their rules, and they regulate you with their regulations — you can't drive too fast or too slow — you keep in line and don't complain and don't rebel or else they take you away to the looney bin or maybe even jail, and then they'll really go to work on you. Oh, and the time just never stops! They neutralize you and they make you logical as a clock, expiring. And what is it that everybody wants? Huh? To get ahead, right? And what do they need to do that, what do they really need? Money. If you get lucky, cheat on the test, have your dad get you a swell job, you can get a little bit more money than the rest, and then you can go out and bang Courtney Roundapple if you like or go blow a few grand at Vegas or develop a drug problem and then talk about it to *People* magazine. Come on, man, you know I'm right! This money has no worth anymore! That's why people use it to abuse themselves and to fuck up everything, everything that was once sacred, dignified law and order put up by our founding fathers, now crumbled and dirty in the pockets of dead, burnt-out gang members gone against the system. America was never totally innocent, but we have grown grossly far from it."

"So what exactly do you propose we do about it?" asked the leader cynically, standing up and dusting himself off.

"Well, we can't just do nothing, can we? We can't just let 'em roll over us. And we can't just keep on trying to get ahead by getting money 'cause we both know that won't happen—"

"Speak for yourself," said the outspoken critic and original leader of the bohemian clan.

"Hey man, come on now, nobody's going to publish your goddamned book, man!" the dreamcoat guy said, and he went over to the leader.

"Speak for yourself, I said," said the leader.

They were now face to face. Dreamcoat held a sharp look as the dichotomy formed right before everybody in the shape of two men beating out their ideas and conflicting naturally. Finally Dreamcoat backed off and went back to his crowd. They were waiting, looking up to him like lost children.

"What I propose we do..." he said grandly. Then he lowered his head as if his great plan had escaped him and vaporized into thin air, and now he hadn't the foggiest idea of what to say. The leader let out a dry whinny of a laugh and walked off toward the Volkswagen.

Dreamcoat put his hand in the air to hold the attention of the bohemians, almost as if to call back the leader or rather to show how he flees.

"Well, what we must do...is find something to replace money. Money...it's the root of all evil."

The leader heard this, cocked his head back and let out a big laugh as he walked away. "I thought TV was the root of all evil," he mocked and flapped his hand at him in dismissal.

"But what about *Frasier?* I like that show," someone said.

"That statement is fallible in itself, for there was evil before there was TV," another criticized logically.

"Metaphorically speaking," Dreamcoat defended. "Besides, money goes back to the Bible, like having to pay 30 shillings of silver to the devil and all that."

"You can complain, but you can't solve anything," the leader scowled shrewdly. "You can't solve; that's the problem."

Dreamcoat ignored him. The bohemians started to ignore Dreamcoat. Dreamcoat pushed on.

"It's simply lost its moral value. This money. It holds so much of our culture. And the advertisements — everything in America has to have the caption of the world's greatest.

"And then on our deathbeds, so many of us will find ourselves swallowed in regret, having been sucked in by a superficiality which is so ingrained in our system that we don't even realize it anymore when we send our children spinning, splintering of their innocence in the social cycle of consumerism, commercialism, a college of normalcy: money. Money is freedom. In this system, true freedom is lost in movies, games, replicas, stories of rebellion, grand old American stories still hissing out with the few unhinged examples and the widely publicized little scandals...How many people have died in its path? How many have killed for it? All blind attacks at this great manmade shield.

"Everyday people are born into their classes and automatically restricted; everyday innocence is lost — I'm not talking pure, divine, biblical innocence. I'm talking the American innocence with all its scarred resiliency — but boy what a terrible price to pay for innocence, for beauty. And that's what we must get back to, man! Remember when we were kids? People were not leaders 'cause they had money; people were just natural leaders. And everybody else was just naturally what they were. We must return to this. Imagine everybody waking up and not worrying about any dress code or lipstick, well, unless you're into that, but I mean just relying on their own values. It'd be kind of scary at first after depending on the government all these years. But just think of how wonderful it would be! We'd have our own ideas truly, and we wouldn't have to watch the news to wait for the experts to tell us what to think. I'm talking about for the first time having our own opinions. We'd be free then, you know, we'd be free."

The cowboy looked around. Everybody was numb with cynical boredom. He didn't know if the speech was over, whether to clap, what anybody else thought, but something he said sure put the hook in him. The dreamcoat speaker went over quietly by himself, squatted down, grabbed his head and started rocking back and forth. You could just feel the force of revelations raiding his mind and refuting themselves, pounding through him.

"A world without money," someone said in critical shock. "An America without money. That is the most retarded thing I've ever heard. No more drugs for that man."

Originally, the cowboy was going to grab some weed and the kid and get out of there before they got into something. But now he felt that he was definitely in something and that he'd have to say something in order to get out. Everyone was quiet, looking at this dreamcoat guy who had just spewed his entire childish philosophy, halting the impetuous bohemian rhapsody.

One sympathetic college dropout bohemian was trying to think of something to say without destroying Mr. Dreamcoat, who now lay down on the dreamcoat, wrapping himself in a little ball in it on the ground, completely ignoring everyone looking at him, as if to make some sort of statement.

"So let me get this straight," the dropout said loud enough. "In your world, instead of going to the supermarket and buying...fruit, say, with money, I'd buy it with...my values...my good intentions...what?"

"Yes," Dreamcoat uttered, disbelieving that anybody had understood him and that he was totally alone, shriveled up against the mad world.

"Well what's to stop me from taking all the fruit just for me and killing others who try to take it for themselves?" asked the critic. "You see, people need something they can hold in their hands and call value. They need to be measured this way. Don't you see? Without the system it'd be chaos. Greed would take over. It'd be every man for himself or worse — one man over all. Money is not the problem; it's us that's the problem, man. But hey, it's a good, sound humanistic — I mean I think we've all thought the way you do every day, man, dealing with this bullshit but..."

The dropout critic saw Dreamcoat's disgruntled face as he sat up. The conviction had been sucked dry out of him. "Hey, man, at least your heart is in the right place, and it's a fabulous idea, if only people would jus—"

"People will see it my way!" he snapped like an aspiring tyrant. "You'll see. Like I said, they'd be scared at first, but they'd get around it. Everybody deep down is suffering and waiting to break loose, ya know? You don't know, do ya? Well you will. Soon." He tipped back and leaned his head up on a smooth rock on the desert ground. He slanted his hat down over his face. His mouth remained in the sunlight. The cowboy watched him speak in his hypnotic, paralyzed voice: "Everybody's just dying to break free..."

The cowboy looked at him for a long time. He wanted to ask, "Break free from what?" But he knew that would just open another long, rambling confusion of an answer. Furthermore it would seem as though he were challenging him theologically, and he was never one for that sort of thing. He was a simple man, just looking for his woman and his home. The kid stepped up to his side and asked when they would leave.

"Now," said the cowboy, with a crazed, stricken look in his eye.

"What's the matter with that guy?" asked the kid innocently.

The cowboy looked at the kid, relieved at once from the craziness of the bohemians, remembering his steadfast partner all over again. It was the first time the kid had asked with such pure naïve concern for another. Man, there was something about that kid. The cowboy wasn't going to ever let him down. No bureaucracy or society or money or anything would ever cut him or hold him down or grow him up and take his innocence. That's a promise, he thought.

The kid spat on the scorched red earth and waited for his partner's reply.

"I don't know, kid, I don't know."

"Well, why don't you go talk to him, see if you can figure him out," the kid suggested.

The cowboy looked down at him in admiration. "And why the in the Sam Hill would I want to do that?"

"Well, on account of him lookin' all sad and lonesome like. Can't you just go see what's eatin' him."

The cowboy chuckled and looked about him. Then he pressed his lips together and dimpled his cheeks and twinkled his eyes at the kid and said, nodding, "All right. I'll go have a word with him."

He went looking for the dreamcoat bohemian a little later in the orgy cave. He sat on a rock and smoked a cigarette. The musty smell of the leftover lust hung in the air. He was looking at the smooth, shadowed stone floor, picturing the raw sex scene that had finished only hours before, when he heard a voice.

"Life is not that simple," said the voice.

It was Dreamcoat. He was very close, in the darkness.

"I think it is," said the cowboy. "It's more simple than most folks make it out to be."

This, and a cigarette offering, summed up all that the cowboy ever said to the bohemian. In return for his advice, the bohemian invited the cowboy to stay one more night. And he accepted.

Through the day, the cowboy slept through an apocalyptic speech, washed, smoked some, drank some, flirted with the tired girlies.

The kid had the love of life in him. He was talking to a pirate, sitting on his knee. The pirate had given him a few puffs of his pipe. The kid ran out, running around the desert, which twisted and bent and swirled about him as the lone red stones of the desert became the stones in his eyes.

Night slowly fell. Dreamcoat emerged from his cave, the dreamcoat replaced by a red cloak, transformed, due for redemption. He wore a huge, stiff, velvet red, Shakespearean suit, with the tightly pinned collar, the tights for pants, and the light slipper-prancing shoes. The red spread glow of the setting sun roused the heads of the bohemians simultaneously like flowers sprouting from the earth. Dreamcoat solidified his cloaked form before them. He raised one cloaked arm and pointed his finger to the horizon, like an apostle's symbol under the cloak. The last tremors of ecstatic spasms sizzled out through his veins and out his tuft of a fake white beard. He raised his head and looked out over all.

He appeared mad at first, as though he'd jump right off that cliff, and then he calmed with the tender falling night. He went down to the ridge amongst his children. "My children," he began. And they all crowded him, touching his face and body. "Get back!" he snapped. And they darted back as if a blast had thrown them. But they crept back in, mesmerized. A guitarist strummed the first high-pitched note from atop one of the mountain's fingers, as the speaker bohemian spoke:

"Behold, the cowboy!

(All heads turned to the cowboy, who rested out yonder on the rocks.)

> *He hath seen the heart of America, and she is a*
> *Bruised and battered*
> *Illegitimate child.*

(The guitarist had long, scraggly hair and tattered clothes, bare feet, and a red electric guitar. The amp plugged into an adjoining finger peak. He played his solo long and hard, smashing with the bohemian's words.)

> *I have seen what he has seen, or will see,*
> *This cowboy character,*
> *His silent vision penetrates through me*
> *In all its strength.*
> *He is I. Mine is his. His is mine.*
> *We are one...*

(Dreamcoat paused, bowed his head solemnly as he collected the prophecy. Then it lashed out in mad reverberations through him.)

> *I want to feel the cold shaft*
> *Of appropriation.*
> *I want to wriggle and moan and yelp*
> *On its axis.*
> *And the little girl...*
> *He thinks about her every now and then.*
> *Wonders if she's still alive.*
> *He should go to the authorities about it,*
> *But that would put*
> *Away his good friend, the sick bastard.*
> *And this he cannot do.*

So what does he do?
He sucks it up, man.
He pays his dues.
Freedom must be won, son.
You come here, you either work and
Take part in the economy, or you run,
Unless you are above —
Inherited in empiricist facade.
But he is not,
So he fights and runs,
But what is there to escape with
That is not temporary?
He's tried the drugs, the girls,
It's all fake, man; it's not real,
Just like the kid there.
As beautiful as he is, he is a lie.
The more he thinks of him, the more he loves him, and the more he
Hates lies.
He says there are so many lies out there,
And people consume them like ether,
And human life detaches from their spines.
Spineless...

An age of blockbusters and best-sellers,
The classic is dead.
Spoken like a true whore,
The girl next door
Shoved out onto the stage...

He hath seen the end
Of the American dream.
There is a thin clerk behind a register
In a striped shirt, plastic visor,
Red suspenders, and a nametag,
Asking, "Would you like to hear about our special?"

People are out there
Selling their kids, waiting in line.
Man, you'd be lucky if you got

Your kid in a commercial! Experts say 30 percent
Go on to succeed in Hollywood.

This America, man, is slumbering
And swelling at the same time,
Swelling with something big,
And its bureaucratic belt can barely hold it in.
How is buying a Cadillac going to keep
America rolling, can you tell me that?
They tack on 'America' in these commercials,
Throw it around like loose change.
Well, I have traveled this land, and I have seen
The rugged land and the soft land,
I've seen the rich and the bums and
The big fat middle class...
Go ahead; get your money.
Build your pipe bombs,
Get on TV.
Nay, not me.
I DO NOT WANT TO RETURN TO NORMALCY!
I SHAN'T
Think of all the people. The lies. The actors.
Hey, you going to watch the Oscars?
Think of all the scandals yet to come.
Crazy mother drowning her children,
Everyone is planning to
Kill each other, and they're all going to do it
At the same time.
Sadness stalks happiness.
Sin eats innocence.
This is the way the world works,
It's fucking pagan idolatry!
Positive fucks negative and creates life,
Can you imagine two negatives?
Anti-matter disintegrating you at touch.
Two positives?
The world an untouched forest, man, I'm not
Lost. I'm lost.

(His hand shook up by his face. He trembled.)
I feel we're close, though. Tittering on the edge,
Just waiting for the right
Wind to push us off. Damn,
I should have known.
Can you imagine
America without currency?

("I can," croaked a bum.)

Without capital?
Behold!
Viva la revolution!
Down with the capital!

Can you imagine the ungoverned world
Reborn from truth
After the lie expires,
Without laws? Without anything
That governs you? You measure a man by
His heart.
How do you know? You just feel it, man,
You feel it. Remember? REMEMBER!
I know you can!
There is no resume, no references,
Just a trust, a divine
Human bond.
And then he breaks it and tarnishes
Everything and betrays you.
Forgive him anyway.
What would we do today?
Release the hate; sit behind
The glass, all fat and skin-dry,
And watch him sit there and die.

Parched, white-collared pricks,
Ignoring the warnings, cocky and complacent,
Tweaking the reports,
Insufficient cover-up for the cover-up,

The obsequious clandestine service...
WAR!

It's gonna be war, man.
Let's get out now and conquer it.
Wake up, America,
Before it's too late.
And out come all the flags,
All of a sudden, a new regime has its juice.
Remind you of anything?
military meanness,
Thrashing rage,
The sound and the fury —
Broken sovereignty.

I know what you are thinking:
This is like man knocking
On the doors of paradise,
With the riddle remaining unsolved
In our iniquitous efforts,
Two million years too late.

But hell, I say we are innocent, the way we were made.
And yet we're killing our children.
I don't know. Let me just say this, he
Has been there, he has seen
The end of this shielded America,
He has broken through the thick glass,
He hath seen the American communism at
Child labor in the factories,
He hath seen the end of money's worth,
He hath broken through the vault,
Seized the American dream
And run with it.
Yet so quickly did they
Take it away, with
Their laws and uniforms,
And I say unto you,
For all the unborn, for

All the fetus' torn apart at the eyes by the tongs,
For all the whores, the
Nameless Pepsi generation 'x' or next generation
Of youth CNN will call 911, for the killers,
The rich, the
Poor, the good students studying case files for
The Bar, for the
Fathers who love yet abuse, for the mothers who
Love yet kill — she drowned
Her family — it's all over the news! For the people in the
Cubicles working
Hard at pretending, all those faking it, planning
It, measuring the details for their great expatriate:
IT'S NOT WORTH IT!!!
Stop! Put down the pen!
Daydream a bit, tell off your boss and go break the
Law, and I'll see you in jail.
It's either in here or behind the screen:
The TV plight, dying with regret, and regret is
For life. The middle word is if, and if you take out the 'f', it's a
Lie.
Nay, he will not regret her. He will not lose her.
He will break this law,
He will fight; he will fight anyone, anything
That prevents him from reaching her,
Loving her. He will take all his rage, all
His mounting anger of the whore-ship of this
Country, and he will attack full throttle,
Straight at the heart,
And he will save her.
He will love her,
And they can never take that away.
And the taxes will go.
The red-blooded souls will glow,
And slip, and slide up and around,
Spiraling, withering, reaching,
Screaming in the bureaucracy,
In the sludge of hypocrisy.

The cowboy will free us all.

And America will return to the basics:
Loving hunger, riding all day,
Sitting around the campfire telling stories.
Then again, I am one man,
One human American. What
Difference can I make?
Besides a budge in the stock? I am a killer,
A sinner, a liar; a lean, mean,
No-good , murdering son-of-a-bitch.
Lock me up; shut me up; write up a story
About me for the papers.
I am sorry for betraying you, but I am weak
And my heart is broken.
I am sorry, America. I cannot go on.
But you keep on rollin', singing your song,
Drop the bomb; sell the gun,
A rollin', rolling, rolling away over me,
And all else insolent souls
Who declare to be free.
Nay, I say,
Come ye,
Follow me,
Together we will
Coup this hypocrisy!

The guitarist jumped from the peak, landed and finished his solo. The speaker fell with the pull of the chord and crashed beside him against the red rock platform. He then swung his guitar around by the end of its neck and smashed it — sparks flying — into the side of the rock and the ground.

And then all was silent for a moment as the sparks fell and fizzed out. Then a bohemian in the crowd cried: "Behold! There! The cowboy cometh!"

The groveling crowd gasped with awe. The cowboy's tall, lean shadow danced forth, bending over a big boulder out to the clear. He walked along the ridge to the speaker bohemian whom he had influenced so. They shook hands firmly. The cowboy hadn't heard much of the speech, except the part about keeping America rolling. He liked that. But he was unaware that the speech was full of satirical bullshit, an inconsolable challenge to the post-modern American constructs.

The bohemian looked confidently into the cowboy's distant, colorless, torched eyes. He gestured fervently, sucking air through his teeth, booming his big English-accented voice through his bearded scholarly cheeks. His head sat back in his stiff cloak collar like an upright grandfather clock, with his goatee bending crustily over his collar and jutting out with his boyish chin as he spoke with such incongruous vigor that the bohemians attracted inward in a systematic swirl to the bank of the ridge. He threw his right arm out straight to the sun. "Cowboy, can you see?" He stepped up on an overlooking plank of rock and pointed west into the setting sun. "A little stirring on the horizon there! A song that vexes me! America, America, God shed His grace on thee!"

The cowboy pierced his eyes to the long red sunset. He put one foot up on a rock, leaning in on his leg a bit. He looked and nodded. He looked sharp and quick at the bohemian and said nothing.

Dreamcoat went on.

"Look there to the golden template, the red strong chest; behold the breaking point, the vintage overgrown and wild, the ultimate chronoscope and the ultimate complaint, collide. He is born. Salvation is now. Man invited, few chosen. The bohemian revolution! Dive innumerably suicidal into the cauldron. Alas! The freed man stands! Betwixt democracy's slaves, and the human, bloodied creviced stave! The American republic stands at attention. Violence halts. Usurpers cease. Voices hush. As time and space separate!"

The multi-colored heads of the bohemians rose to the ridge around the cowboy. Dreamcoat let his huge arm hang out past their stellar icon to the sky. His long classic cloth hung from his arm like the emblem of a prophet.

The cowboy stood up, further out into the ultimate birthing sunset that all the bohemians feasted upon. "She sure is purty," he said at last. And he turned and started walking away.

The bohemians repeated the cowboy's sacred words and wrote them down on the walls of the mountain.

"You said it all, man," a bohemian said to the cowboy. "You said it all."

It was a very bad speech. The fellow they called Dreamcoat had no idea what he was talking about, and you could tell if you actually tried to listen to his words, but he told it so well, with such sloppy yet supreme authority — some sort of sublime existential prophecy — and the others pretended to believe him. So that night the bohemians held a great ceremony, naming Dreamcoat as their leader of the revolution against American communism, which included the imperialism of consumerism and commercialism — the two big C's of the enemy shroud, over the true, unscathed, virgin child called America. Their mission was to save America's childhood, whatever the hell that meant.

In the meantime, the cowboy sat on the range while the bohemians got tight on absinthe and signed their new constitution for America. As the ceremonies died down, the night became very starry and romantic. The kid had passed out on a broad's bosom. The cowboy went up to a lookout point at the mountain's western edge. He sat in a hollowed out hole in the rock, with one leg bent up and the other dangling out the side. He slid his back down a bit against the smooth, weathered stone. The very strained sinews of rock he could see stretched above him in the open circle. The moon settled and silhouetted the cowboy sitting up there in the rock. Drawers, writers, and painters recorded the cowboy. One lady sketcher caught the exquisite details: the hand every now and again gently bringing the stick cigarette to the mouth, sucking back the glow of the cherry and exhaling straight out, head back, hand loose on the bent knee and the idly spinning spurs, and the stark way the hat was outlined against the moon.

The cowboy heard a small group of bohemians riveted around the fire, talking slow and hypnotic like, and then fast and driven with all fear against the world like, singing and laughing, telling stories, talking about some guy named Kerouac.

Soon singers came along and took over, singing old, lonesome cowboy songs, tinkering with the lyrics here and there.

"There is a young cowboy, who lives on the range, his horse and his saddle his only companions. He works with the cattle and sleeps in the canyons, thinking about women and glasses of beer..."

One just kept on examining his hand outstretched before his face, watching the line of life in his palm and the way it reddens when stretched, and all the prints and dips.

A crazy Brazilian guy sang: *"Short and fat and bald and ugly, the boy from Impanema goes walking, and when he passes, he passes the gas, and the people go: aaaahhhghhggghhh! Pee-hew-weee!"*

A poet walked by, grabbing the air saying, "And man thus is thrown into the flux of perpetuating eternity…"

A redheaded, leprechaun dwarf ate some spotted 'shrooms and cut them up and sprinkled them on a rare weed and smoked.

On the rock platform below him, a sculptor polished his masterpiece: an iron hand, depicting mankind reaching from the slime, with the slime all bubbly and strands of it strung tight between the fingers, and snapping at the reach of creation.

From his view, the cowboy could see lanterns dissipating into the night. He figured they were all lovers, claiming their land in the uncharted territory.

"Hey there, cowboy," came a young woman's voice.

She startled him, and he nearly drew his gun and jerked himself out of his little perch up there on the 30-foot peak. But he calmed at the soft touch of the lovely young woman, who looked uncannily like Marilyn Monroe.

"Evening, miss," he said.

"Good evening. Did I startle you?"

"Little bit, try'n to be alone up here."

"Oh, I'm sorry, I'll go."

"No wait, stay."

"Stay?"

"Yeah, come here. It's too late to go now, now that you're here."

"What are you doing up here all alone?"

"Oh, just trying to clear my head from all those crazy bastards down there," he said.

"I understand. Would you like some absinthe?"

"Ah, no thank you."

"Sure?" She sat down on a rock with her drawing. The cowboy put his gun on his lap.

"Is that that green drink?" he inquired.

She presented a bottle from her satchel and quickly made two glasses. It was the real wormwood stuff, and soon the green fairy danced in the pretty girl's starry eyes. The cowboy didn't see no fairy at first, and then she came from the constellations riding the old the pink elephant.

"Is that your gun?" asked the girl.

The cowboy held it in his lap. He picked it up, and she sat down in its place. He told her all about his Colts, and she asked about what it's like to kill a man and rob a store and all that she'd heard about him. And she asked why he was on this crusade. The cowboy explained everything with tired, long-sighing answers, but when he looked her in the eyes he almost figured his crusade for love and home was over. "American girls...the cutest girls in the world," he thought aloud.

"What?" she asked.

"You're beautiful," he said. "Let me see your drawing."

She showed him. He smiled. She laughed, and they perched the drawing up against the rock, and she moved over and cuddled up on him.

The girl felt very special to get this close to him from among all the others below. She knew that the cowboy was a violent, crude man, and he knew that he soon would not care for her, yet she felt special with him for that moment in the moonlight. The cowboy reached under her dress and ran his hand along her belly. The girl became vexed with lust and guilt. She kept on shoving his heavy hand off her, saying something about her platonic love. The cowboy's hand kept coming, until she screamed and pushed his hand to the rock floor.

"What the hell?"

She got off him.

"I just wanted to kiss you," she said. And she kissed him on the cheek and whirled her hair around her shoulder, buttoned up and said, "Happy New Year, cowboy."

The moment after she said this, she backed off and looked at him tenderly in the night; and fireworks sprung up from behind her in the distant dark, where the lanterns had dispersed.

"Wait a second," the cowboy said. "How long have I been here?"

"Three days. It's New Year's, cowboy. Got a resolution?"

The cowboy sat stoic, figuring fast. There was no way it could be New Year's already. He put his arm on his knee. He let his cigarette hang loose in his lips. Then he bit the filter up and took one long last drag as he scanned the crowd for the kid.

"I get it now," said the girl. "You think you're a real cowboy."

He said nothing.

"*Cogito, ergo sum*," the girl said.

"What?"

"I think, therefore I am, Julius Caesar."

"Yeah, well I don't think, therefore, I ain't. And you can quote me on that."

She laughed. "You are truly hollow," she said. "You know what you need, you need some T.L.C."

"Huh?" The cowboy looked to the stars.

"Tender loving care, cowboy, that's what you need — or a mother. Say, where is you're mother anyway?" she giggled.

He kept looking off and she kept talking.

"Anyway, every New Year's we come out here. The bohemian New Year is in May, by the way. I don't know if you realized that, but anyway I don't know about the speech this year. Nobody really knew what the heck he was saying. They just want something to believe in and follow. Bunch of childish followers, you know? Don't worry about that constitution. Every year they sign some sort of revolution, but they never commit to it. Tomorrow they'll wake up from all of this like it was all a dream, and they'll go back to their jobs. Boy, you shoulda seen them when the millennium rolled around. All talking about the end of the world — nobody listens to me much, other than looking at my drawings. But I think when masses of people fear the world will end because they can't get on the Internet and the computers crash, then I think the human world is ending, but no, this..."

The cowboy looked west and saw lights. "Is that what I think it is?"

"That's Vegas, baby," she said.

"Shit, I gotta get the hell outta Dodge, doll-face. I'll see ya." He couldn't believe he hadn't even escaped the lights of Sin City yet.

He shoved by the girl, went down and grabbed the kid from dancing and drinking wine from the bottle around the fire with the bohemians in masks of ancient gods.

"Hey, what the hellya doing?" said the kid.

"Come on, we're leaving."

"Oh, hey, yeah, let's get the hell out of here. I'm tired of these animals, but one more drink—"

The cowboy grabbed the kid by the collar and dragged him out to the truck.

Down the road, they slowed to talk to a man walking on the side of the road. It was the fallen leader of the bohemians who had been so cynical of their new revolution. He said he was going out on his own to sell his book and prove everybody wrong.

"Hell, I don't care if I have to go door to door like my brother did and beg people to read it. It's gonna get read and it's gonna get published."

"All right, man, you do that. Where is this book of yours anyway?" said the cowboy, leaning out the window.

"Huh, oh the book? It's right here." He pointed to his head and patted his heart. "I've got it in me, see. It'd be like aborting my first-born son, if I didn't get it out. I completed the story in my head tonight, see. Now it's only a matter of time and punching it out the way I like it."

"Haha! Yeah, well good luck to ya, man. We've gotta hit the road."

"Yeah, good luck to you also! I hope you find your lady friend!" he called after them. Then he was running after the truck, waving his hands and yelling and totally emasculating himsel. The cowboy pulled over and waited for him, out of an ounce of draining pity for the poor fool.

"Hey, what about Carmen?" the author asked.

"The Indian girl?" the cowboy said.

"Yeah."

"Shoot. I never got her name."

"Yup, Carmen Penny — well her real name's Wunpen Zaborek. Yeah, she was one of those poets that just have to splinter out of orbit, they just can't survive in this world."

"Yeah, and what are you?"

"I'm kind of a divergent myself. No, I'm more of a sprawling malfunction of a human being that needs to be put out of his misery."

"Cool, man," he said as he killed the thought of shooting him right there and driving off. "Funny, seems Wunpen (One-pen) ought to be a fine name for a writer," the cowboy laughed through his nose. The kid imitated him.

"Yeah, I never even thought about that. Couldn't get over how weird it was," said the bohemian. "You're a good man, cowboy."

"Yeah, well..."

They were driving slowly now. The bohemian jogged like an idiot alongside, huffing and puffing.

"She kept on talking about this John character," the cowboy recalled. "Sounds like he'd get in the way, you know. She just couldn't stop talking about him. Hey, what is it with writers and this platonic love anyway?"

"Ha! Who knows? If I could figure that one out, I'd be a millionaire!"

He sent him off with a smile and a bullet for the grace of mankind. He could almost picture him jump up in the air and start walking again. Never had he seen a leader fall so quickly.

They came to an intersection a few miles down the road where they would have to turn right to go east behind those big, postcard-red buttes corroding up like uneven curtains against the night sky. Behind the curtains they could barely see the bohemian's cove in the distance. The cowboy looked back once more. What a place in the middle of no-where. Nature's miniature playground, like heaven fallen on earth in a patch for all those lost and rambling souls.

As they swerved around the bend, the cowboy thought about the Indian girl. He checked the rear-view mirror and glimpsed through the sliver of night between two thumbed, red curtain rocks the crazy Indian lady stepping over the ledge of the bohemian summit and falling into the jagged red rocks.

◆ ◆ ◆ ◆

That night the cowboy and the kid camped out by themselves in the desert. They parked the truck well off the road and built a fired from some wood the cowboy had loaded in his truck.

The truck didn't look good. It bent down lopsided on the front left wheel and dragged its muffler. "Damn thing's falling apart," he said. He had a lot on his mind through the remainder of the night, instigated by what he thought to be the crazy Indian's suicide.

He looked over at the kid. He was sitting up, looking at the fire as though it were the sun fallen to the earth. He wasn't talking again.

"Goddamn it, kid, how come you never talk?" asked the cowboy after a while.

"What the hell you wanna talk about?"

"I wanna talk about why you don't talk."

"That'd be pretty hard to explain if I'm the type that don't talk."

"Yeah, yeah. Funny, funny. You know what I mean. Around people, you're mister big shot, kid. With me, you ain't never talking. 'Taint right being a different person all the time. You gotta be yaself. And I don't even know who that is, and I'm your partner, shit. How old are you?"

"Fifteen."

"Aaah, you're lying."

"Eleven."

"Eleven. Well, when ya going to be twelve?"

"June."

"Ya don't say. Mine is in September. How about that?"

And they exchanged dates, and the cowboy tried to get the kid to talk about his birthday parties or whatever, and just really talk to him for once. The kid grudged him off to the point where the cowboy threw up his hands and said, "Damn it, kid. I already said sorry twice to ya about your ma, and that's more than I've ever said in my entire life to anybody, but I'll say it again if I'd get you to talk."

"I don't need sorrying."

"All right, good. How about this one: What's your name?"

"Dusty," said the kid, "Dusty Rhodes."

"Hahhaa, and your mamma changed it to Hill? Why in the sam hill did she do that? Rhodes. That's the greatest cowboy name I've ever heard. I'm ridin' with Dusty Rhodes; ha. I'll be damned. Well, goodnight Dusty."

And the cowboy turned, pulled his covers over him, laid his head on his clothes-makeshift-pillow and started to drift into dreaming under his hat. The kid curled up in his blanket, opposite the small fire.

"Say, cowboy," his innocent, curious, young voice caught the night from fading into dreaming.

"Yeah?" said the cowboy.

"I forgive you."

"Goddamn it, kid, go to sleep."

And there was a long pause when they both lay stiff and wide awake.

"I'm glad you're sorry for all the wrong stuff you've done and all; I'm glad you let me tag alone. Ain't you glad about things?"

"Yeah, kid. Go to sleep now, wouldya?"

"See, the way I figure it, you're making up for the wrong you did. Most people don't think they can do that when somebody is dead. I'll tell you, cowboy, you're real lucky I'm a good kid."

The cowboy tried to sleep.

The kid persisted. "You're gonna find me a mother. Ain't that right? Ain't that right?"

The cowboy rolled over.

"Ain't that right?"

"Yes, kid, I'm gonna find you a mother. Angie, 'member? Now go to sleep!"

"Oh boy, oh boy, oh boy... I can't wait to meet her!"

"Yeah, that's nice. Now would you shut up! First I couldn't get you to talk, now ya won't shut up!"

They laughed and sighed into sleep.

"All right, all right," said the kid.

Silence settled. The kid caught the night one last time.

"Mister?"

"What?"

"What's your name? I mean what's your real name? I think I ought to know if we's to be partners and all."

And so the cowboy told the kid his name. The deep blue night fell at last. And they fell fast asleep, under the stars.

◆ ◆ ◆ ◆

· BOOK III ·

CHAPTER XI

The kid had the love of life in him. He was out yonder, jumping the steppingstones down the stream, nose-dancing with a butterfly that had come along.

They had driven east a good way, and then ran out of gas. So the cowboy ripped his shirt off and pushed the old truck a good five miles to the next station while the kid sat in the back braving him on, yelling, "Push, goddamn you, push yer womanly, thick-nosed soul!"

When they got to the gas station, the cowboy's jeans were ripped at the knees from falling thrice to the kid's relentless encouragement. His pants were sheeted with dust and sweat. His brawny torso was glossed with sweat and glazed a sunburnt red. He had half a mind to beat that kid, smiling and asking if he could steal some damn candy.

"All right, kid," he said to him, breathless. And the kid ran into the convenience store. "Kid," he called after him.

The kid turned around at the curb and kept still his freckly, dirty face for an instant.

"Five minutes."

He nodded, smiling, and went in.

The cowboy filled up the tank. It was a lonesome gas station. In the little window, he could see the man behind the register. He leaned against the old truck, his hand clenched on the gas lever, and he thought of Angie. He turned his head to the sun and the desert as a dust cloud thinned out over him, and he squinted east into the sun in the morning.

The gas clicked to a halt. The cowboy put back the nozzle, dripping gas to the dry, cemented earth. He lit himself a cigarette, leaned back against the hood and waited for the kid. The kid came running out with the man after him. The man had a shotgun and shot a round into the sky, and another just over the truck, spraying pellets into the side of the bed and the door. This was bad news for the cowboy 'cause he'd lit his last cigarette and wanted to sit and enjoy it before grabbing another pack. He'd sucked it down halfway but didn't get a chance to snub it out. The clerk was trigger happy, and shot the truck's side windows out. The kid slid across the hood and jumped in the window while the cowboy reluctantly tossed his last cigarette as they screeched away.

The man with the gun bit the dust, shooting wildly as a line of fire shot behind him. And then there was a bit of an explosion, and all was quiet in the desert. The cowboy was really bummed he had to forfeit his last smoke.

They then sped through the town and the next and off the road into the desert, around and through the red rocks, and they drove on and on without talking, the kid watching the rode fly, sucking his candy sucker, the cowboy keeping one hand heavy, hanging atop, and one foot heavy on the pedal, and his left hand out the window feeling the wind breathe through his fingers.

And now they had gotten on a dirt road, northeast from their desired route, in order to get away from the cops, and the good Americans, and the men with guns sitting behind registers. The truck sat parked with one wheel off the road into the grass. There was a wide grassy field across the right side of the dirt road, lined with trees, and it looked like thicker forest up ahead. On the left side of the road, the truck sat, its roof slanted a little down the embankment under an overhanging tree, so that the cowboy, from his lounging in the rocks by the brook, could see through the trees the white shine the leaves made with the sun on the old truck's roof.

The cowboy sat there on a gray rock with one hand on his gun. He had made some good traps from deep around the perimeter in the surrounding woods to catch critters for dinner, and he was proud of his work.

The kid came over, jumping in the pond. The pond rippled an eternity, the water rushing to the sides and pinching betwixt the rocks to flow out into the channels.

The cowboy sat shirtless with the sun on his chest on the bank. The kid swam over. "Git in here! It's a hot spring!" he cried.

"Yeah, in a minute, kid. You bathe up now. Git your clothes good and clean and hang ' to dry on the rocks."

As the kid spread his clothes over the rocks, the cowboy asked him, "What'd you steal anyway?"

The kid came over in his wet trunks with an armful of stuff. He tossed the cowboy a bottle of sippin' whiskey and a pack of smokes and dove back in the hot spring.

"Atta boy," the cowboy said. And he smoked and sipped that whiskey and admired the kid, until he grew so overwhelmed with happiness and drunkenness that he put the bottle down, snubbed out his cigarette and jumped in the hot spring. The murky warm water enveloped him. He floated around in the warm, perfect haven, dunking the kid and throwing him around in the water. And then he bathed himself under the little waterfall downstream. And the kid, too. The cowboy's hat was so waterlogged that it stuck on his head and he forgot it was there, and he swam underwater without it budging on his head. He felt like he had a headache because his head was so heavy.

"Take yer damn hat off," said the kid.

"Right," the cowboy said, and he flung his hat spinning across the hot spring to land atop a big dry rock, which looked out over their drying laundry and the woods.

The sun glimmered down, nice and cool through the trees. Everything was sweetness and light. The cowboy swam on his back across the spring, whistling an old Western song. The kid climbed out on a little island by the falls and started skipping stones.

After a while, the cowboy said, "Ain't this the life, kid?"

The kid didn't answer.

The cowboy assumed he had heard him. "This is what I'm talking about: happiness. Natural happiness. If I stole a million dollars, I wouldn't build no big house. I'd live right here, in this hot spring. We'd live off the land, and we wouldn't have to worry about nothing, not a damned thing.... kid?"

"AaaaaaAAAoIAaaaa!" the kid screamed, flailing in mid-air from above.

The cowboy stood and turned in the greenish sunlight through the trees, his bare feet cushioning into the soft creek bed, to see the kid jump out over a cliff and swing out on an old rope and branch swing. He let go and plopped into the water. Before the kid could get his hair out of his eyes, the cowboy was running up to the swing, giddily. He found the old wooden swing platform littered with amorous carvings of teenage make-out sessions, and one interestingly displayed an exotic position wherein a couple swing out, grinding upside down and you swing until you climax and fall in.

"What are you waiting for?" called the kid.

The cowboy laughed to himself and felt his whiskery chin. Then he ran out and jumped off the cliff. He caught the old branch swing and swung out high up, trying to flip and dive but belly-flopping loudly

"That had to hurt," said the kid. And he helped his friend out of the water. His chest was beet red.

"Never felt better," the cowboy said in exhilaration. "Nothing better to wake you up than a big old belly-flop."

They had a good laugh and took a nap. They awoke, made a fire and went out to check the traps. That night they sat around the fire chewing on cooked beaver. The cowboy skinned it and strapped the pelt to his belt. The meat smelt of coal but tasted mighty good. For dessert, they roasted the marshmallows the kid had snatched from the convenience store. They looked at each other across the fire, grunted in satisfaction and went to sleep.

The next day, they bathed again in the spring and were very happy. Turned out, the kid didn't really know how to swim until the cowboy threw him in the deep part. Soon he could tread water with his feet while cupping it with his hands. He'd throw the water high in the air to the sun and watch the sun light it crystal clear and translucent, falling down on them like heaven. It was one of the happiest simple times they'd had their journey. The cowboy wished Angie could have been there.

Anyway, it felt good to get wet and alive again — wash the gritty backs of their necks. Their skin had been so dry and crummy. That hot spring cleansed it all away. The water didn't seem to get dirty at all. It all dissolved and sank to the bottom, like a baptismal renewing spring where you get born all over again in it.

After swimming on their backs, they got out and hung their clothes up in the brushwood to dry. They wandered down the stream a ways and sat on a big, gray overhanging slab of rock shaped like a turtle shell, skipping stones across the pond.

"Any minute now, this big stone turtle is apt to stick his head out," said the kid.

The cowboy laughed and stood up, all brusque and slightly grizzled in the sunlight. He examined the woods for movement. "Don't worry about the turtle, kid," he said. "He's got two humans settin' on him."

"What the hell's that supposed to mean? This rock turtle's huge."

"Yeah, but we're smarter; we've got guns," said the cowboy, one hand on the butt of his Colt in its holster, the other pointing to his head. "If I ever learnt one damn thing from all the crap I learned in high school, it's that humans are dominant over critters or everything that crawls upon the earth,"

"Yeah, well least the turtle don't get all cocky about things," the kid said.

The cowboy laughed loudly. The kid always knew how to make him laugh. He always knew how to make some greater tranquil sense out of what he tried to teach him about life. He didn't totally understand what he was trying to tell him, but he did. He knew it better than he did, in his own way.

The cowboy looked down at the turtle rock with a broad smile after catching his breath from laughing. "You know, you got a point there, kid," he said. "I reckon you'll make one mighty fine philosopher. I mean you're right. The turtle, or the rock, is bigger than us but he can throw us off him if he wanted to, but he's not afraid to...be afraid...keep his head tucked in, like we never do, not afraid to hide and pretend to be a rock, I guess. Kid? Come on, I'm shooting ya pearls here." He looked up from the turtle's shell that he'd been scraping with a rock to see if it would move.

The kid had wandered off again, into the trees. The cowboy took his time alone, shaving, using the hot spring as a mirror, lying belly down on the dry turtle-shell rock, his head over the edge, looking at himself for the first time in a long time. He barely recognized the rugged, lost, boyish face. He finished shaving but nicked his chin at the very last stroke of the blade. He felt the blood stream down and dribble into the water, rippling his reflection. He took a nap in that position, and when he woke, the blood had dried. He sloughed off the rock, slid into the stream, cleansed his face and drank some water. He heard steps and turned his head to catch wind of the kid yonder. He was after that damn butterfly again, trying to grab hold of the mocking creature, leaping at it over the water from stone to stone and coming up empty, hugging the crisp watery air, feeling its wings flicker at his very cheeks and eyelashes.

The cowboy looked down the stream at the kid and wondered if there'd been some sort of death of innocence in him on account of his mother being a whore. Eleven years old, he thought. The splitting age. At twelve you're a man. But eleven you're like a wild child — vanilla serpent, slithering blind through the thickets of death and youth intertwined. As he watched him, the kid leaped, missed the steppingstone and fell head under in the water between the rocks. The cowboy rolled over and looked at the sky. He laughed and shrugged off any surmise of death in the boy.

That next moment, after having thought-tinkered on the verge of an invisible danger of the death of youth in the boy, a very real and present danger came shooting their way. It was like a snap of a twig, followed by a metallic click that he heard. Then there was no sound. He turned all the way around and lay very still on his belly. The rock felt rough and cold on his water-softened skin. He peered through the trees and then yonder where his hat sat drying on the top of the big sun-baked rock. The rest of their clothes were down there, too, hanging on tree branches and on his belt (which they used as a clothesline) and spread out all over this one big flat rock on the shore. All this was only about twenty feet from the cowboy's lookout point on the turtle rock along the shore of the pond. Beyond the little laundry spot was the wood, where the cowboy's keen ears told him the sound came from. He crept up on the rock and peered over. There was only silence. A deer bowed his head out from shadow and crept forth. The cowboy ducked back and kept still, watching between the rocks. The deer arched its head down elegantly and licked the salt off a rock by the stream. A ray of sunlight shed down through the trees, blessing the deer. It was a magnificent sight.

The very next moment, as if they'd crossed some forbidden line, the old vengeful reality for the fugitive duo caught up with them. The first shot struck the deer broadside. The cowboy heard the sound of breaking cartilage. The deer wobbled out into the woods as its family sprang out of the shadows and away to safety. The cowboy wondered if it were merely deer hunters. The next shot answered his question as it skimmed with a spout of dust off the tip of the rock before him, sending his hat spinning out to the ground. He could not see the shooters. He kept under cover. Then he caught the silver glimmer of a rifle in the sun with just time to duck down before the shot rang out. The shot chipped off the edge of the rock that had held his hat and zinged off.

He poked his head out in the open and saw his hat spin around the edge of the rock and fall onto a small sandy patch of the shore. He sprang down to get it. As he stopped and grabbed his hat, turning all in one motion and kicking up sand, three more shots crackled against the rock before him, one zinging right by his ear. He crouched under the laundry-service rock. Some clothes now were scattered in the sand. He grabbed his jacket and put it on. He figured the shooter must've been reloading or reckoning whether they'd shot up a decoy at the hat. He didn't know. But he didn't feel like waiting around to find out. He could hear them walking forward in the woods. He jumped up on top of the high-ground turtle rock and blazed away at the wood line, palm-cocking and gritting his teeth.

"Run, kid!" he called out down the stream over his shoulder. He got up and ran as fast as he could around the rocks, firing his last shots. He ran over the stony shore and down the stream as bullets whizzed over his head. They were closing in all around, hidden in the woods. He could see the kid now up ahead. He was skipping stones, hopping on the damn steppingstones as if nothing had happened. "Run, kid, run! God-damn it! Run!" he hollered.

He came a'running in an all-out sprint, splashing down the stream. It looked up ahead like the kid was still lost in a daydream, chasing that butterfly. He turned and looked back at the cowboy, all innocently dumbfounded and scared-like. He had wandered a good way from the stream. When the cowboy got to him, the kid started running cautiously. The cowboy grabbed him up, slung him over his shoulder and ran like a soldier. He heard the kid warning him about something, muffled through his wind-flared jacket. But he kept right on trudging through the thickening water over the stones.

His foot landed on a shallow-looking puddle surrounded by stones. His step went straight through into the water. The water rushed up to his chin, having to tilt his head back to breathe. The kid pulled himself out and looked down at his partner in loving mockery. "Why do you always have to be right?" The cowboy wrenched from his stomach. Dusty reached down and grabbed his hand to help him out.

They ran to the end of the stream and up the embankment. They hopped the guardrail and crossed the road, looking over their shoulders every now and again. The cowboy wanted to escape, get away to safety; but a wilder part of him wanted to know who the hell those guys were and why they had tried to kill him. It couldn't have been that dumb sheriff's son. He'd never be able to track him this far. Damn, the cowboy was angry and dying for a fight. He'd been getting mad as hell throughout the whole trip. And then when it finally opened up and they got a few breaks, these unknown bastards barged in and started shooting.

They could hear no more shooting now as they ran across a farmer's field and through some trees. Yet they ran and ran. They ran until it started to get dark. And then the kid had to stop. He was breathing hard and raspy. The cowboy patted his back to help him cough it up. "Spit it out now," he said.

The kid seemed ashamed that he had to stop.

"You run like a deer," assured the cowboy.

"Thanks," the kid said, his little lungs moving up and down.

"Just got winded is all."

"Yeah, gotta quit smoking."

"Hell, I'm a little winded, too. Let's rest here awhile."

The kid nodded in agreement.

There was the smell of pesticides and pollen in the air. The cowboy figured maybe some sort of allergy had gotten into the kid.

The kid didn't want to run again. He wanted to walk now. The cowboy told him they'd only trot and they did — out through the trees, into another open pasture, and then through another barren wooden hedge. They passed a small yellow POSTED sign nailed to a tree a while back. The sign forbade trespassing on the land. This clicked to the front of the cowboy's mind after things had calmed down, and he figured that might have something to do with the whole show. But he still wanted to know for sure who was after them. So he went to the top of this grassy crag to look over a few acres with his old-fashioned, single-scope fold-out and see without being seen. There they were, still on their trail, directly southwest about three of those square cut-out fields away.

The sun in the late evening was dying but still hot, raising the day's last tendrils from the earth. The cowboy could actually see one man out front take of his hat and rub his face and his bald head. They were all in dark blue, old-fashioned uniforms — the hot, thick, marching-band, wool kind — a whole battalion of them, it looked like, on horseback. He and the kid had tired them and beaten them on foot. But the cowboy didn't wait to see if they'd quit or if they'd go in the wrong direction. He took advantage of their halt, and he and the kid continued running.

They ran through the woods and came to a field covered in mist.

The sky had grayed, and the tall grass on this meadow was a tempting, lush green. It all seemed too quiet to be true. Seemed like a trap.

"Wait," he said to the kid. "Be very quiet."

They waited at the edge of that mysterious field for several long silence-stretched moments. Then they heard a soft, slow thumping moving toward them. They crouched down in anticipation to kill, the kid's face simply blank, tired, and ruthless. And out through the lighter shades of mist, trotting with a friendly snuff of the nose, came their beauty in black: a dark, perfectly groomed thoroughbred, its muscles tight and shiny, moving effortlessly about the field. As they approached it, they could see other horses grazing in the sleepy pasture. The black horse caught the kid's eye with its big, dark, one-sided bulb and it caught the cowboy too in its peripheral. But it didn't run away. It didn't move. A white horse stepped out of the mist next to the black one and grazed with her. The cowboy signaled to the kid, 1,2,3, with his fingers and they ran for the horses and jumped on from behind. "Hee-yaa!" they shouted as the horses jolted off into the mist.

They heard voices behind them: "This way! Over here!"

But the voices faded out quickly, as the two rode bareback, fast over the hills and through the pastures. The horses must've been dying to run. The kid held on tight to its neck, leaning forward like a jockey. He caught up and passed the cowboy. The kid was a natural rider.

They rode on a long pathway through the woods. The path was trodden with car and even wagon tracks, long grass in the medium. Man, they rode a good quick distance on those pretty horses. The cowboy looked over at the kid. He had his excited face on, bumping along on the agile steed.

"Hi-ya!" he yelled and surged ahead. The kid kicked up his horse and yelled and followed.

They set up camp by nightfall, atop an upper lip of a hill so they could keep a lookout. The cowboy tried to make a fire with some leaves, sticks, and some dried-up old matches that he had, but the fire only burned for a few minutes before a meek wind put it out. All his stuff he'd left at the pond: his Zippo lighter, his smokes, even his shirt. But he had his guns and his hat at least.

The matches were no good, so he tried sparking together two stones.

"It's useless," he said. "Looks like it's gonna be a cold night, kid."

The kid had no complaints. He was so tuckered out that he just went right to sleep, lying on his side, cuddled up at the trunk of a tree.

127

He only had a T-shirt and shorts and no shoes. The cowboy could see him shivering himself to sleep, however temperate the night did fare.

"Kid, quit shivering," he said. "It ain't that cold."

"I ain't cold."

"Then why're you shivering? You're rattling the ground with that shivering."

There was silence. Then the cowboy asked. "You scared?"

"Nah," said the kid. And he was still. He turned his head and saw the cowboy through the embers of the fire. He was whittling a stick. He looked up and saw him watching. The kid closed his eyelids, leaving a sliver open to watch him through his eyelashes. He was a tough kid, but every now and again he'd start shaking and picturing what he could only imagine the men did to his mother behind the doors.

The cowboy picked himself up, went over, put his jacket over the kid and started with the stones again, trying to get a flame. That didn't work, so he tried shoving the whittled stick between the grooves of a hollowed log. The log broke. He went out into the dark forest and stumbled over another. Deep into the night, when he was about to quit, he gave one last friction-forced rub against the wood out of sheer madness. The tip of a leaf caught aflame. The fire grew to a decent size. The kid awoke at its mild roar in the night to find his partner smiling, sweating, and dancing around the fire like a Neanderthal.

The cowboy didn't know what to do about the boy's horse. The black beast neighed and kicked up it hooves, going crazy in the night for some reason. The kid got up and walked over to her outside the firelight. The cowboy saw him disappear into the dark forest. He heard the horse calm and still.

"Stay," the kid told her; and she did.

◆ ◆ ◆ ◆

The cowboy couldn't sleep that night on the ground. It was too damn cold without his jacket, and his teeth clattered automatically, keeping him awake. But that was okay. He had a lot on his mind to stay up and think about. So he sat with his back against a tree and thought.

His mind was just as restless as his body. Every now and again he'd hear something in the woods — a crack on the ground or a brushing, running sound as if some animal was out there stalking. He kept trying to think about this thing he wanted to say to the kid to boost morale, but every time he'd hear something, he'd whip his head around, then stop and breathe slowly, then quickly pounce around to the back of the tree. He'd see little shadows of something moving in the dark, outlines of goblins and creatures moving in the forest — but he knew it was all just sheer paranoia. He was just pissed off 'cause it wouldn't let him think.

Finally, he grew too tired yanking his head all over, slouched down under the tree and thought peacefully. He thought about himself and how he kept remembering his forgotten life in little bits and pieces, like how he used to clatter his teeth automatically and uncontrollably after getting out of the swimming pool in gym class. It's funny how the order of these little meaningless shreds of detail come back. He could remember that he was a clatterer, but he could not remember one book or teacher, not one profound quote.

Then he looked up to the stars. The pine trees overhead parted their arms in just the right places so he could see a perfect triangular piece of eternity in the stars, and he fell asleep.

◆ ◆ ◆ ◆

When he awoke, the kid was still sleeping and the stars had faded. He wished he could've wakened him earlier when the sky was brilliant. Then he'd give him his grand spiel on their mission to raise the morale.

"Kid, you're never going to believe this — what a dream I've had!" he announced anyway.

The kid stood stretching and yawning.

"Look, you know why we're doing this," he told the kid.

The kid looked at him, rubbing his eyes. "Doing what?" he asked.

"Why we're traveling so fast, and where we're going, what we're after, our mission on this little escapade, kid…"

"Mission?"

"We're heading home to my old lady!" he blurted. "Don't you remember? I need a wife, you need a mother; that's why we ride together. We're both after the same damn thing, so we can help each other shoot through all the bullshit and make it home, complete the great American family out in old Kansas. Ring a bell, kid?"

"Oh yeah, I know all that," the kid said with another yawn.

"Come on, ain't you excited at all about this thing?" he asked as he gathered his stuff and found a cigarette and a match.

"What thing?" asked the kid.

129

"The moth—" He refrained from lashing out as he lit his cigarette. "Angie," he said.

"Oh yeah, I know. You told me. But aren't we gonna stop and help folks along the way? Seeing as how we'll be stealing so much money and all."

"What? Yeah, sure we are, I mean we'll try. Help folks, yeah! We're good Americans, kid. Great idea. I tell you, we're going to cure this country yet! We're gonna get Angie and we're gonna cure America!"

"Sounds dandy," said the kid. "So what kind of dream did you have?"

"Ah man, what a dream. The angels slept with me last night, kid."

The kid leaned forward, sitting Indian-style with his tired, droopy, cherubic face perking up, ready to listen.

"Ah, I'll tell you later," the cowboy said. "Come on, the day's growing old."

◆ ◆ ◆ ◆

The cowboy wanted to get moving fast that day. He felt her out there, calling him, waiting in desperate condition.

Luckily the kid's horse hadn't wandered far. They found her grazing a few yards away. "Boy, somebody sure trained her!" the kid exclaimed. She knew when to ride and when to stay. And what muscle and endurance did she have. Yes'm, they rode a long way that day — through the farmers' fields and the woods and over creeks, and then they found the road. And for the first time, the kid noticed the telephone poles as they passed them. It's funny; he just never noticed them before. But there they were, spaced out and tall, planted in the earth, cutting through tree lines and sloping down mountains, lining throughout the country.

"Hey, it looks like a little planet got stuck up there in the wire," the kid observed.

"Yeah, it does, or maybe a ball or something," his partner said.

And there were those orange round balls transferring currents of information or alien brains of god knows what pinioned at the center and hanging down in the wire, spread out between the poles.

The kid asked the cowboy why they have telephone poles.

"Phones, kid, for communication, connecting folks," he told him, uneducated as hell.

"Well how do they connect people in those little black wires?"

"It's a signal, kid — hell, I don't know — they shrink themselves inside there by going through the phone-shrinker machine and then they crawl around in there and talk to each other," he told him.

"No, they don't, do they?"

"Yeah, sure, kid."

"Really?"

"I don't know. It's like a chain-reaction, electioneering thing I know nothing about," he admitted. "Here, I'll tell you what: once we reach our destination, I'm gonna get you the finest education around. I'm gonna learn ya upright! You little dirtball! And then you won't have to ask me about every last goddamn thing."

The kid galloped along, thinking for a while.

"Then I'd be telling you the way things are, and you'd be asking the questions," he pronounced.

"Damn right, kid. That will be the day," the cowboy said. "You ain't ever gonna stop learning."

"Never?"

"Never."

And he kicked up the horse and sliced across a grassy field before a cop spotted them on the road or some punks in their cars tried to bother them again. It's not important, but someone had thrown a bottle at them and yelled, "Ride that bitch, man, ride her hard, cowboy, whooooweeee!" as they sped by in their punk car. The kid sneered at them. The cowboy tried to shoot out their wheels, but his guns misfired. He threw them to the road to become history. And they rode out to the square, cut-out, property-owned country to cross another road.

The cowboy reckoned there was nothing worse the kid could hear to harm him than what his raw life had already cut out for him. But still he had to ask himself, couldn't them punks have seen that he had a youngster with him? 'Taint right to cuss around women and youngins, he thought.

Anyway, the bottle smashed at the horses' hooves and didn't cause no real harm, so the cowboy bit back his intemperance once again and let it go, and they rode on.

But man, he wanted to kill them punks. Man, that pissed him off — when people can't extend common courtesies or any type of chivalry. He had to ditch his sawed-off piece back at the spring. What he needed now was a gun. A big gun.

So the cowboy rode on, faster and faster through the country, thinking about what he'd do if anybody ever harmed his boy. He also thought about getting a better goddamned gun.

◆ ◆ ◆ ◆

They rode along a dirt road eastward until they reached an intersection. The dust swirled about in the wind at the desolate crossing. The cowboy saw something white fluttering on the telephone poles. He pulled up his horse alongside one of them for a gander.

"Hold up, kid," the cowboy said. And he dismounted, went over to the telephone pole, pulled off the paper and looked at it.

"WANTED, Dead or alive. $100,000 reward," read the paper. And it had a gray-stenciled faded outline of the cowboy's figure.

A guy in a big truck drove by, looking at the cowboy. The cowboy walked through the dust and mounted his horse.

"What's it say?" asked the kid.

"It says you're in trouble," he said.

"How much?"

"100,000 bucks."

"That's it? You reckon we'll meet any bounty hunters?"

"I reckon we've made history," he said.

And they rode on.

◆ ◆ ◆ ◆

Toward the afternoon of that day, it had turned out to be another scorching hot one. The strange thing was that they couldn't really feel the heat. The horses ran so fast that they kicked up a furious wind in their faces so that they couldn't really feel anything 'cept the numbing chill of movement. This was good. It was like they were riding through the world protected behind their own secret shield, not feeling the heat like all the rest. Also, it kept the time going best and natural. They never wanted to stop till they got there. The cowboy wished they could've kept on riding like that in fast invincibility all the way to Kansas.

Eventually though, the horses did tire. Their big snouts flared as they rode, twitching and sneezing — shaking their heads in request for a rest break in high-pitched neighs. Yet still the kid's horse kept the pace, its hooves clattering louder and its legs stretching less at each stride. But man, she was one hell of a horse, and riding on her freely like that, knowing she'd run for miles for the trusty stranger at the word go, and with the trees and the land and everything whishing by — and they hardly had any clothes on still! Riding bareback, man, it was great. Can you imagine riding like that, nakedly in this land? The cowboy would admit his crotch was killing him from the constant jamming and pounding on the strong-boned, unsaddled beast. But he still had his trousers at least, (damp from falling in the watering hole); but the kid only had his undies on. He didn't complain. The sun was out and the water drops streamed back over his face as they rode fast under the sun.

They rode this way, drying off, for a long while until they got to an old broken-down barn out in the middle of nowhere. They rode along the tree-shadowed path into the clear light of day that seemed to lift up from the ground, and there it was right out in the open: this brown wooden barn that looked like it'd been there for centuries. It seemed to make a face at them. Its mouth was the black door cracked open and long. Its nose was a cracked hole. And its eyes were perfectly square-shaped black gaps framed by concrete. The cowboy figured they must've funneled the hay in the concrete squares. A concrete strip lined the bottom as well, where there were a bunch of cracks and holes and one dirt path leading out from the inside far corner.

They rode all around it, looking at it carefully, as if the cops were hidden in the barn, waiting for them to come along into the ambush. The big front door was boarded up. Only way in from the front was the cracked hole in the corner.

The cowboy dismounted to take a closer look. Besides the hole from the far corner, he saw a white blur fluttering like a lady's eye in the wind and dirt, stuck on a splinter of the barn wood and the roughly weathered concrete. He reached down and grabbed it quickly, holding it out away from him as if it was a snake. It turned out to be a little girl's dirty underwear. He threw it down and let the wind take it away. Inside a wide crack above the hole was only darkness and silence. The dirt path from the corner led out over a green pasture and a hill.

The barn seemed strangely cut off from everything. The trees engulfed it, pinching in tight at the opening, allowing just enough room for it to stand out of the shade of the trees at high noon. And the only door that opened was the back one, facing the woods. The cowboy thought it'd make the perfect hideout for him and the kid.

"All right, girl," the cowboy said to his horse. "Get along in there now." And he gave her a smack on the rump and led her to the barn door. He opened it wider for her. The wooden door was cold. He had to pull it to get it loose from the ground. It finally shuddered open. Dust kicked up a dissolving cloud into the darkness; and a sliver of sunlight shed in through the trees, but he did not see anything inside.

Just as he was about to step in, he felt this strange, familiar wet snout sniffing at his hand. He looked down, and there was a black and white dog — an English springer spaniel, not barking but pointing from his tail to his snout excitedly at the cowboy.

"Hold it!" came the voice of the dog's master. "Hold it right there!" And out from the trees emerged a rancher with a little girl in his lap, riding an imposing stallion.

This ranchman had a red mustache, a sturdy build, a strong-willed face, one arm around his daughter and the other loosely holding a shotgun straight at them from the side of his horse.

"This here's my property," said the ranchman. "You wanna tell me what the hell you're doing standing on it?" With this he cocked the gun.

The dog went over and stood by his mounted master.

The cowboy admired the ranchman. He knew that's the best way to do things: Don't try to convince them that you're serious; just point the gun and cock it. He liked his style but was ticked off again about the (near) cussing thing in front of the kid.

"Watch your mouth, goddamn it," he said. "Can't you see I've got a kid here?"

"Well aren't you the special one? You've brought your childhood along with you! Annie, wouldn't the world just be perfect if we would all bring our childhood along?" he asked his silent daughter. His crazy face lit up in smiling. He waved the gun back and leaned it on his shoulder. The cowboy's instinct was to draw and shoot, but he restrained on account of the little girl in his lap; and on account of his imagination getting the better of his nerve. The rancher had one of those strange looks to him, as if he was one of those renegade, shameless assholes, similar to the cowboy's game, belonging to the breed that could kill on instinct without feeling he had to.

The rancher stopped laughing. "All right now, goddamn it! Step away from the barn and close the door."

The dog had sneaked in there.

"Don't worry about the dog, just close the door now."

The cowboy obeyed the crazy rancher.

The whole time, the little girl in his lap kept staring straight at the kid with a little, austere smile. And the rancher's horse kept its black bulbs right at the cowboy. The tired rancher's horse looked as though it had been hit in the face with a board — so stiff and blank. But the rancher collected some wild character. The cowboy saw it in him and decided that he might make a good friend. And the girl for the boy. And hopefully there'd be a lady for him somewhere over the grassy knoll.

"Hey," said the rancher, bringing back the cowboy's attention. He trotted his horse slowly around the intruders in circles, observing them and growing a wild smile, still covering them loosely with the shotgun. "Lemme take a gander, ha haaaa!" He had a terrific laugh. "You have no clothes, no job, no occupation whatsoever, no family, no wife, nothing, right? You're just a drifter. You're free! Hell, I envy you! Yeah, that's right. I envy you! No clothes, no money. Hell, you should run for president! Ha HAaaaaaa! Start the country afresh!"

"The kid and I are looking for—"

"Love, right? It's always love! You're free and you're looking for love in this great land! What a perfect bedtime story." And he gave the laugh again.

"We only need some shelter for a few days—"

"Yeah, sure you can stay with us. Of course! Hobos used to come here for anesthetic during the Depression; right in this very barn we had our own little family hospital anesthetic service going. See there...that's the sign carved on top there." He pointed. Sure enough, there was this crazy sign carved above the barn door. The cowboy couldn't believe he'd missed it.

"Well, come on inside! Yeah, go ahead, ride the horse back to the house; it's just over the hill yonder. My girl Annie here will make you some lemonade; she's selling it from her cute little stand. But she'll oblige you boys for free, how about that?" He shook Annie on his lap and she smiled shyly. He then uncocked the gun just as loudly as he'd cocked it and put it in the holster on the side of the horse.

Man, did that rancher talk a hell of a lot. The cowboy wished for a second that he would go back to the impression of a cold-blooded killer rather than an annoying idiot. But hell, he needed shelter and a friend to laugh and drink with for a change, besides the kid and his innocent little questions. Anyway, he thought the kid might've fallen in love with the little Annie girl so he was as good as gone. The cowboy was happy for him. And something gave him the feeling that he'd too find a little work and pay and contentment from the crazy ranchman to help him get back on his feet money-wise, while keeping low from the law just like he'd reckoned. So they went along.

CHAPTER XII

That night the kid and the cowboy sat around a big wooden table at the ranch owner's house, playing cards with a couple of guys the rancher called the "good old boys," and they ate plate after plate of hot beans and meat that the ranchman's good wife cooked up from the kitchen.

The cowboy hadn't even taken time to look around at the place. He caught some time in between plates to swallow and look up for the first time to find the good old boys and the lean-faced, red-mustached ranchman staring right at him. And for the first time he realized that they were strangers and that he had accepted an invitation into a strange place. It's funny how hunger can pull people together, and then once you get some food in your belly, you lose all trust in the very hand that feeds you. It's a vicious cycle, the cowboy reckoned.

"Hungry there, cowboy?" said one of the good old boys, who was actually a bald, fat man with gray whiskers and red suspenders.

"Yes," the cowboy said. "Much obliged. We owe you a case of beer. The kid and I, we don't forget good hospitality. Matter of fact, cowboy, this is the only real hospitality we've gotten yet."

"Don't call me that. You're the only cowboy here," said the rancher. "Besides, you'll pay me back. I'll see to that." And then he just looked at the pair again, and the whole gang went back to the staring routine. For the first time the cowboy noticed the silence in the room.

The rancher's wife, wearing a white apron and a humble smile, came in and put another plate of food under the strangers' noses. The cowboy picked up his fork. But he caught himself before digging in. It was the quiet that did it. And suddenly he grew somber, looking down at the dull plate of food and thinking about that girl he had talked to back at the bohemian's cove. Man, he hated these kinds of killing silences. As soon as he knew it was there always, he knew no chewing noise could swallow it out. The food wasn't all that good anyhow. He and the kid just got all excited there, for it was the first hot meal they'd had in a long, stomach-dry spell.

The cowboy told them a good yarn about his days driving cattle to Kansas up from Texas. He told them how beautiful Oklahoma was, but he didn't even really know.

"Dig in," said the other good old boy. He had red suspenders, too, bulging and outstretched, barely holding in his big beer belly from flopping over onto the table.

"Naw," the cowboy said, "I ain't hungry."

"Not hungry?"

"No, I'm full, thank you," he said.

He didn't feel like explaining. The rancher in the cowboy hat sitting across from him seemed to understand. He sat there under the dim table light with his hands folded and his eyes glinting with a nostalgic smile, as though he'd known the stranger before him for years.

Without looking, he yelled into the kitchen, "Wendy, that's enough. The cowboy's finally full!"

Wendy didn't answer. But the clattering of pots and pans stopped.

"Shit!" she said at last, cutting the silence. "What am I gonna do with all this food!"

"Give it to the dogs."

"Willis, you know I don't like wasting good food. You know there's people in China starving right now—"

"There's people starving all over the world, honey. You should feel happy you fed one of 'em."

"Well, maybe I'll stick it in the freezer for tomorrow—"

"Damn it, Wendy! Don't get all self-conscious about it — you're giving it to the poor starving dogs!"

"Ah shit, bunch of mongrels…eat all the damn food anyway. Why do I even try…?" And she grumbled off out the screen door with a slam, to go feed the dogs.

The whole argument was yelled through the swinging, thin wooden kitchen door.

"Your wife is a pretty good cook," the cowboy lied, trying to keep up the talking.

But the good old boys and Willis the rancher just sat there, looking over the cowboy and the kid.

The cowboy then told the kid to drink his milk and finish his dinner and head on up for the bed they had set up for them in the guest room upstairs.

"Who in the hell are you talking to?" Willis asked.

"I'm just talking to my boy here, telling him to eat up, we've got a long journey ahead of us."

The good old boys started to chuckle. Willis let out a quieting gasp and then released a broad smile.

"Well, hell, you don't have no journey; you've arrived, son!" he said.

"I don't understand. You want me to stay?" the cowboy asked.

"You're looking for love, right? Well, this is the place! We've got plenty of love right here, just look around ya!"

The good old boys seemed like they could barely contain themselves from laughter as if some practical joke was in play. Willis was serious though, and he shushed the boys and told them to go get drunk.

"I ain't looking for love," said the cowboy. "I'm looking for work. Work first. Then I'll go fetch my girl back in Kansas, but I ain't going back unless I got a little hard-earned dough in my pocket, you got me, rancher?"

"Call me Willis, Willis Mitchell at your service," he said with a wink.

"Henry Dunn," the cowboy said.

"Looks like your boy's all tuckered out."

"Yeah," Henry said. "This here's Dusty Rhodes. He's come a long way with me."

Henry took another look around. The house was big, frail-framed, dark and hollow except for the light from under the kitchen door and the dim lamp over the table lighting up the strange smiling faces on the other side, flickering a red burning semi-darkness in the air and casting a mysterious white light against the far wall of the house. He saw cascading picture frames going up the stairs with the cursive caption: "daughters" arching over them in wooden lettering. "Well sir, this here is a very nice house. I understand you and your wife have been very lucky. What is it, seven daughters?"

"And one boy, yes, we are indeed blessed," Willis said, shrieking his eyebrows back with a crazed, dripping sarcasm. "Usually that's considered unlucky in my family — if you believe in the whole, 'may your first child be a masculine child' thing. Usually it'd be the other way around: 7 boys, 1 girl — now that'd be lucky. But whatever. She has the dominant gene; I get it. I don't approve of gene tampering, mother nature first, and all that macho stuff is for the birds anyway. I love my girls! Oh boy, wait till you meet my girls. They're very special, not like any other girls. See we're different than most families, and so are you, you know that? That's why you're sitting here."

"I'm not sure I know what you're talking about, friend," the cowboy told him, "but how about one last hand of poker and then I'm gonna cash in for the night—"

"Call me Willis," Willis reminded cordially.

Willis kept on interrupting the cowboy, which he loathed out of strangers.

"And then what?" Willis said. He brought his face in over the table, close to the light. "And then you'll be off, find some place to hitchhike to or sleep...brother, it's here, man. Your wandering days are over. Here, come on, let's go outside and talk."

As he got up to go out, Wendy entered the room. "Where are you going?" she demanded.

"Ah, I'm just taking the young cowboy outside here to chew on some snuff and shoot the shit — you know, man talk, Wendy," he answered her with the big dropped jaw, 0-gape mouth look of a schoolboy whose mom just caught him whacking off.

"All right," she let him go. "But don't be filling his head with no nonsense, ya hear?"

"Yeah, yeah."

"Snuff — nasty habit," she mumbled as she sat down and lit herself a cigarette.

"Don't listen to a word she says," Willis whispered to the cowboy as he closed the door behind them. "The old battle axe can be a real bloody sow sometimes..."

140

"Don't worry about it," Henry replied, and they stepped outside.

Willis sat down on the top stair of the porch. Henry sat on the other side square wooden pillar with his feet dangling down over the ledge. Willis drew his can of snuff from his back pocket and packed it. Then he pinched a large wad and offered the can to the cowboy. Henry looked at Willis with his lower lip protruding and stuffed with tobacco like bits of black turds on his lips, and he nearly burst out laughing in his face.

"What's the matter? Never done dip before?"

"Hell, yeah, since I was 13," he lied proudly.

"Well here, take a pinch."

The cowboy took a pinch and stuck it under his lip.

"Good shit, ain't it?" Willis asked.

Henry couldn't answer. He felt woozy. A strong mint taste had already trickled down through his gums and into his bloodstream. His own spit tasted nasty. He hated mints.

"You gotta spit, though," Willis instructed. "Like this." He grabbed a tin basin from somewhere behind him and spat a loud clank into its empty belly. The cowboy spat, too, and they heard the hollow clank.

"If you don't spit, you're liable to throw up yer dinner ya just ate," Willis said.

So Henry kept spitting. Willis held his in his mouth for a long time, building up a big clunker; and then he just started talking, the big youthful bastard.

"Yeah, I know Wendy keeps a pretty tight leash on me, but I still have my fun, keep a leash of my own on her you, know what I'm saying? I'm still the man of the house, goddamn it, still head of the household, putting food on the table. We both keep leashes on each other I guess, in a way. That's marriage. Compromise. Sacrifice. Man, she just don't know how to have any fun anymore. She's older than me, ya know? Yes she is. And ever since we had kids, she got all domestic on me. It's always: 'take it outside,' take it all, all the fun, outside and keep it away from me, keep it away from the kids. Keep the kids from having fun, but that's not possible, is it?"

"Sure it is, given the circumstances," Henry coughed, and he remembered his pappy beating on him for having too much fun.

"Well, it certainly ain't natural," Willis said.

Finally, Willis spat out a big one and they looked off and out into the sky, only dreaming now, their own separate dreams and not talking for a while. The stars were out again and the sky was a deep black with thin gray clouds moving massively like ships across the moon.

"Hey, Henry," Willis said whimsically, "lemme ask you something."

"Huh?"

"That kid of yours in there..."

"Dusty. Yeah, what about him?"

"Ya ever touch him?"

Henry jolted forward and spat out his tobacco to the ground. "What?"

"Oh never mind."

"Touch him?"

"I meant it only in a philosophical sense — feeling like Homer tonight under the stars, and you're like Ulysses I got here, on his 10-year whimsical journey across this crazy land and out come my sirens...angels, you know?

"No, I don't know," Henry said.

Silence grew between them. They both let it and tried to forget what had just been asked and consequently revealed about this sick bastard Willis.

Willis fingered his whiskery chin, looked off and began talking again.

"Or she doesn't understand that you can't protect them from what she calls bad habits," he began, still looking off. "What a crock of hypocritical shit!" With this he looked away from the wide-open night sky with some secret remorse in him. "You saw her in there smoking a cigarette?"

"Yeah, I saw her," the cowboy agreed.

They could hear the good old boys cursing quietly and playing cards through the big thin window. But as they talked, that card game slowly drowned out as the slush tobacco feeling kicked in. Then Henry heard them wheel away nosily in their big hick trucks.

"That there's Earl and Buck. Finest boys left in Wyoming. Teacher used to call 'em Pearl S. Buck back in grammar school to get 'em to remember her name. You know, when we had to read that book about all the locusts and concubines and shit. You read much?"

"No," the cowboy said with a little edge.

"What's the matter? Don't like the snuff?"

"No, it ain't that, I just didn't know we'd gone all the way north to Wyoming."

"HaHAAA! You don't even know where you are, do you? See, I love that about you. You're free. You lucky bastard. Most Americans these days don't even believe in simple things like luck and dreams; it's all networking, connections, money and sheeit — but you, you're free man, you're free chasing your dream, man."

"Everybody's free," the cowboy said with a spit.

"Horseshit!" Willis shouted. "That's the biggest lie of them all! The land of the free — that is the fuel of this whole mad thing, man, this hypocritical blind shit we're in, man."

"I don't know what the hell you are talking about."

"Oh, but you will, man. Nobody believes in anything anymore. You just keep your head down and stay in line and work hard."

"Damned right, you work hard — nothing wrong with working for your piece under the sun. You know what, man, why don't you save it? I believe I've heard this bullshit before."

"Of course you have, it's spreading around — everybody's starting to feel it. I just can't believe you're here, man, I mean you've come right to my home, you're like a modern American knight, searching for love, helping the common man, the dreaming man. You are the last surviving article of the American dream."

"What the hell you talking about?"

They could hear Wendy inside turn on the TV and sit down.

"Come on, let's go to the fence," Willis said.

They went out and leaned on the ranch fence and looked at the sky.

"You are the last cowboy of the great frontier," Willis said to Henry.

"Hold up, I ain't here to lead no crazy revolution, and I ain't no hero. I'm just a guy trying to get on back home," Henry said.

"Ah, well, still you've got it, whether you want it or not you hold America's burden on your back. Oh, my girls will love — wait till they see you — the real article. I can't believe it. We've got the persona of the great American cowboy here!"

"So I'm a persona now?"

"Yeah, man, take away all that traditional fighting the Indians and working on the ranch and rodeo cattle shit, and what do you got: a young man with no clothes, a stolen horse, no money, his kid, and his dream traveling across America, looking for love."

"Yeah, whatever you say, but that horse wasn't stolen."

"Yeah, it was. It's mine."

"Can't be, I found it grazing out in the wild, miles from here."

"There ain't no wild horses, cowboy," he laughed. "This here's a big ranch. She's mine. Her name's Marla. She has it burned on her arse," he told him. "I own six thousand acres of my corner of Wyoming — it's the heart of America. And I don't like trespassers. Hell, I sent a whole crew out looking for ya. I didn't know it was gonna be you. Hey, what'd you say yer name was again?"

"Henry Dunn," said the cowboy.

"Well, Henry, I heard you were shot at — my boys can get a little trigger happy on trespassers. Sorry about that."

"Don't worry about it. I'm alive now, ain't I?"

"Yes, you are, my friend," he said, giving him the old awkward nostalgic look again.

"If you shot me, I reckon I wouldn't have been sore about it anyway, as long as we could get some good eating," Henry said. "Hungry as hell out there." And they laughed and joked and grew tired. The moon found its way out from the clouds and looked down on them with a quarter of its face turned and shaved off into the night.

"You should see the harvest moon come Halloween. Boy, I wish I could have you around to work the harvest!"

"Well, I'll go to work for you tomorrow," Henry told him.

"Yes, I know you will," Willis said.

◆ ◆ ◆ ◆

CHAPTER XIII

The cowboy slept himself that night a wonderfully deep and dreamless sleep, sunken down in a feather bed, awakened only by the soft morning light. He lay there in that baby sky-blue painted room, immobile and without worry. He looked over and there was the kid under the sheets of the other bed, his hair bristling out, the rest of him disappeared off somewhere in a dream.

He let himself fall back asleep then. He was pretty tired. It all would have been sweet and perfect if she was there, he thought, watching the purple fuzzy worms crawl across the black behind his eyelids. What a worthless dreamer he was!

The next thing he felt was the old familiar push of the wet snout in his limp hand that hung off the bed. Murphy, the rancher's dog, was there looking at him with his big dreamy eyes.

"What do you want, boy?" he asked him.

Murph went over to the kid and put his front paws up on his bed.

"Kid! I wanna go for a run!" he told the kid in wagging his tail and perking up his ears. He whined and bowed his head, poking his nose at the kid under the covers.

"You wanna go for a run?" asked the kid, waking up.

"YES!!"

His snout drooled a puddle on the bedside. His tail and his hinny shook rampantly, and you could hear his big paw toenails tapping and scratching at the ancient brown, museum-waxed oak floor.

Oh, what a whimsically moving day! It started out this way with them all groggy with the Murphy dog, for it was only around six o'clock when the sun woke them and it wasn't even the sun when they thought about it, but it was the wind and the fog that had come in. The guest room of that old country house had an open window that they couldn't get closed. The winter years had frozen the wood together, and now it would not slide down so there was always a draft. And that's what woke them: the wind, not the light, and of course the dog.

The cowboy found an old-fashioned shaving knife and some lather in the little room's bathroom. He filled up a basin with hot water from the faucet, balanced the big wooden bowl on the mantel and shaved by the window. Man, he needed a shave. He shaved calmly and gently, seeing through his slight glassy reflection in the half-open window. The white dream light of morning softened on his face and stretched in beams glimmering through the fog. The kid called it a dream cloud, which must've fallen from the mountains and filled the valley; and now it was coming in the window a little, too.

And somewhere in the cloud the cowboy could hear children laughing, running around, playing hide and seek in the fog. Then he saw one of them, one of Willis' little girls. She appeared out at the edge of the fog by the house and saw the stranger looking at her from the window. She put one little finger to her lips and gawked up her big, home-grown, beautiful blue eyes. The stranger in the window smiled at her and kept her secret. She was an adorable, about seven-year-old child in a pink flowery spring dress. She had a shyness about her that just made her mother cringe to look at her and capture the picture of her forever, ever time.

Willis kicked in the door.

"Don't make 'em like they used to," he said. He was thirty-three years old, had light blond hair that glistened gold in the sun, that reddish mustache and blue-green eyes most opalescent in his daughters. But here and there, his wife would take her genetic right with strands of brown and an austere stance in the lively girls, all so unsettling and uptight. What a perfectly productive couple! You've got the young and the old, the free and the tamed, life and death all rolled into one perfectly

146

stubborn, capricious child standing in the mist, and seven other reasons to live (including one boy somewhere), running wild or still sleeping in their beds.

Willis went to the open window, put both hands on either side of the wall and sucked in a big hit of life from the dream cloud. Holding it in, he turned to the cowboy and exhaled and said, "Come on, cowboy. It's huntin' time!"

"Yeah, yeah," Henry said, and he went and got up the kid.

The kid put on his boots and was ready to kill.

Willis was plush white with exhilaration, rushing mad ecstasies bearing the weight of the born day, looking off into the clearing fog, hysterically juxtaposed — whatever.

He laughed terrifically. "I knew this fog would come. It's always good and dangerous hunting in the fog!"

So they went downstairs and downed plates of eggs and bacon and hash browns. Then they went out to the stable, saddled up and got all ready to hunt. As the cowboy mounted his horse, Willis tossed him a rifle that was light as a stick. It was only a BB gun on account of the ranchman not fully trusting his new ranch hand, despite his idolization for him.

The stable was a shady red color inside. Dense smelling wood hung heavy with rainwater, and the whole structure seemed drooping like it was about to collapse. And man, as soon as they stepped foot in that stable, they wanted to get riding out, out in the fog and feeling good and lost with the cold dream air refreshing them from the rancid stable of horseshit stepped on and smeared on hay.

The kid was gone again, in love with that Annie girl, running around with her in the fog probably, but the cowboy could just imagine what he'd say.

"EEEEeeeewhoohooooweee!" he found himself whooping. "Smells like huntin' time already!"

"Hi-yaaah!" Willis agreed. "Happy huntin', boys!"

And they pummeled out the shed into the lifting clear fog light, Willis, some other hunters, and the cowboy. They rode out deep into the fog to hunt in a mystical spot right in the middle of a meadow. There the fog hollowed out, spreading its dew on the outside lengths, drizzling down the inside of the tall bent grass.

However, as Henry would recall, it took them quite a while to get to this glade, quite the little journey, slowly trotting their horses through the visible air. Every so often a tree would appear. Willis nearly bumped his head into one. Trees would emerge from the fog, inches away, the tops vanished and the mist licking around them. Willis would yell back to the boy behind him, "On the left!" and the boys would know to watch out.

Soon it was just Willis and the cowboy riding up front, leading the way on a narrowing path through the harrowing, ghost-covered forest. The roots were hardened with a coat of frost. In his fantastical mind, the cowboy imagined all the lost souls fallen to roam for living loves. Privately he said hello to his grandpa on his mother's side. He wanted to tell Willis about this, but he knew he'd go nuts at his first will to concoct such nonsense. So they rode on through the souls and the trees, the silence shimmering in crisp space between them.

"Hear that?" Willis asked.

"No," Henry said. His horse bumped him up as it lethargically climbed over a thick root.

"Sounds like God's doing his laundry," Willis said. "He's unfolding his socks. Hear that static energy separating?"

Henry didn't know much about God, and he wasn't very religious. But he believed in Him. He didn't like talking about Him because he knew he'd probably pissed Him off too much, and admitting that he believed wasn't exactly his style. But for some reason he felt that he wouldn't mind talking about God out there, hunting with the crazy rancher in the mist. He rode gently thinking of a way to bring Him up without cramping his style. Thankfully, Willis started about religion, which some folks believe is pretty close to knowing God without having to die.

"My wife is a Catholic," Willis began. "And I just don't get it. My side of the family was always Methodist, and I don't remember ever going to church except on Christmas. Now look, today is May 4th, 2001, and a Wednesday of all days, and where is she? Out to church early in the morning, when she should be a cooking the kids' breakfast. Ya ever go to an early weekday Mass? Well man, let me tell you it is, it is — I can't even say — just a bunch of old guilt-stricken fogies drooling and dropping their dentures and carrying on. She's the youngest one there. I bet she gives 'em all a boner, that's why they keep coming back — free Viagra for all. But what's her reason?

"Man, I just don't get it. I don't get the whole thing at all. You know what it's all about, don't you? The whole religion is about waiting. Waiting all the time. At church, at home praying, just waiting. Waiting for

Christ to return. Now, the first generations of Christians believed he would come back in their lifetime. I bet you didn't know that. Ridiculous, ain't it? Then it just went on and on. There's no way he'd come back. Hell, last time He was here, we humiliated Him, tortured Him and nailed Him to a cross — can't blame the guy for not wanting to come back. And how would we know when he arrives? Hell, man, who knows? You could be the Christ in disguise! Yeah you, cowboy. Or maybe that kid of yours, and maybe you don't even know it yet. I'm not saying they'd nail you to a cross or anything. But imagine if you started saying you were Jesus Christ, the Savior. What would they do? They'd throw you in the loony bin, boy! Write a crazy article for the tabloids and get you all lobotomized, laying around the hospital like a piece of meat."

The cessation of Willis' voice lasted and then cut briskly in the thickening forest air as the fog rose. The cowboy got to figuring hard about Willis' words. It all seemed to make such common sense to him now. He felt like God was laughing and agreed. And he remembered a picture of his late grandmother praying the rosary desperately over her dying husband. Gad, if only she'd known.

"Hey, what are you thinking about man?" Willis asked then.

"Aaaah, nothing," the cowboy said. "'Taint my place to talk of such things I know not of,"

"Good man. I don't know where I get my ingratitude. I'm such a lucky man, really. You, cowboy, are a good man."

"Thank ya."

"A very good man. I don't care what the TV says you are."

"Yeah, don't listen to that bullshit."

"It is so easy to criticize something you know not of. But when you go to meet eternity, you better pray that eternity ain't mad at you."

◆ ◆ ◆ ◆

They stopped at a bog to pee. Then they trudged into the low marshland and sat on a large log and talked. They realized that they were lost. They had strayed beyond the property line into the unknown marsh. "We are lost!" Willis called out to the mist-strewn trees. "Where are you, cupcakes? Where are you, my love?" His voice squeaked and rang out, echoing through the faded mist, throughout the land, idiotically.

Henry sat knee-bent, balanced on the end of the log leaning against stone. The sound of his partner's voice shot back sounding manlier like his own, and somehow he knew his love had heard him through Willis. So he tried not to think about too much bawdiness.

Willis came over and confirmed that they were lost. They laughed about it, and Willis started with the calling again.

"God, where are you faggots?" he shouted. And he went on climbing out of the bog through the underbrush calling out obscenities and come-ons, trying to get a rise out of certain hunters. "Tom Morris is a raving homosexual! He packs the fudge with Pete Hamlin! And Butch Bo-Koo — HaaaHAaaaa! Butch Bo-Koo and the Sundance Stroker — aaahhh you guys are worthless." He threw up his hands, turned around and walked into a mountain. Henry leaned against the mountain with a half-smile, lighting a cigarette. Willis had stepped down into Jackson's Hole and scrunched his nose right up into the Tetons. He gazed up at the cold rugged slate of rock shafting up into the mist.

"Well, I'll be damned," he said. "Who put this mountain here?"

Then they heard water trickling. Willis stepped sideways and forth into a surreal, thin-cut vertical cave. They found at the quick end, water trickling from a spout between the crevice of two huge, jagged rocks where the mountain had created and joined with its brother centuries ago under ice; now trickling cold water onto their faces as pure as heaven. They found themselves pushing each other out of the way in the narrow hollowed cave, like boys fighting over first dibs on a chick, to drink unquenchably from the Tetons' crystal fount.

◆ ◆ ◆ ◆

Willis pulled out a bottle of whiskey. They sat and drank, tossing the bottle back and forth, Willis sitting down on a rock on the bank of the bog, the cowboy on the thick, hollowed bridge-made log that lay over a trickling creek. Willis talked and drank himself into a nap. The cowboy remained quiet, thinking and waiting for something to shoot. He took the bottle out of Willis' limp hand and drank. After a while, the fog cleared, and Henry remembered his truck.

"Man," he said loudly.

"What?" Willis said sleepily.

"My truck. I gotta get my truck."

"Don't worry about it," he said, falling back asleep.

"Let's get heading back."

A deer pranced close by through the forest. Henry heard, saw and got down smelling the dense, rain-softened, pine-coated forest floor. Willis napped with his hat over his eyes under the sun. Henry watched it raise its head in an acute silhouette in the forest. Henry aimed his gun, supported over the log. He pinched his right eye shut and shot and missed. The deer didn't know what to make of the BB shot. Probably thought it was a tick or something. It stepped forward, saw the cowboy stand and raise his stick gun, and it ran away. The cowboy sent one after it, snapping through the branches, missing again.

"Damn it," the cowboy cussed.

The second shot woke Willis.

"Save some critters for me!" he said.

"Ain't no critters," the cowboy said. "Let's get on back now, I gotta git my truck."

"Whatever you say, cowboy."

On their way back, they ran into a lumber crew. Willis fired off a few shotgun rounds over his shoulder, cracking and crashing down a big tree branch to the ground. The opportunity had come where he could play the lunatic kid he really was and stick it to the man.

"I want you boys off my property now! You get down from there! You say 'timber' one more time, I'm gonna cut you down myself, boy."

"Now, Willis we have authorization rights signed right here, by Mr. Limberg of the —"

"I don't care if the president signed your goddamned papers, you're on my property, you are trespassing, and you have already cut down one, two, three of my darling trees. How'd you like it if I came onto your land and started killing your darlings?"

The lumberjacks left, but Willis was sure they'd be back. He knew he was losing his land. He was losing everything he loved and ever dreamed and earned. On the way back he told all about how when he was a boy he'd play in those woods and hunt with his old man and bring back deer, slung proudly on the hood of a '57 Chevy truck for his mother to gut, skin and cook. This reminded the cowboy about his truck, which he had forgotten about already. He had hidden it under the trees off the side of the road outside of town by that pond. He figured the police had confiscated it already, but he wanted to go back and check for himself anyway. Maybe they'd be waiting for him, and there'd be a good gun-slingin'. He always loved a good fight in the morning.

Later on he recollected the fact that he had no firearms, but he figured he'd go anyway, use his fists if he had to, or borrow some guns

151

from Willis. He was somewhat fond of that truck.

Finally they crossed out into a clear meadow at dusk, and they walked right into it casually. They had been there before. The cowboy was thinking about fighting when Willis halted him with a tightened, steady hand at his chest.

"Rabbit. 10 o'clock."

"See him?"

"See him."

"See him?"

"I see him!"

"Ssssshhhh!"

They crouched down behind the grass. Willis gave the shot to the cowboy. Willis sat back, smiling mischievously and watched.

Cutting through the tall grass, the cowboy's muzzle crept out. He aimed up the little critter, aligned with the two bits of iron sights on the long, smooth black barrel. Closing his eye, the feeling rose in him that he had him. He squeezed the trigger just before the feeling broke. And immediately he doubted his shot. The rabbit stopped stiff, and they could see from afar blood squirting — a gushing outpour staining the white fur. The rabbit fell broadside and out of sight in the grass.

"Holy shit!" Willis said, biting his fist. "You done did it! Dead with one shot, and with a damn BB gun!"

"A gun's a gun."

"Ha," Willis said, squatting down looking around in amazement. "Well you don't know much about guns, but you sure can shoot!"

The cowboy smiled, happy with his kill. They walked across the meadow as the sunlight broke through the dusk. Turned out the poor critter was only a tike, baby rabbit.

"My, my. The Easter Bunny is going to be pissed!"

They brought it back anyway. Willis was drunk. The cowboy had gulped more whiskey but felt okay. He was on that stasis whence everything slows down to its proper speed, and you see the world crystal clear coming at you.

The cowboy carried the bunny carelessly by its hind legs, swinging it back and forth, whistling and feeling it brush against his trousers. He wondered if the little critter had a soul, and if it did, where did it go? Something gave him the feeling that the bunny was content. He looked down at it and told it so. It made no argument.

"What a way to go out!" Willis said. "Hit by a BB in the soft of the neck!

Never knew what hit him, quick and painless. One moment he's walking around in the late morning sun at an innocent little nook from the forest, and the next he's fallen over feeling the blood gush out from behind his eyes. And now he's flopping around at the cowboy's side!" Willis reached down drunkenly and felt the sure hole in the soft, cold pouch neck.

"What the hell you so curious about? He's dead," the cowboy said.

They agreed to roast it and eat it over the fire that night, but Willis warned the cowboy, as they finally humped over a big water-dense log out into the clear of the wide backyard rolling up to the house, not to let Wendy know or she'd throw a fit. She always hated it when he and the boys would come home hooting and a-hollering up a whole town with a few bloody carcasses slung that they expected her to cook. She especially despised the killing of little critters. And it didn't help that she still had Easter decorations to take down and children to look after while her husband snuck off with the boys, hunting.

Some quiet set between them as the cowboy and Willis approached the house. Up yonder they could see the girls and Wendy taking down plastic Easter eggs from the leafless twig-branch trees. Willis grabbed the dead bunny and tossed it into the wood line for later, and the day kept rolling.

As the laughter of the children filled the air, Willis said, "Look at that, man, the American dream alive! It's the original little house on the prairie, ain't it?"

Prairie surrounded the tall white house along with a big blue-graying sky, rolling hills and cuts of forest, and a light purple mountain range in the distance. As they walked toward the back end of the house, the thin road came into view and they could see a single truck coming to the house. The cowboy looked to his right. He could see the tip of the barn over the cleft of the hill. And straight ahead, he hadn't even noticed it before, was a baseball field, a homemade sandlot with an old skeleton of a fence behind home plate. The fence slanted at the top and hung over, protecting the house from popped-up foul balls.

Henry wanted to ask Willis about the barn, but he found himself so dismally enthralled for some reason by that field. They walked in through the outfield, and all the kids were out playing ball. He brought his hand to his brow as they reached the dugout and saw through the caged fence, Dusty heading up to bat.

Beyond the game, he could see Wendy now talking in her motherly, maid-like role again, calling the girls and everybody in for some lemonade and sandwiches. She did look lovely, the cowboy would admit, standing on her toes and calling out. Then she let her naked heels sink into the soft cultivated dirt of the little garden out front. Willis, beaming with joy, called out to his wife. All the kids quit the game and ran in for a picnic lunch.

When Wendy saw her husband walking with the cowboy amongst the children, she'd done caught him chucking the dead rabbit off into the grass near the woods.

"We'll get him later," Willis had said under his breath. "You shot him. You deserve him."

"Hell ya," Henry agreed.

"Goddamn it, Henry, you kilt the only goddamned critter in Wyoming."

Wendy had overheard. Consequently, when her husband went up the porch to kiss her, she pulled away, returning straight back to being the trapped wife and the old uptight, hard-working, vein-bulging, homely look took her. It was as if Willis was her most troublesome child. The cowboy found it quite humorous to watch such a marriage, wield it in his own dumb and innocent way, and not get involved.

Inside, the house blew and shook and rattled with the wind coming down howling from the mountains. The doors in that house were thin, and the wind pushed them closed each with a slam like a ghost sweeping through.

Outside, the picnic blew away, the tablecloths up and the paper plates sailing, sending Willis chasing in vain with the kids, the crazy bastard. Then the kids grabbed what they could and ran into the house. And then it started hailing. The hail did not last long. The kid said that he was ready to crush the ball into the woods and that earlier he was playing left field and some kid hit the ball into the woods, but he ran down there and grabbed the ball and threw a bullet in to hold him to a triple. And he kept on rambling excitedly, "I loved it! I loved it, I really did! I want to be a baseball player! They're letting me pitch next inning 'cause I'm a southpaw and 'cause Red says I got a good arm!"

Red Tucker was the forty-five-year-old senator who was good friends with Willis and commissioned the whole beautiful little backyard league. He was a serious man. The cowboy took one look at him and decided so. A serious, scrunched, red-faced little cherry of a man, and he liked his kid.

Oddly, Red came over to the kid, sat down and kept on talking about his ability while the cowboy ate. Henry just kept eating and talking, man, the truth, only the truth the way he'd seen it: "Yeah, man, I never noticed it till today! What a talent. He can really hum that ball."

"You know what you need to do now, need to tame his talent and get some money out of him," the senator said, talking with his hands.

"Yes, yes, yes!" And the cowboy went on nodding and rocking in his seat at the thought of money, as he stuffed food into his mouth. The next thing he knew, the food was gone, the game was over, and he looked over to find them all, the whole crazy family with Willis in the center, waiting and calling his name. "Henry, come on! Git over here, cowboy!" So he went over and stood in the back of the big huddled group with all the sweet, shorted and skirted, beautiful girls lounging around on their bellies and with their arms around each other for one big, happy, family photo. And there they all stood! The wind blowing the sandy infield sideways in the background with the flow of time. All but one.

"Dusty, come on, get in the picture," Henry called.

He was running away over the hill because they had lost the game.

"Can't hold that kid still, can ya?" said the senator.

And they all laughed it off and stared into the automatic red blinking character on the tripod, the cowboy looking off as it flashed.

This was about noontime. The afternoon was all work. Willis and the boys got down to business. The cowboy went along just for the ride and sat in the bumpy back of one of the trucks. They went out and gathered up some stray cattle and horses that had wandered off and gotten stuck in this big mud creek yonder, just beyond the trees. Coyotes were liable to get them sooner or later. Sure enough, as they drove down there into the mud, they saw the coyotes, a whole scattered pack of them, running across the field to the cattle, gnarling. They had the big dumb cows stranded in the mud. They got there first and were ripping at their legs and throats, daring to attack at the will of the cowboys and their shiny black guns. The cowboys fired shots echoing to the end of the sky. And Henry thought while watching them in their big Ford trucks, sliding around with their raggedy-doll heads hanging out the windows, whooping at the top of their lungs, and with their radios blaring some country slang, and the boys in the back hanging on to the ledge and sometimes bumping off and rolling around wilding in the mud and then running and falling and running and screaming like a chicken with its head cut off — he thought now these are what's left, these are the real cowboys. He was just a jest, an act, a commercial cowboy for these suckers con-

155

fusing heroism with idolism. He couldn't figure out why they all seemed to look up to him in a certain way and call him one of them. To hell with them, he thought. Henry took off his old hat while standing there alone and looked at it, all dirty and muffled, yet rugged just the way he liked, the way it was supposed to be. Smiling, he put it back on, leaned against the truck, his hat tilted down and to the side; and he closed his eyes and dreamt of love while listening to the whole yelling, neighing madness of man and beast wrestling.

When all the brutes had been lassoed up and clumped together, they took them back to the stable.

Old Willis made himself a good profit on that land. He told the cowboy all about it on the way back, how he dreamed of bringing back the old family distillery making whiskey, too. They bumped along the dirt road with the speedometer tittering around 85 and the dashboard rattling as the wheels went airborne for split seconds in between sentences that told the meaning of life — the simple life on the land with his own ranch and family, the one the cowboy wanted — but he couldn't hear what it was his friend said over the constant thrashing of the ride. The truck crashed down and evened out going uphill toward the house, and Willis looked over at the cowboy smiling and said, "Bumpy road, huh?" Then: "Ooops, bit of pothole there — remind me to patch that up."

The cowboy nodded always and replied, "Sure, yeah, yeah, right, right."

When they got back from the roundup, Henry took a nap on the hammock that was there on the side of the house, tied between two oak trees. He tipped his hat off over his face and rested his head full of thoughts on his interlaced hands. The docile weather in the late day gave a slight gust of wind every now and then.

He awoke to the sound of a black bird crowing. He could see the bird setting its weight, bending down the thin naked tip of a pine tree. It crowed, "Ka, ka, ka," as crisp and nasty as awakening to the sound of time's ruthless beat. The cowboy wished he'd had that BB gun.

In the distance he heard the call of Mrs. Mitchell. "Chillins, come on in and get washed up for supper now! Come on, chillins, inside now." She bent over at one and said sternly, "Leanne! You git a shirt on you! Come here. You can't go running around in the dirt with no shirt on. You're becoming a woman, nearly 11 now. 'Member what we talked about?"

"I don't want to become a woman, mama! I wanna be a boy!" she protested.

"Oh stop."

One of the littler girls then came a wandering over, reading and writing in her diary, and she nearly bumped her head right into the lump Henry's bottom made sunken into the hammock. Yet she traced the obstacle before her without looking up and she ducked her head to the side, walking right under the cowboy without a sound. Henry sat up. He watched the little girl walk off, sensing things coming and meandering around trees without looking up from her book, and finally settling down under a big shady oak. After a few minutes she closed the book and went to sleep in the sunshade. She was seven years old. She had no shirt on, only dirty pink pants. All the others had gone away. So it was just the cowboy who fell asleep with his hat tilted over his eyes as the little girl seemed to throw stones at the bird and scare it off. And for a while it was just the cowboy and the little one napping.

The little one came over after a short while and plopped her elbows into the cowboy's hammock. She ran in the trodden dust spot under the hammock and suspended her legs, bent, and crossed at the heels, swinging back and forth. The cowboy did not wake. She went down to his boots, tangled in the thick rope. She went underneath them by the tree and spun his spurs with her fingers. The cowboy awoke and grabbed for his gun. The little girl giggled. He looked over at her and joy took him with the sight of the cute young one. He pointed his finger gun up at the sky and fired for the bird who was back already with friends, and he fired at make-believe bad guys and even at her, playfully; she giggled vivaciously and shot him back, cringing her face and shrieking back excitement within. Then she had a full smile as he pretended to croak from her shot. And her big French-green eyes glowed full at the little spectacle.

"Is your name Leanne?" asked the cowboy.

"No," she said, shyly.

"Well, come on, what is it now, you don't wanna tell me?"

"Candas."

"Kansas?"

"No, Candice."

She had a little lisp. Her skin was pale and her face smudged with chocolate and dirt. Her hair was a sun-blazed, dirty blonde. She walked right up to the cowboy and handed him her diary. He found from the first page that she had named it "Kate." The little, brown, leather-bound book was full of pictures and big, beautiful, simple writing saying how she loves her family because they are special to her and how everybody is special. Henry began to love the word. He asked her what she wanted to be when she grew up.

"I don't have to be a woman yet. I'm too young. When I get eleven, I'll have to be like Leanne and wear a shirt all the time even when it's hot out."

"Oh, I see. But I mean, what do you want to do when you grow up?"

"Um...a writer," she said, twirling her hair with her finger.

"Yeah? Wow. Writing what? Letters and such?"

She looked at him funny.

"I don't know much about writing, but I know you can get famous that way. Anything else?"

"Um...the president of the United States of America..."

"Yas! Anything else?"

"And...a bunny rabbit."

"A bunny rabbit!"

"Yes, because I like to hop."

And she giggled away, hopping around the hammock in circles and catching Henry's eyes under the hat for moving moments, searching for his adult approval that he'd provide in smiles and laughs.

Just then, after he lifted himself up from the hammock to hop around chasing her and to give the trees a break, he heard the sputtering of an old car coming in the dirt driveway out front, and their special time together was up.

"I have to go," Candice said. And she grabbed back her diary and ran away around the house. The cowboy didn't think much of it then. He walked around the house and saw her climb, at the graceful boost and a harmless pat from behind — as if she needed help homing into that truck — from the one and only good old Mr. Senator Red Tucker. Willis waved her off as she looked sadly out the window.

"Smile," Willis said to his daughter through the car window. "You're young, darlin'. Smile while you are young." He pushed his lips back with his fingers and made a funny unnatural smile and that got her. And she smiled her little cute self away, her teeth tiny and dirtying yellow a bit and growing away with the day, to spend the night at the senator's house.

"That senator got kids?" Henry asked Willis standing next to him at the end of the Mitchells' stone driveway, watching the truck kick up the dust.

"Yeah, he's got a little girl," Willis answered casually.

"They friends?"

"Yeah, she sleeps over there all the time — they're inseparable, I probably won't even see her for a couple of days." He glanced back at the house and saw the glassy, blank glare of his wife standing in the window.

"Must be good having a senator as a friend," Henry said.

"Yeah," Willis said, long and dry. "Come on, let's go inside. Tonight is family night."

"Family night?"

"Yeah, come on, cowboy, you're part of the family now — a regular household name — Haaaahaaaa! The last cowboy!"

"What about Candice?"

"Sheeit! Candice man! She's a big girl, a lot smarter than you'd think. Don't worry about her. Sometimes not everybody can make it. You should know that. My only son hasn't made family night since he left for the Navy. You can't be home and happy all the time. You got to go out and fight for your piece and then bring it back, spend it up and go out again, catch my drift? Ya picking up what I'm laying down? Hahaa! Tonight my friend, we spend, spend the goddamned night away! Got me? Come on, you don't even know what home is, do ya, cowboy?"

Well the cowboy did not understand, to this day he would not understand, but he went along anyway. What the hell else was he supposed to do?

◆ ◆ ◆ ◆

CHAPTER XIV

The next morning, Henry went to get his truck. He walked the three-mile straight shot down the road as Willis had directed him to and found his truck where he'd left it. It seemed like a hell of a lot more than 3 miles when they'd run to that ranch. He figured so on account of the chasing all over the property.

On the windshield he found a yellow slip of paper, tucked under the rusty wiper. Driving, the cowboy turned on the wiper to bring it up as he reached out the window and grabbed the ticket. He crumbled it up and threw it away.

Then he saw a hot little girl walking gawkily in the dust on the side of the road. She wore short shorts and had skinny legs with little kid bumps for knees. She had brown hair with red streaks of highlights. She slung her backpack over her shoulder, flashing her young sweaty profile and a firm set of amply developed breasts pressing against her shirt. He drove slowly up alongside her. The girl kept walking, peeping over and keeping back a smile.

"Hey there, sex-on-a-stick," said the cowboy.

The girl looked over and smiled.

"It's a hot one," the cowboy said. "Why don't you hop in here, sugar, I'll give you a lift."

"Sure," she said. He stopped rolling and she got in.

"You like the music?" the cowboy asked.

The girl was shy.

"I can change it if you want."

"No, I like it. I love country music, are you kidding?"

They drove on. The cowboy felt good and relaxed to have his truck back. The engine didn't sound so good, but it would get him where he needed to go. He hung one hand over the wheel and the other out the window, whistling along to the song on the radio.

Then the girl built up her nerve. "You're that cowboy," she said.

"I'm that cowboy."

"You're that cowboy on TV. My Pa said he would've turned you in for the reward if you weren't so nice."

"Did he now?"

"Yes sir."

"And who's your Pa?"

"You know my Pa — it's Willis, Willis Mitchell."

"Well I'll be — you one of Willis' girls?"

"Yeah."

"Oh man! Good thing you told me! I was about to get myself into trouble. I figgered you was like 17, 18 years old. What you doing out here anyway, ain't you got school?"

"I'm skipping today. You were thinking about getting into trouble with me?"

"No, I'm only kidding, darling."

"You think I'm hot?"

The cowboy looked over and saw her breasts in a push-up bra. He looked back at the coming road. "Yeah, hell ya," he said. "But don't get any ideas; you are way too young, honey."

"Love knows no age," the girl said.

"Yeah, maybe, but lust does," he said.

The girl had the audacity in her now.

"How old are you?" she asked, with her young, pink glossy lips.

"Twenty-five. Why?"

"We're only nine years apart."

"Sweet sixteen, huh?"

The girl nodded slowly, smiling. She wet her lips and pressed them together.

"My name's Leah," she said.

"Leah, not Leanne, right?"

"No. I'm the oldest, Leanne is…the third oldest."

"Which one of ya'll's Leanne?"

"Why?"

"Just wonderin."

"She's not hot like me. She's still a good girl. She's messed up. Don't even wanna be a woman, don't even wanna be in the family anymore."

"Why's that?"

Leah shrugged. She pursed her cute, little, baby-chub cheek in and tooted her wet lips. When she started licking the tiny beads of sweat from her fair skin around her mouth, the cowboy forgot the subject.

As they rolled through the Wyoming countryside, Henry tried to kill the thought of making a pass at her. But before he could, she offered him some "road head." And before he could get out a word, she unzipped him and went down with her dainty pony-tailed head into his lap. In the middle of it, they'd hit the big intersection that turns left towards the Mitchell Ranch, and the truck sputtered up a cloud of smoke, overheated and broken down. Henry pulled himself together, pushed the truck to the side of the road and popped the smoking hood. The ranch was only about 300 yards away. She told him that Willis and his boys could come out and haul his truck in later and take it to the garage for repair; and she convinced the cowboy to go for a walk through the high country toward the mountains.

So they meandered off through a daisy field. Leah didn't care where they went. They eventually settled on a hillside in a soft patch of grass. "How was family night last night?" she asked.

"Family night? Yeah, it was all right, I guess. You weren't there either, huh?"

"No. Did you sit around the fire and eat s'mores? Did you roast that bunny and eat it? Did Dad tell his stupid Indian stories? He always does, the one where the Indians are all prowling at night looking for their body parts."

"Right."

"And that one when he's like, one Indian went to law school and went berserk and stabbed his client in the throat with a pencil, and the other went to the Marines and started blasting everybody away. And the third, 'who turned into a white rancher somewhere in Wyoming,'" they said together.

Leah giggled incessantly, trying to talk. She kicked her feet up in the air and wrapped her arms around her legs to squeeze the giggles out. The cowboy looked over at the ball of youth beside him as he sat smoking, and he thought she was so small and beautiful that he felt a twinge of guilt already.

"And the third Indian," Leah said, catching her breath, "the third Indian...is...ME!"

"Yeah, that was pretty funny."

"Funny? It's scary. I jumped out of my bunk the first time I heard that shit. Awww, my dad's awesome, ain't he?"

"He sure is," said the cowboy. He didn't know if he should reprimand her young cussing mouth or kiss it. She went for the kiss. He kissed back. She slid her little tongue in. And they kissed with the blue mountain background pleasant beyond the green hills. While kissing, she felt him up and unbuckled him.

"Are you sure you shouldn't be in school?" the cowboy asked between kisses.

"No. My teacher's a dick. I'm skipping today." And she dug her fingers into the thick hair behind his head and pulled him in and kissed. This led to the cowboy springing out of his pants and grabbing a handful of hair in the back of her head and pushing the little doll wet mouth down, down, down as she'd come up and gasp for breath. It was beautiful. Really hit the spot. But he felt pretty guilty seeing the young girl all glazed and cum-faced. But she said it was all good to her. She got out and spat and used some grass to wipe her face. She was a pretty good kisser.

The cowboy spent the rest of the day with Leah. They went to a meadow and lay about, dappled with love, touching each other's skin, rolling around in the grass and looking at each other for long periods of time, then running after one another. It was a precious young love, spring fling for the cowboy. They came to a stream at the edge of the meadow.

"What are your sister's names?" asked the cowboy after a while. He leaned his face in his hand. His elbow pressed into the earth. The light of the stream glistened on them.

Leah looked at him drowsily. "Awwww, okay there's Melissa, Dorothy, Leanne, Kimberly, Ashley, Jessica and Candice."

"Their ages?"

"No, don't make me do that."

◆ ◆ ◆ ◆

When they arrived back at the house for dinner, it was around 5 o'clock. Leah had called her dad on her cell phone and told him about the truck breaking down. Willis' boys had already gone out and hauled the truck in the garage, which sat out front to the left away from the house by the road. The good old boys got to work on the engine, putting in a new muffler and filling up the radiator as Willis had instructed — part of the cowboy's benefits for working for him, and well, being a cowboy. Leah and Henry went into the house. Henry thought Willis would be suspecting something between them, but he was too busy fighting with the wife.

"It's over. We're done. Sell the land. I'm bringing the goddamned documents over right now, and I'm gonna sell this land, and I'm gonna move us outta here. Move to the suburbs. Is that what you want? You want our children to grow up in the suburbs? Going bored out of their minds. Watching the niggers on TV! Talking to strangers on the computer? Then they'll get into drugs —"

"No one wants to buy our land, Willis! Don't you see? They want to sell us. Nobody needs farmland anymore. They want to put up a middle-class residency here. They're gonna cut down the trees and drill in pipes in your land, and then they're gonna shit in it. Or they're gonna put a park here for movie stars to escape to. Grow up, Willis. And don't you tell me how to raise my children! You know anything, anything, would be better for them than this!"

Wendy went down the stairs. Willis chased after her.

"Wendy —"

"You are selling our children."

"It's the only way."

"Bullshit."

"All families in bad times must make a sacrifice to—"

"Bull-fucking-shit!"

He nodded at the cowboy and his daughter who stood in the doorway, and he followed his wife to the kitchen as she slammed the swinging door in his face. He pushed through into the kitchen.

"How do you think I feel about this?" They heard him continue to argue from inside. "Did you ever once stop and think about me? I'm the one that had to save us. I'm the one that had to get sacrificed!

"You're sick, you know that."

They heard a slap and a thud and something glass shattering on the floor. Willis flung open the kitchen door and came out, defeated. He put his hands on his hips and looked like he was about to cry. He saw the cowboy and Leah standing in the foyer.

"You have to sell the house?" Leah asked.

"Go upstairs and do your homework," Willis said.

She went, turned and smiled at the cowboy. He smiled back in a half-smile and then looked at Willis.

"Wendy!" Willis called through the door. "Our guest is here."

Wendy said nothing.

"He'd probably like some dinner."

"No, I'm fine, really —"

"Woman, git out here and fix the cowboy some dinner!"

"Dinner's on the table," she replied finally.

There was nothing on the table except a shine.

"Wendy!"

Wendy slammed open the door against the wall and came running out. She knocked past her flailing husband and pushed out the screen door.

"Crazy woman," Willis said. But he didn't chase her. He put his hands on his knees and looked after her, at the closing screen door. "She won't do it," he said. The door made a whishing sound of compressing air as it caught and slowed and then slammed shut with the wind.

"Goddamn it," Willis said.

"You better go after her," Henry suggested.

"Yeah," he sighed. "She's lucky I'm a nice guy." And he patted his friend on the chest as he passed him out the door, screaming something about the apocalypse.

◆ ◆ ◆ ◆

The house was quiet then. Henry went upstairs to visit Leah. School pictures filled the wall cascading up with the stairs. And in the upstairs hallway, all the old folks' pictures hung, a crucifix in the center, and a picture of Willis and Wendy — a couple of kids in love atop a mountain, their hair wind-blown, Willis holding in his wife from the cold, Wendy with her forced smile, Willis with his sure one.

Henry wanted his family big and beautiful and raw like that.

He saw a light creak through a door around the banister. He carefully pushed in and found Leah lying belly down on her bed reading. She kicked her feet back and forth, slow and steady like a pendulum.

They had a great talk, cuddling, and laughing. Leah explained then about her family's financial problem. Some company wanted to buy them out, and they were doing poorly on making any kind of profit off the land, but they didn't want to sell out. They loved the land and knew it would come through for them, or the market would change and demand what only their land could supply. And they loved Wyoming. Willis' great grandpappy always said, "A man ain't nothing without his land." It became the family slogan, engraved on a plaque in the den.

"Well," said the cowboy, "I'm sure you'll work it out."

Something about the way he said it made Leah believe.

"You think so?" she said.

"Yeah, if he don't, call me and I'll rob a bank for ya."

She laughed. Then she asked. "Seriously, have you ever?"

"Honestly, no. I've never hit a bank; knocked off a couple of convenience stores though. I've been thinking about doing a bank though. Knock off some small bank out in the dust bowl — there's money swirling around out there, you know you just gotta go grab it. Me and the kid, maybe, knock off a bank. He's great, the kid."

"Yeah, I know."

"You should see him with that gun, and that lip of his — he snarls it up — it's the meanest no-shit-taking look I've ever seen!"

"Dusty?"

"Yeah, Dusty. Good old Dusty. Say where is he anyway?"

Just then the door opened with a cold breath of wind from downstairs.

"Candice?" Leah called.

"I'm home," came the tinniest voice.

"Oh, god," Leah said, "wait here."

She went down and fed Candice and brought her up and gave her a hot bath. She had come back from the senator's house. She didn't say a word and went right to bed, all bathed and snug, the heavy wool covers up to her chin. All the other sisters were out, mysteriously, and it was just little Candice in the giant bed. Henry watched the scene of the big sister kissing her little sister goodnight and figured Leah just might make a good mother.

The child went fast to sleep, and Leah swept her motherly air away back to the room with the cowboy. She asked him how it feels to break the law, to steal, to kill. "I don't know. Good, I guess," was all he said.

She was in awe of him. She wondered how many men had died by his gun, witnessed now out to the living in rumors and by his nonchalant shrug under the word "good" — all the bad things they said about him on TV.

"You're so...I can't even say. You're an American hero. Straight from the heartland, the cowboy comes to kill the fake and the corrupt and save America."

"That's original."

"You don't like it?"

"No, that's real good. I like that."

"Oh my god, you could be like a movie. What was it my dad called you? The last cowboy. Yes! I'm going to write it, send it to Hollywood and get rich! You don't mind if I write about you, do you?"

"Not at all."

"You'll take the attention right? This way everybody will see what you really are."

"And what's that?"

"You're the cowboy, Henry. You're America. Now, stop asking questions. Come here, let me see you with this shirt on. It was my brother's."

She drew a fine plaid blue shirt from the closet and put it on him. She buttoned it up from the neck down and down further unbuttoning now to caress his little Henry, which quickly grew, as he held back the impulse to shoot another one in her eyes long enough for her to tuck the shirt in and fasten his belt. She stood behind him and presented him to the mirror.

"Oh! How romantic," she said.

She wrapped her arms around him. Then she stood back with her hands folding together up to her face and her eyes cringed. The cowboy stood looking fierce at his own mysterious reflection, pretending to have a gun at his side, his fingertips dancing around it — he drew and fired.

"Oh nice! The fastest gun in the West. Oh, Henry, will you do something for me?"

"Anything."

"Sweep me off my feet."

The cowboy did and looked at himself holding the young chick in the mirror.

"LEAH!" Willis shouted as he came in downstairs.

168

Henry dropped the girl. A thud stamped through the frayed wooden house and the china downstairs jumped and clattered. Leah was picking herself up when Willis pushed in, drunk and enraged, pig-eyed in his stooped-over walk.

"Leah," he said and creviced a yellow smile. "Git off the floor. We need to talk."

"Wait here," Leah said to the cowboy, arching her thin strained neck back to him. The cowboy sat down on her bed.

Willis went over in his tunnel vision, touched Leah's arm and then grabbed it. The cowboy saw his yellow fingernails dig into the child's skin. As he took her away, he heard him say, "Your mother left me. It's just me and you kid. You, me and —"

The door slammed. The cowboy lay down on Leah's Barbie bed. He stared up at the posters on her ceiling of some modern pop boy bands. He got up after a while and turned off the lights. He lay in the room with the little glow in the dark moon and stars on the ceiling.

The door creaked open, and Henry sat back up in the dark. A line of light spilled in the room and hit his face. A tall lady figure in a maid's dress approached. She took two baby-steps, then ran across the room and clung crying to the cowboy.

"Oh, I'm sorry, I'm sorry. I'm weak. I'm sensitive. It's all my fault. You know, I remember when I worked as an aide with the kids at the special school, there was this one girl named Kaylie who just wanted to run away. She was autistic, and whenever the door opened she'd run out it. Once her parents caught her out on the highway running away at night — if only the girl could just run, run away — I'm having a stupid memory. Oh, cowboy, give me your strength. I'm weak. Forgive me. This never happened. Let's just pretend like this never happened, okay?"

The lady pulled back and looked at the cowboy's hard, confused face. "I will be strong now," she said.

And the cowboy saw that it was Wendy clinging to him.

"Where's Leah," she asked.

"Willis took her out —"

"Oh no!" She broke into tears and befell her head to the cowboy's shoulder. She picked up again and dried her tears. "This never happened," she said. "You want something to eat? I'm going to cook a late dinner."

"Aaah..."

"Oh of course you must be hungry. I'll fix you something. You just rest easy. I'll call you when it's ready."

◆ ◆ ◆ ◆

That night, when Henry came down to eat, Leah sat across the table from him, her eyes blank and sad. A cold sweat filmed on her forehead, and she smelled strangely organic.

"You want some tea, dear?" Wendy asked her daughter, almost pleasantly.

"Yes, please."

Wendy went and made the tea. The pot whistled loudly into the silence. It was late. Wendy brought the tea kettle over, poured a cup and placed it before her daughter without looking at her. Leah drank, brought the cup to the sink, said goodnight to her mother and Mr. Henry and went upstairs to bed.

Soon after, Wendy went out, drying her hands.

"Well, I'm gonna go to bed. Did you have enough to eat?"

"Yes, ma'am. Quite enough. It was very good," the cowboy said.

"Just leave it there. I'll tidy up in the morning. Well, goodnight."

"Goodnight."

Henry sat in the darkened dining room. The table seemed to glow red under the lamp. He could see the cupboard across the table against the wall. The white drapes of the two tall, open windows blew in, dancing ghostly with a gentle night wind like cold white eyes looking out from the dark den. He leaned back on the chair and looked around some more. He looked at the ceiling. The texture was coarse with drops of dried paint hung — like a mountain from a bird's-eye view — the upside down jagged world. He looked so long that he convinced himself that he didn't know where the hell he was. He really didn't know these people. He didn't know what their problem was. He just wanted to work on the ranch and get some money to go home. But then he figured he shouldn't have any ingratitude on account of their hospitality, however strange. It was a good place to hide from the law, let things die down on the outside while he worked up some money. But when would he start working? He figured he'd ask Willis about that first thing. He really hadn't done a damn thing or gotten paid, except in food and shelter. But he didn't need any crazy chicken chase, just some cash to go home with.

Such entanglements kept him looking at that cupboard, wondering if there was any whiskey in it. He figured those boys from that shithole where he'd shot that sheriff were still after him. He'd wait them out.

Outlast the bastards. But he wasn't sure about the one who'd shot him, the sheriff's son. He might've been the patient type. Nah! He thought. He'll never get me, the big, ugly, bucktoothed bastard.

He was wondering about the kid and where the hell he'd run to when Willis came in. He moped over and sat down. He looked down at the table, guilty as hell.

"You know," Henry said, as he creaked his chair legs back down to the floor. He leaned his elbows in on the table and looked Willis square in the eye. "I can sorta understand why you are going crazy, if you don't mind my saying."

Willis grunted and looked up at the cowboy.

"Hell, I'd go crazy too if I was the only man in the house!" he said.

Willis coughed up a good laugh.

"I mean, goddamn, it's 8 against 1 here!"

"No shit. Ha Haaa!"

They laughed long, then sighed it out and grew somber again.

"Thank god you're here now, Henry. I feel like you're my son. Seriously. My son, he left, he got out. Government took him. I'll never forget when he got into that car with that Navy recruiter and off he went. Aaaah, man, cowboy, I only wish I could go with ya, you know."

"With me? Where?"

"Home."

"You are home."

"Here, nah. I mean I wish I could go with you to America, man, the real thing, but I'm stuck here in this domestic disposition."

"This is America, you crazy bastard."

"Well, wherever the hell you're going, where are you going anyway?"

"I ain't going nowheres yet. Not till I work a good coupla months, get some pay outta yer cheap ass, daddio."

"Yeah, you wanna work, huh?"

"I need the money, partner."

"You help everybody, don't ya, cowboy?"

"I guess you can put it like that, as long as everybody pays me."

Willis smiled. They went into the den and talked, chewing snuff, spitting into the tin basin by the hearth. A small fire warmed them. Willis got up, went to the bookshelf and retrieved a book. The bookshelf was old, dusty, and classical looking. Willis sat down and held out a book called the *Grapes of Wrath*. The fire danced upon the frayed cover.

"They say it's immortal," Willis said.

171

The cowboy looked at it and nodded as though he'd read it a thousand times.

"Immortal. Ha. Do you think when everything is over, this book will remain in our ashes?"

"I'm gonna hit the hay," said the cowboy, and he spat his snuff out.

"No, the answer is no. What we got in our veins is more immortal than the ink on any old book." Willis tossed the book into the fire. He went after the cowboy. "You know there's some creativity in my daughters. Candice wants to be a writer. Leah wants to be the next Courtney Roundapple, but I can't help that."

"Good night, Willis."

"Good night, Henry."

Upstairs, the cowboy went in to say goodnight to Leah. She was still up talking to her friends on her computer. She signed offline when the cowboy came in.

"Hey, look at you! You've got the spurs and everything! That blue shirt is perfect for you."

She took him over to the mirror again. She wore jogging pants and a Wyoming State University sweatshirt. She looked comfortably clad and acted rosy again. The cowboy wanted to have sex with her. She told him about some 24-hour dance marathon the next day, and that she had to get her sleep for it.

"You wanna go dance, cowboy?"

"Yeah, sure, darling. Let's dance."

The cowboy danced the young chick into bed and kissed her goodnight.

He went out of her room and found Willis and Wendy standing in the doorway of the littler girlies' room. Willis' arm was around Wendy's waist, and they seemed to be smiling. The cowboy went up to them.

"Look at my angels, cowboy? Have you ever seen anything more beautiful? The fruit of my loin!"

Henry looked in over their shoulders. The six little daughters slept, in one big bed, their heads denting the pillow softly, their bodies crunched in fetal position in soft warm humps under the blankets, lined up from biggest to smallest. And Dusty the kid, was right in the middle of the sleeping babes, wiggling around belly down against the bed. The room was drowsy and full of dreams. The moon cast rippling light over the covers; and then a cloud covered it, and the soft moonshade washed the room.

The proud parents stood in the door and admired their offspring.

Henry went down the hall, washed up and went to his room. He tossed his jeans over the chair and placed his boots under the bed. He took off his hat on the desk. He lay in bed under the sheets and stared at the ceiling for a second before he closed his eyes. He was glad Willis and Wendy seemed to have made up. They were such a lovely couple.

◆ ◆ ◆ ◆

In the middle of the night, a screaming awoke the house. Willis and Wendy were really making up. Their room was right next to Henry's, and he could hear them sighing and moaning and yelping; the mattress springs squeaking. He stood and stepped out into the hall. He was sure that they must've woken all the children. He looked down the yellow-lit hall. There was the kid at the end of it. He'd heard the noise he knew. Henry gestured to him to get back to bed. The kid stood frozen, his eyes not drowsy but wet and absent. He looked like he'd peed his pants.

"Come 'ere!" Henry whispered through the thick lust.

From inside, Wendy moaned and screamed, "Oh, Willis! Yas! Fuck me!"

The kid walked fast down the hall past the screaming room. Henry closed the door, and Dusty jumped right in the bed.

"Those damn girls keep moving around in bed," he said. "I can't sleep."

"Watch your cussin' now, you can sleep here, just stay on the edge of the bed and don't start tossin' around either, you hear me?"

They lay in bed, eyes forced shut, then wide open as the screaming climaxed to a halt and a long sighing aftermath, as Willis emptied the essence of his being into his reluctantly horny wife. And then it was over. The cowboy sighed. "You know what that was all about," he said to the ceiling.

"Yeah," Dusty said.

"Good."

And they went to sleep.

Yet later in the night, a cold draft from the stuck-open window came a'chilling in. Henry awoke, saw nothing and pulled the covers up to his eyes. Then he saw her standing in the faded-blue night room, right at the foot of the bed. She walked reverently to the window and placed her hands on the pane. The kid awoke from his dream of the girls, smiled at the ghost in the room and closed his eyes. He opened them again and began to scream. The cowboy cupped his hand tight over his mouth. The kid's eyes bursting out.

"Shut up, kid," the cowboy whispered in his ear, "just lay still."

Wendy's nightgown floated over her skin. She stood tall and slender. Her fingertips bent delicately on the pane. Her face glossed a soft blue-white under the moonlight. A lone coyote somewhere out there yowled to the moon, as she gazed out the window. The cowboy saw a tear swell in her and fall streaming hot and wild down her cheek. She bit her lip, and quivered and tried not to cry. Henry didn't think he'd ever empathized so with a woman, although he'd broken many a-womanly heart.

A strong wind blew in, her hair and her nightgown back; her tears dried up. Her arms crossed tight, her face cringed, as she shriveled up and within. Then she reached up, dancing her finger over the glass and grabbed the top of the pane. The wind, the damned wind, she thought. She pulled down on the pane. The veins in her skinny arms tightened out like strained rope. She stood on her toes and used her weight pressing down on the pane, her slippers leaving the floor for it. She cursed and bowed her head over the pane. She went back at it. The window wouldn't budge. And then the pounding began. Standing on her tippy-toes, she pulled down on the heavy window with one hand while also pulling herself up and pounding on the top of that pane with the other. The window only let out one notch of movement with a mocking, halting, toot screech. The window would not close.

Wendy gave up. She put her throbbing hands back gently on the pane. She looked out to the mountains and challenged the wind, and she hoped the coyote would sing out his lonely song again.

And then: Snap! Down came the window like a guillotine. Wendy's fingertips snapped under the wood. The sound resembled a gunshot. But no one came to her side at first. Everyone waited, stiff in their beds. Henry could've seen it coming. Wincing, he got up and went to her. The kid sat up and dropped his jaw.

Wendy lifted the window an inch and released her broken hand. She crushed down against the wall to the floor.

"Oh, man, let me see that hand," said the cowboy.

But she snapped her hand away into her chest. Her mouth opened wide. Her eyes filled with fear. She felt so much pain she couldn't recognize anything around her. The cowboy stood over her. Her eyes bulged with fear. Willis came in. And then came the screaming.

"Fuck you! Fuck you! And fuck you, and you, get away from me!"

"What happened?" Willis asked.

"Her hand, the window fell, closed on it."

She wouldn't stop screaming. She saw two shadowy figures of men before her and one boy in the background. The men were probing her, trying to look into her eyes, but she wouldn't let them. She kept screaming wildly without knowing it. The hard floor and the hard walls and the men surrounded her in the tiny room, closing in on her. She couldn't stop screaming. And then she yanked her head into the wall of the closing corner, and her eyes sucked back, fluttering out and she was out cold. Her broken hand fell to her lap. Willis tried to revive her, shouting her name. But she wouldn't move, no matter how hard he shook.

◆ ◆ ◆ ◆

CHAPTER XV

The next day, Wendy had her hand patched up. Willis used popsicle sticks that the girls had sucked clean and dry as splints for her fingers. They didn't go to the doctor's or anything. They were the kind of folks that did things for themselves.

She stood on the porch with her three middle broken fingers on her left hand, looking out to the sunny day at the children running and playing. Willis and Henry came out the screen door after a few beers for breakfast — that thousandth of a second good and killed which they agreed to feel necessary when living domesticated. The cowboy had never stayed in one place for more than a week for something like the last 10 years. Yet he admired the country home and wanted to get himself a slice of country heaven one day with Angie, and hopefully not get all crazy like this family.

"Good, morning, honey," Willis said, cheerful and portentous.

"Good morning," Wendy replied coldly, with her back to him.

She let her hand fall from the post to her side. The wide bandages felt heavy. The popsicle sticks jutted out a bit like wooden nails.

"How's the hand?" asked Willis.

"Wonderful," she said.

Willis chuckled.

"All right, darling. Good news is: you got the window closed. Ha-Haa! Leastways, we won't feel that terrible draft in the house no more."

He kissed her on the cheek as they passed down the porch steps to the open country.

"Yes, things will be much pleasanter now," she said. She smiled a little. "Especially for you, Henry, now you don't have to feel that wind in your room when you're trying to sleep."

"Yes'm," the cowboy tipped his hat. "Thank you, ma'am."

They left her watching on the porch and headed down to the barn. The cowboy figured they'd do some work now, but Willis stopped in the middle of the bare, yet rich brown, cultivated field that rolled out of sight. "Let's see how fast you are, cowboy."

He called out to Leah. Leah came out yonder from out the barn door. She pushed the door closed while holding a half-full carton of milk. The cowboy figured she must've milked the cows or something.

"It's over on the other side," Leah called.

They inclined over a slight hill in the field and walked sideways a bit until they found a makeshift shooting range all set up. Leah put down the milk by the barn and came running to them.

"Thank you, darling," Willis said. "Come here and give me a kiss."

He went to kiss her on the cheek, but Leah bent her head down and blocked it. He kissed her head, and she smelled his beer breath slobber on her soft hair.

"I can't wait to see," she said, and she backed off, barefooted.

"All right," Willis said. The green hills and the high yellow plains of tall crops gapped with cultivated bareness surrounded by patches of tall grass reflected all corn-yellow in the hazy morning on his slack-jawed profile. "All you have to do is shoot those cans there yonder. I'm gonna time ya on this here stopwatch," he said.

He pulled a gold chain stopwatch from his vest. He was dressed in his Sunday best in a wacky, purple, old-fashioned suit. He twirled the watch around his finger.

The cowboy looked down at the setup. Six beer bottles lined two old picnic benches stacked on top of each other. The wind blew down one bottle.

"Oh, my lucky day," Willis said. He finished the beer in his hand and put the bottle up on the bench. Then he got out of the way and stood by

Leah with his arm around her, looking at his stopwatch in his palm.

He glanced up for a second. "All right, now pretend these guys are drunk, and they just done killed yer — I don't know, they've done something really bad — I'm sure you can picture a scenario. They're about to draw their guns and you have this."

"Pardon me, darling," he said to his daughter. He pulled out his pistol and handed it over to the cowboy. It was an old Scofield model Smith and Wesson.

Willis went back over to stand aside with his daughter. "Now," he continued, "I'll give you 5 seconds. You kill all these bottle men in 5 seconds, considering they's drunk and prolly slow on the draw, I'll say you past the test. Then I'll know if you's a real cowboy or one of them fakes. All right? You wanna do it?"

"Love to."

"All right. On my mark.....FIRE!"

The cowboy was still admiring the gun when he yelled "fire." But the word clicked in him and he grabbed the gun into a twirl, caught it in grip, aimed and started palm-snapping back the hammer into action. The bottles smashed down the line like dancing to music, the cymbal crashing with the drumbeat. The cowboy's knees bent slightly, and he leaned to his left in one motion. The gun roared. The shards of glass exploded, lighting caramel, bright copper glass under the sun. They fell to the ground in nearly perfect circles under the benches. The last bottle the cowboy got a little cocky on. He loosened his grip and jerked the trigger, altering his rhythm. The gun jolted back, and he broke his stance and stood up straight. The bullet only nicked the top off the bottle's neck. The bottle swirled around like the end of an improvised cowboy jazz solo, ringing out its hollow spinning dying sound on the hard wood and falling to the ground.

This raised Willis' eyebrows. Leah applauded. "Whoooo," she let out with her little pink mouth wide open to the sky. So damn distracting, the little devil. She was like a feeding bird or a scurrying squirrel.

"Goddamn," Willis said. "I ah, I stopped the watch when you hit the last one in the head. Nobody's gonna mess with you after you shoot 'em in the head. No cognizance. No nothing. Boom, boom out go the lights, eh cowboy?"

The cowboy blew the smoke out of the barrel.

"Oh aaah, three and a half seconds. Six men, three and a half seconds, with an old gun like that — not bad. Pretty impressive. I don't reckon we need to buy that home security system after all, huh honey?"

"No, sir!" Leah beamed at the cowboy. She ran over and hugged him, and giggled into his chest.

"Watch where you step with those bare feet, darling. There's glass all over."

The broken glass glistened like treasure in the dirt. Willis came over, and the cowboy handed him his gun back. The pistol had a nice feel to him when he shot it; hadn't enjoyed shooting a gun like that in a while.

"This gun is a family heirloom," Willis said. "But there ain't no more cowboy's left in this family. You be good working for me, and I might just let you have it — I'm sure you'll put it to good use."

He went on showing the engraved picture of a cowboy on a leaping horse, firing to the sky. He said a few things about the Mitchells who have died and thrived holding that gun. The cowboy couldn't stop looking at Leah. She radiated some ulterior bliss that he could not fathom, never from a girl so young. He watched her bare heels arch up in the soft dirt to attend to her mother's call, and he thought he'd fallen shamelessly in love with the girl, although she was only a youngin'.

"You want the gun?" Willis asked.

"Absolutely," the cowboy said to Willis while looking at Leah.

Willis saw the cowboy looking at his daughter and looked at her too with a smile. "Now that's gonna cost ya extra," he said with a chuckle.

Henry looked at him. Willis smiled his yellow chipped teeth.

"Hey, cowboy, you wanna go ridin'?" Leah asked. She pranced up to them.

"All right," he said.

"Ma's getting the horses for us. She's been really nice since she got hurt."

"Sure has."

And they left Willis and went to the stable. On their way, Dusty crossed their path. Henry overheard him talking to that little Annie girl by the tire swing under the willow tree.

"What's the matter," Dusty asked her.

"Boy, stupid boy, stupid, stupid boy," she said swinging. "Go away, stupid boy!" It was very cruel. The cowboy figured the kid must've gotten his heart broken right then on account of him falling in love with that girl at the first sight, then just standing there not knowing whether to cry or run when she was mean to him out of the blue. He stood all sad and stiff under that tree. He'd told him not hang his heart on a skirt and chase it all around. About time he learned, he reckoned. And the girl just kept on her mean face for some reason, swinging back and forth.

◆ ◆ ◆ ◆

That day the cowboy and Leah rode out through the woods and the fields all the way to the Tetons. They crossed a shallow stream, washed a bit and rode back fast, drying in the wind. They got back around 4 o'clock in the afternoon. Leah went to get ready for the dance. Henry had a shave. Wendy bustled about, turning off lights and closing doors.

"Wendy, will ya stop!" Willis said from watching TV in the den.

Wendy poked her head out of the kitchen. "Do you know how much money I'm saving? Your gonna thank me when we get that bill." And she turned off the kitchen light, the dinning room light, the living room and the hall, and she went and sat by her husband on the sofa. The whole house was dark except for the soft lamp in the den. Willis had decorated the room with some bought stuffed game and hides: an owl in the corner, a deer head above the fireplace, a bear fur below it, and an otter skin spread out smooth on the floor under the TV. The girls came in and wrestled with Willis on the bear carpet. His change fell from his pockets as his daughters pinned him down. The girls picked up the coins. "Daddy, can we keep the money," one said. "Yeah, sure girls, keep the change," he said. And the girls divided it up and went to their bedroom to put it in their piggy banks.

The same old news was on TV. Wendy watched it blankly and turned it off with the remote. She looked at her husband lying knee-bent on the floor.

"Honey, do take your boots off. I just vacuumed."

Willis complied. Wendy picked up his boots and went and scraped the mud off them over the laundry room sink.

Willis sighed. "Honey, I was thinking," he called to his wife, "we need one more kid. That's what we need."

"Ha!" Wendy laughed one dull syllable.

Then she said: "We have one more kid darling, remember?"

Willis closed his eyes.

Wendy got off the final layer of mud and started scrubbing his boots under hot running water. "And don't you forget her, that little bitch," she said.

"She's mine. I have her."

"What you have, I have. We have. That's marriage, dear."

◆ ◆ ◆ ◆

Now, the cowboy had been noticing several oddities about the Mitchell family. After they fought, they went to complete, perfect manners, seemingly. The house was cleaned. Nobody complained. The kids went to their friends' house and came back for dinner. Then they all dressed up for the dance and sat on the bench at the dinner table, lined up and ready to eat. They weren't any typical, easily excited kids. They didn't have the jitters in their legs waiting for food. They simply sat on the bench, looking at their plates, waiting. Like flowers, their heads seemed soft and gentle under their combed, shining, dirty-blonde hair, blossoming at the sight of food and growing day by day.

Willis watched them. He liked to look at their eyes and how the skin cuts off in perfect half-ovals and begins the white and then the blank outlook of the soul. He remembered his daughter, Dorothy, the curious, plain one with curly hair, once asking him if the eyes were the windows to the soul like her English teacher said. "Why sure, if you believe so," he'd told her. And she said, "But what about blind people? With the gray eyes and such. Do they have souls?"

Willis gave his lazy, one-eyed, crooked, whiskery smile of nostalgia at remembering the conversation. One of his daughters — he did not remember her name — turned then to her father and stared unblinking into his beady eyes.

"Honey, you want to say grace?" Wendy demanded flauntingly, closing her eyes.

"Yes, mother. Our Father, who art in heaven, hallowed be thy —"

"No, not the Lord's prayer, grace!" Wendy said.

"You just said it," Willis said. "Rubba dub dub, thanks for the grub, dig in!"

Wendy scowled at her husband. "Grace, dear," she said again.

"Yes, mom. God bless us, our Lord, for these thy gifts, from thy bounty, through Christ our Lord, Amen."

"Very good, sweetheart, but it's 'and' these thy gifts not 'for.' God bless us and thy gifts, right?"

"Yes, momma."

And the family began supper.

In the middle of it, Willis looked up and saw one of his girls telling secrets to the cowboy's kid, Dusty. Willis looked down and ate. Wendy smiled a little at her husband from across the table. "There are no secrets in the house," she said. Willis looked up, his face besmirched under the yellow dinning light. He glanced a plea to his wife. Her glare shielded it off. "Candice, darling, you wanna tell me what yer whispering about?" he asked softly.

"I'm telling him about our family. How our family has the most love." The child stood up on the bench. She measured the air with her hands. "Not this much." The space widened between her hands. "Not this much." She held as much width as she could, stretching her arms all the way out. "Not this much... but soooooo much!" And she wrapped her arms around her body, hands clamped on her tiny shoulder blades.

Wendy smiled mysteriously. "But we don't love each other too much, do we Candice?" She looked up at her daughter.

Willis swallowed hard.

"Why not too much?" Dusty asked.

Wendy looked at her daughter sternly, lowering her chin and raising her eyebrows. The seven-year-old Candice looked down sadly into her lap. "Because too much of anything is bad," she said.

◆ ◆ ◆ ◆

Meanwhile, Leah and the cowboy were out riding. They came across the kid as he headed back into the woods with a shotgun on his shoulder and a knapsack tied around the end of the barrel.

"Whoaa!" the cowboy pulled up his horse. "I'll catch up to you!" he called to Leah as she galloped by. "Kid, where the hell do you think you're going?"

"I'm goin' huntin'," he said. He smiled in the sun and ran into the forest.

On his own, the kid ate a flower he'd stolen from the bohemians. He played with magical tarot cards with a group of pretty girls in white dresses in his living fantasyland.

He left the girls and the forest and came to a hill. He ran across the daisy-pecked pasture, stood at the foot of the hill and squinted up into the sun. He thought he saw someone up there. He brought his hand to his brow. Yes, it was the lady, it was Her. She stood at the top of that hill. He would've called out to her, but he figured he'd have to save all his breath for the run. He ran up as fast as he could, gliding his hands over the daisies. Just as he made it to the top, he saw her wave, turn and start to descend into the fading sun. He ran as fast as he could to catch her, but that hill was so steep, especially at the very top.

Walking back down, he picked a handful of daisies and popped their heads off, singing a song. Then the daisies were all gray at the base of the hill — and some wind-sucked piston bulbs already. He ran through the gray patch, swirling the seeds up with the wind.

◆ ◆ ◆ ◆

The kid came back and went right to sleep while Henry got ready for the dance, shaving in the upstairs bathroom. Wendy came right in with her overuse in straightening everything in the house, her elbows bent up and her hands flopped like a kangaroo's. She went to the sink, leaned over across the shaving cowboy, turned off the water and went out, as if she hadn't even noticed him. Henry thought, shook his head and turned the water back on, but turned it off when he wasn't using it.

They arrived early to the dance. It was called the Dance for Love, a 24-hour marathon raising money for kids with cancer. Henry and Leah each signed a $50 vow and placed their ballots in the box. They went in the gym door. The school was small, but the gym was big. Nobody was there to welcome them with a cheer. They were too early. So when more people came and the pastors and the cheerleaders formed a circle around the door, the cowboy took Leah's hand and brought her outside. Then they came back in again and everyone cheered. A priest with motorcycle gloves on gave the cowboy a high-five. The inspirational music filled the gym. The bleachers were all pushed back so they had extra room. Banners and balloons all over decorated the place. Prizes were raffled off on a stage, and a band played, and there was Irish dancing. A kid named Mitch requested Nirvana's *Smell's Like Teen Spirit,* and he climbed the folded bleachers and pretended to jump into a crowd, but only hit his knees hard on the floor. Kids ran around hot and wild. There was a separate, small, matted gym where they could play dodgeball and wrestle. Teenagers jumped up and touched the nets of the basketball hoops and danced with girls, nervously, their palms sweating. The cowboy stood off to the side. After a while he went looking for a beer, while Leah went into the racquetball court to get her hair cut to give to the kids with cancer. There were a couple of them: young dancers wearing hats to cover their heads. They were all very shy and welcomed in dancing circles.

The cowboy went out and had a cigarette. When he came back in, everyone was huddled around someone. He pushed through the crowd and saw that it was the seven-year-old Candice Mitchell. They were all clapping and cheering her on. She wore sparkly pants and a tight, belly-showing shirt. She kept on pulling up the shirt with her fingers and rubbing her belly, closing her eyes under the lights and pleasuring her young self. All the faces to her kept cheering wilder as she danced sexier. "Wow, the next Britney Spears," a guy said.

Some guys sat on the one jutted-out bleacher on the side, eating off paper plates and talking.

"A little fuckling, that's what that is," the cowboy heard one of them say.

"What?"

"A fuckling. That's what I call that chicken right there."

"Man, she's seven. You sick fuck."

"Best part is, ya comb her hair back in the shower, she looks like a boy."

They burst into laughter.

"I don't care," the pervert continued. "She wants it. Look at her. The cute little fuckling. Can't condone it. Gotta admit, though, you'd spin that ass around your cock like fucking the globe on an axis — all the virginal world unclenched and open, screaming in orgasm, moose and woman, snake and man, automatically, magnetically, whatever, just fucking, man, that's the free world —"

"Give it a rest, Willis, you're drunk."

"We've given birth to the end, man."

"The end?"

"The end. I'm crafting a new guild in this slumbering country. I even got the cowboy on my side, and I've already given birth to the end. She's growing in my barn."

"What a crock of shit? Do we really have to listen to this shit? Willis, what in the hell are you talking about?"

"I'm telling you, 'taint mattering anyway. My girl Candice will be sucking cock in a few more years."

"You're sick."

"I heard the senator's already bought her."

"Shut up. Don't interrupt. What I am saying is, it ain't a bad way to raise yer kid. Think about it. You teach them the way the world works. They learn certain things, so that they don't get hurt or have any awkwardness about them like most youngsters. They're strong. They're like adults. The only thing worth living for is getting money and getting fucked."

"Getting laid and getting paid, huh, Willis? What is the travesty with you?"

"No, there is no rhyme to it. It's getting money —"

"Yeah, I got ya. You're all twisted backwards man."

"Get it straight."

"I got it."

The men laughed and sneered at the dancing seven-year-old, saying, "I'd hit that," as they slugged back their beer. The cowboy turned to them. He'd heard every word and he recognized the voice.

Just then, Leah came jumping up to him with her new do. Her hair was chopped off at the ears and cropped up. Her head looked like a sweet bell. Through the laughing and dancers, and Leah in his face, Henry spied a languid figure exit the gym.

In his burlesque trance, the cowboy denied a young girl a dance. "I don't dance," he said, gruffly. Then Leah asked him, and Henry danced her up good. Then she got in a group of black fellows dancing circle. They bobbed their heads, housing her and rubbing up on her.

The cowboy wasn't one for such group dancing. Two black guys housed her from front and behind. She sliced a look up to him. The damn gang-banging animals were all over her, flopping her back and forth, and sexing her up. A teacher came and broke it up before he could.

Leah clung to the cowboy's side. The guys came after her again, but he brushed them back with one look. Leah went off again on her own. A thirteen-year-old blonde came up and asked the cowboy to dance, as she saw him standing alone in the middle of the floor.

"Sure," he said.

And he danced with the pretty, young, blonde chick in the white shirt. He could feel the outline of her bra on her back. The girl was nervous. So he moved his hand to the small of her back. She had her arms up high on his broad shoulders, and she smiled to the break of laughter every time he looked at her.

"How old are you?" asked the cowboy.

The girl immediately slid her arms down off him at the question. One of her friends who had apparently been dancing right next to them overheard and came wheezing excitedly up to her, and the girl leaned back and whispered to her friend for a while, keeping one hand slowly falling from the cowboy's shoulder, to be polite. The hand fell. And she was totally detached. The cowboy stood waiting for the girl. The chubby black one stopped talking and smiled her big, red lips at the cowboy. The thirteen-year-old girl turned to him finally and yammered, "I just saw you and wanted to dance with you because I thought you were lonely. But if you don't want me, I mean if you don't want to dance with me, I'll go, oh iieeiieah, I better go." She curtsied and ran off giggling into her friend.

"It's been a pleasure," he called after her. "What kind of show are they running here?" he said under his breath.

At dinnertime the next day, they ate in the school hall. The cowboy was truly not hungry for the first time in his life. He sat against the wall and let his sweaty back slide down. "Goddamned dance marathon, what the hell am I doing here?" he asked himself. The floor was nice and cold. He looked at paintings of pastures and seas and penguins drawn by third-graders. Someone kicked him. He looked up at the kicker, feeling no strength to get up and kick him back.

"Ever been to a marathon before?"

The cowboy shook his head.

"Boy, you better get some food in ya. I don't wanna have to pump an IV in your ass. Come on, man, seven more hours."

The doctor helped the cowboy to his feet and brought him over to the food line in the corridor. He heard some foreign language hitting dull against the side of his head. He turned his heavy back and found two girls with shiny-silk skin and hair and big, wet, lively eyes, biting their lips at him.

"*Hola*," the cowboy nodded. "*Como esta? Quien es?*" He knew a little Spanish from his time in Mexico.

The girls laughed. "No. We are not Spanish. We are Russian."

"Oh, Russian! Of course!"

Later in the night, the cowboy danced with the Russian named Natisha. He took her hand, but she said no. She didn't dance like that. Rather, she put her arms over his shoulders and swayed her hips close into him. She wore tight jeans, a black blouse, and had sprinkles of glitter on her rosy cheeks. She had these clairvoyant eyes like deep green seas, and the cowboy swam in them unafraid as she moved fluidly. Then he had to look away. "Sorry, I have this blindness, I can't look into most peoples' eyes too long, I get all cross-eyed in it after awhile."

"What?"

"Never mind."

The music was pretty loud. She laid her head on his shoulder and told him she had a boyfriend watching from the bleachers. He said he had a girl back home. Then a rock band lit up in fluorescence and ripped their first riff on the small stage behind them. The boyfriend came over and took the girl into the crowd.

The band rocked out to the end. The guitarist would jump up and cross his legs and land in the crowd, banging his head. They dressed in suits but got them all messed up. That was their thing. And they kept telling folks to buy their CD on the way out.

The final song was a line dance they'd done every hour, and all had entrenched in them. They all held hands in one big circle. Some girl named Nicole tried to connect with the cowboy. Her good family was around her. When he told her he was staying with the Mitchells, the good family gasped and brought Nicole away.

The final festivities kept him from getting the hell out, with a crowd milling in his way waiting for raffle announcements and speeches praising how much money they earned, a bunch of other shows and acknowledgments. That Dance for Love was a pretty big deal.

The doors plugged up with sweaty dancers trying to get out. The cowboy went to the concession stand and had a cold juice in a plastic cup.

"So how do you like that hospitality so far, cowboy?" a fat man in suspenders asked from behind the table.

The cowboy glanced up at the man. "Never was much fond of high school dances," he said.

"It's for the kids, man."

It was one of Willis' good old boys.

"Yeah, I guess."

"You're staying with the Mitchells, right?"

"That's right. How's my truck?"

"It's good. Tuned up and ready to go. New muffler. So you didn't answer my question. I said how do you like the hospitality?"

The cowboy said nothing. All he could think about before he did anything was finding Willis, telling him what he'd heard about his daughter, and find out what the hell was in that barn.

He made it out of the gym, and the cold Wyoming night purged all the sweat-congested smell of the dance away. He walked through the parking lot. Leah was there.

"Hey, we're going to a party," she said.

"There gonna be beer?"

"Yeah, of course."

The cowboy could not refuse. He'd been looking for a cold beer all night. "I'm there," he said.

They got in Willis' truck and drove to the house party a few blocks away. Henry was disgusted about what he'd heard those men saying about the daughters. On the other hand, he was just trying to lay low and make a buck; he really didn't want to get involved. So he figured he could drink it off and hightail out of there in the morning.

Leah and Henry sat in the garage at the party, sitting on the door-step of some kid's house, getting drunk. The cooler of beer was next to them. Drunken youths were running out into the rain and swerving back into the garage laughing. They'd go out in couples, kiss and roll around in the slush-puddled rain.

Leah looked down at the cowboy. "Too much for ya, cowboy?"

Henry looked up at her; the cowboy said nothing.

"Ain't really enjoying yourself — ya wanna go somewhere?"

"Yeah," he said and got up, finished his beer and went to the truck. He smashed the bottle to the driveway and got in. Leah hopped in shot-gun. They drove in silence back to the ranch; Henry parked the truck and got out. He stood in the rain looking at Leah. Then he looked off. "I gotta see what's in that barn," he said. And he started walking out to it, across the cultivated field. Leah ran after him and got around in front of him.

"Wait," she said, putting out her hands. "There ain't nothing in there. Here, don't you want me?"

She kissed him hard and tried to get him down to roll in the slushy columns with her, but he ripped off her shirt and pushed her off to the ground.

"I gotta know. I need to see for myself," he said, and he left her muddy and shirtless in the rain.

"You bastard!" she screamed after him. "I'm gonna get my father!"

The cowboy kept walking toward the barn. Leah picked herself up and ran inside. A light in the house flipped on. An antique madam's dress, a long and rigid outline with tiny feet at the bottom, was impaled against the light in the big window. Leah tripped and lost her shoes in the mud. The cowboy walked briskly on through the rain.

He got there. A lantern hung from the drainpipe on the outside corner. His shadow running slanted with the rain against broadside, he made his way around to the back door. He yanked it rattling open —

scratching against the dry spot of earth beneath the barn's short arcade — and he went in. He stepped into the blackness and could smell sour milk. And there in the corner, under the broken light of the moon and the lantern through the cracks, sat a little girl on a tin pot. She stood up before him. Her skin was pale, her pale eyes crossed inward, her nose straight, mouth small. Her head looked like it'd been beaten in with a baseball bat. Her dirty blonde hair had been ripped out in patches and she held some in her hand at her side. She stood short, naked and chubby, yet malnourished. You could see the bones curve out from the paper-jaundiced skin around her neck and vagina.

"Had to see for yourself, didn't ya?" Willis said.

The cowboy turned to see him standing there with his arm around someone, lurking in the darkness. He stopped and pulled a string of a single, hanging light bulb. The bulb swayed and flickered on, a yellow light dissolving into the surrounding darkness. An electric box buzzed near the naked girl at the light's edge. The girl had bruises around her inner thigh and her arms. Her feet were chubby and her toes curled up. Her mouth hung wet and stupid.

"Look into her eyes," Willis said. "You can look in them forever and still never see her. She's got her own little world in her. The heart of America. Our daughter."

He stepped forth under the light, his arm under his daughter, Leah.

The cowboy cringed his face in disgust.

"It was the only way," Willis said.

"Oh, god."

"They were coming down on us — those bureaucratic bastards — we were losing the house. I had to do it. I had to...sacrifice my children into society...to survive. And then I got a little sloppy..." He nodded to the retarded child in the corner.

"You sold your children?"

"Yes."

"You sold your children!"

"Beautiful livestock, aren't they? Only livestock we got anymore. Blonde hair, blue eyes, pretty faces, soft skin, ample young breasts, tight clits..." He lifted Leah's chin and looked into her eyes. "These girls could lust over any good man's heart. Even a senator. No matter who brought them into the world. Even a poor old rancher like myself."

Rain lashed the roof. The cowboy stepped forward to leave.

190

"Aaht, not so fast, cowboy," Willis said.

The shotgun protruded from the dark, a sprinkle of yellow light along the black, wet barrel. Leah held it steady in her young hands.

"You can leave if you want, cowboy. Just don't tell anybody, understand? Or you can stay and live off the fruit of the land," he said, and he ran his fingertips up through Leah's hair. She smiled playfully and ruthlessly, without taking her eyes off the cowboy.

Henry didn't know what he'd do if they kissed right then.

"Or you can leave and go on your way, and I'll never see you again, right, cowboy?" Willis said. "It's your choice. What's it going to be?"

The cowboy looked at the hay against the wall behind them. He smelled human feces and urine. He didn't know where to look.

"You wanna get the hell out of Dodge, don't ya, cowboy?"

Henry felt a cold touch on his hand at his side.

"Don't ya?" Willis repeated.

Henry looked down at his hand. The incestuous breed gazed up at him, the embodiment of all banked taboo lust relinquished into existence, breathing seeing, feeling, pulsating blood, and already sin-smitten and snared, having never known innocence or the foul human taint of her makers. But for some reason, she reached out to the cowboy and touched him.

"Ain't she a darling? Little trouble at birth. Young Leah's hatch weren't exactly like Jackson's Hole at the time —"

"Shut up, shut the hell up!" the cowboy said.

"Just think what it'd be like to see from behind its eyes," Willis went on.

"Why do you keep her in the barn?" Henry asked, looking at the child.

"Oh, ah, Wendy, man, that cruel feminist bitch! She won't allow it in the house. Says it ruins the family name! This whole thing was her idea, man. She wouldn't even let us abort it. She never forgives, never. She lets Jesus do all that and to hell with us."

The cowboy pierced him a look, then softened his eyes back to the child. He lifted her cold, limp hand on his for a closer look. The yellow skin spread over her frail hand, and he could see the stretched cells and the blue vein lying idly underneath.

"So we kept it in the attic for a while," Willis continued. "Leah had to swivel her breasts through the crack above the door to feed it. Wendy caught her one time and put it out in the barn. She won't let us clothe it on account of her not wanting any clothes of our legitimate children touchin' it. But we feed it everyday."

"Does it have name?"

"Her name's Anna," Leah said proudly. "She's five years old."

"Anna," the cowboy repeated. He pulled his hand from Anna's. The soon-to-be government-labeled illegitimate and unwanted child's slab of arm flopped lifelessly as the tall cowboy figure jerked away from her. She stepped back into the corner. Only her battered yellow thigh sliced out from the darkness, as the child slumped down in the darkness and whimpered.

"She don't cry 'cause Wendy beat her every time she did since she was one year old. She'll be five next week now, but Wendy don't hardly ever come out here anymore..."

"You sick son of a bitch..."

"You can leave, cowboy. You're good at leaving, ain't ya? You wanna leave?"

"Fucking-A-right, goddamn it!"

"All right." Willis took out the Scoffield 45. He unloaded it, letting the bullets thud to the hay-scattered barn floor.

"Consider this a small consolation for you keeping your mouth shut, all right, partner?"

He tossed him the gun. The cowboy caught it and holstered it. He looked back at the child and almost wanted to grab her up out of there.

"I can't go with ya, cowboy," Willis said. "Naw, I'm stuck here. So is she. I wish I could go, I wish I could." He and Leah stood to the side. "But I got a family to look after." The cowboy saw the rain outside and walked out into it.

He went back up to the house and got the kid. He woke everyone up in the process, and all the girls wanted to know where he was taking Dusty. Wendy came down and saw his face stricken with the fear of being alive, and she smiled.

"Won't you stay and have a cup of tea?" she asked pleasantly. "Did you meet Anna? In the barn?" she persisted.

The kid looked up at his partner. The cowboy couldn't talk. He looked over all the girls jumping and running and screaming — the rancher's cattle, the senator's afternoon snack. And then he saw the door. He grabbed the kid, and they got the hell out of there.

They went to the garage by the road. His truck's hood was still propped open. He knocked it down; they got in, and he jammed the key in the ignition.

"Start, goddamn it, start! Come on!"

The truck choked up to a start. He saw Willis walk out to his mailbox, wait and wave as they passed by, down the hill and out into the long narrow stretch of road.

After they had driven a ways, the kid asked the cowboy drowsily, "So what was in the barn?"

"Nothing, kid," he said, "nothing."

The kid went to sleep. And they drove on. The cowboy had everything he needed: his restored truck with a full tank of gas, his hat, a good gun, the kid and his dream still intact: Angie, Angie, Angie! He was going home to her — forget the money! Forget trying to work for it from these damn crazy ranchers — but of all the ranches, he thought, of all the ranches in the West... The miles flying under his wheels made him feel all right. The truck climbed up a hill, and he leaned his head out the window in the rain and watched the tire spinning back road as they descended down a long hill. The rain died then, and the mid-May night hollowed out cold. Then there were the mountains, jagged against the weathering night sky. And what he'd seen didn't scare him anymore. But he couldn't help but do the math. And good god, she was only eleven years old.

◆ ◆ ◆ ◆

BOOK IV

CHAPTER XVI

In America, when the wind sweeps across the prairie, a young man tosses the empty plastic bottle to the car floor, a mother will cry and her baby will die, a team will lose and the coach will say something a little iffy and have to apologize formally, the daughter will get high and the son will slip by. The taxes will arrive. The sinews of hair roots will stress and thin, and the eyes will strain under the TV commercial and gin; and the movie will come out about the white rapper with the miserable life who just found out that every dying moment is another chan — there will be news about violence and who is pregnant. And then people will get up again and try. The professor will talk about X and Y. "I don't wanna fail; I just don't wanna do any work," says Cal the student. "That's like the dichotomy of mankind right there."

Yes, several things happened in America. An orca-fat black woman from Harlem wrote a book of poems about her mourning for her uterus lost in her fat and her miserable life growing up black. All the bald white critics swung sucking on her tits and nestling in there at night, like the lost children of the color white, aware of all sensitivities, idolizing subjects of victimization, American and legally human.

And the whores will come out, and the men will fight.

The law will orphan the children and vice versa. And they'll be American Trickster Legends. Break a paradigm or two. Be on *Time Magazine*. Rave around until their money runs out, and the proper institution catches them.

Newsweek will surround arrows and bold print and the color beige around the balding talking heads of the cynic and the bureaucrat at the bottom of the page.

Society inflates and bursts, hemorrhaging out miscarriages. And the land holds it all. And the song on the radio in the motel keeps on a-buzzing about the girl singer with the miserable life.

"Whoa! Whoa! Wowww! Girl, are you choking?" the cowboy asked, and he jumped over the bed, pulling up his pants.

The girl crouched down by the bed, snapped out the plug with her foot, and the bedside radio cut out. The girl nodded her head yes that she was choking. The cowboy's children were all stuck in her throat and oozing down her chin and neck. He knocked on her back and spat up his kids on the motel floor. The door was open, and it was a nice day in Tennessee. They sat on the floor leaning against the bed and talked, the cowboy and the whore.

"Sorry about that," the cowboy said after they'd laughed about it. "I've spread my seed all over America — man — now that I think about it. My kids have died in toilets, on motel floors like this one, all places kids should never be."

The cowboy's kids again had been shot into the blinding light of wild consciousness and then died as the white light stretched thin, looking up at their smiling master from the motel floor.

"It's okay," said the girl. "Gawd! You really had a cupful!"

"It's been a while," the cowboy admitted. He was still in an absent-minded spell from Wyoming. He and the kid had driven far and fast away from there, and they passed right by Kansas and into the East on account of the law giving chase. When they needed something, they took it, but the police were getting harder and chasing them farther. So that's how they made it all the way to Tennessee, the cowboy going sober without women and an empty gun. He explained all this vaguely to the girl. "Then I saw you," he said, "and I just had to stop."

She laughed. She was a pretty, young, skater-punk singer before fame. She wanted to talk about her dreams to the cowboy. She wanted to tell him more than ever after all she'd heard about him, but she feared that if she told, she'd lose it, as it always goes. Now, the cowboy didn't care for this superstition. He moseyed right up and spewed out his big romantic dream of finally getting on back home and marrying Angie.

"Then I'll bury my seed where it belongs, and it will live! You get what I'm saying?"

"Yeah," the girl said sadly.

"No offense or anything."

The girl was quiet.

"What's the matter, darling?"

"Can I ask you something?" she said.

"Sure."

"What do you think about America?"

"I love America."

"I know, I know, but I mean what do you think about...the American dream?"

"I love that, too."

She sighed and withdrew. The cowboy caught her chin.

"My American dream is my girl, Angie. I'll do whatever it takes to get to her."

"Yeah, but you don't think it's like shielded?"

"What? The American dream?"

"Yes!"

"Shielded by what?"

"By—"

"Bullshit."

"Yes!"

"Yeah, I see that all the time. I just shoot through it."

"See you can do that, but me I'm caught up in it — trying to make it in this business with all the scandals, commercials, societal norms, and stupid TV shows — we actually got a reality show about being someone you ain't; hundreds flock to get in this show and they act like complete asses just to get a shot....aaagggghhh! It's bullshit. I can't even talk about it anymore. Why does everything have to be so damn complicated?"

"Damn, girl. You sure do have a bunch of ideas. And you got the words to back 'em up, too."

"Thanks."

"You're gonna be a singer someday."

"Awww, shucks."

"I ain't kidding."

"And I'll owe it all to you."

"Now what'd I do?"

She smiled fully at him. The sunshade twinkled through the leaves and across the lawn outside through the open door and in her eyes.

"I don't get it. I don't deserve none of this attention, and I don't want it. What do people think they see in me?"

"It's you, it's just you. You're the cowboy. Come to break the shield and wake us from this commercial slumber before it's too late. You're America."

"No, no, no, don't start with this. I've heard this everywhere I go. I ain't no savior. And if I'm America, then America is in big trouble, let me tell you."

The girl giggled. "I mean you're a symbol," she said.

The cowboy furrowed his brow.

"Here, let me show you. "Don't you watch *Donahue*?"

She went over and turned on the TV. They sat on the bed watching for about five minutes. The girl knew the channels well. She flipped through till she found a political talk show just coming back from commercial. The cowboy didn't know what the hell he had to do with politics.

The hard-talking host led off the discussion.

"All right, we're back: the ongoing story is this unidentified cowboy..." He introduced the expert talking heads going around the table.

"And last but certainly not least, our beloved satirist, Professor Howard Stoker. Howard, you seem to be very aggressive on this issue. Why don't you start us off?"

"This cowboy must be stopped. He's on a killing spree, a, a robbing, murderous spree, and America is loving him for it! This is an outrage. We are feeding our own hypocrisy."

"Steve, what do you think?"

"I think the guy's a hero."

Steve wore a cowboy hat. It halted the discussion just to look at it.

"Yeah, buy Stetson; the stock is at record high and climbing. America can't get enough of this guy, whoever he is — I heard McDonald's is coming out with a cowboy action figure—"

"The guy is a killer!"

"Who'd he kill? A corrupt cop. Couple of whores maybe."

"There is no evidence that sheriff was corrupt. This is ludicrous. I'm not gonna sit here and listen to this."

198

But Howard stayed seated. His face reddened.

"Howie, Howie, come on, man. You gotta let go. Look at you; you're about to have a heart attack. This cowboy has inspired thousands of Americans. In our society of victimization and impartiality under our scandalized and fragmented old American ways instigated by the nullified '50s, he stands as a symbol, a man of will, simplicity. He keeps his own law in his head, and his own love in his heart. I hear he seeks a lover. Come on, Howie, capitalism has fallen! You no longer have to be its slave and hold back. You're free! Speak, man!"

"Capitalism has fallen?"

"Figurative speech."

"Right. Well, first of all, you're nuts. Second of all, the only slaves of capitalism are the indolent and—"

"Who wants to work?" Steve asked the crowd out of the blue.

"Oh and now it's the fall of diligence — don't interrupt me," Howard snapped. "There are those who can't work, but the government insures them—"

"Just the amount, too."

"Shut it, ya damn commie!"

"Whoa, that came out of right field," said the host.

"Well, I mean there's the liberal left and then there's this — this unfocused, whining, un-American, hippy crap. I mean what if people really started believing and acting like this cowboy nutcase, just start killing people that get in their way? Crime has already spiked, and it is his flagrant disregard for human life —"

"Howie, the cowboy ain't like that at all."

"Ain't?" Howard looked at the host, who sat shaking his head in his hand.

"He's helping people," Steve argued. "He gives people peace of mind. In his graceful, altruistic—"

"He's giving these people death, Steve."

"He's setting them free. He avenges a lost childhood love; from the heartland of America, the cowboy strikes at the heart of hypocrisy. And hey, if you got it coming, he'll get you, too!"

"What is that, a threat?"

Steve started riding his chair like a bucking bronco, a-flailing his hat wildly over his head.

"This is absurd," Howard said.

Steve ran out into the camera. The screen cut to multicolored blocks and then a "Please stand by for technical difficulties" blue screen. The girl turned off the TV and looked at the cowboy.

"I never asked for this," he said. "But I sure ain't what anyone on TV can say."

"Like you said," the girl exclaimed, bouncing a bit on the edge of the bed, "America's got something coming."

"You ain't hearing me, girl," he said. He tugged his hat down and went out.

◆ ◆ ◆ ◆

"Say, why don't you go on down to the river and get yourself some of that good, old, wooly, rank Tennessee pussy, eh, cowboy?" coaxed the old nigger who ran the motel.

"Naw, that's enough for me today," he said as he walked by him.

The old-timer kept on. He had a big, wrinkly, gray-whiskered face.

"Awww, it pains me to see you turn them down! I can't let you. Come on, on the house. Goddamn it, if I was a fine, young white boy like you, I'd jump right in them women."

"Go ahead," the cowboy said.

"Can't."

"Some white chicks dig black fellas these days, old-timer," the cowboy told him.

"Yeah and we dig them right back, but a crusty old man is a crusty old man."

"Never know."

"They're college girls…"

The cowboy stopped dead in his tracks.

"Just take a look. Just one look."

A flock of brunettes bathed in the river, washing each other. One walked in to shore, and the cowboy watched as the water shimmered down in levels from her body with each step.

"Aaah, Barry, right," the cowboy said, as the girl emerged from the shallow water, shaking out her hair.

"Yeah?" said the old-timer.

"Hand me that whiskey, will ya?"

Barry, the old-timer, handed the cowboy his bottle from under his jacket.

"Sure do have a good eye," he said to the cowboy.

The cowboy slugged, handed back the whiskey and walked back in surrender to the river. The girls lined up against the motel wall outside his room, and he took them one by one. They soon grew restless, and all flooded in. The cowboy had four at once. After each time, he'd go out across the road over into the yellow, sunlit meadow and lie in the soft grass, close his eyes and sigh, "And that's all it is. All it is." And then he'd collect himself and go back for more.

The kid came running up to him while he sat under a tree smoking. He brought him a piece of paper and recited the words on it like the old-timer had told him to. It was all about some religious club for men about keeping promises or something or other.

The cowboy shrugged.

"Looky here," the kid said, and he showed him the paper. "Says here we get a reward if we join this club."

"Yeah, what kind of reward?"

"Says here an everlasting spirit —... a really big reward!"

"Money?"

"What else kinda reward is there?"

The cowboy reckoned. Then he got up and said: "Hell, yeah! Kid, you're a genius! We'll go to the church for money. They've got tons of it! Gold crosses, gold challises, gold candleholders...all sorts-a-shit! Just gotta hit the right church. I ain't saying we're gonna hold up a bunch of priests; I'm just saying we'll go along with their club like you said, then I'll tell the priest about our situation, wanting to get home with a little money and all, and he'll likely pay us double our reward. I ain't saying we'll take charity or nothing, just our hefty share — what we deserve, boy. Nobody's seen more misfortune than us."

"The way I figure," the kid said, "this is our chance to do some good and get money, too. That way the law will see that we ain't all that bad, and we'll take our money and go home."

"Home...."

"Home."

"Sounds mighty advantageous," the cowboy said. "Ya done good, kid." He smiled at him. "Come on. Let's get a move on." He put out his hand, and the kid grabbed it and helped the cowboy pick himself up. Henry brushed off his jeans, and they headed for the truck.

◆ ◆ ◆ ◆

CHAPTER XVII

The semi-trucks swayed massively like ships vrooming in the dark night. One changed lanes and boxed them in. Henry cruised along at the 65 mph speed limit over the smooth blacktop road, nodding off every now and again, and coming to in full alert, slapping his face to stay awake. The lights from the trucks smeared and stretched long their shining beams piercing through the rain-drizzled window and his droopy eyes.

He turned to the kid.

"Kid, you awake?" he said. His voice sounded all hollow and lonesome in the cab, with the vrooming of the trucks, and the highway muffled and ceaseless through the thick plated windows.

The kid rustled in his seat, his head leaned tilted against his clothed arm and the soft plastic arm ledge of the door. Henry couldn't see his eyes.

"Good," he said. "You sleep, kid, you sleep."

And there was a long silence, broken by the bellowing of a semi-truck horn. Henry awoke in the lights and thought he'd been abducted by aliens. He gathered himself in a heartbeat and swerved away from the truck. The sides of the big, industrious trucks moved in the night like stone walls with faded advertisements.

"Jesus H. Christ," Henry cursed. And he wondered what the H stood for as he wandered up to the front wheel of the 18-wheeler, his foot limp and heavy on the gas pedal. He saw the giant double wheels before him, sucking in, eating the road. He swerved violently to the right, stacked up on the gas and drove along the body of the truck, like a guppie on a whale.

The kid slept on. The cowboy looked over at him, then back at the road.

"Damn, kid, I don't know how you do it," he said. "All tuckered out, huh?"

The kid was silent, and for the first time the cowboy felt lonesome as they drove east away from the Mitchells in the uncertain void of the night and the morning coming with the beautiful, unscathed, and innocent America waiting; the rugged land conquered, yet now a good stretch beyond home, which he only hoped was still there.

And so, after acting such an evasive life, unknown under his hat, elusive to the public yet plastered on billboards and made into action figures sold at fast-food restaurants and fictionalized in movies — "the ruthless cowboy-killer" — the epitome of America himself was lonely.

"Hey, kid," he said, staring blankly straight ahead at the empty road. His voice echoed lonesome in him and hollow in the dark cab. The headlights threw a short slanted light to the passing pavement. The truck on his right moved up in position with the one on the left, creating enough room diagonally between them for him to gas it up and slice out free.

He tried it, but the bastard truck drivers speeded up. And his old truck didn't sound completely healthy still. He actually figured the stunt too risky on account of his sleepiness, also. He hadn't been driving but five hours or so. Damn college girls had drained him good and sucked him dry. A thick drowse sank in his gut, tingling its effect throughout his innards. He felt it like a weight sinking down in his gut and his arms, and his heavy eyelids closing.

He nearly veered off the road once more and awoke to a searing wail of the horn and the flash of stretching lights again. The strings of light waved up thin in his sleepy eyes, stretching out and in.

"Goddamn it, kid, wake up. I need to talk to you. I need you to talk back to me. This damn radio is shot."

He fumbled with the machine in the red dash light. And then he punched it but felt no jolt of pain.

"I'm gonna fall asleep and we're gonna fly right off the damn road! Goddamn it kid, talk to me; come on."

Sleep dappled his voice and penetrated only as characters in the kid's dreams. Henry looked over slowly at him. He was out like a light.

"All right. All right. Got it. Not a problem. Seeing as how you's sleepin' and all, I guess I'll just do all the talking then. One-sided conversation. Just need to keep awake. The more I talk, the better. I have a voice, too, goddamn it. The more I keep silent...the more, the more.... the more I am liable to crash us both into the unknown. Ha Haaa, ain't that a hoot, kid? The unknown...

"The great unknown...kid, I wanna tell you something. I wanna tell you again — damn it — I'm sorry. You know when you do something that just don't make no sense? You don't know why you do it; you just do it. And you think you're actin' all cool by not thinking about it — ain't got no weak nerve or fear, countenance as cold as the snow...and you beat up a punk, quit your fake job and start blowing holes in folks, speeding like a bullet, leaving 'em in pools of blood and one long trail coming straight back to you. But this is the tricky part: you're really hurting your damn self. Think about it, we're all related going back to Uncle Adam and Aunty Eve, if you believe in that sort of thing, all one big, pulsating, bloody heap of mixed skins like one huge, ugly, strewn, speckled pelt, one big heap of flesh and bones and blood and hormones shooting through sin and water... all connected. All one big family. I mean like, look at the truck on my left. My brother drives this truck, and I am separated from him, separated by velocity and metal and space and an advertisement for, what is that, apples? And if I wander off this straight path into his, I'm bound to crash in his metal — hell, kid, I don't know what the hell I'm rambling. Goddamned bohemians, man! They got that crazy shit stuck in my head! What do they call it? The human condition? I don't know, but I'd say the best one to deal with that would be a doctor...

"Anyway, what I'm trying to tell ya, kid, is that love is worth it. I know I been whoring and drinking and killing, but love...is what binds us, man, breaking all barriers, even the ones we make for ourselves. It's worth the trip, kid, the fighting, and the shooting through all the ugliness and bullshit. The chances we take, breaking and running from the law. I ain't no Billy-bad-ass, kid, plain and simple, ya got me. I'm just a man who's had enough, trying to cut back through everything, against the wind. Just, wait till we get home. Boy, I remember chasing her out through the meadows to the tree, and we'd lie in the grass once I caught her…playing and chasing and lying under the sun through the tree. And riding… It's just really good stuff. You dig me, kid? Damn it, I love ya, kid! And I love Angie. Kid, you love Angie? Wait till you meet her. All right, I'll get off my goddamned soap box, but this is working…"

Henry twitched his arm on the wheel as he talked. His hand fell over the top of the wheel, his fingers dispensing his boogers onto the dash. His other hand stressed out in the cab air between him and the kid at all the points of emphasis and then relaxed to let the slow, dry-spoken words sink in.

"Yeah," he said after a while. "You know, kid, I've never felt more awake."

He rested his hand on his shoulder and patted him. "I know you love her, I know you do. That's the one thing I know is true. The one thing you gotta hold on to and fight for. I ain't kidding, either. Don't ever let anything hold you back. You stand up and fight. But don't be like me going around killing people though…aww hell, let's pull off and get some shut-eye, huh? Forget all the stuff I just said. Hell, I don't know… All I know is that all that love bullshit is true, kid. You find a good one, hold on to her."

The cowboy shifted in his chair and sat up. The truck to his right exited the throughway. The full moon shined large on the brim of the road. He pulled off into a rest station provided by the wonderful government and the taxpayers of America.

"All right, kid," Henry sighed, good and surrendered. "No more talk. Time to go back to being the cowboy again."

He'd parked under a tree, which overhung the small lot. The pavement seemed like it had been stamped down on the scraggly grass, which rimmed the edges like gruff hair around a bald man who's paid his dues. The yellow space lines sat quietly beside the car, fading down the rows. A car drove by slowly on the throughway, with the cold engine noise like a dream coming and fading out, with one headlight thrown ahead at the road. The cowboy turned off the truck. He tipped his hat back down over his face, folded his arms and slouched back as far as he could in the seat. His booted feet went limp beyond the pedals. And he slept. The kid opened his eyes. He watched his partner start to snore. Henry snorted up and tossed around to face the window. He grabbed his waist, but no gun was there. He looked at the kid and went back to sleep. The kid smiled into the soft cloth on his forearm, gazing out the window at the moon.

CHAPTER XVIII

When the cowboy awoke the next morning, he was still sleepy. "You drive," he said to the kid. With only a nod of assistance from under his partner's hat, the kid drove clear to the far eastern reaches of Tennessee. It was a hot, sunny day. Henry stuck his bare feet out the window and felt the wind between his toes, sleeping with his hat over his eyes.

The rumble of shaking boards woke him as the kid flew by a weight-warning sign, through an unimproved, wooden house bridge.

The cowboy roused up and said, "Slow down, kid, slow down." And went back to sleep.

The kid slowed down.

The noise of cars passing them then woke the cowboy.

"Speed up, kid! Up!"

The kid's head barely reached over the wheel. He sharpened his eyes and slanted his brow, driving like a racecar driver up to the minivan that had passed him.

"There ya go," the cowboy said, going back to sleep. The kid jolted past the minivan and screeched to a halt at a red light.

"This is where we all end up, at the goddamned light," the cowboy said. The lone light sagged low on the wire over the wide, dusty inter-section. The roads all ways shot out to their horizons. The heat hazed around in the dust under their noses.

"Go on," instructed the cowboy.

And the kid crossed under the red light. The middle-aged man in the minivan sat and waited it out.

"Why'd you stop?" the cowboy asked. "Come on, boy. I wanna get there sometime this summer. Next time you see a red light like that you—"

"I got it."

"Good."

"Pull over here, will ya?" said the cowboy.

The kid pulled into a gas station. The cowboy stood pumping gas, leaning against the truck, surveying the sky. A tall, puffy cloud sailed across the clear blue dome. It connected to a horizontal cloud like the mast on a ship, but it puffed up like a creamy beard, only upside down. Then he turned and pierced his eyes to the cracker-box town yonder. And then he checked the old-fashioned, beat-up gas station. He could not sense one shred of danger. That's what scared him.

"Where the hell are we?" the kid asked. He sat on the hood.

"I don't know," the cowboy answered, still looking off. He slapped his arm for his lighter and his pack of smokes tucked in his rolled-up sleeve. He lit up as the gas pump clutched to a halt. Shuffling his pack, he saw that he was running low on smokes. He put them away and pulled out the nozzle under the burning cigarette held loosely between his parched lips.

The cowboy went into the station still smoking and came rushing out with a case of beer, saying, "Come on, kid, we've passed it for sure. This place sure does look like home, but it ain't. We gotta turn around and backtrack west for Kansas."

"I thought we were gonna get money from the church club thing?"

"Yeah, right."

They switched drivers. The cowboy stepped on it. On their way through the yellow country, the kid sat wondering what the hell kind of spell came over his partner when he heard the sirens. The cowboy drove for miles going ninety over the long hills, apathetic to the policeman.

"Hey, kid," he said after a while.

"Yeah?"

"See that cop back there?"

"Yeah."

"You think you can shoot him from your window?"

The kid took a good look, sticking his head out the window. He came back in with his face red with life. "Naw, I reckon not," the kid said.

"All right," said the cowboy. "Let's just see what he wants."

They pulled over, and the cowboy put the gun in the glove compartment. The kid itched and sweated. Just from stopping, the thick hot air halted in the cab. They wished again they could've kept right on riding with the air beating into wind against the windshield, riding aimlessly with the current now of billboards advertising products of America's best, the law pushing them onward past home in a gritty odyssey.

"Come on, get out of the car," the cowboy said as he watched the police car from the rearview mirror. The policeman kept sitting in his car, talking on the radio and taking notes, as he prepared to approach the car, step by step by the book. He radioed in, "I've got a '95 red Chevy truck. The truck is slightly rusted, with white streaks on the sides."

The cowboy could not wait. He grabbed the gun out of the glove box and got out of the truck. The man in the minivan drove by smiling, waving his cell phone. The cowboy stuck the Colt in his pants and waved back.

He closed the door.

"Can I kill him?" asked the kid.

The cowboy turned real slow. He smiled a half-smile. His whiskered face cut yellow against the sun. "You wanna kill him?" he said.

"Ain't got no gun," the kid said, hopping up and down on his knees on the seat.

The cowboy said nothing and went over to talk to the policeman. The policeman did not notice that his suspect had left the vehicle until he stood right outside his window. The cowboy nodded and said, "Hey," but the policeman just kept on taking notes, rocking in his seat, double-checking everything.

The policeman glanced up at the truck again. "Okay," he said aloud. "There's only one of them." The kid looked back, his head perched atop the back seat, smiling his yellow teeth through the dust-strewn rear window. The academy-graduate rookie had checked everything. His partner he'd left back at the doughnut store. "I can handle this," he'd told him when the call came in. "Yeah, go take care of it, will ya — ya sure now, right?"

Then it hit him. "Wait, there was two—"

The cowboy tapped his gun against the window and said, "Howdy, Deputy. Can I get ya to roll down yer window real quick? Wanna talk to ya about why you're chasin' me and my partner with them sirens."

The young policeman looked at the cowboy figure in the dust outside his window. As he tried to close his jaw, he saw the gun glistening. It gestured him to come out and talk. He fumbled with the car door and complied.

The cowboy saw the young policeman shaking like a leaf.

"Relax, man, it ain't loaded," he assured him. "But if it was, my kid was ready to use it on you. Can you believe that? Little tike wanting to kill his first cop? What's the world coming to, right?"

The policeman pulled out his gun, dropped it and sprawled to pick it up. The cowboy stepped on his wrist.

"I just wanna talk to you," Henry said. He picked up the gun and tossed it away.

The policeman calmed down. "I pulled you over for speeding," he said. "95 in a 55 mph zone."

"Yeah, well the town kinda runs up quick on you."

"There is no town."

"Yeah, there is."

"Are you—"

"Yeah. I am."

"Oh, well...wow. If it ain't the convenience store bandits? Huh?" he said.

"Is that what they're calling us?" the cowboy asked.

"Among others. Listen, I ain't got no beef with you. I pulled you over on account of your truck; it's leaking gas. Could be dangerous. You ran a red light, but what the hell, right? And you, ah, forgot this back at the station." He held up the truck's gas cap.

"Thanks," the cowboy said. He put the cap back on and kicked a break in the leaking gas line on the dusty road. He looked at the policeman as he pulled out his cigarettes. He winced a friendly tacit to the policeman as he searched for his lighter.

"Got a light?"

"Yeah, sure."

"I left mine back at the truck."

"Not a problem."

The policeman's hand shook as he lit up the cowboy's cigarette. He had heard the stories about the cowboy's signature move of dropping his last cigarette on a line of gas and blowing up the robbed convenience store as he drove off. He watched the suspect shake his pack around and look inside.

"Ha, still got my lucky one left," he said. "You smoke?"

"Ahh, no, I quit."

"You're a good cop, ain't ya?"

"I try," he chuckled.

"You're just trying to help me, ain't that right?"

"Right."

"You know, I've always had respect for cops. Not the damned sheriff I kilt or the one that beat my brother senseless, but generally—"

"Hey, can I kill him or what?" the kid called from the truck.

"The kid," the cowboy chuckled. "He's got one humorous mouth on him."

"Hilarious. Well, you know leaking gas can be dangerous. I'm going to leave now, if that's all right, I mean, I'm going to..."

"Let me off the hook this time?"

"Yeah, let you off with a warning," he said with a wink.

"All right," the cowboy said, about through with his cigarette. "Hey, you want a beer?"

"A beer?"

"Yeah, come on, have a cold one."

"No bars open at 10 in the morning around here."

"Hmph." The cowboy went over to the truck and grabbed a couple of beers from the case he'd just stolen. He tossed one to him, and together they drank standing out there on the road, the cowboy and the cop.

"So you are that cowboy then, right? The one they are looking for," asked the policeman.

"Yeah, ain't you supposed to be looking, too?"

"No way, man. That's a federal thing now. But man, that's the kid in the truck with you, right?"

"Goddamned right," said the cowboy.

"Hot damn," said the policeman, laughing, looking down in disbelief. He looked up in elation, his young eyes smiling in his sweaty uniform. "My kid loves you guys."

With this the cowboy let him go. He exhaled mighty cold and enjoyable-like after that beer. He tossed the can and went back to the truck.

"What he say?" asked the kid. "You didn't even shoot him?"

"He's a good cop."

"Yeah, that's what I figured. Ain't all lawmen bad?" said the kid. "That's why I didn't really want to shoot him."

"You just keep talking, kid," the cowboy said.

Before they speeded off, the cowboy decided to bum a light off his lit cigarette. He didn't think he'd be able to find that goddamned lighter, so he'd double tap into his lucky. Turned out his last lucky was broken. "Ah, shit," he said, and he tossed his cigarette out the window.

The policeman had just gotten his gun back from the side of the road. He sat in the patrol car to watch a line of fire shoot under it and back over the hill toward the gas station. The cowboy half-smiled as they speeded off. "Luck is out," he said, lowly.

All the same, he reckoned they'd head on into town, see if they could get some money out of it before they crossed down southwest toward Kansas. No more bouncing around. He was going to do it the right way. He was going to go straight, seething against the commercial current.

◆ ◆ ◆ ◆

As they drove into the small town of Buckley, Tennessee, the cowboy and the kid noticed strange signs of some sort of religious upheaval. First, just before the town, a naked cowboy came rampaging on his horse, kicking up a trail of dust, and a-yelling and a-hollering up some sort of heretic havoc. He ran right alongside the cowboy's truck, and the cowboy stopped and rolled down his window. He had to meet this guy. The drunken, naked cowboy directed his horse to carry him to the open car window. The snout of the horse shook and whinnied and sniffed its hot breath into the truck cabin; then stood erect, holding the nude cowboy's head well over the roof of the old truck.

"Back up, man, back up," said the clothed cowboy.

The naked cowboy backed up his horse. And there he sat mounted alongside the road, buck naked, his burly, blond chest hair swirling in the wind, his package plopped neat and raw on the back of the beast, and a whimsical smile curled on his face. He lifted his hat in the air, waved circles around his head, shouting, "Yawweeeeh!" And as he said this, the horse, a perfect thoroughbred steed, raised its torso fully extended, neighed and danced its hooves gloriously. The naked cowboy clung to its neck with his scrawny white arms. The horse came down, clattering its hooves like thunder on the roof of the truck. The cowboy

212

and the kid took cover. The roof dented above them. The naked cowboy finally pulled the horse, sliding its heavy-shoed hooves off the truck and onto the road. It was a beautiful beast. The truck's roof dented inward a bit now, but the cowboy didn't care.

"Howdy, stranger," he said.

"Howdy-do, Mr. Cowboy. Name's Rylan Rice. Folks call me Yahweh 'cause unlike most other cowboys, I ain't saying yeehaw to get up my horse, I say "Yaaaaaawweeeeh!" And the horse stood on its hind legs again, magnificently.

"I see," said the cowboy. He stuck his red slab of muscular arm against the hot sheet metal of the door, leaning out the window. He squinted up into the sun at this Yahweh cowboy. He saw the naked flesh out there against the sun and could hardly believe, yet at the same time, expected to meet this Yahweh out there on the road.

"I don't know how you do it, man," the cowboy said. "Your balls must be killing you."

"I have balls of steel," said Yahweh. "Besides, I'm used to folks breaking my balls by now."

"Yeah, hey, stranger, what's the deal with this town?"

"Oh, Buckley is a good town."

"Tough cops?"

"No. Not really."

"I reckon so."

"You reckon right. Buckley is the perfect place to lie low, gain some spiritual cash and shit."

"Yeah, man, that's what we're after. We just need the money."

"Cool, cowboy. But I wouldn't go in that town if I was you. Now if you're running from the law, and money trouble and what have you, it's a good place to go, but if you're running from the risen Lord, I would not suggest that town 'cause that's where He's at right now."

"In Buckley, Tennessee?"

"That's right."

"Well, I best go and see him then. I need to confess my sins," the cowboy said and he laughed savagely.

"Hey, stranger, I'll tell you all about it," said Yahweh, his cowboy image cast golden in the sun.

"What's that now?"

"I'll tell you what happened here in this town," said Yahweh. And he told the story about how the town was once all strictly Catholic and the church was the center, second to the mini-mall, so it was a pretty big deal when Father Joe stepped down from the podium one day and went into the stultified people. It was a long story the cowboy didn't care for. He nodded through it, admiring the horse, throwing a thousand, "Yeps, and right, right, right..."

"So the main thing is," finished Yahweh, "the religion thing is kinda unsettled right now. The Man's in there craftin' incongruity, like the fall of Babylon or the punishment of Sodom. You got the Catholics and the Presbyterians, or Evangelical, or protestant, or heaven — I don't know what else!"

"Quakers?"

"No. No Quakers."

"You head on into town, you'll see." Yahweh turned his horse to ride off, then looked back.

"Cowboy," he called. "You can make a lot of good dough doing God's work."

"Yeah, well, yippidy-fucking-do. God is awesome. Go cry at a youth group retreat and fall in love with a slut."

Yahweh smiled his big toothy simile and his beautiful stead rode off with him.

The cowboy turned suddenly to the kid. "Did you hear that, kid? Working for God will pay off! It will save us from our money troubles. I'll be rich, and I'll go back to Angie, and she'll marry me, and we'll run away and start making babies!'

"I told ya there's good money in God," said the kid.

The cowboy stepped on the gas, screeching to the dusty cracker-box town. The kid rolled his eyes. He broke the filter off the last broken cigarette and lit up with the cowboy's lighter.

◆ ◆ ◆ ◆

As they drove onto the wide, old-fashioned Main Street of the town, the cowboy looked over and saw a man holding a sign that read: "Fear the Lord." The man with the sign looked right at them as they passed. The cowboy looked right back at him, his face grimacing in the light sun. The town looked like a wooden Hollywood setup, with the old-fashioned, box building fronts on stands, including the lumber house and the saloon.

"Say, kid, maybe this ain't such a good idea," said the cowboy. "I ain't one for fearin' no lord."

The kid flicked his cigarette out, his young arm undulating in the wind out the window. They saw another sign down the road, this one not written on a slab of cardboard but neon-lit and flashing implacably to the hot day, raised in the air on two black metal poles.

"Let's go see a movie," said the kid.

"Kid, you read my mind," said the cowboy as he spied two, black and white dressed Mormons walking on the sidewalk. "What do ya want to see?"

The modern Blockbuster Theater was just opening. The cowboy paid 15 bucks for him and the kid. It could've been less, but the kid wouldn't say he was a kid.

In the empty theater, Dusty told his partner Hank that the day was his birthday. Henry thought he was bluffing to get something, but then he saw the kid remember himself all over again, telling of past birthdays in the small outlet of complete and simple happy days he'd had when his parents were together and no so bad off. Guilt scythed his heart. The kid kept on talking of old happy times and then some sad ones, like how he'd wait in the parking lot of motels for his mother. Then he saw that the cowboy was quiet, and he grew quiet, too. They sat there watching the previews for outstanding, computer enhanced special effects of explosions, shooting and what not, flashing in their young unblinking eyes. And then as the FBI warning filled the screen, the cowboy said to the kid, "Well, happy birthday there, Dusty."

"Don't worry about it," said the kid with a wink.

"Naw," said the cowboy, "Come on, I'll buy ya whatever ya want from the concession stand."

The kid filled with joy.

At the concession stand, the cowboy stood digging for change out of his pockets before the pimply-faced teenager behind the register. Although the theater was empty for the matinee show, except for the cowboy and the birthday kid, the theater employee wanted to get back to his magazine about how to be cool, fantasizing scenarios with Courtney Roundapple. The cowboy glanced at him and could tell the dude was an asshole, stuffed with bullshit.

"All right, hold on," Henry said.

"Would you like to try our Marshmallow Chocolate Candy Super Fudge combo with nachos and a medium drink for only 10.99?" said the clerk absently.

The cowboy slammed a bill down on the counter and threw the coins at him. "I got three dollars," he said. "What the hell can I get for three dollars?"

The clerk dropped his jaw slowly.

"Do you think I want to try your super bullshit special," he continued, chewing his ass.

The clerk looked like he ached a bit with guilt. The cowboy stood before him, looking him right in the eye from the other side of the counter. The kid peeped up over the counter and gave his mean look.

"Well," said the clerk, looking around for help.

"You can get a small soft drink for 3.50," he said.

"Is that right? So I'm 50 cents short?"

"Yup."

"Look, buddy, it's the kid's birthday here. How about letting it slide just this once, huh?"

"I can't do that."

The cowboy looked at his nametag. "Rick, come on, man."

"If I let you slip by, then other people will want to slip by, and I'll get fired," he said, picking up his magazine.

The kid looked around the empty court. An usher was sweeping the floor, a couple came in the double doors and gawked up at the movie times. The whole place was decorated with cutout cardboard characters and posters for the new blockbuster $300 million film, which would ironically inspire a $3,000 documentary about the 300,000 thousand children who suffered in the industrial bowels of manufacturing, which the cowboy had paid $7.50 each for him and the kid. The title of the movie was ——, another one of S——'s bullshit movies full of lousy jokes, special effects, sex, violence, ADD cuts and a world-saving plot.

The cowboy now had his killing look, and he was on the edge. "Well, let the others go free, Ricky. Let the cattle out, goddamn! We're gonna start with you, ya no-good son of a bitch, and they're gonna put your pizza-face on the new dollar."

"Can't do it, man."

The cowboy punched him in the face. Rick fell back and slammed into the popcorn machine, then slid down to the floor.

The cowboy then went to fetch the goddamn 50 cents. He went around the arcade, scratching his fingers against the empty metal slot to the video game machine. He finally busted open the backside of the change machine by kicking repeatedly at the metal box. The change poured out onto the fake cobblestone courtyard floor. The good American couple looked on awestruck, as the cowboy took two quarters, went over to the concession stand, resuming his place before them at the counter, and paid for his small soda. Rick's nose was all popped and bloody. He was taking a while to get up. Finally he stood, leaned his head back and plugged his nose. They all knew what this was about.

"Get the kid a coke," the cowboy ordered, and he tossed the quarters at him. Rick had to bend down and pick the money off the sticky floor. It took some time. Then he had to call the manager about which button to push to open the goddamned register. The manager helped him and the drawer opened, unveiling under the cowboy's eyes a slice of legal tender. His tongue nearly lolled over in his mouth at the sight of money.

"Is Pepsi okay?" asked the clerk, closing the register drawer.

"Who gives a fuck? Just get me some goddamned sugar water, now!"

The kid enjoyed his sugar water. He sipped it slow. He let Henry drink, too. It was a pretty well spent birthday as far as the kid was concerned, forgiving the bullshit movie that they saw.

Special effects danced on Henry's snoring face. He just couldn't follow the one-liners, copying and mocking and trying to outdo countless symbols of bullshit in the American pop culture.

"How'd you like the movie?" asked the cowboy, after snorting awake at the closing credits at the kid's nudge.

The kid thought for a second. He didn't want to offend his partner, so he told him truly, "That movie sucked my left one."

The cowboy laughed and then took the kid out to go to the old Catholic Church to get money so he could buy him a real birthday gift. The kid was twelve years old.

Henry took off his hat as he walked in through the heavy chestnut doors. As soon as he walked into the little cathedral down the red carpet aisle between the pews and saw the shiny chestnut altar at the end, with the distant white fans circling high up on the ceiling, he knew he'd come to the right place. The richest damn church he'd ever seen. He walked slowly down the aisle with the kid at his side, both gazing round and round at the surrounding white stone columns and the intricate, sculpted fringes at the top of them. A rope hung from the ceiling against a wooden post in the middle of the church. The kid touched it.

"Don't touch that, kid, you'll knock the whole church down," Henry told him.

The kid gawked up at the square brown post. It crossed ¾ of the way up to make a gigantic crucifix, holding up the center of the church at its heavy belly of a roof, which was all white, with castle-fashioned lanterns hanging from long chains over the pews. Behind the white marble altar were three white marble steps, red-carpeted at the center, leading to a golden chalice on a table.

Henry told the kid to go over in the front pews and wait and pray while he stood in line for the confession box on the side. "Just pray for my girl, Angie, will ya, kid? Ya know, that she don't got any troubles, and that we can get to her with some money soon and run away — you know how to do it? Cross your thumbs...there you go, close your eyes, get praying."

Henry went over and stood in the somber, short line at the confession box, leaning against the unleveled stone wall. Inside the box the arid air held a deep scarlet color, in the blackness and the red carpet and shiny furniture, like the dissolving composite of sin shedding.

In the box, the cowboy didn't know what to say. He leaned forward in the red velvet chair and thought of asking about the promise-keepers club thing with the reward, but the priest went into a whole formal thing, asking his son how he had sinned and such. "I killed a woman," he said through the yellow ruffled window. He had much more to say, but this was all he could muster. He sat still with a shrill, chill shivering through him, his eyes lowered. It killed him to stop and think and admit to himself for the first time since he could remember, before he started drinking and killing and whoring, before he left home.

"Do you know who I am?" Henry asked the father. "I'm the cowboy they're looking for, the one on TV."

Henry shrieked and half reached for his gun. The father had reached around the wall with his old, hairy hand and touched him on his trigger finger. Henry held himself suspended, stuck in the box. The old priest put his hand around the cowboy's and held it firm.

"Yes, I know you, my son," he said.

His hands were paper-thin. Henry's hand sweated into the papery one. He took a deep breath and closed his eyes. Sweat filmed over his eyelids. He clenched his jaw and slowly let go.

Afterward the father suggested procedurally and hopelessly for the cowboy to turn himself in. The cowboy stood in the light by the door where the priest could see him.

"Now don't look over your shoulder," the priest said, seeing the cowboy's laconic face. "Regret is a trick of the devil. God has forgiven you. Now go! Make good."

◆ ◆ ◆ ◆

He found the kid asleep in prayer in the front pew. He nudged him awake.

"You wanna try this confession thing, kid?" he asked him.

The kid shrugged.

"It's the real deal," the cowboy coaxed. "You just go on in there and you tell the father yer sins, and he blesses you and God forgives you. It's really the greatest thing, kid, I'm telling you. You're not talking to Henry Dunn — this is the awakened soul of the cowboy; ain't that some shit, kid! I'm serious: the soul of the cowboy stands before you straight up from the heartland!"

"Don't start talking bohemian again," said the kid.

"I'm awake, kid. I'm telling you, I've never been so wide awake!"

The kid reluctantly went into the confessional box. The cowboy watched him and then looked up at the ethereal dome-decorated ceiling above the altar and the painting of Christ with a chorus of angels, the dead horns of the devil under his feet. He hadn't been in a church since he was a kid. He was glad, especially after coming from the Mitchell household, that there was a good Catholic church to escape to from the pervert's incestuous, sex-obsessed Americanism. He watched the kid go in and close the big wooden door to be alone in the chamber of residued and subdued sin, alone with the priest.

Now the cowboy thought the kid wouldn't be long in the box, being the innocent kid and all, but he took a bit of a longer time than he'd expected. Then the doors started pounding out. The cowboy and everybody in the line all went to the pounding door.

"Dusty?" Henry called through the door.

The door stopped pounding. It had pounded so hard, dust sprang out from the hinges.

"I'm stuck," said the kid through the door. "The damn door won't open."

"Watch your cussin', kid," the cowboy said with a laugh. "We're in church, for christsakes."

Early Saturday churchgoers had arrived, scattered all through the hollow church, praying. They all heard the pounding, echoing off the high dome ceiling. Henry tried the door knob. It squeaked around, completely detached and useless.

"Kid," the cowboy called in with a smile, "you ain't forgiven yet. God ain't gonna let you out till you 'fess up!"

And with this, everyone in the line and a few pews back laughed. The man at the front of the line, waiting for the kid, contributed a deep, fearless laugh filling the high ceiling and bouncing off the walls of the church. He was a bricklayer. This was the first thing he told the cowboy on account of his status in the trade. He took great pride in helping people build their homes and corporations their buildings. He was a good American. He had broad shoulders, a square, shaven face, and a chiseled build bursting from his neatly tucked-in plaid shirt.

"Here, cowboy," he said, in complete and abrupt crystal cessation of laughter, "let me help."

The bricklayer also knew a few things about mechanics and architecture, naturally.

"What you got here is a criss-crossed secondary mechanism — disabled — the springs are tangled, either that or they're not even there — disabled somehow."

The bricklayer pressed his ear against the door by the knob.

"Ok, Padre," said the bricklayer through the door. "I'm going to fix the door so you can slam through it, just hang in there, and when I say, pound away!"

He turned to Henry.

"Suit you, dad?"

"Suits me fine," he said.

"All right."

As the bricklayer did his thing, sticking a golden keychain slim-jim into the door and clanking around the mechanics of it, freeing the kid, Henry let the uncorrected "dad" reference go sinking in.

"Okay. Now, padre, now!"

The priest threw himself into the door and broke through on the third strike. The big heavy door came shattering and splintering open. The church people let out cheers and applause as the kid and the old priest emerged from the box. It was one hell of a sight.

◆ ◆ ◆ ◆

CHAPTER IXX

Now, I really hate to rush the story, but my time here is running out. Several things happened in America at this time: The President got on the air and said, "All sympathizers and misguided Americans who deem this cowardly murderer of men, women, and children a hero of some sort will be charged with harboring a fugitive if discovered that they have or are sheltering or assisting the cowboy — I mean, aaaa (he looked down at his notes)...*the suspect* in any way. I am reconnoitering America of this unthinkably blasphemous fiend — sanguine only in a violent expression of anti-Americanism. You know, you've galvanized this guy, who is nothing more than a sheer criminal. He is in fact a terrorist. Now, I call on the American people to do the right thing. Not only is there a reward, but it is the duty of every American to inform law authorities of his whereabouts. Make no mistake, we will round up this cowboy, whoever he is, and we will bring him to justice."

However, in private at his Crawford ranch, the President stood at the window and felt the presence of service behind him.

"Jim, I'd like to meet this cowboy," he said.

"Yes, sir."

◆ ◆ ◆ ◆

Meanwhile, back in Kansas, Angie dated Ken at the will of her mother on account of Ken putting out a $50 cut of his check for working with his old man down at the auto shop, saving them from eviction. With her husband out of the picture, this deal was the only way, Mrs. Sherman thought.

Ken soon knocked up her daughter. Her mother agreed with the abortion, and they told no one. And then they got her on the pill.
Angie slit her wrists with a kitchen knife one night. She survived and wore a watch. She worked and dated Ken for enough money to go to Fort Plain Community College. She felt like a whore, and therefore an artist, so she majored in the humanities.

One night, while sleeping on her mother's lap on the sofa, dreaming from bits of white noise and commercial stimuli, she felt the warm flickering light of the TV go solid and she sat up. It was a tornado warning. She ran out across the road and stood in the grass in the still air. She stood waiting for the thing to form and touch ground, yet thank goodness that before it could, her mother had scurried out and collected her, and brought her back in through the cellar door.

◆ ◆ ◆ ◆

Back in Tennessee, the cowboy and the kid found the priest who promised a reward for joining his religious club, but the club was gone.

"Yeah, this is the place," said the fat priest, "about three months ago."

But they stuck around for a while. The cowboy took the kid to the movies again — an old rickety theater that the blockbuster age had forgotten. They slept through a black-and-white scary movie. And the old man, Charlie, who ran the place let them have a freebie. As they were walking out, he said, "Gentlemen, how about one more show, eh? An unscheduled special before we close: *Superman IV*, in color, the one with Nuclear Man!"

"Yeah!" cried the kid.

"Hold up, now, no freebies," he said initially.

"We ain't got no money," said the kid.

"Aaah, what the heck! On me!" cried old Charlie, and he tossed a nickel into the box.

The theater they watched *Superman* in was the nice one with red walls that cascaded sideways up to a bulk in curtains surrounded the screen. They waited anxious and giddy and shaking around to get comfortable, yet feeling comfortable shaking in their seats. Then the old usher Charlie dimmed the lights slowly off.

"Awww, this is it kid. This is it!" cried the cowboy.

"Enjoy the show!" Charlie called out from above, and he began the reel.

The kid jumped out of his seat at each outdated coming attraction and said, "Oh boy, oh man, I have got to see that one!"

During the movie now, when Nuclear Man was born out of the sun, the kid cried, "Get - Me - OUT OF HERE!!" And he ran out all the way to the end of the parking lot outside and stood breathing hard on the scrawled section of grass.

"Damn it, kid!" said the cowboy after running after him. "Look what you done to my hand."

He held out his hand and scrunched it in tensely, yet not a whole fist.

"I was squeezing on your hand?"

"Yeah."

"Gross."

◆ ◆ ◆ ◆

They walked across the parking lot by the grocery store to the truck. The kid caught his breath. The cowboy told him, "Dusty, I've been thinking: I'm getting too old for this. Yeah, I've had the young crazy bulk of my life; I'm going on what, 27 years of age now. And I've fought hard against all the system, haven't broken it yet, but I figure I'll settle down, have sons and let them finish the job with glory.

"I've kilt many-a guilty man and many-a innocent man — yet they were all no more guilty or innocent than you or I. Hell, they're all better off dead. And those damn whores, but God has done forgiven me for all of that. I've got a clean slate. And I'm going home."

He looked down at the kid, who sucked on a cherry lollipop and wore a Davy Crockett coon-skin hat.

"Where'd you get that hat?" he asked him.

"Stole it," said the kid, between licks.

"Well, quit stealing things, would ya?"

The kid bulged out his cheek full with the sucker. "All right," he said.

"The world is yours, kid," he said. "You don't have to steal nothing."

◆ ◆ ◆ ◆

Forgiveness stood the cowboy in good stead. The next day he went through the trees and walked along the stream to the lake. He walked across the lawn to the Promise Keeper's bunker behind the church under the roughage of pine. The lake nestled against the Appalachians, and a mining plant smoked across the lake in the valley.

He went in the bunker and found some men sitting in a circle in a room praying. The head priest said, "I want each of you to find your eternal moment, that moment when your whole life falls into place, when you realize everything all at once, the epiphany like Saul to Paul, the tax collector to the prophet, the servant of God."

The cowboy went out and had a cigarette, looking at the lake. Soon they finished and he went in to say goodbye. The priest sat alone, his big gray robe draped over the chair legs. The cowboy talked to him about what he'd heard about him getting kicked out of the church and all for being rebellious in his manner of preaching, coming down from the podium into the crowd and all. He told him about his son, Rylan, who came in just then fully dressed sharp in a suit and hat. The cowboy had to look twice to make the connection. He even had the little priestly, white rectangular piece at the throat. And then the priest just wouldn't shut up, talking about his criticism of the church and how people just stand around mindlessly and sway and step forth and receive the body and blood of Christ for our salvation and sit down and stand up and say, "Amen."

"His body is broken for thee...think about how powerful those words are?"

"Yeah, no offense, father, but a, could you just give me my pay and I'll be on my way?"

"What? Your pay?"

"Yeah, I mean, I did join the club for a few days didn't I?"

"Oh right. Stick around. I'll give it to you later."

And the priest spilled on. Rylan went in the back den, opened the top of a Jacuzzi and drank a martini. He loosened his white-and-black priest necktie and called over some girls on a phone. The girls and he all got in the hot tub in the background as the priest spoke his so-called allegorical oratory.

After a few drinks, the cowboy threw up his hands.

"All right, where's my money!"

"Money?"

"Hey, don't make me do this. I've done some things, but I ain't about to hold up a priest!"

"You've got it all wrong, son. There is no money here."

"Well, what's this about a reward?"

"Your eternal reward."

"Aww, snap! Don't give me this salvation crap. I need to put gas in the truck, padre, at least cough up a couple of bucks. I know you're good for it."

He picked up the priest by the shirt. His son stirred in the Jacuzzi. The big man of the cloth gently unhanded himself from the cowboy and sat down.

"What's your hurry, cowboy?"

"My goddamned hurry is get some money and go home," he said in best restraint.

"Aggh! You ain't got no money? Empty your pockets."

"What, why?"

"Because you're wasting my goddamned time!"

"If there is such a thing as eternity, then there is no such thing as a waste of time, now is there?"

"For the living there is."

"Yes, yes, living, dying..."

A rat scuttled on the empty, dusty bookshelf in that gray room. A girl got out of the Jacuzzi, came over, kissed the fat priest on the cheek and looked at the cowboy. Henry went out, got the kid and got the hell out of there.

◆ ◆ ◆ ◆

They hit Memphis that night. They went all up and down Beal Street, robbing everything and everyone. They came to a wholesale store. They piled food, water, a case of beer, a carton of smokes, a bottle of whiskey, and even ammo in a cart. There weren't any jobs for the register clerks at this modern store.

"Please place items on the scanner one by one to be charged," said

225

the lady computer-standardized, polite voice.

"Please go fuck yaself," said the kid.

And the cowboy shot the computer lady, sparks flying from the screen.

Yes'm, they hit Tennessee pretty durn hard. The cowboy was mad as hell, at God and the world, society and the perversity of that inbred Willis. But he didn't know it. All he saw was lights, and people waiting in lines and cussing into phones, and the big pervert leaning into the little one coming around the corner, saying, "If you wanna fuck a girl..."

He went into a bookstore for directions. He figured someone might have some intelligible sense in a bookstore. But the red-lettered sign on the door read: must be 21 to enter bookstore. There was a black man in the aisles and a white bald man on the phone behind the counter.

"Say, fella, which way's west?"

The big, bald bookstore dude gestured for him to hold on a minute.

"I ain't got time for this shit, just tell me which way is west."

The big pervert ignored him and kept on the cordless phone. The cowboy left and caught the western wind. The kid dropped the movie he was looking at and ran out after him. He walked just like the cowboy down the street. Then there were the jazz people all around. They walked through it and arrived at a lowly looking tavern at the end of the strip. Outside the bar, a buffalo stood grazing on a grassy hill at the end of the road. Its tuft outline cut out temptingly against the night wind.

The cowboy went in the tavern. He did not talk about the buffalo on account of his suspicion that any one of those men in the tavern would be liable to go out and kill it for himself. He was out of bullets again, but he just kept on a-pointing that gun. And they lived off the fear of the already-dead humanoid heads, and all they said back to them was, "Gimme the money."

Now in the tavern, folks were friendly. The famous bank robbers Max and Sam sat at the bar talking about their next score. The cowboy went up and had a drink. The kid sat up beside him, and there was a little trouble getting the kid a drink, but the bartender obliged kindly after one look from the cowboy.

"A man ain't a man till he's had his first legal drink," someone said from down the bar.

"A man is a man who makes his own laws, takes his own goddamned drink," the cowboy disagreed, turning to the stranger.

"How are ya, cowboy?"

It was the policeman that had pulled him over. He was off duty. They all shot the shit and drank and laughed. But the cowboy never laughed much lately. Then Max, the short, chubby bank robber, said, "Hey, is it true you banged Courtney?"

"True as the blue sky," he replied.

"Oh shit," Sam said, and he handed over some cash to Max.

"Never doubt the cowboy," Max said. He said the women fancied him on account of his stocky cuteness and his quick hands that took in all things he wanted around him like a gambler pulling in chips. He said a whole bunch of things. Sam, the lean one, smoked a pipe. Max had a cigar stub in the corner of his mouth. He idolized the cowboy, tried to make the compliments go to his head so he'd ruin him that way. He told him about some TV show about American idols was going nuts to get him on the show. He said they pay big money and give free residency. He offered his card. The cowboy took it, burnt a hole in it with his cigarette and handed it back.

While Max was trying to think of something, Sam went in with his con.

"Hey, cowboy, see that old-timer over there?"

"Yeah."

"That there's Bumbling Joe. Been in the war, got crippled. Now he sits there all day till they close. In the morning when I get in, he's already there. He spends his whole life at the table."

"I hear he was in the Klan," Max added.

"Yeah, he's a racist. You'd like him. You should go talk to him. He's full of money. Just look at that electronic wheelchair, man; that thing must've cost a pretty penny."

"Yeah, what the hell," said the cowboy.

He finished his whiskey, went over and sat down across the table from the withered, crooked-faced, scrawny old man who seemed to flex himself inward as if retreating from the cold.

"All right, here's the deal, old-timer. You tell me your life story and get all healed and shit, and then you pay me 50 bucks so I can get a tattoo."

The old-timer rocked back and forth and did not glance up.

"All right. Now, I hear you're a racist. Old Mississippi ghost — well that's fine. I used to hate them niggers, too. I mean, I ain't racist against blacks, just niggers. There's a difference, you know, them loud-ass, cocky, pecker heads and those whiny, punk niggers like that one fucker on the radio all the time: 'I'm sorry, momma...' and shit. Actually, when

I think about it, I think that nigger's white. I don't know. Anyway—"

The old-timer suddenly pounded his fists on the table and jolted forward. "You wanna make money? You gotta fight, boy. Tomorrow, be here. I'm yer fucking manager!"

"All right, easy, old-timer. Sure I'll fight for money; hell, sounds good to me."

Then old bumbling Joe went back to rocking back and forth like he had autism, bumbling about how he'd done killed, raped, and pillaged some family in a place called My Lie.

Anyway, the cowboy got up pumping iron the next day at a high school gym, getting ready for the fight. He knew when an old-timer said anything with sincerity that it was probably true. But he didn't know who he'd be fighting or how many. The bartender had said something about a little fist-fighting club they had going on at the tavern. So he and the kid lifted weights in that little workout room with the red rubber floor all day. This fight night could pay off, he kept thinking as he got in a weight-lifting contest with this crazy-haired, country, buck-toothed boy named Billy Wantuck. They both about dead lifted the same. Billy would let the small crowd slap his face with chalked hands as he'd dead lift and squat thrust. His brother in the crowd kept yelling, "That's my bro, man!"

Then walking around the high school, the cowboy had to maintain discipline in good stature from slapping the asses of all the cuties in tight clothing. The popular fashion was tight pants or high skirts. Butts. Butts were in. Boobs were nice, especially the tight, snug, bouncing jugs. But butts, oh man, butts.

The superintendent had quite the problem trying to issues a school dress code.

"You wanna blow job?"

"No."

"Come on. In the bathroom, real quick." The weird looking skinny girl sat against the wall doing her homework.

The cowboy went up to the library. The girl followed him. She crept up behind him in the comfy seat and touched his muscles up his sleeves, till the cowboy upt and left, down to the exit, only to stand in front of a yelling head.

"You can't be in here, what do you think you are doing? Well then, you need to sign in as a visitor..."

The cowboy wandered around the high school some more and

found the kid munching on cookies and drinking soda in a formal lounge area. The cowboy dipped a nacho in a heap of salsa and was chewing on it when the lady with the stick of knowledge surgically stuck up her ass came over.

"Are you a teacher?"

"No, ma'am, I ain't," he replied through his chewing mouth.

She acted like she couldn't understand.

The cowboy swallowed. "Excuse me," he said.

"Yes, ma'am, he's a goddamned teacher," the kid said for his partner.

"Really, from what school?"

The kid looked over and saw the name of a school on somebody's nametag.

"Clouberg High," he said.

"Yeah, I teach Western History," said the cowboy.

"Really?"

He leaned in close to get her name from her nametag.

"Well, Betsy, no. I ain't no teacher."

"Well, then I'm going to have to ask you to leave."

The cowboy stood still. "Well, then ask me."

"Will you please leave?"

"Surely, ma'am. Just let me finish eating. I like the food here."

"This food is for teachers."

"So tell me to leave woman, what's the matter with you?"

"Leave!" she screamed. And all the heads in suits turned to her. She seemed on the verge of tears.

"That's more like it, lady," he said and slapped her ass. "Now get a damn dress, will ya? No man's ever gonna wanna court ya if you walk around in a damn business suit."

On their way out, the kid snatched a soda.

That night the cowboy entered the bar ready. Bumbling Joe was rocking in his wheelchair in the corner. He buzzed it over to him. "Let me look at ya! Aaah my fighter!" He slapped his face. He'd removed himself from the urine-soaked bench that he'd occupied on a daily basis for the last 20 years, all to watch the cowboy fight.

A big black man came in first.

"Take that ape," Joe told the cowboy.

The black man's name was Hal, and he could dead lift 350 pounds. He sat at the bar. The cowboy went up to him and picked a fight. Hal smiled hugely. "Put your arm up here, haus," he said.

And they arm-wrestled. Hal laughed as the cowboy struggled, then he slammed his hand down and flapped his arm back and forth saying, "Yeah, I feel some resistance there..."

The kid looked on, eating his dinner in the booth.

More men came in, and fighting and betting began, and the cowboy started making some good money. All the time, Hal looked on laughing, drinking a tall beer. The men crowded around, cleared out the tables and chairs for the fighting floor, waved money and shouted across the floor; throwing money down to Joe, on the cowboy's side, as the cowboy just kept on a-knocking them down.

That night Henry made over $500, hardly breaking a sweat. He sat at the bar, and Hal bought him a drink. Everyone dissipated out, raving of the cowboy into the night. Joe was dancing around.

"I thought you couldn't walk, you old fool!" said the bartender.

"I can't, but I sure can dance. Look at me go, Johnny!"

He was drunk and sat down for a cold drink.

The TV in the upper corner showed advertising for a big fight up in Detroit.

"Now, that's where the real fightin' money's at," Hal boomed.

So the cowboy hitchhiked up to Detroit. Well, at first they walked the railroad track to try to hop on the next train coming through, but that didn't work — they had to dive out of the way of that speeding train with no conductor — this was 2001 man. But they made it by asking for rides jutting out a thumb and sometimes sticking a gun to their faces, and the kid tagged along. They asked around for the arena, and they took a bus to it. There were a lot of blacks in Detroit. All the white folks lived in the suburbs. One coon put his stoned, squinted, hooded face up in the cowboy's and asked him if he wanted to buy some drugs. The cowboy didn't hear him and punched his face back in his hood. His scrawny body flung into the garbage cans. There were a few more scuffles after this.

And then the cowboy began the walk through the parking lot to the arena. The parking lot was big and dipped down where the arena lit up, and they could hear sounds of thumping music and fans cheering all faded out yet growing as they made their way. The cowboy made it through one section and saw only more parking lot. Well, he was downright sick and tired of walking around cars so he walked over them. He walked right over those cars, his spurs scratching the paint jobs and his boots cracking the windshields on some. A straight line is the best route, he thought. He'd go straight to the fight, get his money, and then he'd head straight home to win his love.

Ah, man, terrible pictures cut into his head — pictures of the bad men chasing his girl.

"Hey, you that cowboy, right?" said the man at the back door, and he let them in. They were led through the hall to a room with machinery and lots of TVs and guys with headphones on.

All in the halls, wrestlers in costumes walked through, talking loud to their agents and banging against the walls to get pumped up, then disappearing through a big black curtain.

The short, sweaty man with the ponytail in the control room looked familiar.

"Tony, put in The Last Cowboy on the screen. Put it big and bold, oh this is going to be perfect. The flag as the background, perfeito!"

"Yeah, but why The Last Cowboy, boss?"

"I dunno. It's good symbology or sumptin."

"All right."

And the cowboy took off his shirt and stood by the curtain.

"And now...ladies and gentlemen...a very special surprise fight... straight from the Heartland! Weighing in at 215 pounds...The Last Cowboy!" boomed the announcer.

"Kid, you stay put. I'll be back," Henry told him.

"Get out there! What's he doin'? Get him out there!"

A man in an orange security shirt touched his arm. "Come on, cowboy, time to go."

The cowboy jerked him off and went out. He wore his jeans, boots, hat and a ripped T-shirt with no sleeves, showing some old tats. The crowd went wild. The giant TV behind him made an image of the American flag, as his shadow cut out in it. The lights came on, and the cowboy climbed in the ring. Some big guy with a ninja mask on grabbed the mike and mocked the cowboy. Then he came up to him and whispered, "high punch," and he fake punched the cowboy. Henry punched the fake fighter, smacked the mask off his face. He bled from the nose, wobbled backward and hit the ropes.

"What the hell!" screamed the broadcaster. "That's real blood!"

"Look at those special effects, man! I told ya wrestling's the bomb!" shouted a teen smeared in the crowd.

"You had him sign a contract, right, boss?" said a man in the control room.

231

"Yeah," said the pony-tailed man.

"I don't think he read it."

"Ya think."

"Cops are getting pissed off at people making money off this guy."

"We're gonna turn him in afterward. It's all taken care of, don't worry about it."

"Yeah, boss."

The cowboy continued to beat the shit out of the wrestler. Then he grabbed the mike as the wrester lay bleeding and unconscious. Breathing heavy, his voice thick with excitement, he intoned throughout the arena: "All you fake Americans...you better give me my goddamned money, or I'll come back here and kill every single last one of you sons of bitches."

He dropped the mike. The crowd went wild. Another wrestler dressed like a cowboy came out. The broadcasters raved, "The Last Cowboy is in cahoots with Mad Dogg Sodder!" Someone threw a folded metal chair into the ring. The cowboy grabbed it and beat up his fake partner. "No, he's not in cahoots! What betrayal!"

Someone threw the standing cowboy a beer. He caught it and chugged it. A flood of orange-shirted security came running down the aisle to the ring. The cowboy enjoyed his beer, then punched through the security and mounted the corner pedestal. His chest was beet red from the fight. Some of the wrestler's blood was on him. He jumped into the crowd. They carried him to the top aisle, where he picked up the kid. "Come on, kid!" And they ran along the aisle till they hit a security block, so they barged in a box of rich people and grabbed some shish-ka-bobs to go.

They made it to the service elevator, where the old elevator man praised them. "Boy, I've been waiting for that. Oh man! Black Wrath sure is a fag, ain't he?"

"Is that the belt?"

The cowboy had forgotten about the belt. The huge gold belt he had slung over his shoulder. He'd used it to beat through some of the security, and it was speckled with blood. He gave it to the old man. The kid looked back as they ran out of there and saw the old elevator man finally happy — the doors closing and him standing between them with that championship belt.

Security blocked the service exit. The cowboy grabbed a fire extinguisher, extinguished it and beat his way out, leaving them coughing in the white cloud. He told the kid to go on ahead while he got the money. He went into the control room.

"Wow, cowboy! What a show!" The TV guy that had put up the whole thing was on the phone.

The cowboy threw the phone across the room and said, "Where's my damn money?"

"It's here. It's here. Let's just sign a contract and get you all—"

"I don't want no contract." He ripped the papers to the floor. "Sheit!" he said as he saw the police stacking up outside.

He grabbed Phil, the pudgy TV guy, and he put his gun to his head, standing behind him for cover as they shimmied past the huge, open truck gate into the hallway. Myriad police lights flashed from the huddled cars, an officer talked on a PA cone, and a chopper hovered overhead. Phil led him to a back way out, where he met the kid and hid behind the cars. They hijacked a semi truck at the edge of the parking lot and blasted through the barricade, sending police cars flying with sparks and screams in the night.

And then all was quiet again on the road. They sat high up and pushed on with that big-ass truck.

◆ ◆ ◆ ◆

CHAPTER XX

Now as to his whereabouts after this, there are many distortions and speculations. No, he wasn't that naked cowboy in Times Square. He wasn't that cowboy who stole a $3 miniature, plastic American flag from a puddle in NYC. He never was in New York City; that's a totally different movie.

Rather, he was in a field, running and laughing and singing, popping off the heads of daisies and sighing…

The red slice of her baby-smooth cheek held the breath of summer. It sliced and dissolved away in his memory as she swung sadly back and forth, back and forth, on the rickety swing. "You feel that whush tickling between your legs when you swing high up into the wind?" he said. She looked down sadly, playing some game with her feet in the dirt. He asked and she told him, but he didn't understand. And then the swing swang empty beside her. He climbed in the truck from the sliding back window, and she watched him disappear down the road.

"Henry!"

"What!"

"You were dreaming up something, man."

"Where the hell are we?"

"In the back of this big-ass truck on the side of the road some-wheres."

The cowboy put his hands on his forehead. It had turned out the truck was a beer truck, and they'd cracked open a case in the back. Henry had fallen asleep thinking there was always some good fellow or luck to get him out of situations. But now they needed to dump that dead giveaway, big-ass beer truck. Take as many as you can fit in your pockets, but get a damned car or something, he thought.

The cowboy was still sleepy and his head hurt.

The kid talked him up.

"I say we go back to Tennessee, get our money," he said. "It's on the way."

"There ain't no money, kid. What the hell are we doing?"

He lay still in the aisle with his hands dug into his brow. The kid leaned up against the beer cases. He looked at a *Life* magazine that he'd found.

"Say, Henry, where does money come from?" he asked.

"A money machine in Washington."

"They just make it?"

"Yup, big machine spits it out."

"Then why do we have money trouble if we have a machine that makes money?"

"What?"

"Says here that America is in debt."

"Because we ain't got money."

"Exactly. That's why I'm saying, why don't they just print out some money and give it to America, then people won't be a-dying on *Life* magazine anymore."

"Kid, you are a genius."

They ditched the truck and hitchhiked back. They were pretty popular to get picked up by a fan of theirs. But the circumstances of the law being highly present in the area kept them away from the tavern in Tennessee, and they wandered all the way up to upstate New York, where they stayed with a policeman and his family. The policeman was happy to oblige the cowboy and his big gun. But soon his wife and the daughter Lena, he'd noticed, were a bit attracted to him. The cowboy noticed it as well. He might've been down for wife swapping, but he didn't have anything to trade. And he didn't want to break any good cop's heart about the incredible sandwich he'd had while he was at work, so he happily left and went home searching elsewhere.

He remembered once looking for shelter house to house way back when in the Southwest. But all those houses were in the middle of the desert, with artificial sod lawns cut out square in the desert, and the sympathetic, coke-head, out-of-work actresses all loved to take him in. But this was upstate, suburban, bureaucratic New York, man. He used the kid and knocked door to door, saying honestly, "Hi, we'd like to ask you for some shelter from the law, if you don't mind." He was being real polite about it and not stealing anyone's home after how bad he'd done that cop.

The cowboy made it all the way up to Rochester and saw a sign that said these TV people were looking for actors to stay and live and be on some sort of reality TV show. So the cowboy applied, and the kid tagged along, and they got accepted. The TV producers thought the cowboy was great for the show. "So you're gay?" they kept asking him.

"What? No! Hell, no!"

"But you're a cowboy."

"That's right."

The TV producer leaned back and whispered to his associate, "I think this is perfect. We'll get him to come out on the show."

So they started living in this big penthouse with big windows like walls. The TV job even gave them another job working at some art/choreography facility. The penthouse had a Jacuzzi and everything. And the cameras were everywhere inside, and everyday the screaming fans lined the streets out below the glass walls. It was just like the real world.

At the end of the day, all the young participants were required to sit in a room and talk one on one to the camera about the group dynamics of the day. The cowboy would go in there and smoke and sip whiskey on camera. But this faggot went in there and spewed his forlorn love story for the cowboy to the nation.

"He won't even look at me! He never talks to me! He sits there drinking and smoking, and then he gets up and goes to the window and flirts with the girls screaming to him on the street! Ohhh!"

The next morning the cowboy awoke to the faggot's morning lumber in his face. He castrated him with his flint knife and slung his stiff one eye to the big window. And he and the kid got the hell out of there.

Eventually, these two college dudes picked them up and let them hang out in their dorms. There names were Cal and Wade. And Corey lived in that box room, too. They all dreamt of life but didn't have the balls enough to quit their inhibitions and go after it. See, it was a very ordinary college, wherein if you didn't succumb whatever marvelous eccentricities you may have, they'd give you a responsibility lecture, kick you out and send you a formal document in the mail that would put the fear of the world in you. So they went to seminars and sat around in circles talking in turn about ordinary things. They lived in a triplet suite on the ground floor of the private Catholic college. The hallway was all ripped up and full of trash coming out of the phone booths as they went to the room.

They played a few hands of poker for kicks. Then Cal showed the cowboy how to pick up a girl through the computer.

"Ya gotta talk, man, you gotta keep talking! See, look at that, ellipses, that means she's bored."

"All right, well, tell her my name ain't spooner32."

"Dude, she knows."

"All right. Well tell her…I don't know what the hell to tell her."

The instant-message screen popped up with a little jingle.

"Piece," read the message in red on black.

"Piece, dude, she wants to give you a piece!"

Cal asked her to the movies. She asked what he'd like to see.

"You on my cock," said the cowboy.

The college boys opened their mouths about to laugh and looked at each other. "Ohh! Dude, you are the man!" They typed it in and pressed enter.

Someone came in the room playing the guitar. Someone in the hall shouted "fuck." Cal explained that freshmen just need to get those out sometimes. Corey was cramped in the corner at his laptop. He was applying to transfer to another college online. His bed was perfectly made with blue plaid and several pillows. He had posters of inspiration and good Christian things. He had several Civil War figures positioned carefully on his desk. He kept saying things that nobody heard. Then he said, "Can you please stop playing the guitar," while stressing his hands around his head.

"Corey's gay," Wade said.

Someone had put a dream catcher made of condoms over Corey's bed. He was having a nervous breakdown. Last night, the screams of a drunk awakened with marker writings all over his body kept him awake. They'd locked the drunk in a room for everybody's safety. He kept yelling how he hated college. And then the security opened up the room and tranquilized him.

As the tongue-pierced Wade and the cool Cal made fun of him, Corey focused for a few minutes and wrote a journal entry on his laptop — something about being the angriest, most shunned and rightful roommate to topple this tyrannous social disposition.

"Core, are you going to come with us to get high, or are you going to just sit there being mad about the world?" Wade said.

The question was never answered and soon forgotten. Cal and Wade played a video game of a man stealing cars and shooting people. The video game man kicked down a woman in a bikini and beat her head till she bled dead on the street as Cal gritted his teeth. "Take that, bitch, you like that, huh, you like that! Bitch!"

That night, they went out and smoked up on Wade's bong. Corey gave in and came along. They sat on the hood of Cal's old Cadillac in the parking lot of some mining factory, smoking J's. Wade flipped through a magazine. "Man, New York sucks," he said. "I swear, we're going to be the last state to legalize."

Back at the college, Cal and Wade used their ID cards to buy late-night garbage plates. While eating in the little lounge, a guy gestured for money at Cal. He came up and said, "Twenty bucks, for the inconvenience." Cal flipped him off. While they were sitting down eating, three guys including the money-asking one, approached. One complained that he had to sit around all weekend on account of Cal stealing his fake ID, and for that he owed him 20 bucks.

"I don't have it," Call said. "Sorry you had a bad weekend. Now fuck off."

"What? How much money do you have on you?"

"None."

"Lemme see your wallet."

"Dude, were you socialized to be an asshole or were you born with it?"

"Harsh," Wade commended.

The money-asking kid crossed his eyes in confusion, contemplating the insult.

◆ ◆ ◆ ◆

Now, a slew of things happened from here. The cowboy actually got a quick random job as a gardener for a household on a normal-looking street in Missouri. He made friends with the crazy Brazilian nanny who dealt with the spoiled brats and the old lady's lizard-dry disposition on account of her dead husband.

The boy made the cowboy play video game football with him, and the girl swore at the nanny. She blurted that all Brazilians were a bunch of monkeys.

"Isn't that awesome? Look at that, I just dodged your guy! Oh, yeah, I'm the man, you suck! 200-7!" the spoiled little bastard would say at the Playstation football game.

The cowboy sighed and looked at the real kid, who was dying, and the kid and he and the crazy Brazilian upt and got the hell out of there. They stopped in Kentucky for a rodeo. A clown said, "Seggggguuuuuura peaom!" to the cowboy and the crazy Brazilian as they walked by him on the sidewalk.

Then they stopped in Tennessee. In the old tavern, none of the old gang was there. But Scott Garrett burst in the door with the fear of the world in him. He said he'd just gotten out of a long spell with the Merchant Marines and had come to help the old posse — the Texas 7 as the TV called them — break out of prison.

So they all hitchhiked down to Arkansas, where they dropped the crazy Brazilian off. She had some friends there able to pay for the airfare for her to get home. Oh, yeah, the crazy Brazilian girl was pregnant and had a baby, and the cowboy caught the red-cringed beauty and handed it to her in the back of a pickup truck.

"Well, now, let me see this fine lad! Yes, he's about 60% Brazilian, 20% French, 10% Italian, and 100% American, and a hundred percent beautiful!" spoke the cowboy grandly.

And then he was off. He and the kid hitchhiked along 66 in the back of an ordinary car driven by the driver with no name who never said a thing. Well, they slept through their destination, the cowboy trying to hold on to every dying tendril of dream he had left in him, and they found themselves somewhere in the Southwest, where there was a motel and a gas station and a big wooden dinosaur.

The kid went up into the dinosaur and looked out to the west through its teeth, while the cowboy tried to communicate to the prison through the pay phone. He gave up, but before he could leave the dust-strewn booth, it rang.

"Tomorrow at 8," said the voice. "You down?"

"I'll be there," the cowboy said. "Is that you, Will?"

The phone clinked and rang again. The lady came on: "If you want to make a call…"

He cursed at her and hung up.

Now, they needed a car. Luckily, not too long after the need, a red Corvette convertible pulled in, driven by a man whose white hairpiece flapped back in the wind. Well now, the cowboy figured the old-timer would be more than kind enough to oblige. But he wasn't, and there was a bit of a struggle. The cowboy explained to him, "Sir, it ain't right wasting a beautiful car like this on an old-timer like you! I mean, look at you; you ought to be home with your wife and grandkids."

"I worked hard for this car! My wife's dead! Her insurance paid for this damned car!" He was about as mad as an old-timer can get and blurting out things.

"Aah, I see," said the cowboy. "I knew you were a fake. This is your dead wife's car. You shoulda stole your own when you were my age. Now, either step aside or bust a hip."

They drove it through the panhandle of Oklahoma and into Texas. He saw the tall yellow crane jut up against the sky as they came around the bend. The cranes were all over the place, like a construction site in the middle of the desert. The cowboy pulled by slow and leaned out his window. "What the hell is all this?" he called.

"Diggin' for oil!" shouted the man in the construction hat directing traffic.

The cowboy recalled when he worked on an oil rig in Texas back when, but he'd thought the frontier they were digging up was once a national park or some kind of land that couldn't be touched.

"President's orders!" yelled the traffic controller in the construction hat. "The man figures we can still get oil out of here, cheaper than the Mideast, so he's digging up here and Alaska."

"Gotchya."

◆ ◆ ◆ ◆

They drove on, got there right quick and parked the car off the hillside road overlooking the prison. The breakout was already happening. "Sheeit!" They drove down the hill and busted through the fence and the bar at the gate that dropped in front of them. Their wheels blew out

241

at the spikes as they flew through the secure entrance. The cowboy got out and ran into the prison. It was chaos. He went back out, turned the car around and went straight through the jail. He drove right down the aisle, flopping his tires, sparking his car against the bars. The seven rebel sons of Texas all jumped in, and they busted out the other side of the jail and rolled down the hill, busting through one last barbed fence and onto the highway.

They went to a gun store and robbed it. The police surrounded the store. The shootout lasted hours into the night. The cowboy said to the kid, "If anything happens to me, kid, go back to Kansas. Tell Angie I love her!"

An outlaw rolled a barrel of gunpowder out to the police and shot it. Cars flipped high in the air at the explosion.

"We gotta get outta here!" cried the kid.

"I can't leave," the cowboy said.

They were covered behind a desk.

And then the police smashed in on ropes through the windows. They had bulletproof vests and semi-automatic rifles. The outlaws shot one them eleven times in the head. The cowboy figured they'd have to head for Mexico after they'd killed that policeman.

Then the snipers started taking out the outlaws one by one. The cowboy watched his posse fall and die.

"Kid! Let's get the hell outta Dodge," he said. "On the count of three, ready? One…two….aww screw it….aaaaghhhh!" And they ran out shooting back and under fire. They climbed over a wooden fence, crossed the sewage stream. The cowboy and the kid separated there in the gunfire. "Meet me at the Badlands!" he shouted, and he covered him while the kid made his escape. The kid ended up riding on top of a semi, behind the big slanted, metal windshield, driving fast and protected against the rain. As other kids passing by saw him up there on the truck, they awed and knew exactly who he was. Now the cowboy, he ran down a long dry hill. Run-off water slipped him up as he slid down to the road. He held up a car. The woman was most generous to oblige. Hers was a red convertible, too, but hers had a hemi. He riled that hemi up and drove criss-crossing past home once again all the way up to South Dakota, where he waited in the Badlands, living off prairie dogs.

Somewhere between this time, the cowboy had made it in to a gun shop on the northern most tip of the panhandle and bought some ammunition for his Scoffield 45. The woman who sold it to him looked like he'd just kilt her son. She wouldn't sell it at first, just stood there behind the counter with her big body and her black and blue eyes. Then her big husband came a-lumbering in and said, "What can I do you for?"

"Well, sir I need to buy some ammunition for my six-shooter here, but this lady won't let me without no ID."

"This lady here is my wife," the gunsmith said, with an edge. Then he smiled. "Gotta have ID, son."

"I already have the gun."

"All right, all right, ya talked me into it. Let me tell you a joke first."

His wife went into the back.

"What do you call a woman with two black eyes?"

"What?"

"Nothin', ya done told the bitch twice!"

The gun seller let out a long hissing laugh with his mouth stuck open.

The cowboy bought the bullets and went out. He missed Angie. There was also some trouble buying cigarettes. "I have a moral obligation not to sell you cigarettes."

"What the hell, woman?"

So now there he was, armed, chewing on dog's meat around a sparse fire, high in the Badlands with the kid, wishing he'd had a cigarette to burn through his missing for Angie. He stood rugged and unshaven against the car, the western wind and the dust hitting him. He'd talked once about the Badland rendezvous with the kid, just in case they ever had to split up. But he wasn't sure he'd ever make it. Then out of the blue the kid showed up, like walking straight out of the setting sun.

Meanwhile, Old Bucktooth Miller and his gang, slumped down the mountains into South Dakota. They've been through Montana, Texas, and Utah with those damned Mormons. And now they were ragged, but Bucktooth pushed on. Their carbines and assorted arms shot up against the night sky with the pines.

The cowboy heard them coming. Just as he'd escaped from the legitimate law, the vengeful sheriff's son came finding them in the Badlands. The cowboy saw their shadows dance on the sun-burnt rocks. They ran through the Badlands down to the road. Shots hit the rock behind them. The cowboy stayed to finish his business with old Bruce Bucktooth. He told the kid to go on. Now that old road provided roadkill meals of all kinds — you'd be amazed at how many critters go to die crossing that road. And the kid was hungry.

◆ ◆ ◆ ◆

Bucktooth was crazy. He shot everything he had at the cowboy, the man who had murdered his Pappy. He'd gone all across the country in just an unorthodox, gun-carrying-idiot fashion as the cowboy, yet the cowboy got all the popularity and attention for his lawlessness. When he ran out of bullets, he grabbed the gun of one of his dead men and fired it at the slightest movement of shadow under the smoldering sun. The cowboy attained the high ground and knocked off his men left and right. He ran into a deserted, unimproved, dust-covered town. Killing the rest of the men in there was like hitting pop-up bull's-eye targets. He used the alleyways well and then went up to the roof of a building. The last of the men rode in, and the cowboy shot from on high and hit up the side of one of them. The man flipped over sideways, yet his feet remained stuck in his stirrups and his horse dragged him, his face scudding across the earth.

The cowboy jumped down from the ledge of a saloon, stole that man's horse and relieved him of his dust-eating. He rode down a draw and up a spur, across a ridge and between a low saddle back into the Badlands. Bucktooth caught him at a cliff. He dragged his wounded leg out through a weathered rock underpass.

"Turn around," he said.

The cowboy turned slowly.

Bucktooth saw his face and pulled the trigger viciously. It clicked.

"Out of bullets," said the cowboy coolly.

Bucktooth swung the butt of the gun to the side of his head. The cowboy dodged back and rocked forward, punching him hard. His bucktooth popped out. "'Bout time you lost that damn tooth," he said. He held him over the cliff, blood and spit drooled from his mouth. Disparaged, Bucktooth, watched his tooth fall as the cowboy stood over him, one foot clamped on his chest. And then he left him for dead and went to find the kid.

The kid was about to cross the road. Henry waved to him. "Let's go home!" he shouted. But the kid was pointing behind him, trying to warn him, running out into the road.

Then the shotgun blast came from behind. The cowboy turned, drew and emptied lead into Bucktooth's chest snapping against the stone, the 45 roaring throughout the Badlands. Bucktooth fell, flipping far, and cut into the jagged rocks.

It all happened together. The cowboy turned again and heard the horn. The red sports car hit the kid and clipped him to the side. The cowboy fired his last shot after the sports car. And then went over to the kid on the side of the road. He picked him up with his gun still in his hand and held him in his arms. He was hurt bad. "Go home," said the kid, "go home..." And the kid died right there on the side of that road. And the cowboy wept.

He could've understood if he'd died in the fight, but not like this.

A horse circled the scene slowly. The shadow of its tall rider fell upon him. The cowboy looked up and saw the bearded lawman on the horse, pointing idly, his shotgun down at him. The lawman saw tears in the cowboy's eyes. He rode back to the men and said, "It ain't him. This ain't the guy we're looking for."

The cowboy buried the kid where he died by the road, and that was the end of their adventure together, the cowboy and the kid.

◆ ◆ ◆ ◆

Now, there are also several blatantly erroneous mistakes as to the cowboy's whereabouts after the tragedy of the kid. No, he was not that cowboy dancing around the gate, shooting at the White House. Rather he wandered, distraught, back east. He knocked on a door late at night.

"I need shelter," was all he said.

The bald man had a good humor and took him in. And for a while the cowboy stayed with the middle-class Newton family on 123 Meedy Oaker Lane, outside Nashville. He hung out with Mr. Newton's teenage son, going up to college parties, getting high in cars and losing gaps of memory and time, driveling monologues of collected pain.

Mr. Newton was an accountant. He came home from work and watched CNN until he had a headache.

"Are you going bald?" asked the TV. And it showed the top of a balding man's head.

"Yes, I am," replied Mr. Newton.

Then the family had supper. The family had two twin beautiful daughters. The cowboy hated it that he still wanted them.

Mr. Newton never said anything out of the ordinary. He chuckled if you said hello to him. He chuckled after everything he said. He wasn't odd, just really normal — so normal it was as though talking to somebody was a new and embarrassing thing.

His wife kept a modest and prudent home.

One of the twins asked for money while Mr. Newton was doing some tax work at the table. Henry sat across, looking slightly down into a gap of space. He saw the father discipline the daughter about money from far down the table, heard it all like a blur.

Mr. Newton straightened a one-dollar bill drum tight in his hands. "This is money, baby, it don't grow on trees…no buts…All slithering, withering, undisciplined humanity is abrogated handsomely, cleanly cut, under the authority of this legal tender." He went on lecturing about the importance of money.

Then his daughter left when she saw her dad exuberant with his new discovery about money, which he'd probably repeat for a month. He put the bill under the cowboy's eye, "Here, look at that," he said with a chuckle. "Look at Washington's face. Seems like he's mad about something, right? I think he's saying, 'Stay out of foreign affairs, America! Stay isolated.' He's warning us, right with that stern and shrewd face of his…"

The cowboy had no insight on this. In his head he thought sadly, "And this is your great discovery…gad, help us."

◆ ◆ ◆ ◆

That night, the cowboy took Mr. Newton's luxury car and went into Nashville. "Goddamn it, I can't get enough of this state," he muttered. He sat in a smoky back booth listening blankly to the soft country guitar swing. A girl came up and asked him to dance. He'd seen her all in slow-motion like, leaning back, and holding on and tossing forward with her hair all over under the red light, riding well on the mechanical bull in the back. He figured he'd put in some quarters and show her a thing or two. She had a little cowboy hat with a lasso around it tattooed above her ankle. He showed her his smoking guns on his chest, the bleeding heart on his arm, the burning skull on his forearm, and a few others. She had some more in other places, too…

He stood up and dressed and looked at himself in the mirror. The bed had dented as he sat down to put on his boots and his last one-night-stand girl aroused and tried to coax him back to bed.

The cowboy left her sitting up in bed, waiting for the next guy to come along. He drove back to Buckley for his money one last time. The old retarded kid, Mick, was sitting out front of the tavern in the dusty day by the icebox, playing his harmonica and messing around with an old typewriter. He drew a small silver pistol and stopped the cowboy in his tracks.

"Well, well, looky here. I got the drop on ya! I got me the last cowboy: Hank Dunn — got him dead to rights!"

"How ya doin', Mick?" the cowboy said, and he walked towards the stairs.

Mick tried twirl-holstering his pistol but dropped it, letting a round zing just off to the cowboy's side. Unflinching, Henry walked up and picked up the pistol and twirled it in the kid's holster for him.

"Sorry about that," Mick said.

"Stick to writin'," Henry said.

"Yas sir, the day Stephen King dies will be a great day for literature," Mick said out of the blue. And he hammered it down with the paperless typewriter. "That thought right there might be my opinion, and nobody might be able to understand why I said it, but you ever read Faulkner? I can't understand a lick of what he says except in feelings, and he's a classical guy. Just gotta be ambiguous, ambivalent, yet weave a pattern and puncture a feeling in a sweeping show. A statement...a stand....you mark the page and give it life...

"You know, one time a skeeter was a-sucking on my hand, and I wouldn't kill it, even though it was sucking me dry and getting all fat like about to burst with my donation. Sometimes I wish the whole clouds of skeeters would die, but I reckon that'd be a break in the food chain and come back on us. Don't listen to me. I just have some idio, idio, idiosyncrasies I need to get out.

"Anyway, in writing a classic...always say hitherto and thitherto instead of here or there, and use words like whilst and doth and hath. Make sure there are certain parts of the book where nobody knows what yer talking about. And call blacks niggers at least nineteen times. You do that and you got a classic. Not a bestseller, a classic, that will get you some money, cowboy."

"Many fine books were written in prison, I guess," the cowboy said, smoking before he went in. "But I can't write to save my life."

"Stephen King writes phony bestsellers with the twenty-page introductions. I have a right to mock him. The bastard wrote bad things about my dad — he's the guy that hit him with that minivan. My dad ain't had no say in it, no twenty-page chummy introduction. What the hell was he doing walking out there anyway? That fake bastard thinks he's special. Talk about bourgeois, hypocritical American bullshit! But I guess he did rise up from nothing, and *The Shining* was pretty dang good. But I say he's sold out by now. I think him and Danielle Steele should have little phone babies. My dad—"

"Mick, I got it," the cowboy said.

"You don't wanna write no classic?"

The cowboy leaned over and typed, "I love Angie." And that's all he could write.

He went into the bar and got ready for one last fight.

◆ ◆ ◆ ◆

The fights at the tavern lasted long into the night. They had the old mechanical bull going again, tossing babes all over the place. Bumbling Joe was there. He whispered into the cowboy's ear, "Beware of that one."

"That guy just sitting there?"

Joe squirted water in his face and wiped his brow with a cold towel. "Wife left him; ever since he's been one crazy son of a bitch."

"He don't look too crazy."

"Oh he's crazy, and he's like a piece of iron, did a stint in the Army while back."

Later in the night, the quiet-man fighter named Mark blasted in riding a bucking buffalo — the last one on the prairie the cowboy had seen when he first got to that old bar.

As he rode him, knocking over tables and chairs, he leaned in on him stabbing him in the neck until he sloughed down and died. The blood seeped out thick and dark.

"Get that thing out of here," Joe said.

Mark climbed off the dead-twitching last buffalo and ran in the makeshift ring, which was only about a 20-by-20-foot area with some rope wrapped around four wooden posts in the center of the room by the bar. The man on the side rang the bell and the fight began. Mark attacked for the stomach. He had bull's blood on him. The cowboy couldn't get a handle on him. Then he landed a hook that sent Mark's head banging into the post. Mark snapped back. Another hook from the cowboy, and Mark dodged it, watching the punch break the post and sweeping under him with a quick punch to the gut followed by an uppercut. They cowboy slid out of the corner, then went in and popped him on the kisser. He had time to wind up and follow through with a right. Mark bounced back off the ropes and hit the floor, out for the count. The cowboy cleaned himself off with a towel and had a drink. He collected his money and left. He'd purged away everything he had in that fight. And now he had $25 for gas money. He'd spent and lost the rest of his 500 the last time.

◆ ◆ ◆ ◆

The next day he went back to the Newton's house. He saw a cowboy figure leaning against the neighboring house. He drew his gun and shot up the wooden black cowboy figure in this lady's garden. It was the middle of the day. Kids stopped riding their bikes, and everything stopped, and everyone looked at him.

He grimaced. "Damn wooden cowboys," he said.

And he went to the Newton's door, but it was locked. Mr. Newton came down squint-eyed and worried. "My God, what happened to you?"

The sight of Mr. Newton made him want a drink. He pushed past him and went into the basement where the liquor cabinet beckoned. He sat watching TV and sipping whiskey out of the bottle until dinner.

"Little whiskey, huh? You like it?" chimed Mr. Newton.

They assembled for dinner, all but the cowboy. He heard them talking about how Mr. Newton would have to ask him to leave tomorrow. It was a good charity lesson, but not a very responsible method, Mr. Newton expressed.

The news came on low volume on the TV: "Good evening, America. We have breaking news about the cowboy who has been on the run since April...The FBI has discovered his identity and they say he is still at large, armed, and to be considered extremely dangerous, possibly lurking in a neighborhood near you. More details after this..."

They cut to a commercial. The cowboy polished off the bottle.

"And we're back. Yes, the breaking news is, the mysterious cowboy/killer unveiled: His name is Henry Dunn, an out-of-work actor from L.A., ran away from his home in Texas aa, about 10 years ago. Authorities believe he is delusional and very dangerous."

"So all this time the guy was just some actor who decided to put real bullets in his gun?" asked the female anchor.

"Apparently so, Sue. Well, I wonder if this news will quell his popularity."

"Oh absolutely, Bob. The guy's a fad, a farce; he will pass like everything else."

"He actually played a drunk as an extra in a western film, which never made it to theaters — now here we have some footage of a convenience store robbery in Arizona where we get a good profile picture of him, which is ultimately how the police..."

Henry stood and fell back to the couch, drunk. He passed out and awoke in his underwear under a blanket. He made his way upstairs. Mr. and Mrs. Newton were up talking.

"Where the hell are my clothes?"

"Aaa, sit down, will you, Henry?"

"No, where the hell are my clothes?"

"Henry, we think you better sit down and talk to us, and then we'll give you your clothes," Mrs. Newton said.

Henry sat in his underwear in a comfortable chair between the good American parents. The room was dim. As they spoke to him, he knew what was happening and felt his skin getting sucked in as they looked at him with those fixed eyes.

"We think you should seek help," said Mr. Newton.

"Help?"

"Yes, son."

"I ain't your son."

"Okay, Peter, let's not force him. It's his decision," Mrs. Newton said, and she took her reluctant husband upstairs.

"Your clothes are in the dryer," said Mrs. Newton as she passed and went upstairs.

"Thank you, ma'am."

He went downstairs, yanked out his clothes and dressed. Then he found some more liquor in the bottom corner kitchen cabinet. He drank that, then got into their Mexican liquor and drank it all until he was hammered, sprawling around downstairs of the good American household. He went out back into the shed and brought in the gasoline. He lit a cigarette and the downstairs and went up and had the good American family slain, leaving the twins spread-eagled and bleeding.

He busted out of the flaming house. No other sleepy houses noticed the flaming one. Mark was outside waiting for him, his face broken and bloodied.

"I'll follow you anywhere, cowboy," Mark said.
"Go back to your wife," Henry said.

◆ ◆ ◆ ◆

The cowboy drove west till he ran out of gas and money. He sought shelter behind a Marlboro billboard on the side of the highway. It worked out all right, keeping him from the wind while he smoked in the crisp orange horizon, sitting up with one knee bent. He then walked across a road and into Bill's Bar in the middle of nowhere.

All the furniture and everything in the bar seemed miniature. The bartender waited. The place was empty.

"You Bill?" asked the cowboy.

"Yes, sir," Bill said.

"Good. How about a whiskey, Bill?"

"On the house," Bill said. And the whiskey appeared. He drank it and looked up at the TV in the corner. There was a long friendly ad for the lottery on account of the economy. Then there was advertising for jewelry. "Get the complete set! 'Rings of humanity' is on sale for only 359.99! The set includes seven covetous themed rings: Love, honesty, ooh betrayal, greed, death, life and home! Call now or visit our website at www.humanity.com!"

"Tell me sumptin', Bill," said the cowboy.

Bill leaned in and listened. "Which way is Kansas from here?"

"Kansas...well if you head out that door right there and go directly that-a-way, you might make Kansas in a couple of days."

The cowboy stood and thanked Bill. He headed out that door and down those steps, heading west for Kansas. The long desolate fields he knew would become familiar. Hell, it was already nearly August.

Bill yelled out something, but he kept walking.

◆ ◆ ◆ ◆

Reprobate, having defied all law of superficiality, hypocrisy, economy, etc.; having lost the kid on the journey; having been sheltered by good Americans all stuck in their dispositions and jobs; having exploited the illegitimate heart — now only seen as the child actress pulling a heartstring — having been used up and drunken and wasted to the core; having whored more women than any can imagine be whored

251

without his heart breaking but only piercing on the thorn, and starving his heart strong, the cowboy scourged on through the tall grass with the wind at his back, his breath liquor-tainted, his gun loaded in his holster, his spurs scratching the earth, seething his intemperance through his teeth.

◆ ◆ ◆ ◆

⬥ BOOK V ⬥

CHAPTER XXI

The cowboy went west. Hot days passed in that late July. He acquired another beat-up old truck and scrounged for gas money. An old man he saw pumping away, looking at him from behind cool shades.

"What's this guy looking at?" he said in his head as he pulled into gas station the wrong way. All the other people clenched their hands around the nozzles and stood by their modern cars with sublime apathy. The old man looked right at him and approached.

"You need some money?" asked the man. He'd seen the cowboy counting his change at the pump.

"Yeah, money would help," Henry said.

The old man handed him a dollar bill.

"Thank you, sir," he said.

When he went in to pay with his $1.74, he saw the old man and he thanked him again.

The old man slapped him on the back.

"Where you headed, young man?" he asked him.

"Home — Fort Plain, Kansas."

"Now how the hell is $1.74 gonna get you home? Fill her up, it's on me."

"Mighty obliged, sir."

"A buck seventy-four won't get you a damn mile."

"Thanks again, sir. I appreciate it. I gotta get home to see my girl."

"See, I knew I was helping a good cause — you love her?"

"Yes, I do."

"Wife?"

"Not yet."

"Well, don't worry about it, young man, I can afford it. I'm sure you would've done the same thing."

"35.57," said the young clerk behind the counter, taking the change without counting it. He believed the cowboy.

Henry turned to the old man, "Well, I sure do appreciate it." And he shook his hand.

The old man smiled and saluted him off. Everyone in the gas station had heard their little conversation on account of the old man's loud voice, and they all swayed in line behind the register, smiling and understanding.

Then his old truck drove smoothly for a while. He drove on a straight, empty road lined with trees. The sun glimmered on his face through the gaps in the branches. He came out of the trees and turned left into the clear day. A big, green lip of land inclined gradually, stretching into corn stalks at the crest with their soft yellow tips shimmering and the whole field moving with the way the wind ran through it.

Henry drove around a bend and a farm and saw the field, looking over in seconds to his right and then back to the road. He grew contemplative. His brows creased. As he drove through a section of small old structures — an inn, a brick house with weeds and grass all over it, a huge farm — he felt the familiarity off it all like a good drink he liked to take when he would think about home. But this was no drink.

The truck sputtered and scooted around a bend cutting into the field. He pulled off the road and got out. Everything seemed like a tornado had come through. A car whizzed by. The field on the other side of the road went out to a tree line and halted. He could see tall, thin metal towers connected by wire. They skimmed along the trees, cut across the field and somewhat connected back into regular wooden telephone poles lining the streets, connecting into the roofs of scattered houses, back into the town. The trees bent around the poles. Henry peered up across the street to the one closest to him. It was a leafy tree and an arm swirled out over the road along the wire, a'pointing out to the field.

Henry tilted his head to look at it. The he looked over to the field, and he remembered the way by the old pointing bush in the tree. So he set out walking, running through the corn. At last he made it to the other clear — a road trodden by tractors with a grass median tall between the ruts. Some farmers raised their heads to the cowboy as he passed. They were just along the opposite field of rye. One was squatted in the field checking the earth and talking to himself, as a few other men hacked away weeds and one tractor rolled up hay yonder. The one squatting heard the footsteps, and he stood up slowly.

"Hank, is that you?"

"How ya doing, Mr. Johnson?" Henry said to his old neighbor, and he waved.

"Welcome home!"

"Yeah."

And he began to walk down the rye field. A kid riding his bike on the dirt path, with his arms outstretched high on the handle bars and his skinny self all leaning lazily back on the seat, gave the cool semblance of summer.

"Hey, kid," Henry said, startling him a bit. "You know of a pretty girl that lives around here?"

"What you mean, Angie?"

"Yeah, Angie."

The kid said nothing but pointed straight down the path, as Henry had expected.

"Thanks," he said.

The kid rode off.

Henry closed his eyes as he began to walk, feeling the soft, dry tips of the rye on his fingertips. He opened his eyes and walked steadily. It was dusk. The sky was a soft, graying yellow, the sun a strewn gash in the clouds, hazing its light down the mild slope across the thin road to the blue house on the prairie — the home of Lady Angie.

Henry brushed his hands over the edge of rye and came under the shade of a tree. The withered tree had its roots all twisted, and its leaves were sparse and dry in tangled branches, the same branches he once swang and dangled from in his hot-squabbled youth. He squatted for a moment and brushed away some dust on the trunk to find the faded carving, "Henry loves Angie." The words were in a cut-out heart with an arrow through it. He remembered she wanted him to carve "Angie loves Henry" on the other side, but his knife had dulled.

"I already know you do," Henry remembered saying as a kid. "But I have to remember it," the child Angie pleaded. "You'll remember," the young cowboy assured her. And they'd kissed under the tree and chased each other laughing through the field at the dinner bell.

Now, the cowboy stood, took a step from the shadow and into the sunlight. Angie rose from her corn husking, dropped a stalk to her side and looked to the distance. All of her family and old relatives were waiting for her with the corn at the picnic table beside the house. A wind picked up the tablecloth a bit and blew a paper plate up and over. An old, craggy aunt caught the plate and smacked it against the table. "Angie, get that corn husked yet?" her aunt asked.

Angie ignored them. Henry walked briskly through the dry, dusk-whitened field, feeling the crop splinter off at his touch and step, sending its seeds sailing. He halted as he saw Angie from a distance, her blue dress blew back against her legs in the wind, and she lifted her heels and looked out across the road, digging her toes curled into the earth. She saw his hat brimming as he walked forth, and then she saw him step out of the field.

"Angie," he whispered.

"Henry..."

And they ran out, wistfully and freed. They clasped and clung together, and they looked each other over, kissed and held each other tight. "Oh, I have missed you," Angie said.

"And I you," Henry said. "Let me look at you."

And he held her before him, his hands on her bare smooth arms, her face like he'd always known her and kept her in his dreams. He couldn't contain himself looking at her for too long, and he pulled her into his chest and looked out to the sky.

"I can't believe I have you now," she said into his shoulder, "Oh, Henry, you're finally home!"

"Come eat with us," Angie said.

Henry looked off as Angie led him down to the house, and he saw her mother, a stale portrait scolding from the small window in the kitchen. Angie lowered her head to Henry's chest, and his heart leaped as she looked up into him.

"There is much to tell you," she said sweetly.

The cowboy smiled down to her, and they were kids again, and they ran and chased each other, dancing in the rye.

CHAPTER XXII

That evening, Henry dined with Lady Angie and her family. They made a place for him at the head of the table. Old Grandpa Sherman gave up his seat as he went inside. Henry humbly accepted. All were merry and fond of his return, as they laughed and told stories — all except Lady Angie's Ma, whom Henry called Madame Sherman.

As twilight set in, all the other folks retired, and the mothers put the kids to bed. Henry and Angie went out for a walk. They cut through the field and lay in the grass, head to head. They could see the stars settling. Light orange heat ascended in the horizon, dissolving into blue, purple, and then the black of nightfall.

The cowboy told Angie of his adventures. His face awed boyishly as he highlighted all the exciting parts. Angie laughed and listened dearly.

"Yeah, and then this one guy," he said, "this guy, Willis — normal fellow. Got a wife, family — seven beautiful girls and a boy — and a ranch right up by the Teton Mountains of Wyoming, but everything seemed a little strange. He had one hell of a twisted disposition —

turns out, he sold his daughters for sex to folks like politicians just so he could keep his land!"

"No!" Angie gasped.

"Yup, he was one sick son of a gun. He even had a child with his own daughter."

"Figures," Angie said. "Damn rednecks don't know when to stop."

"Anyway, that was just one place. Angie, I have been all over. Such a crazy trip. Stayed with these bohemians out in the desert. Went down to the Grand Canyon. Went to the middle of nowhere in Nebraska, damned law chased us al the way up to the Badland's of South Dakota, where we laid low for awhile. That's where the kid died."

The cowboy couldn't talk anymore.

"How'd it happen?" Angie asked. Her face stared placid up at the stars. She placed her hand like a feather in Henry's.

"He was hit by a car," Henry said. "Hit-and-run sports car out of the blue."

"Heavens!"

"Yeah. Damnedest thing. Wished you coulda met him, or at least he coulda died in another way bravely fighting, but the fight was already won. He didn't need to come a-running across that road. Then he got knocked back to the side."

"Oh, Henry—" Angie sighed.

"Angie, I'm so weary." Henry stood up, went to a large rock and put his foot on it. He leaned in over his knee and lit a cigarette. He turned to Angie, who lay before him. He tossed his cigarette and patted it into the ground with his foot.

He watched her lying on the prairie looking at him. She stood up and looked at him watching her in the soft starlight. He got down on bended knee.

"Angie, will you marry me?"

The cowboy waited for her to freeze and drop her jaw with the overwhelming excitement of trying to say yes, but she just tipped back his hat and looked into the scarred, human, thick-wrung, hard-cut face that if she looked at too long she'd see the boy she knew. She put his hands around his face. His eyes searched hers and caught, and they saw the kid souls of each other, and she looked away.

Henry picked up her chin with his hand. "I know you prolly have some boyfriend — or you prolly haven't ever—"

"Yes!" Angie said.

And Henry elated from his doubting. Lady Angie was right before him, her face glowing and taken aback, holding the moment under the twilight, her hands folded at her heart. Henry smiled at her, and she broke and hugged into him.

"Oh Henry, we will be happy! I have been so lonely," she said.

And she went on whispering sweet somethings in his ear. And they went their weary way, happy together, across the field down to the brook to the cool water and the grass.

◆ ◆ ◆ ◆

CHAPTER XXIII

The next day was the first of August. Angie hung her ungirdled white dress in the window. The cowboy pulled right to her door driving a two-horse carriage.

"Lady Angie!" he called. "I have come for you!"

Angie ran her dainty self out and hopped on. Her mother looked on from the window, shaking her head.

"Where'd you get this carriage?" she asked Henry.

"An old friend owed me one." he told her. "So I traded in my old truck. Damn thing is about to fall apart anyway."

They rode in a small parade in that carriage. The cowboy saw the new Main Street and the new Commercial Avenue. He saw the police everywhere. And he saw the new bank — the big vault being closed as they passed.

They strolled the carriage out to the saloon for some fast line dancing to the old violin, stomping up the dusty floorboards, swinging and swirling her dress around. Then they went to get ice cream. Folks waved to them and called out. And some kids chased them, chanting for a kiss. Henry pulled up the horses, and they gave it to them and watched them run out to the willow tree.

Then he saw an old friend. He pardoned from Lady Angie and left her with her girlfriends. He followed his friend into the saloon to buy him a drink and talk back through the miles and the years. The cowboy told him he was going to marry Angie. The old friend told him that she was Ken's girl now.

"Yeah, she's a lil, dainty piece, ain't she?" said his old friend, Colby.

"What the hell has happened since I've been gone, Colby?" Henry asked him.

They sat at a table by the window — full with memories looking out on Main Street. Only now more cars outside passed along. Colby had a new air about him that Henry could not decipher. He saw him talk fast and lean back and break eye contact, and Henry wanted to grab him and shake him out of it. Colby must've sensed it. He leaned in and said, "Hey, man, it's been ten years, I thought your disposition would've sweetened up by now."

"I don't know what you're talking about."

"Forget Angie, man. That's what I'm saying."

"I can't do that. I love her."

"Might be true, but she's Ken's girl now, man."

"Who's this Ken character?"

"You want a girl? Come with me tonight to this party. I got plenty of tight high school ass lined up for ya."

"No."

"What do you mean no? You ain't even tempted?"

"Got a date with Angie."

"Yeah, yeah, Angie, Angie…"

"Say, Colby. Where's Billy and Jeromy, Hawk and Quincy and the rest of those guys?"

"They all moved away. Why?"

"Goddamn it! Well it's high time everybody starts moving back."

"Nobody's coming back here. You're the only crazy bastard I'd ever expect would."

"Well, I figure this Ken prolly has friends so—"

"Aw, man, you're still thinking about Angie. Let me put it this way: all right, the girl ain't the same girl you grew up with, Henry. All right, the girl, sucks cock like a baby sucks a bottle."

Henry punched his friend out the window. As he sprawled to his feet, he called after him, "Goddamn it, Henry! Grow up!"

◆ ◆ ◆ ◆

That evening, Angie and Henry strolled out through the high plains and parked the carriage by the brook to talk.

"Who the hell is Ken?"

"Oh, shit."

"Did he hurt you? I'll kill him."

"No. He's just a guy that helps me and momma get by, that's all."

"He works for you?"

"Can we talk about something else. Everything was so romantic."

"I'm sorry, darling."

"Ken is nothing to me. I'm sure you must've had some girls that were nothing to you."

A twinge of guilt hit him. "I have," he said. "I've done a lot of bad things."

"No need to tell. The past is gone. We've got each other now."

"Yes, and we got no need for Ken."

"Of course, darling. But you must understand, we were going to get evicted—"

"You want money, baby, then money is what I'll get you."

"Where you going?"

"I'm gonna get a job. You stay away from that Ken, ya hear! Don't worry, baby. I'll come back to ya. I'm gonna get some work around here."

"Will I see you tomorrow?"

"I ain't coming back till I get you some money, girl!"

◆ ◆ ◆ ◆

The cowboy went out and got drunk with his old friend, Colby. They went into a school bus by the school of their youth. They sat in the back among the ripped-up seats and talked about old times. Henry remembered watching Angie out the bus window, as she'd get off at the public school and get on a smaller bus to go to the Catholic school. They went up the aisle, and Colby sat in the driver's seat. Henry punched the front windshield and cracked it.

They wandered over to a wild bar and took part in the revel. Henry told his friend about the crazy Brazilian chick he'd met. He woke up the next morning under a luscious American slut. He shoved her off and went home to see his old man.

The shack sat far up the east part of Pearl Street out of town, past Angie's house and the sunflower fields. He camped out, hunting around the area first, remembering all his boyhood forts and where he'd kilt what and hid from whom. The next day he went in the old shack of a house and found his Pappy among beer cans on the recliner. The sun reddened his 58-year-old face. Long lines creased his cheeks and his brow. His hand lay limp off the chair. Dust shed stale about him in a column of sunlight coming in. His mouth hung open.

"Henry, is that you, boy?" he called, hearing him step in.

"It's me, Pa."

"You got a job yet?"

"No."

"I thought you were dead. Figured they'd done electrocuted you by now."

"Still alive, Pa."

"Well, git over here, boy! Give your old man a hug, for Christ's sake!"

Henry went to hug him, but he sat back limply. He patted him on the shoulder.

Then his father got up, went to the kitchen and washed his face under the faucet. The door was open and June bugs were everywhere, coming from under the old TV, which was on a talk show at low volume. Weeds grew on the back steps and into the house a bit. The view of the lush land was still there, sweeping out, but only so far. And then there were some tree stumps and a half-constructed residence section.

His dad walked back in and sat down and watched TV.

"My half-sister's dating my step-brother, but I am pregnant with his baby!" read the caption of the talk show.

His father seemed immensely interested.

Henry stood by the door. He stepped forward onto the rug.

"I'm gonna get a job, Dad," he said.

"Well, get one then. Quit standing around! Go be the first Dunn ever to hold a job. You know your name is all over the news."

"How'd they…"

"They tracked you down. They got computers and shit, son. Goddamn it. Take off that stupid hat."

"Henry, is that you?" came an old voice.

"Grandpa?"

"Yeah, go on, go say hello to old man Ulysses before he passes," his dad muttered.

Henry went outside and sat on the thin line of concrete porch next to the 95-year-old, brittle man. They sat in busted wicker chairs.

"What are you going to do, Henry?"

"Well—"

"You gotta get a job."

"Yes, sir."

"You don't know what you're gonna do."

"I was figuring maybe—"

"The law's closing in on ya, and you don't know what to do. You don't even know who you are anymore. Aah, that's okay. I get that way every now and again. How's that girl?"

"Angie?"

"That's the one."

"She's good. We're getting hitched."

But he didn't hear. He sat looking off nostalgically, his hair like a small cloud fallen on his head, stretched out thin with the wind. "You know, I remember a girl by the name of Gertrude. Called her Gurdy. Don't laugh, damn ya. We used to play in the mud together, ride together, all day...."

Henry's father came out and lit a cigarette, and they all looked out to the land. There they were: three generations of men, beaten down and broken, the youngest still fighting with the strength of contempt in him. He'd kilt many'a law and man on his way across, but if you asked him, he wouldn't think twice and wheeze dryly back at you, "Yeah, they're all better off dead." He didn't care for any of it, save Angie. But he'd have to bear it to get her back.

◆ ◆ ◆ ◆

That night he went to call on Lady Angie again. They talked lying side by side out on the prairie grass. The cowboy told her how he'd gotten a job that day in the construction business, and how he went to work tomorrow extending that new Commercial Avenue. He told her that he went right up to the boss and said, "I need work. I'm a hard worker." And he told her about how he was before, just to show how much he was willing to change for her.

"Hell, I'd sooner break the system before I sell into it, baby," said the cowboy.

"Henry, the system ain't that bad, honey."

"I know. I thought I could break it. But I only broke myself instead. And for what? Now they're gonna come after me."

"Oh, don't talk like that, please."

"I'm sorry. You got nothing to worry about, baby. I'm just saying."

"I thought you weren't going to call on me till you got the money."

"I know, I said that, didn't I?"

"I'm kidding with you," she said. "Money is nothing to me."

They lay waiting for the stars.

"Although there is one thing that needs fixin'..." Angie said.

"Anything," Henry said.

"Well, Dad left Ma, as you know, but Ma won't accept no alimony on account of pure stubbornness — you know Ma — but I think Dad still wants to come back."

"You want me to go talk to him?"

"Yes!"

"I will."

"Oh, you are the best."

The next day Henry worked hard for the construction company and then went to talk to Angie's dad. He lived in a small house closer to town with an overgrown garden all around it. He called his name through the screen door. "I'm in the back end!" came the old familiar voice.

He went back to find Angie's father among a cleared-out space in the garden, drinking wine and reading the paper. Just inside the screened door, his mistress sat in the kitchen having tea and breakfast. "Papers keep talking about this last cowboy guy," Mr. Sherman said to her

"Last one?" his mistress said as she got up and checked her makeup to go out.

"That's what they say."

"Thank gawd!" his mistress said, and she came out and kissed him and left the men to talk.

Mr. Sherman gave Henry his blessing on marrying his daughter, but he wouldn't budge on going back to his own wife. Then they talked a bit more, and Henry mentioned the kid.

"Shame, ain't it?" said Mr. Sherman. "Had to happen, though. I read about it in the papers. Damned tragedy. He was a wild one, wasn't he? Oh, no, couldn't keep that kid alive, no sir, not in this world."

The cowboy looked up at him.

"He was kinda like you," Mr. Sherman said.

Well now, the cowboy set aside all past grievances and talked him up quick and strong, trying to persuade him to return to the house and patch up the old Sherman family. Mr. Sherman admitted the main reason why he'd left to begin with was the money that he figured his wife was using him for. The cowboy told him a thing or two and left him to think about it. He was beat tired from work. He went home and slept in his old room.

The next day, he went to call on Lady Angie again after work. He overheard her mother talking to her in the kitchen as he climbed the porch steps.

"...that damned crazy boy comes back after debauching and murdering all across the country in a drunken stupor, and all the sudden you're in love with him again, like you was kids — he just whisks you away, sweeps you off your feet like you're in a fairy tale? Well, I don't like it; I don't like it one bit!"

"Henry!" Angie said. "Come in."

"Ma'am," Henry said to Mrs. Sherman. He tipped his hat and then took it off and gave Angie a light kiss.

"Oh, you're all sweaty," she said. "I have to run out to work myself. Stick around, though. I'll be back by 9." And she was out the door.

The cowboy looked at Mrs. Sherman's grim face at the kitchen table.

"You got a job?" she asked him.

"Yes, ma'am."

"You better not hurt her."

"No, ma'am," he said through a child's call.

"Angie!" called the child from upstairs.

"Why don't you make yourself useful and tend to the youngin in the tub."

Henry went up and played with the little neighbor Emily and kept her company, sitting by the tub. His big legs shot out of the little chair, and Emily used them as highways for her toy cars. He leaned in and splashed her and poured a cup of soapy water on her head. She said she wanted to be a cowgirl and go to cowboy land and shoot bad guys.

"Sounds like a plan," said the cowboy.

Then she was playing with Barbie dolls. Henry was Ken. His mind wandered.

"Henry, play! Pretend! You're Ken! Talk! Do the voice!" Emily demanded.

Then she held up the blonde Barbie. "When you find her, will you marry her?"

This got him thinking who exactly this Ken character was. He looked at the plastic doll in his hand. The child's voice reverberated in him: "When you find her, will you marry her?"

Angie didn't come home at 9. The cowboy swung little Emily around in circles in the grass, holding her by her wrists. Then he put her to bed and went to see Angie at the gas station. She was having a hard time slamming the register drawer closed.

"Hold on, girl, let me get that for you," he said.

Angie slammed the drawer closed and caught her finger. "Easy, girl!" Henry said. As she sucked on her finger, he went around behind the counter, put his arm around her and said, "Come here, darling."

She sucked on her finger and put her head to his chest.

"Oh, no," she said, as some guys walked in with Ken.

"Hey, girly," Ken said. And then he saw the cowboy. Henry pulled in Angie tight and glared at Ken.

"Boyfriend's back, huh? I see how it is."

"You stay away from her," Henry said.

Ken chuckled. He gestured for his gang to gather in.

"Please don't fight, Henry. No fighting in here, boys. Go away!"

The cowboy stood steady, unarmed, holding Angie. A police car rolled by and parked among the neon-lit gang cars, and Ken and his gang began to disperse.

"If I ever see ya again around here, I'm gonna shoot you into so many pieces, your friends will get tired looking for ya," the cowboy said to Ken.

Henry went back to the house and got his gun. He met up with Ken at a party and pistol-whipped his muscle man, then decked Ken flat out to the ground. He picked him up and continued to beat the shit out of him up against a car as the rest of his gang ran away.

He went to work and stayed away from Angie till he had some money to show for it. Then he went to work drunk a day before pay-day and got into a fight with his fellow workman. "Come on, man. You gotta wear the hard hat, for your own safety," said the fellow workman. "Take off that stupid cowboy hat and put it on." The cowboy cussed him out and disobeyed. The fellow workman went to the boss. The cowboy cursed the boss and disobeyed. He was fired. But he got to go home with his good old hat on and finish a 12-pack with his pop.

Through all the working in the noise of construction and under the hot sun, and fighting and getting nowhere, sweet children's voices kept ringing in his head: "You know when my daddy's yellow construction company truck is in the driveway that he's home. We used to love to ride in the back, remember? Going out to the fields looking for arrowheads. Oh, Henry, do talk to him! He sends us money, but that's an offense. We want him. Help us, Henry, help us!..."

"When you find her, will you marry her?"

◆ ◆ ◆ ◆

The summer grew late and the sky condensed and hemorrhaged its last summer showers.

Instead of getting drunk one night, Henry went to her house. The stars were out and the streets were wet from the latest shower. He knocked on the door for a little time, and when no one answered, he went in. The house was empty and dark. The linoleum kitchen floor gleamed white at the other end of the hall. There was one light on in the kitchen over the sink, waving down in semi-darkened ripples over the quaint curtains. He looked around. All else was pitch black. In front of him he knew was the mirror. He reached out and touched it, then slid his hands across it and found the stair rail as he started climbing the steps. He didn't know what the hell he was doing just coming into her house, although he'd done it thousands of times before on secret sleepovers.

The rail was cold.

As he got to the top, he shook his head of all doubt. It was her. Angie. The girl he knew always and had come all this way for, killed for, stole for, broken the goddamned law for; the girl he'd sneak out with in the night as a kid. And there she was, sleeping in her room in the bed by the window. Moonlight shone in softly white on her blankets. He lay down on top of the covers next to her. She lay awake looking out the window at the moon.

"Look at that moon," he said. "Seems like we could toss a lasso up and pull it down."

"Or you could just pull yourself up and sleep on it, with your legs all dangling off the end," she said dreamily.

"Yes, that is where I'd like to go with you. If the wonderful cosmos would permit me, that is where I'd go."

"If you got really rich, you could buy a trip up there like that billionaire did. But if the world could put you anywhere, cowboy, it would be in jail, darling, to tell you the truth."

She lay still. He watched her hand fall limp in the air and cast a shadow on the wall.

"No," he said, "don't you worry; they'll never get me. Even if they do, they never really get me."

"They'll get you. They'll break you. And you'll be like me, staring out a window somewheres."

"I wouldn't mind being you."

"Yeah, well, enjoy the view."

"I will." He stared lovingly at her laying on his side. But she wouldn't let him drift into dreaming.

"You know, I think I've got a hollow heart," she said.

"Quit talking that way. You ain't sullied, girl. 'Taint nothing that can sully my sweet—"

"They're gonna kill you, Henry."

"Won't happen, won't let it. Besides, they think I'm in Texas."

"They'll find you. They'll kill my father, too. Just like they killed that kid of yours."

"You don't know what you are saying. I've been all across this rugged slab of land and I've seen its wondrous people and love, just dying to break free. I don't know why you can't see it."

"Quit talking like a damn Indian. Go away or go to sleep, but don't bother me. I have to work in the morning."

"All right, sweetheart," he said. "Let me just ask you this one last question: if you could go anywhere, where would you go?"

She was silent, her face turned to the window.

"Well, I'll tell you where I'd go. You wanna know, girl? I wouldn't go nowheres. I'd stay right here with you right now and forever."

And he left her in peace, and he went to find a motel.

◆ ◆ ◆ ◆

CHAPTER XXIV

The next evening, the cowboy went to call on Lady Angie once again. She was working.

"Again? Man, that girl throws her whole life into that gas station!" he said. But Angie's mother told him not to go and disturb her. They needed to save up every penny they could, now that Ken was beaten out of the picture.

"Well, come on in and have some apple pie," Madame Sherman said with a little smile.

"Why, thank you, Madame," said the cowboy.

"We missed you at Fourth of July. My pie won the best in the town."

"Is that right?"

Over pie, Angie's mother remembered the boy Henry as she watched the deluded cowboy before her. Henry said he was working on getting Mr. Sherman to come home.

"Oh, no, you didn't."

"Yeah, I believe he's coming around."

"What'd he say?"

And they talked, with Mrs. Sherman cheering up and leaning in over the table and getting some life back in her, instead of staring sadly out that window all the time.

Then there was a knock at the door. The man stapled a yellow piece of paper to the screen door. Madame Sherman said to be quiet and make like no one was home. But the cowboy had to see if it was Ken.

The eviction man stood at the door and looked tiredly through the screen at the cowboy. Henry looked on over Mrs. Sherman's shoulder. No words were exchanged between them, but the threat tinctured from both ends through the screen. The man turned to leave, and Mrs. Sherman started yelling and hooting up a storm about the eviction notice stapled on the door.

"You got three days to vacate the premises, ma'am," said the officer.

"What the hell does that mean?"

"You got three days to get out," he said, and he left.

After Mrs. Sherman yelled him off, she and Henry sat down on the bench on the porch, looking off across the plains.

"We need that money, Henry," said Madame Sherman after a while. "We still need that goddamned money."

Angie came home for a break from work. She played on the *Heart and Soul* on the old piano, in the living room — the simple song Henry remembered that she always used to play. He stood behind her and rubbed her shoulders. Then he sat down next to her and played the simple duet.

Then she went back to work, and Henry got up to the construction site to collect his severance pay. He cashed a $55 check and had a shave and a haircut.

Gary pulled out of the auto shop. He'd just gotten that boom-boom stereo system installed with his high school graduation money. He had some $500 in his wallet, $300 in his clothes, $3,000 in his decked-out car with tinted windows and a spoiler and hydraulics. He had a scholarship for one of the finest colleges around. His parents were proud of him. He'd broken up with his girlfriend after high school and was completely free to waste and spend himself away all summer. He'd had a haircut and got fancy colored contacts for his eyes. His allergy medicine had cleared up his head. His Luvox had cleared out the obsessive demons in him. He was done with doing homework and sitting in classrooms and listening to parents. He was a good all-American boy. He'd paid his dues and earned a summer's slack-cut of freedom. And he was one week shy of getting his braces out, and the acne medicine had done wonders for his complexion.

Gary drove through the stop sign along the mini-mall. Some cowboy walked out of the barbershop and right in his way. He screeched his tires to a halt. The cowboy looked at him. Gary stuck his head out the window with his stereo pumping and yelled, "Get out of the way, dick sweat!"

The cowboy stood firm and furrowed his brow at the youth.

Gary put his head back and beat on the horn.

The cowboy drew his gun and shot one shot through the windshield. Gary rocked forward and bled to death in his new car. His braces and his teeth shot out the back of his neck and implanted into the leather-cushioned seat.

◆ ◆ ◆ ◆

That evening, Henry stayed in his shack. His Pa and Grandpa left for Texas so Grandpa Ulysses could die. His Pa took one last look at his son, knew where he was headed and didn't want to stay and see it. He told him he was taking his grandpa to an old ranch owned by a friend. There, he'd work a hand and Grandpa could die in peace. And his father embraced him and left him.

As soon as Henry was alone, he went to Angie's house. There, he had a quiet dinner with Lady Angie and Madame Sherman. And then the little girl, Emily, played with Angie and Henry after supper. Henry swung her around in the green grass outside and even inside, watching the child's face elate as her legs flew over furniture and her wrists stretched and held pink. And she kept saying, "More, more," and laughing until Madame Sherman put her to bed. That was the little one's last night, as her parents were to return from their trip the next day.

There was something on the news then. Courtney Roundapple had died of a drug overdose. The TV people were all over it. Madame Sherman turned off the TV. Angie and Henry went out hand in hand into the lush Kansan night. They crossed the road and walked over a long plain and out into the middle of a sunflower field, and they lay on a blanket in a patch of tall grass on their backs, gazing at the stardust.

"There it is, right here," he said. "All $45. I spent $10 on a shave and a haircut."

"Well, you do look might fine, my cowboy. Sorry for being melodramatic last night."

"Don't fret it. Hey, I was thinking about going over to the tattoo parlor and getting Henry and Angie on my bleeding heart. What do you think?"

"Oh, please don't."

He laughed. "See, I'm being good now; I'm asking you first. But you can be downright mean sometimes."

"I'm mean?"

"Well, a little sometimes."

"I guess I've toughened up a bit, fending for momma and me by ourselves."

"Yeah, well, don't let 'em toughen you up too much, girl."

"I won't." She smiled and kissed him.

She took the money and shuffled it in her hands. "Is this one week's pay?"

"Two."

"Oh."

"Not enough for the tattoo. It's like five bucks a letter down there, but it ain't bad, huh?"

"Yeah."

"I told you I was gonna get you that money."

"When do you get paid again?"

"I don't know yet. I gotta get me another job."

"Why?"

"I got the axe."

"You got fired?"

"Yeah."

"Henry!"

"Least I was honest with you!"

Angie sat up and put her hand back, digging her finger into the ground. She looked up into the stars but saw nothing in them anymore. She hung her head and began to cry.

"Hey, girl, don't cry now. I'm gonna get another job at the restaurant on Main Street. I talked to the guy — Colby said he knows him and he can get me right in."

Angie flapped her hand at him like he didn't understand. She turned from him and covered her face with her hand.

"Oh, come on, girl," Henry said. He leaned in over her. He tried to touch her face, but she snapped to him.

"Henry, do you know how much money we need just to keep our house? Pappa's never gonna come home."

"He'll come home."

"You'll never get a job."

"I'll get one tomorrow."

"We're never gonna get the money. The government is closing in on me and Mamma. And the law is closing in on you. Oh, Henry!"

She wept into his shoulder.

He calmed her and then said, "You know what I think you need, girl? A vacation. Go on an adventure with me. We'll climb the Sierras, walk through Death Valley, dip our feet in the ocean and come back. If we run into law or anything, we'll just shoot through them bastards."

"Just shoot through it?"

"Yeah."

"Henry, you need to get realistic here."

"I am."

"No, you can't just go off on another damned killing spree. You can't be a racist, you can't keep stealing, and you can't be a cowboy!"

"Hey, baby, this is America. It's a free country."

"No, it ain't. That's the big lie. And you ain't no cowboy either. You're an actor. You ran away from home when you were fifteen, ran away from me, never succeeded as no actor, got a cowboy get-up from somewhere and went crazy!"

"Girl, you really need a vacation. That's what I think. And just to get it straight, I ain't no racist against blacks, only niggers, them loud-ass niggers."

"Augh. You just don't get it. You can't get it. You're dumb. A big dumb cowboy."

"Girl—"

"Henry, no. You're not gonna run anymore. You're gonna stay here and face your problems. You're gonna get that goddamned money. And don't you kill anyone anymore, ya hear? You haven't have you?"

"No."

"Henry, you lie. How many have you killed just to get to me?"

"I don't recollect."

"Augh. You are going straight to hell, cowboy."

Henry stood up and leaned against the only tree out there. "Well, so what if I am? I'll go right down there and kick the Devil's ass, free the world of sin, yes sir! Then we won't be arguing!"

Angie laughed and looked at him.

"What?" he said.

"You," she said, smiling.

"Yeah, and another idea is that I could write a classical book about my adventures."

"Henry, Britney Spears will come out with her road-rip movie be-fore anyone will ever care about your crazy trip."

"Damn it, girl! What is with it with you? Used to believe every damn thing I'd say!"

"Okay, maybe you'll have a lot of time to write in jail."

"I ain't going to jail."

They smoked the last of a pack of Winstons and got everything talk-ed out that night. They lay around that dying tree out on the prairie.

"I ain't never seen a tree die on its own before," said the cowboy at last.

Angie was looking off, pondering.

"You know, we all have it comin', Henry. We all owe a little heart-break, a little sacrifice to make it."

"I never figured you for a tragic character."

"It's true. Most people don't even realize when it happens. For me it was when you left. Said you was going out to Hollywood to become a star. Now look at you. Come back to me running from the law — yeah, yours Henry, is gonna be the biggest break of them all. You're long over-due. You keep on dodging it, but it will get ya."

"Stop it, please. We are getting out of here. We're going to Mexico."

Angie rolled around in the cool grass with the cowboy then. They got up, ran back to the house and sat on the rickety swing set behind the house, swinging gently in the dangling conversation.

"I used to wait for you here," she said. "Every morning I'd watch the sun break like a healing wound in the sky, stretching between your house and mine...

"Henry, did I tell you there's a twister bound to come?" Angie said, catching her breath.

"Looks like it already came," Henry said, and he touched her wild hair and face.

"Not yet. But the TV says it's gonna be big."

"When it comes, you just hold on to me, baby, and I'll hang on to our tree, and we'll be all right."

Angie hopped off the swing and sat Indian style in the grass. The cool green and the lush blue night haloed her. She picked herself up, and went to her cowboy. She kissed him behind his ears, and he lifted her hair and kissed her behind her neck and all over, slowly.

"The kid woulda loved you," he said.

"There was never no kid," she said. "TV says you're delusional."

He kept kissing her on her chest, on the little dimple in the center of her collarbone and up to her ears and her cheeks. "Why you always listening to the TV?" he said softly. "Girl, you know they ain't got nothing on me." And they made it home to the mouths, and he realized he hadn't really had a real good kiss since he'd gotten home.

"Angie!" called her mother.

"Oh," she pulled away.

"She's okay," Henry said and tried to kiss her again.

"No, I must go." And she took off running around and inside the house. The moon was big, and everything shadowed crisply over the fields. Henry ran after her over the hill, their shadows small like children chasing.

He caught her in the doorway. Her back was to him.

"Angie!" her mother called from upstairs.

"I'm here, Mama!" she said.

"Just checking," her mother said. She crossed the stairway upstairs and glared down at the cowboy. She'd heard about the killing in town. Henry looked up in his desperate face to her, and she went to bed.

Angie kept her back to him in the vestibule, her head down.

"Hey, Ange," he said. "I love you."

"Henry, do you know what it feels like to have something die inside you?" she said in contrition, touching her belly.

"No," he said. "That Ken is dead."

"No!" she turned to him and put her hands sliding down on his chest. "It's been so hard with you gone — I am so sorry — but I do care for you..." she said. He held her around the waist. Her hair hung in a ponytail. Henry touched her face lightly over with the rough back of his hand.

"So when do you want to get hitched?" he asked with a smile.

Angie handed him back the money.

"Henry, we can't get *hitched* out of no desperate circumstance," she said. "You need to get out of town."

◆ ◆ ◆ ◆

The small light in the doorway shed a dim yellow stage in the big, black, silent house.

Before he could speak, she said, "Get gone, Hank. Your love is useless to me and your money is not enough."

277

"You want money? I'll get you your goddamned money!" said the cowboy as he slammed out the door.

◆ ◆ ◆ ◆

He didn't want to sleep in his pop's old shack on account of his lonesome, empty feeling that throbbed in him. He wanted to be with his girl. He'd take anything but the old shack. The place reminded him of lickings he used to take and hanging around watching TV getting bored as hell, wanting to be a cowboy. But he couldn't afford a motel room. So he went home and sat out on the old rickety chair he used to sit in, drinking whiskey and looking at the sky.

He thought about how far he'd come and everything, and how he could satisfy Lady Angie. He just wanted to pluck her up out of the damned town and run away with her.

The field off to the left of the shack descended out into a little or-chard. He walked a ways into it and picked an apple. He sliced off a piece with his knife and ate it. The apple was dented and bruised and brown, and a damn worm slithered out. He chucked it up in the air and drew his gun and shot at it in mid-air, but the safety was on. He cursed and took it off.

He believed it was Angie's dad who'd actually made that chair back when he was a carpenter. He remembered teachers and folks telling him not to sit back in chairs. He leaned back and dreamt anyway until the chair broke.

◆ ◆ ◆ ◆

CHAPTER XXV

The cowboy awoke at daybreak. He picked himself up. The flattened grass where he had fallen was dried with speckles of blood. The chair that Angie's father had made for him had broken into splinters in the grass. He reached back and itched a dry burning itch on his back. His hand found the rusted nail sticking out. He pulled it out, looked at it and chucked it away. He felt the blood-dried crusted scar on his back and itched it till it burned. Hence, the cowboy stood scarred front and back.

He stood long, looking out of the tomato and onion gardens and the dry wheat fields in the distance. He knew what he wanted, and he knew what he had to do.

The crisp morning bit his face. The wind nipped his eyes wet. He turned his head and looked down to see the home of his love. He could see it just barely over the curve of the road.

He broke stance and went down beyond the shack, past the tipped-over surrey and down to the pond to wash.

He then went to his shack and got dressed: new spit-shined, fancy boots; dust-beaten trousers; tucked-in red plaid shirt — the one Leah back in Wyoming had told him he looked handsome in — his leather jacket; and a fresh, clean bandana. He strapped on his heavy gun at his side just in case he ran into trouble during the day.

And then he retrieved his hat from hanging on the broken bed-post. He put it on snug and directed it in a perfect shape on his head. He checked himself in the cracked, rusty mirror in the shack and wiped away the dust. But all he could see was his outline.

He went out and checked the sun. He figured he had a good three hours before he had to go to work. He went back in the shack — the slanted, dilapidated home of his boyhood. He lay back in the shade; a sun ray hitting in stronger; his hat tilted over his eyes.

Three hours later, he awoke again and kicked out the door to the day. It was 10 o'clock a.m., August 17, 2001. He needed a car. He saw his neighbor waxing his new red truck across the street. He crossed the street to greet his neighbor. Although the liquor had him hung over, his contempt bulled headstrong and allowed no swagger in his step.

"Morning, cowboy," said the neighbor.

"Morning," said the cowboy. "I need to borrow your truck."

"What?"

The cowboy did not break stride. He punched his neighbor down and stole his truck.

On his way to work, he made a little stop at the bank.

"Give me the money," he said to the teller, and he drew his gun at her.

The woman didn't move, but the man understood. He opened the register drawer and placed the money on the counter. "Keep it coming," the cowboy said. He emptied all the registers and then he made the man go to the vault. He came back with a cube of money wrapped in plastic. The security cameras rotated and stared at the cowboy. The cowboy glared right back, looking around at the frightened people. He cut through the plastic with a knife. An old lady fainted, the rest kept their hands up like he'd told them to.

The cowboy exited the bank with a bag full of money and more stacks of it in his arms. He heard Troy strumming his guitar, and he looked down at him. The homeless, black, old good-hearted Troy of the Town leaned against the bank building, smiling.

The cowboy tossed a stack of hundreds in his open guitar case of small change from passersby. Troy stopped playing, "Oh, boy, you've done it now, cowboy!" The cowboy grabbed a fistful of dollars, reached down and pressed some more money into the homeless man's chest. Troy received it graciously.

"Now go on, Troy, my friend. Get out of here," the cowboy said.

"Yes, sir. Thank you, sir. Hahaaa!" And he went off dancing and laughing with his money, running down the alley singing "God bless America!" with the money in his hands. He left his guitar on the sidewalk by the bank with his hat filled with change.

And with the money, now, the cowboy went to call on Lady Angie, one last time. As he drove out of town, he looked over at the money piled on the seat beside him and overflowing out the glove compartment.

He saw some wild roses and pulled over, ran out and grabbed one. The thorn pierced him and he cursed but went right on clenching the thorny stalk, and he yanked the flower out and broke its stalk.

"Hey, mister, what are ya? Some kind of cowboy or something?" came a kid's voice.

He looked over and saw the chubby, dirty kid.

"Yeah, I'm the last cowboy, kid," he said. "Goddamned Indians killed off all my friends."

The kid ran away. The cowboy got back in the truck.

Then he was there. He pulled off the road, slanted in toward her house. He grabbed an armful of dollars and ran to her door. He had to run around some guy's yellow truck and under the cherry tree and up to the porch. Before he could knock, she opened the door with a smile. The cowboy put out his hands, showing her the money. Angie frowned and pushed out through the screen door.

"Henry, what have you done?" she gasped, and brought her hand to her lips.

"Baby, I got the money," Henry said, showing her an armful of dollars. "Come on, baby, let's go! We gotta go, we gotta get of here. We're free! Come on. It's ours. We're free. Let's go. We can run away and raise a family and be happy! Come on, baby, let's go now!"

The cowboy could barely hear the sirens. Angie heard them. She stepped out and looked down the street. A swath of police cars roared in the haze.

Just then, some guy in a bathrobe came to the door and interrupted them. The cowboy drew his gun and shot him dead without thinking twice.

"Oh!" Angie cried. And she covered her mouth.

Henry hadn't even seen his face from the shade in the doorway. He'd assumed it was that damned Ken. But then he looked in at the man he'd shot. And then back at Angie.

"I am sorry."

"No..."

"I love you," Henry said.

"Oh, Henry!" Angie couldn't say it.

And Henry threw up the money, grabbed Angie and kissed her. Angie dug her fingers in the thick hair in the back of his head. They kissed so hard that his hat pressed back against his forehead. He backed up for a moment and smiled and tipped his hat back. And he kept with the kiss. He picked her up and swirled her around. Her dress swirled beautifully. He raised his gun skyward, still kissing, and fired off his last shots to keep back the cops. The bullets hit the porch ceiling, and bellowed and whizzed, battering and ringing out through the country. The debris from the ceiling and the burning bits of money fell upon them like cinder; and that was what the boys back in the bunker would call his eternal moment: kissing her in the cinders.

Henry dropped his gun and kissed her with both hands. He finished the kiss and backed up to savor one last, good look at her. A policeman slugged him in the side of the head with a knife-stick. They read him his rights as they dragged him, unconscious, to the car.

The cowboy came to at the airtight slam of the car door. He looked around, parked beside the road. He could see the policemen gathered at the porch, confiscating the money, trying to catch it in the wind. Two stood on either side of Angie. She stood in the doorway looking at Henry, her white dress dancing with the wind.

"Did he hurt you, ma'am? Did he harm you in anyway?" asked the policeman.

"No," Angie said, still staring at him.

A few policemen were in the house, staring over the dead body. Henry couldn't move. His hands were cuffed behind him.

A policeman tapped on the hood of the car. "Take him away," he said.

Another bent down and looked in at the cowboy. There were so many uniforms. The driver policeman got in and looked back at the cowboy through the glass.

"Little trouble with the lady, cowboy?" he chided, and he closed the car door.

"She is my wife," said the cowboy, keeping his eyes on her through the window.

The day's humidity swelled and broke into a light rain. Henry could see the rain hitting his hat outside on the ground. He clenched his jaw, his hands useless in the cuffs.

The car jerked into drive, and the cowboy felt that sure break in his heart. "Well, cowboy, this is the end of the road," said the driver. And the car jolted forward and rolled away. The western wind swept across the land, scraggling the grass growing sideways to the east, whistling numb against the edges of the cars. And the people in their homes just kept on a-watching the news. And the people in their cars just kept on a-driving along. And he watched her disappear, through the rain-drizzled car window.

THE END.

◆ ◆ ◆ ◆

Great Fiction Titles from Robert D. Reed Publisher

Call in your order for fast service and quantity discounts!
(541) 347- 9882

OR order on-line at **www.rdrpublishers.com** *using PayPal.*
OR order by FAX at **(541) 347-9883** *OR by mail:*
Make a copy of this form; enclose payment information:
Robert D. Reed Publishers
1380 Face Rock Drive, Bandon, OR 97411

Name _____

Address _____

City _____ State _____ Zip _____

Phone: _____ Fax _____ Cell _____

E-Mail _____

Payment by check /_/ or credit card /_/ *(All major credit cards are accepted.)*

Name on card _____

Card Number _____

Exp. Date _____ Last 3-Digit number on back of card _____

		Quantity	Total Amount
The Last Cowboy by Daniel Uebbing	$14.95	_____	_____
The Small Business Millionaire by Steve Chandler and Sam Beckford	$11.95	_____	_____
Trash and Other Litter by Richard Bellush, Jr.	$24.95	_____	_____
The Jade Head by Patrick Grady	$12.95	_____	_____
To Wear the Badge by E.A. Machado	$14.95	_____	_____
The Shadow Mouse of Everjade by E.A. Machado	$24.95	_____	_____
Forty Acres by Gerard Murrin	$22.95	_____	_____

Quantity of books ordered: _____ Total amount for books: _____

Shipping is $3.50 1st book + $1 for each additional book: Plus postage:_____

FINAL TOTAL: _____